THE CREST

MENTOR CHRONICLES

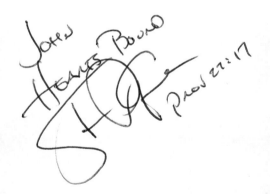

STEVE GERALI

The Crest: Mentor Chronicles

Contact may be made at: www.stevegerali.com

Artistic Direction: Mark Novelli   www.imagocommunity.com

Cover Art: Jack Stockman   www.artbyjack.com

Marketing: Jen Howver   www.vodcommunications.com

ISBN 978-1-4507-5993-9

Printed in the USA.

PREFACE

This story is true! I assure you that the events in this book have occurred. You will need to determine what parts of this story should be read literally and what part should be read allegorically. For those of you who will take it all literally, you may be missing out on the deeper meanings of things. Those who read it all as allegory may be missing out on the mystical encounter with the supernatural. The story will take you on a journey.

My life passion and career has been spent mentoring youth and young adults. These young souls are navigating their way through an age span which allows them to explore who they are and who they would love to be. I began to discover that every young person deeply desires to walk this identity defining journey with a mentor. Some have the wit and insight to intentionally seek out a mentor. Others are blessed by being surrounded with virtuous mentors from their extended family and faith communities. These young men and women journey alongside their mentors without ever, formally discovering the powerful input that the mentor has had. Still others come to connect with mentors who take them down dangerous and destructive character paths. They emulate the twisted, unwholesome and seedy values that corrupt character. Whether consciously or unconsciously knowing, young people seek and find mentors to assist them in their character development.

On my life journey, I had many virtuous mentors who poured into me and instilled a strong value to pay it forward. I became a lifelong student of the process of identity formation and the powerful role that mentoring has in that process. I was particularly intrigued with this, as it shaped the character of young men. You see, in Western culture, the messages that guys receive about being a man run counter to a virtuous character. I trust that you will discover what I mean as you read this book.

So I became a mentor to young people, and more specifically young men. Guys need a mentor to help them see the internal qualities they possess, dream of the men that they can become, and then help them succeed in that quest.

The desire of a young man to have a significant male mentor in his life causes him to search. He first finds, and deeply connects with masculine archetypes (warrior, sage, king, wildman, priest, etc.). He imitates the character of the archetypes he discovers in literature, the arts, culture and religion.

As he continues his journey, he may see the character traits of these archetypes embodied in real men who he labels, *role-models*, *heroes* or *leaders*. Like the masculine archetypes, these real life figures in history and present media, remain distant. His heart, mind and soul crave a connection to someone more existential. He longs for a flesh and blood, real live mentor who will walk alongside him through his journey.

Mentoring is not just a role it is a sacred lifestyle. It is the charge on every life, deeply instilled in us by our Creator - that we contribute to the greater good of mankind and nurture generations that follow us, to do the same. Mentoring has existed from the dawn of time. Yet at the onset of the Industrial Age, it became convoluted. Virtuous character was replaced by quantifiable outcomes, accolades and net worth. Rugged individualism superseded the metanarrative of community. Ancient fraternities became suspicious organizations, and rites of passages, which were strategic tools in the mentoring process, became minimized and obsolete. Still, young men have a deeply rooted desire to be mentored into great men. They crave an adventure that will shape and mold them. They lustfully desire a significant brother, father, mentor who will speak powerfully into their life journey.

This book is about that journey; it's about the development of virtuous character in a young man and his passage into manhood; it's about mentoring and becoming a mentor, and finally; it's about the adventure of discovering one's created purpose and design. As I mentioned earlier, this is a true story of a group of young college guys who became men of great integrity. The events recorded in this chronicle may seem sensational to you, but I assure you, many great men will tell you that they really happened. You be the judge.

PROLOGUE

Every boy is set upon a path to manhood. That journey is a complex adventure hewn in time and space, and requires conscious, intentional decisions whose outcomes will shape the man he will become. Common boys can choose a path with little resistance and become common men; or common boys can choose a path that will take them on this great journey that will cut, mold, shape and refine them by fire. These common boys emerge as uncommon men.

When a boy travels this journey with like-minded companions, he is blessed. He comes to understand that he will be sharpened like the razor sharp edge of a sword when iron meet iron, crafted in the Master's hands. So it is with virtuous men – one sharpens the other. Great men are never self-made, nor are they rugged independent individuals who take their place in the world. Becoming a great man starts with a commitment to be inter-dependent.

This journey offers peril and peace, trauma and reconciliation, discernment and whit, courage and faith. But there comes a point when every boy is faced with a pivotal question, "What kind of man do I want to be"? As he takes his steps in the direction of his decision, he will find others who have gone the same way. And if he seeks carefully, he will encounter great mentors who will see him as a valuable treasure, worthy of investment.

The second question that every boy encounters early in his adventure is, "What legacy will I leave?" He should begin to think of how he will be remembered, early in his journey rather than in the twilight of the journey. He should also contemplate how long he desires his legacy to last. This question should cause him to seek the Eternal.

An emerging great man will find that the marriage of the two questions yields a life that is not so much defined by what he does but by the characteristics, that God instills in him. That boy must cultivate those characteristics, which determine who he is. Who he is then shapes what he does. If a young man's *behavior* defines who he is, he falls as a weak man; but if a young man's *character* is qualitatively shaped and developed in a way that informs his behavior, then he stands as an impeccable man.

The remainder of the journey becomes a quest to stay on that trajectory never allowing what he does to define, him but letting who he is mandate his actions. When the journey ends people will see a great man, a God honoring man of integrity, who leaves a legacy that impacts and influences his children's children, his community and society.

This type of man may be marked by many character traits, but there are four, that commonly mark a God honoring man of integrity. These characteristics are love, goodness, wisdom and freedom. While one may be more dominant, all four can be traced.

Now you stand at the threshold. You are invited to embark on this great adventure. Remember that not everything is as it appears to be. A man of great character looks for things unseen, listens for words unsaid and discerns that there is always more than what is happening right in front of him.

Hearts Bound!

King Elyon

Acknowledgement ⟶

Many friends and protégées helped make the Crest a reality. Above and beyond their help and support, I am grateful that they are a part of my life.

Thanks to the many men who have allowed me to be in mentoring relationship with them. This is our story!

Thanks to Jay and Jen Howver for their loving support, wisdom and guidance through this project. You have been a clear example of paying it forward, all throughout your lives. I am certainly blessed that you are in my life and a part of this journey.

Thanks to Mark Novelli. I remember when . . . and look where we are now. Your insight, support and design with this project has encouraged me every step of the way. You are a loyal friend and I am rich because of it.

Thanks to Jack and Kathy Stockman, long time friends. Jack your artistic design is amazing as is your life. Thanks for your faithfulness to our King. Kathy, I'm so grateful for your editorial coaching. Your insights only made this better.

Craig Massie thanks for your gracious spirit and your willingness to jump in and bail me out! I'm blessed to have you in my life.

David Deck I love your dream and your vision. You encouragement prods me on. When we met years ago, I knew that God was going to keep our hearts bound for many years. Look where it's leading! You are a great man!

Thanks to the many protégées who served as readers of this project. Your ideas, critiques, comments, suggestions, etc. reflected your passion for the narrative and your love for *real* life.

I am especially thankful for the love and support of my wife Jan and my amazing daughters and son-in-law, Alison, Andrea and Matt. Thanks for the hours of listening to, reading and re-reading this story. Thanks for your honest criticisms and creative ideas. Thanks for your encouragement and support. Thanks for your love of literature and passion for fantasy, from which grew your valued insight. Thanks for being my heart and soul.

To all of you, thanks for being people who live out the values and virtues of a great King and His Kingdom. *Soli Deo Gloria!*

CHAPTER
ONE

The weekend before the fall semester classes began at Mason University was always the most hectic and exciting time of the year. The air was energized with the rekindling of friendships that were on a summer's hiatus and the formation of new ones with the emergence of a brand new incoming class. Cars were double parked in front of the dorms, music was blaring from the open windows where an occasional empty box was tossed to the ground below as students claimed their living space. Adams Hall was clamoring with young men who were carrying in suitcases, television and stereo equipment, makeshift bookcases and a variety of furnishings that they pilfered from their family basements, all in an attempt to make their dorm room uniquely *home* for the next academic year. The resident advisors stood sentry in the halls to greet the returning sophomores who resided in Adams Hall. They were also charged to make a pleasant and positive first impression, as well as to watch over and protect the mahogany paneled walls of this historic century old building from the over-zealous, bravado emulating, late adolescent guys who tried to lug sofas and refrigerators up the hand crafted wood carved staircases to their rooms. The stately portrait of the hardened bullfrogged faced late Dr. Phineas Adams seated with his arms folded across his chest, hung on the lobby wall facing the entrance. Old *"Frog-Face Finny"* looked like another sentry guarding the ivy leagued ambiance of the dorm, which bore his name.

CHAPTER ONE

Wesley Litchfield darted into the crowded lobby and dodged his way between parents carrying boxes and residents moving furniture as he hurried up the staircase to get to his room. The excitement of the news that he carried had his adrenaline pumping but it never deterred Wes from politely excusing himself as he squeezed between the sofa movers and the stair rail, or from offering a quick helping hand and a warm engaging smile on the way up the three flights to his floor.

"Wes! Wes Litchfield!" yelled one of the dorm residents, in excitement to see an old friend. The sound of the voice came from the main lobby below.

Wes stopped in his tracks on the stairs and looked over the railing to see Jake Masterson, a friend from last year, holding a box of personal items, standing in the center of the University crest that was inlayed in the tile floor of the lobby.

"Hey Jake, how was your summer?"

"It was amazing . . . I spent most of it working at my grandparents beach house in San Diego."

Wes really didn't want to have this conversation now but he also didn't want to be rude to his friend. "I want to hear all about it. I'll come by your room later tonight after *Move-In* is over," Wes yelled down. He was sincere about catching up with Jake but the news that he carried was far too pressing to stop and chat now. He and his friends had waited six months for this and now Wes carried the knowledge of an event that would change the course of their tenure at Mason University, and possibly their lives, forever. Wes tried to remain undeterred by slowly inching his way up the staircase while still attempting to give Jake his attention.

Wes' charismatic personality, keen whit and an innate sense of responsibility played into this sandy blonde, blue eyed, athletic, nineteen year old boy's persona as a natural born leader. He possessed a remarkable ability to connect with others, on a deep level. Wes often found himself in late night talks that became intimate, quasi-counseling sessions, often resulting in his friends telling him *"things that they had never told anyone before"*. Wes' mom often said that he should be a priest, because people found it safe to tell him their confessions. Wes' loving spirit and unconditional acceptance made it easy for his friends to confide in him.

"That's cool – I'm counting on it. I have a lot to tell you. Some things have changed since our last talk at the end of last semester. Remember what we talked about?" Jake called back, trying to be evasive.

Aware that everyone was hearing their conversation and presented with the prime opportunity to poke fun at his friend, Litchfield's wit flared and he returned, as loud as he could, "Oh Yeah! Did you stop denying that you wear your mother's clothes? That's so great!"

With that, he raised his eyebrows and gave an endearing trade mark grin that uniquely marked Wes. Then he quickened his journey up the stairs before Jake could return a stinging comeback.

Jake stood gazing upward as his friend disappeared among the movers. He chuckled, shook his head and as he started to walk away he realized that the lobby, full of visitors and students, heard their entire conversation. Many stopped their moving and stood nearby smiling and looking in his direction.

"I don't wear my mom's clothes – I mean I never denied wearing them – I mean . . . He's just kidding . . . you gotta love the guy!" Jake snickered as he shuffled off.

All the way up the staircase, Wes encountered the high spirited salutations of friends who were glad to see him after being away for the summer. And all the way up the staircase, Wes had affirming words that made each guy know that he was held in high regard by a friend – even when he was joking. Wes made some exceptional friends last year at Mason and was excited about seeing those relationships grow deeper this year. All the while Wes Litchfield was undeterred from his mission. Bringing the knowledge that he carried from the ensuing events of the morning to his roommate Josiah Nestor, and friends Caden Boyd and Ian Bound would only make it become reality.

CHAPTER
TWO

Wes Litchfield finally made it to the top of the staircase. His new room was the first one on the right hand side of the corridor, off the staircase. Wes and his roommate Josiah Nestor had arrived a day earlier, ahead of most of the students. They conspired weeks before to get settled into their room quickly so that they could go about the business of reconnecting with as many of their friends as they could before classes started. Wes also had one important matter that he wanted to finalize. It was a venture that he and Josiah Nestor, along with two other friends, Caden Boyd and Ian Bound, had begun before they left for the summer break at the end of their freshman year. Wes had diligently attended to this matter throughout the last spring semester and then finessed it throughout the summer, emailing and making numerous phone calls. Before he left home to come back to Mason this semester, he had arranged one last negotiation meeting, which became the real reason why he was anxious to return earlier to school. He had hoped that the plans that he and his friends had begun would come to fruition before the semester began.

All that hard work paid off, I just hope that Caden and Ian are back from break now. We have an early appointment in the morning that none of us can miss. This is going to change our lives, Wes thought.

Wes finally reached the third floor of Adams Hall. When he left earlier that morning, Josiah was busy unpacking and working to make the room presentable.

Josiah Nestor and Wes Litchfield became instant friends on this very same weekend a year ago when they both arrived at Mason University as incoming freshmen. They met as they were standing in line at the *New Student Orientation Fair* in the Harding Athletic Center waiting to get their dorm assignment and room keys. Each stood there, along with hundreds of other freshmen, disoriented, frustrated and growing impatient. Neither had said a word to the other until a beautiful student worker came walking toward them. "Excuse me, boys" she said as she pushed her way between them. She put her hand under Josiah's chin to close his mouth, which was gaping wide opened. "You look like you've never seen a woman before – welcome to Mason U," she said as she walked away. Wes and Josiah's eyes followed her in synchronized form as she strolled through the crowd toward the Athletic Center exit.

"Wow!" Josiah said, as he took a deep breath and then exhaled as if the wind had been knocked out of him. "I've never seen a woman *as beautiful as you,*" he said in her direction but only loud enough for Wes to hear.

"Exactly, and you smell as sweet as you look!" added Wes as he breathed the lingering aroma of her perfume in and shook his head in an attempt to make sure he wasn't dreaming. "College is going to be amazing!" Wes said, now directing his conversation in real time to Josiah rather than to the illusive siren that waltzed in and out of their time-space continuum.

"Yeah, I think I'm going to like it here," Josiah concurred. Both guys looked again in the direction where that vision of beauty walked, but she had disappeared into the crowd.

As hard as they tried to find her, they never again saw that girl at Mason University. Nonetheless, she became the catalyst that got the conversation rolling between them and sparked the imminent friendship Wes and Josiah would experience. Both guys obviously shared similar interests. The long wait in that orientation line turned into a bonding experience as they discovered other things that they held in common besides a similar taste for beautiful women. Both shared similar tastes in music, foods, and sports, which among other things included lacrosse. Both had played in high school and were admittedly just a little better than average. They agreed that they weren't good enough to make it on MU's division one team. The conversation seemed to be very real; not a lot of trash talking, grandstanding or over-inflating one's abilities - like most conversations that guys initially have. There seemed to be a refreshing honesty and acceptance that they each shared. From their initial introduction with each other, Wes and Josiah knew that they could be . . . *real*.

By the time they reached the registration table, they agreed that they would attempt to play *intramural* lacrosse, at least for a year together. When they received their room assignments, they discovered that they were living a few rooms away from each other, on the same floor in Duke Hall, the freshman dorm. But the event that really solidified their friendship occurred days after the orientation when a power generator malfunctioned, leaving most of Richland County and Mason University without electricity. Wes had just stepped into the elevator on the seventh floor of the Archibald Justice Student Center. Just as the doors began to close, Josiah caught it and boarded the elevator. Minutes later, between the fifth and fourth floors the power went out leaving the two guys trapped. After concluding that there was no way to get out of the elevator, both guys just kicked back, sat on the floor and waited for help to come. The only thing to do was talk – so they did . . . about anything and everything! The conversation ultimately took them in a direction regarding their expectations of how college life was going to change them. Neither wanted to be sucked into the shallow conforming grip of being identified as a partying frat boy, although they concurred that there was a lot of appeal to move in that direction. Both agreed that they saw this as a time to leave behind childish things. They wondered if they could still have fun without compromising their integrity. The awareness that they were leaving the childhood dependence of their families and stepping into manhood seemed to be first verbalized in that elevator. Four hours later, there was a jolt as the power was restored. Wes and Josiah seemed disappointed that their deep conversation had ended. They immerged from the elevator on the first floor, changed slightly with an eerie knowledge that there was some grand supernatural design to that event. Over the course of the year, their friendship grew deeper. They road tripped home with each other, got involved in various aspects of student life, played on the same lacrosse team and even had a few courses together. Wes considered Josiah to be one of his best college buddies. He also knew that the sentiment was reciprocated. It just seemed natural that they would be roommates after that first year.

CHAPTER
THREE

The meeting that Wes attended that morning at 8am only took two hours. Josiah had already been awake and was emptying boxes when he left. Wes stood in the doorway of his new room, where he and his best friend would call home this next year. Wes fully expected to find Josiah still working when he returned but instead he found a beautifully clean room with everything in place. Josiah had finished the job and now was gone. *I can't believe that he's not here*, Wes thought as he plopped down on the side of Josiah's bed. Wes looked around his new room. He knew that he might never see the room in this pristine condition for the rest of the school year. As his eyes spanned the landscape of the room, he noticed the blending of the possessions, which defined his life, along with the possession that defined Josiah's. He recognized some of the posters that once hung in Josiah's old room, now intermingled on the wall with his. His eye quickly fixed on a new picture of Josiah with his grandfather, carefully positioned on the corner of his roommate's desk. In all the time that he had spent in Josiah's room last year, he never noticed this one. He surmised that the picture had been taken over the summer. Wes along with many other friends heard stories from Josiah about this grandfather who he adored and respected.

Josiah was third generation Asian American. His grandparents, on his mother's side emigrated from Japan. Josiah's mother was raised in a mix of Japanese and American culture. She married

Josiah's dad, Jack Nestor, after they met in college. Mrs. Nestor tried to retain and pass down some of her Japanese traditions, but they seemed to be fading with Josiah's generation. Many of the traditions that they did hold on to were out of obligation and respect to Josiah's maternal grandfather and only living grandparent. Josiah affectionately referred to him as *ojichan*, the Japanese word for grandfather. Half way through Josiah's senior year in high school, his grandmother passed away. This prompted some dramatic changes and grandfather Takahiro came to live with Josiah and his family in the guest quarters that had been built on the back of their home.

Grandfather Takahiro had a close bond with Josiah, his first born grandson. Josiah admired the character and wisdom of Takahiro. As a child, Josiah spent a lot of time being nurtured and mentored by his grandfather. He had many memories of field trips and outings that they went on together. Those close encounters continued through the years even after he left for college. Josiah knew that every time he came home on break, he and grandfather Takahiro would spend some quality time alone together apart from the rest of the family. Takahiro had an uncanny way of making life lessons from simple, average everyday things that he encountered.

Last spring break when Josiah returned home, he found his grandfather in their backyard with his gaze fixed intently on the ground.

"Konichiwa, Ojichan," Josiah quietly announced as he bowed in respect. Without breaking his gaze or returning the greeting, Takahiro motioned for his grandson to come closer.

"Look ants," Takahiro stated slowly and softly in his best broken English. "They teach us much. All work hard for season. *Not - one - lazy*. When times difficult they live well because they not lazy when they must work. Watch ways of ant; be wise man."

Josiah's friends noticed that he was a bit more industrious in his studies when he returned to school from that break. He often would tell the guys stories about the lessons he learned from his grandfather. Josiah hoped that he could be as wise as his hero, grandfather Takahiro.

The picture on Josiah's desk reminded Wes of the special bond that his roommate had with his grandfather. Wes was looking forward to rooming with Josiah. He had a feeling that big things were going to happen this year. But for now, Josiah was nowhere to be found.

Where the heck is he? I feel like I'm going to explode if I don't tell someone. I'll wait five more minutes, he should be back soon; after all, he knew that I was going to the meeting. Josiah knew the outcome affected his own future too. Hardly able to sit there any longer, Wes thought, *Maybe he's in the shower.* With that, Wes sprang to his feet and walked the hall toward the lavatory located in the center of the floor. As he passed the other rooms of dorm-mates, busy at work getting settled in, he peered in to see if Josiah had stopped to help and hang out with friends. Josiah was nowhere to be found.

Wes pushed open the lavatory door. He could hear the shower running. He walked past a row of showers only to find one in use. "Josiah, are you in there?" he yelled.

The shower curtain opened and a head popped out, "No dude, it's me."

"Oh, hi Chase, when did you get here?" Wes said. This wasn't someone that Wes really wanted to see this early in the semester. Chase Morelock was a self-centered, arrogant, pompous rich boy. He emulated everything that Wes desired not to be. Chase's father Charles Morelock was a very powerful and wealthy Wall Street corporate lawyer and Chairman of Mason University's Board of Trustees. Charles Morelock masterminded corporate takeovers and acquired monopolies in various utilities and trades. He single-handedly brandished his financial influence to leverage many congressmen into office. Charles Morelock's moral compass was strongly defined by his lack of accountability, the fear that he generated and the sheer size of his wallet. It wasn't difficult to see in Chase that the apple didn't fall far from the tree.

"I got here about an hour ago, on my dad's private jet. I'm going to make sure my dad gets rid of this pilot. He got me here fifteen minutes late again," Chase replied. "I partied all night and wanted to grab a quick shower before I started to unpack. Don't want to repel any of the ladies who plan to stop by my room to help me move in. Speaking of repelling women, has your luck changed in that department?"

Not giving into Morelock's insults, Wes curtly asked, "Have you by chance seen Josiah Nestor"?

"No, but I did see your other dim-wit friend, Caden, down the hall in his room earlier. He asked about you and Josiah too. You know you really ought to associate with a different class of people, Litchfield. Those losers are a rather unappealing bunch."

"That, coming from a guy with no frame of reference for discerning character; huh . . . I'll have to give it some serious thought! A little return advice for you Morelock, you really shouldn't be opening your mouth when there is water pouring over your face. You wouldn't want to drown!"

Chase Morelock sneered and came out of the shower at Wes, buck naked and dripping wet, brandishing his chest to intimidate his foe like a deranged gorilla.

Wes just shook his head, turned to leave and said, ". . . and you really shouldn't expose your . . . short comings." The comment caught Chase off guard. He quickly backed down and returned to the warmth of the shower.

"Loser!" he yelled as he whipped the shower curtain shut.

Living on the same floor was going to prove to be a challenge for both, Wes and Chase this year. Wes exited the opposite side of the Lavatory, which was situated in the center of the third floor. Caden and Ian's room was located on the north end of the third floor east wing, opposite of Wes and Josiah's room on south end.

Caden Boyd and Ian Bound were very good friends who were returning to Mason University this year. Caden had the ultimate techno-toys; surround sound stereo, HD TV, computers, and the latest in virtual computer gaming. Wes imagined that they probably would be running wires and mounting screens and speakers to make their room the ultimate techno-palace. All four guys, Caden, Ian, Josiah and Wes had become close friends before their freshman year was over. They had established a fraternal brotherhood that began to give them a unique bond and identity, which Wes quickly labeled a "band of brothers". *Band of Brothers*, the phrase felt good to the guys so it became the descriptor of their relationship. The news that Wes was so anxious to communicate involved all four of them, so he hoped that he could find them together.

CHAPTER
FOUR

Wes' encounter with Morelock momentarily deflated his focus and high spirit. He quickly redirected his thoughts.

I'm not going to let someone like Chase Morelock interfere with the energy that will make this one of my best years yet. I just need to find the bros and get them up to speed.

As Wes exited the lavatory, he almost got sideswiped by a couple guys carrying in an old sofa that they just picked up at a local garage sale. They blocked his exit and his view of Caden and Ian's room.

I can't see if they are there or even make out if their door is open. I hope they are here. Will you hurry and get the damn sofa out of the way, he thought but the movers had a difficult time maneuvering it through the tight doorway into the room directly across from the lavatory. Meanwhile, Wes heard Morelock shut down the shower.

Keep your head and get out of here, Litchfield. Move the eff-ing couch! he thought.

"Here - Let me give you guys a hand," Wes said politely, even though his level of frustration was peaking. He grabbed a corner of the sofa. "We should turn the sofa on its side – it will pass through the doorway a bit more easily." Wes certainly had his share of hauling sofas and large pieces of furniture in and out of rooms as he helped friends come and go. All the while he felt that he was so close to accomplishing his mission as a messenger of glad tidings and yet so far, only to be impeded by a shabby red sofa in front of him and an arrogant jerk who was emerging from the showers behind him. Wes grunted as the weight of the sofa shifted and the moving crew heaved to get it through the dorm room portico.

"Hey thanks for the hand," one of the movers said.

"Sure thing!" Wes replied as he backed out of the room as quickly and graciously as he could. He wasn't about to get caught in a conversation.

Down the hall near Caden and Ian's door, Wes could see boxes stacked outside the room into the hallway. As he drew closer to the room, he could see that the door was opened. *I hope they are there and Josiah is with them,* Wes thought. When he got to the opened door, he expected to see his friends busily working. Instead he found Josiah, Caden and Ian mesmerized in front of Caden's fifty inch flat screen television playing *"Dark Force Overthrow"* the latest warrior video game. Caden and Josiah were seated on the edge of an old orange paisley print, low-backed sofa that Ian had found in the trash on the side of the road near fraternity row. The two gladiators were locked in mortal combat while Ian stood behind them frantically calling directions. They were oblivious to the fact that Wes was standing in the doorway.

A sense of relief and great joy washed over Wes seeing his brothers together again for the first time since they left school last May. Even though he was excited to tell them the news, he felt amused by the scene before him. He decided to wait for the opportune time to announce his presence.

Caden had obviously perfected "Dark Force Overthrow" over the summer. He had grandiose thoughts of actually being like one of the electronic gladiators with which he identified in his videos. While he wasn't delusional and was surprisingly not nerdy, Caden's warrior ideology translated into real life in the form of his strong desire and aggressive actions to champion truth and justice. Not to mention that he was a bit of a hot head, easily set off when someone acted hypocritically or if one's actions or beliefs were in opposition to his own. Caden worked hard, always to do the *right* thing and he prided himself in that.

"Dude, you're a dead man," Caden yelled as he fired his nuclear powered rocket with the flick of his thumb. The larger-than-life high definition graphics accompanied by the digital surround sound captivated the senses of the guys. Caden's broad shoulders and torso moved with each movement of his video persona. It was difficult to know if Caden's reddened face was the reflection of his curly auburn hair or the heated excitement of the game. Josiah's fingers frantically manipulated his laser rumble gamepad in an attempt to dodge Caden's attack. From the gritty determination on Caden's face and the aggressive movement of his body as he barely sat on the edge of his seat, it became evident that he was closing in on his Josiah's last living virtual warrior.

Ian stood behind them yelling directions to Josiah. "Siah move left, watch out for his power blaster, he's gaining on you. NO! Move left; MOVE LEFT, WATCH OUT . . ." His tall slender form, also nimbly shifted in concert with his buddies and the motion of the armed video forces. Ian hardly changed over the summer. His shaggy brown hair and boyish looks, still gave this college sophomore the appearance of a sixteen year old. In order to change his appearance, Ian had announced that he wasn't going to shave all summer. Judging from the little stubble that graced his chin, he was sure to get carded well into his thirties.

Josiah kept yelling like a ninja, occasionally throwing in a few Japanese words to give the impression of authenticity with every counter strike that he made, but the expenditure of all that energy couldn't steer his cyber-soldier clear of Caden's mark. There was a flash of light across the screen and a loud explosion that elicited the vociferous yells simultaneously from all three guys as they fell back into their seats. Josiah's last man was destroyed. Game over!

Before the thrill of the virtual moment had evaded them, Wes stated from the doorway, "Someone had way too much time on his hands this summer. My money is on the fact that you never found a job and spent days on end locked in *OVERTHROW!*"

The guys quickly glanced over their shoulders to see Wes propped idly against the door post with his arms comfortably folded across his chest. The excitement of the game turned into a glad reunion.

"What are you implying? I do believe that you underestimate the *natural warrior* in me," Caden said with his teeth clenched, only to turn it into a smile as he hugged his friend. "It's good to see you buddy - can't wait to school you in the next game," he continued with a wink and a jab to Wes' midsection.

"Where have you been," Ian exclaimed. "We could have played teams. I was knocked out in the first round. I could have used a good partner who could remember the rules of this game."

Wes threw his arm around Ian's neck to affirm his delight in seeing a good friend, "Do you always have to play by the rules, Ian? That's only going to make you more uptight than you already are. Loosen up, dude."

"Yeah Ian, you'd play a lot better if you took a few more risks, dude. You should just go *ninja* and fear nothing!" Josiah added as he struck his most fearsome karate kid pose.

"That really helped you, 'Siah!", busted Caden, who couldn't resist getting in a good dig.

"Well I still could have used you as my partner," Ian replied with a smile in Wes' direction.

"To be honest with you I was attending to something a little more important," Wes responded. He suddenly felt an urgent excitement again. He wanted to cut right to the chase and tell the guys his news.

"I went over to Dr. Ashe's office. I had a meeting with him," Wes blurted out.

"What did he say?" Josiah interrupted.

"We're in!" Wes blurted.

"Yes!" Caden shouted as he clenched his fists in a gesture of victory.

"Are you kidding?" Ian shouted. "That's so great."

"Bro that's so awesome. We owe a lot to you, Wes," Josiah said. "I can't believe that we have been selected to be Dr. Ashe's next mentor group."

"That's right! We are going to become protégés of the renowned Dr. Ashe and join ranks of many great and influential men in society who have done this before us!" Wes said.

Now to an average college guy that may not have sounded like an opportunity that warranted so much excitement, but at Mason University, this was better than being pledged into the most coveted fraternity on campus.

Dr. Darren Ashe or "Doc" as he was affectionately referred to by his students, held the distinguished Andrew W. Mellon Foundation endowed Chair of the Humanities Department. His research on identity development and the formation of *character* in men made him one of the world's most sought after experts on *mentoring*.

Dr. Ashe had a brilliant track record. The men that he mentored became men of great character and esteem. His protégées included Senators and Statesmen, Clergymen and Counselors, Advisors and Advocates; all men of great influence and integrity. Past members of Dr. Ashe's groups included the present Vice-President of the United States, the Director of The United Nations International Children's Emergency Fund and the Crowned Prince of Montenegro. Some of the greatest men who came to Mason University's ivied halls had been part of one of Dr. Ashe's mentor groups.

Doc made it his policy to invest in only one mentor group of guys in any given academic year. He was very strict regarding the boundaries for the mentor group. The group had to be made up of no less than four, and no more than eight guys or he would not meet with them. In addition, the group had to commit to meet weekly in this mentoring relationship until they graduated or left Mason University. When a group graduated out, Dr. Ashe would start another group.

Last year a group had graduated, leaving an opening for the start of a new mentor group. Wes and his friends knew that they each had to commit and that the commitment would span the next three years while they attended Mason. While this appeared to be an unusually demanding requirement for four nineteen year old guys to make, they realized that this opportunity might never come again.

Ian and Wes had become acquainted with "Doc" last year after they had taken Dr. Ashe's course entitled *Personal Strengths and Character Development.* Doc had a way of reaching into the minds of his students and provoking them to deeper levels of thinking, far beyond what they imagined could be possible. He also could grip his student's hearts, igniting their passions like an ember that ignites a great wild fire. After taking his class, Wes and Ian were sold on the idea of trying to become the next group of guys who came under Doc's mentoring.

During the course of that semester, Doc lectured at a dorm event for *"Guys Only"* that involved all the Men's dorms and fraternities on campus. Josiah and Caden attended the event along with Wes and Ian. Dr. Ashe was put on the hot-seat and guys were allowed to fire any question they desired at him. His gentle spirit, straight-forward candor, and amazing wit and wisdom captivated every young man in the lecture hall. At times he had them belly laughing and then his honesty and depth of life experience would suddenly bring the room to a tender silence that made the electrical current in the overhead lights; a noisy distraction. After that event, it didn't take long for the band of brothers to start inquiring how to become Dr. Ashe's next mentor group.

The guys knew that Doc was "graduating" a group out because their resident advisor and senior, Dave Madison, was a member of that group. Dave was a great role model and leader for the freshman guys in the dorm. Anyone who came in contact with Dave walked away knowing that he had just encountered a man of integrity. Dave had a way of building up people and bringing out the best in them. Josiah and Wes immediately connected with Dave after they discovered that he was one of the starting attackmen on the Mason University Knights lacrosse team. Dave had encouraged Wes and Ian to approach Dr. Ashe with their desire to be the next mentor group.

"Do you understand what Doc's mentor group is all about?" Dave asked.

"Yeah, he does something that makes men become great and powerfully successful," Josiah answered.

Dave smiled and calmly said, "First of all, Doc isn't responsible for the way the guys in his group turn out. He never claims that he *makes* any man, although great men can be made by this experience. Secondly, if wanting to be a great man means that you seek status, power or wealth, then Doc won't be interested in mentoring your group. But if you really desire to become a man who internalizes the highest of virtues, then you may have a shot at becoming Doc's next mentor group. You really need to give this some thought because you will not be called to an easy task. The stakes are high and costly."

"Almost every guy on campus wants to be in a group that Doc mentors. Give us some insight that will help us gain an advantage over the other guys who are contending to be his next mentor group," Wes said.

"I can't do that. This isn't a game that you win or some kind of test that you can cram for and pass. Doc will assess many variables to see if he, your group dynamic, each guy's intentions, and a host of other things will line up to create a maximized potential growth environment. All you can do is be real and be yourself."

"What happens in the group? Do you just sit around and talk?" Josiah asked.

"I can't tell you that either. If you are chosen, you will enter into a confidential fraternity. You just need to know that this isn't a pansy group therapy session or weekly social club. You'll be stretched and pushed to your limits. Your relationships will be tried and tested. It will be more intense than anything you have ever experienced. The potential for failure is great and the consequences are dire. You've heard about those who succeeded but there have been others who have failed, who you don't know about".

There was a sobering and pensive tenor to Dave's words. His countenance appeared to fall slightly and Wes detected moroseness in his attitude. He felt as if Dave was speaking out of some personal insight or experience that informed his response. Could it be that during this process Dave came into a greater awareness of some darkness in his soul? Maybe he wasn't becoming the man he had hoped he would be. Or maybe he was reliving the pain of watching a dear friend come into the dire consequences of the failure that he had spoken of moments ago. Nonetheless, it was as if the conversation had been hurled onto a sheet of thin ice. Nobody ventured to move the conversation forward; besides, they doubted that Dave would offer up anything more. Dave just sat contemplatively in an awkward silence, which made Wes and Josiah more uncomfortable.

Wes knew that he had to say something to escape the uneasiness of the moment. "I guess I only thought the mentoring produced great men. I never thought that there could be a downside. It sounds like Doc's mentor group gets pretty intense. Dave, do you think that we have the potential to become Doc's next group?" he asked.

"Sure! I don't see anything that could hinder or disqualify you guys from the running. Besides, Doc often asks his present group for insight – I promise to put in a good word for you guys," Dave said with a smile that brought the room back into a sense of peaceful resolve.

After Wes and Josiah had a series of conversations with Caden and Ian, the four decided to move ahead to secure their future as Doc's next mentor group. Wes spearheaded the venture by meeting with Dr. Ashe who was open to the possibility. Doc had his department secretary, Mrs. Welton set up a series of meeting so that he and the guys could get a clearer understanding of the expectations, demands and design of this mentor group. He wanted to make sure there was a *good fit,* before a final decision was made.

CHAPTER
FIVE

During the final semester of their freshman year, the guys aggressively began to pursue the possibility of becoming Dr. Ashe's next mentor group. Wes had set up the first meeting and emerged as the point person leading this initiative.

"I will entertain the thought," Dr. Ashe announced. "I rarely find a group of young men at the end of their freshman year with the level of maturity and commitment to follow through with the intense rigors of this initiative. But I am passionate about the idea of being a part of a group that stays intact for three full years. They usually can emerge as the most dynamic and powerfully impacting group of men, when all is said and done. I am also intrigued that there are only four of you. Given the proper character traits, your brotherhood could prove to be quite impacting."

That comment kindled an exhilarating hope in the guys. "We certainly are committed and we all are passionate about doing this. What do we have to do next?" Wes asked.

"I would like to meet with each young man individually a couple times before you leave school for the summer. I know that this is a very hectic time with the semester ending; final papers, projects, exams and all."

Doc knew that often the single passion of one or two carried a group. He wanted to insure that all of the guys were as engaging, passionate and committed as Wes was. He also saw this as a test of their commitment. If they really desired this opportunity, they could find the time during the most hectic part of the semester to meet. In short, they would rearrange their priorities. He had seen so many young men skirt around these appointments in the name of academic priority, only to learn that they could find time for more frivolous activities that superseded study. Dr. Ashe knew that the young men he was looking for would not compromise their studies *or* their commitment to being mentored and to each other. These men would forgo other activities to keep their priorities intact.

Over that last month of the semester, each guy met with Doc two times individually and informally in the student commons, over lunch in the cafeteria and at the favorite student hang out, a coffee shop off campus called *Mystery Brews*.

Caden was the last to have his final meeting with the good doctor. That night the band of brothers decided to regroup at Mystery Brews to talk about their experience.

"Man! Dr. Ashe is intense," said Caden. "I felt like he was dangerous, yet incredibly good. I left his office earlier feeling like I was on fire. I'm so stoked about doing this."

"I know what you mean. It was kind of like he was looking right through me. He asked me such powerfully direct questions that I thought he was reaching inside to pull something out of me – I was afraid that he might find something that he didn't like . . . or maybe I didn't like," added Ian.

"For sure!" Josiah interjected. "But it wasn't like he was looking for garbage, I rather had this overwhelming sense that he was . . . mining gold, you know – like looking to bring out the best in me. Deep down, I believed that he would help me uncover some amazing things about myself. That really pumped me up."

"I agree; the experience with Doc is on an entirely different level than other experiences because he doesn't just talk *at* you. He has a way of involving every part of who you are. I left his office thinking that he really stretched my mind but also engaged my heart.

That can be kind of scary but every bit of who I am wanted more. It felt like it was a great adventure. I'm nervous, but I'm excited at the same time. Do you guys know what I mean?" Wes asked.

They all agreed, and each guy came away from those meetings intrigued, challenged, a bit intimidated and more excited about the possibility of meeting together with Dr. Ashe on a weekly basis.

In the days that followed Caden's meeting, Doc alluded that he thought he had gathered enough insight to understand each of the guys' personalities and their passion for this group. He was convinced that each guy was genuine and valued the other guys who were going to be in the group. Now he needed to discern if the mix was going to create an environment of integrity where each member could sharpen the other, like a knife against a honing steel. He questioned how well each guy knew himself and if that guy had a *teachable spirit*, as Doc would call it. He needed time to assess if each guy had what it takes to be a great man. Dr Ashe also needed to assess if he, himself, had what it takes to engage and cultivate those things in this group of men.

Doc believed that mentoring was not about the mentor but about the quality of each guy's character. He knew that a mentor needed to see, affirm and cultivate the best in a protégée. He believed that a mentor served as a facilitator of experiences and situations that would cause common boys to face themselves, dream of the men that they wanted to become and empower them to emerge as great men. Every time Doc faced a new group, he would humbly assess if he was the man who could cultivate these things in the lives of that particular group. Doc needed one more face-to-face meeting before he could begin to deliberate his decision.

CHAPTER
SIX

Exam week had begun when Wes received an email from Doc requesting another meeting with him over coffee at the Mystery Brews. Doc didn't need to meet the entire band of brothers; he thought it sufficient to talk only with Wes.

As Wes walked to the coffee shop he wondered, *Is Doc going to tell me that he made a decision? Maybe we don't have what it takes to meet Doc's expectations! Or . . . maybe he sees enough potential in us to get excited about a three year mentoring group.*

Wes arrived before Doc. He ordered a passion fruit iced tea and sat at a table near the door. He gazed out the window of the establishment and within moments, he spied Doc coming from the parking lot. Wes stood up when Doc came close to the table.

"Sit down, lad. Please, sit down. I'm going to get a strong cup of the Ethiopian Blend. I've been thinking about it all morning. For some reason the coffee in the faculty offices is extremely weak today." He took off his hounds-tooth fedora and placed it on his chair then walked over to the counter to get his prize. Wes watched him and felt endeared to the old guy. *I really hope he tells me we are the next group. There is something amazing about this man.*

Dr. Ashe returned to the table with his piping hot coffee. Before he even sat down, he began, "I haven't quite made my decision yet, Wes. I don't venture into these things lightly or quickly. I do not detect any red flags from you or your brothers, but I need more time to process. I feel like this decision may be the most important of any that I have made in the past, so I want to be diligent and discerning. That may give rise to many more questions. And that's where you come in, my boy. I would like to direct some of my thoughts and questions to you, through email over the summer," Dr. Ashe stated. "I gathered that you are the glue of the group."

"Glue? What do you mean?"

"You were the one who labeled the group a *band of brothers* rather than calling them your homeys, peeps, good old boys, drinking buddies or whatever the vernacular of the day is. I usually find it difficult to keep up with the lingo of a younger generation. Regardless, I gathered, that you believe that there is a deeper heart connection that each of you share, or hope to share . . ." he paused, then looking over the top of his glasses into Wes' eyes, continued: ". . . which transcends mere friendship. It is this deeper relationship that makes you see each other as *brothers*. It looks to me as if you have led them into that relational depth. You have learned to think and lead with your heart, my son. That's why *you* chose to call them brothers," the good doctor surmised.

Doc seemed to read him like a book. Wes felt uncomfortable and vulnerably confessed, "I hate that about myself, Doc. It's a great flaw."

"What do you mean?" Doc returned with a puzzled tone.

"I hate thinking with my heart. On the outside, I seem to be confident, but inside I doubt myself. I'm not a leader or glue as you call it because I'm way too . . . sensitive."

"So you think that it's a flaw for a man to think with his heart?" Doc clarified.

"If they do it like I do, it is. A few weeks ago, I was running late to get to my Lacrosse game. I needed to eat lunch fast, so I didn't want to talk with anyone in the cafeteria. I found an empty table in the corner and deliberately sat with my back to the entire room so nobody could bother me. I had just begun devouring my food when this girl came and sat across the far end of the table opposite from me. She asked me if it was ok for her to sit there. I nodded graciously but hardly acknowledged her, let alone engaged her. She sat in similar fashion, eyes focused down at her tray, not conversational; but I surmised that she wasn't pressed for time like I was. I told myself that she must be the quiet, shy type because she seemed kind of . . . sheepish. I expected that a friend would soon be joining her, but nobody came. Part of me was glad because I didn't want a table full of girls, but then my heart began to kick in and I felt hurt for her. Regardless, I kept my focus on my lunch and the schedule I had to keep. After a few moments, I felt like an ass, thinking that I was going to leave without even acknowledging her presence. It felt so devaluing and cold. I also felt bad that she was sitting alone. She really looked . . . lost. I had to say something so I introduced myself and asked her a few questions about herself." Wes paused.

"Great - that makes you a person of great character, Wes. You did a valiant, compassionate thing," Dr. Ashe quickly chimed.

"Maybe, but that's not the end," Wes continued. "As I asked her more questions, I came to find out that she is very lonely and hurting. She told me her story. She had just come to Mason University this year as a freshman. She was having a difficult time because just four weeks before school began her father had a sudden heart attack and passed away. She was close to him. She was having difficulty making friends, keeping up with course work and a lot of other things. I don't even remember all the details. But here's the bad part - As she told me her story, I started to get very emotional. I didn't know what to say, or how to help her. My eyes started to well up. I didn't want to cry; not in front of her, and certainly not in the middle of the frick'n cafeteria. I was trapped with nowhere to go. Fortunately, she got a phone call from home and had to leave. The minute she left the table, I lost it. I sat there by myself bawling like a baby uncontrollably, praying that nobody would see me. Somehow, I was sucked into sharing her pain. I just left my tray and got out of the cafeteria through a side exit, as fast as I could."

With exasperation, Wes continued, "Doc, I'm such a wuss, I get choked up seeing a chick-flick; there's an earthquake in China that kills hundreds of people and I can be reduced to a puddle. Hell, someone's cat dies and I feel like I'm going to lose it. All my life I've had to work hard to stay in control. My dad used to tease me and sometimes even got angry with me because of my sensitivity. He would tell me how embarrassing it was to have such a sissy for a son. Now I avoid sensitive situations or change the subject when conversations get too emotional. I've even learned to be tactfully humorous when the vibe becomes too deep. Doc, I hate thinking with my heart, I'm too sensitive. Real leaders aren't that weak. A strong man is able to exercise more control over his emotions than I do."

"Ah, Wes did you ever stop to think that that girl may have just needed to encounter a man, strong enough to feel her pain? She may not have needed anyone to fix her or even say anything to her. You may have brought wholeness to her by just joining her suffering. Your tears may have been the very thing that could have brought healing to her broken spirit. It takes strength of character to do that. My son, I have come to understand that truly great men understand the unbridled power they possess when they think with a compassionate heart."

Wes was feeling very insecure but also a twinge of wonder, "I don't know if I understand that, Doc."

"I'm sure you will, someday," Doc replied confidently. Then he looked at his watch and rose abruptly. "I have to run to class, my boy. I'm still going to count on you being the point man throughout the summer."

"Gladly," Wes replied, swallowing his last gulp of tea.

As Doc started to walk away, he turned and said, "One more thing - Two other groups have asked me to meet with them next year. Just to be fair, I've also met with those gentlemen. Over the summer, I'm going to give this a lot of thought . . . with my *heart* as well as my head."

He tipped his hat and smiled as he walked out of the coffee shop. That was the last time Wes saw him, until the meeting today. Over the summer, Wes had fielded questions, gathered each guy's schedules and kept in email and phone contact with Doc. Now Wes stood in front of his three friends with the encouraging news. Dr. Ashe was inviting them to meet with him in his office tomorrow morning at 9am, one hour before the President's Convocation, which officially marked the start of the academic year. The thrill of the adrenaline-producing, "Dark Force Overthrow" virtual reality game and its accompanying background music, still blaring in the room, faded as they pondered the journey they were about to embark upon.

CHAPTER
SEVEN

Morning came quickly. Dr. Ashe's office was on the other side of the University campus. The guys agreed that they would leave the dorm at about 8:40am so that they could be on time. Ian and Caden rolled out of bed about 8:30, dressing as they came walking down the hall to snatch Wes and Josiah before exiting their floor. They looked like they had gotten very little sleep.

"Did you guys stay up all night playing Dark force?" Josiah asked.

"No, Mr. Anal-Retentive wanted to get the room completely set in order," Caden resentfully stated, pointing blame at Ian. "First day of the semester and already he makes me pull an all-nighter."

"I was just afraid . . . (yawn) . . . that we would never get it done if we didn't do it . . . (yawn) . . . right away," said Ian, unintelligibly yawning through the rejoinder.

"And of course I had to help him," Caden admitted. "We got about three hours of sleep – We're planning on sleeping through the Prez's Constipation," he mocked. The President's Convocation was the official kick off of the school year. The pomp and circumstance, the parade of faculty in full regalia, the introductions and long winded rhetoric from various visiting scholars, along with the University President's speech welcoming students back to their scholarly pursuits at Mason University was a boring mandatory requirement for all students. "We'll just sit in the balcony and catch a good nap," Caden continued.

"You guys worked all night getting your room settled? You should have told us that you were planning to finish your room last night before you started the project. A couple more hands would have made the work load lighter and completed hours sooner; I recall a wise man once telling me something like that," said Josiah.

"You mean you guys would have come down and helped us?" Ian asked.

"No! But a couple more hands would have gotten you more sleep," Josiah chuckled.

"C'mon guys, we really don't want to be late", Wes said, desiring to make the cross-campus hike in a timely manner.

The boys quickened their pace and began the trek across the beautifully landscaped University grounds. The morning was crisp and while there was still a feel of summer in the air, the birth pangs of autumn had already begun.

They arrived a bit winded and fully awake at Dr. Ashe's office right at 9am sharp. Mrs. Welton, the Humanities Department administrative assistant greeted them at the reception desk where she sat as the gatekeeper to all faculty offices in that department.

"We're here to see Doc . . . I mean, Dr. Ashe," Wes said.

"Yes, he told me you boys were coming and asked me to let you into his office. He'll be right with you. Follow me."

The guys followed the matronly woman back to Dr. Ashe's office. She opened the door to a grand old room with an ivy-league ambiance. The room was lined with redwood bookcases that stretched from floor to ceiling. Each housed volumes of old hardback books. Some of the bookshelves contained cultural artifacts that Dr. Ashe had acquired over the years. In the center of the room were three leather sofas that formed a cozy horseshoe shaped conversation alcove. A large dark wood coffee table graced the center of this meeting area. It invited visitors to sit back on the couches and put their feet up. There were a few stone carved figurines, some candles and a couple of oversized books on the table.

At the far end of the office was Dr. Ashe's desk. It was a massive piece of furniture, piled with papers and books. One would assume that along with many student essays, there was a gold mine of research on that desk top; an ironic and humbling blend. Behind the desk, on the mahogany paneled wall hung many of Dr. Ashe's credentials. They beckoned a visitor to "come see" yet their position behind that intimidating desk created a foreboding chasm. It seemed that anyone who wanted to look closely at those hanging accolades would have to cross a sacred space to do so. High above, a row of small leaded glass windows, some of which embodied the crest of the University, separated the mahogany walls from the vaulted ceiling. These artistic transoms allowed the only source of natural light to come in. The windows cast a warm and colorful hue into this impressive room. This grand architectural design reminded everyone of the legacy of this institution and generated a reverential respect.

"You boys have a seat and *Doc* will be right with you," Mrs. Welton said. Then she whispered as she walked out the door, "He ran down to the lounge to get some coffee – he doesn't function well in the morning without a java jolt."

The boys positioned themselves, two on each of two sofas and silently looked around. Wes noticed a glimmering object mounted on the wall behind a coat stand in the corner of the office. He hadn't noticed it when he came in because it was concealed by the large raised paneled mahogany door. Now that he was seated, he could see that the object was a beautiful sword affixed to a hand carved wooden wall mount.

The thirty-six inch double-edged blade of the sword glistened in the light of the leaded glass windows. The hilt added another eleven inches to the length. The grip of the sword was wrapped in a deep, midnight blue-dyed leather that made the silver pommel seem like a beacon light atop a high standard. In the center of the pommel set a blue sapphire medallion with an inlayed ruby stoned, Fleury cross.

The quillion reflected the bright silver of the pommel, with the end of the cross guard crafted to look as if two open palmed hands were raised heavenward to receive strength from God. On the ricasso of the sword set a crest. This crest was not the crest of the University, but another beautifully colorful crest, foreign to any that one could find at Mason University. It was divided into four quadrants. The upper left quadrant was hunter green and contained chalice with an ornately designed heart etched on its bowl. The quadrant in the upper right had a deep wine colored background. On its face was a strong man's fist clutching a blooming white lily with light emanating from behind the hand. The lower left quadrant was golden maize and had an eagle with its wings spread wide in flight. The remaining quadrant was royal blue. In it was a flaming torch situated though a gold crown and set upon an open book. Down the center of the sword's fuller was engraved the words:

Hearts Bound: Men of Love, Goodness, Wisdom and Freedom

Without a word, Wes sprang to his feet and headed in the direction of the sword. He needed to see this beautiful object up close.

"What are you doing," Ian sternly whispered as Wes walked toward the sword.

"I want to take a look at the sword on the wall over there," Wes returned. "Don't worry I'm not going to mess with it."

Josiah and Caden quickly joined him leaving Ian alone, in obedience to the *"sit down"* law enacted by Mrs. Welton.

"Dude, Dr. Ashe is going to be here any minute. We were told to have a seat and wait. It's going to look really bad if you're snooping around his office," Ian said in a reprimanding tone.

It was obvious that the guys were intrigued by the magnificent sword. They appeared to tune out Ian's mothering. Moments later Ian was standing with them eyeing this great trophy.

Ian kept looking around the office door to see if Doc was approaching. Wes could see Ian becoming anxious over this. He knew that if Dr. Ashe had walked in during this sword admiring moment, Ian would remain caught in the trauma of that experience for the duration of their meeting. Instead of running that risk, he headed back to take his rightful spot on the sofa. As he did, the others joined him.

"Ian you worry way too much," Wes said, plopping down on the sofa next to him.

An awkward minute of silence passed as the four companions sat in this amazing space. It felt as if Dr. Ashe had left them there for hours when actually it had only been about five minutes since Mrs. Welton invited them to have a seat.

Josiah broke the silence, "Do you think he's read all these books?"

Before anyone could make a retaliating comment they heard, "No not *all* of them, but *most* of them; besides, some of these pompous volumes are so boring they could put an insomniac on a sugar high to sleep," Dr. Ashe replied, looking over the top of his eyeglasses as he walked briskly through the door.

CHAPTER
EIGHT

As Dr. Ashe entered his office, the guys all rose to their feet as this renowned man of high esteem and great social stature entered the room. He looked older and more frail than they had remembered him. Somehow, he didn't appear as larger-than-life as they recalled or had made him to be in their mind's eye. He was a simple, sixty-eight year old, grandfatherly gentleman. His tweed jacket and striped tie kept him locked as a stereotypical professor in a former time era. Suddenly this legend became an ordinary, real-live-flesh-and-blood man.

"Sit down boys, sit down, I'm sorry I kept you waiting, but our conversation wouldn't have gotten very far if I didn't have my morning coffee. The stuff stimulates the brain you know; at least that's what I tell myself."

Dr. Ashe held an oversized hand crafted mug of piping hot black coffee in his hand. It looked like one of the relics that belonged on his shelves. The coffee mug in and of itself was intriguing, but it only served to draw attention to Doc's hand and the ring that he wore. The center of the ring was adorned with the same crest that was on the sword. *The crest must be some kind of secret fraternal order,* Wes thought. He wanted to ask about this intriguing icon but Dr. Ashe started right into the agenda that he had in mind.

"Well gentlemen, I'm curious to know what your expectations are regarding . . . mentoring," Dr. Ashe said as he positioned himself on the remaining empty sofa.

The guys looked silently at each other, all with anticipating glances that non-verbally prompted, *"Say something . . . NO! YOU say something . . . Somebody please say something"!*

"Well Doc," Josiah, broke the ice respectfully, "We want to learn from you."

Dr. Ashe's brow furrowed, he put his hand against his chin and fixed a pensive gaze toward the corner ceiling as if deep in thought. The guys anticipated some profound words of wisdom. Instead Dr. Ashe replied, "You could have just taken one of my courses for that – how will this be different?"

There was silence. Rebuttals quickly formed in their heads . . . *Isn't mentoring supposed to be a learning experience where a younger guy gleans from the life experiences of an older man? Doesn't a mentor bestow words of wisdom on the ears of his protégées so that they become more competent in life?* Dr. Ashe didn't wait for anyone to reply. He just raised the issue then left it unresolved.

"How about you Caden, what are your expectations?" Dr. Ashe said shifting the direction away from Josiah.

"I know that the guys who have been in your past mentor groups became very close brothers. Our resident advisor last year often talked about the deep bond that had developed between the guys in his group. Quite honestly, we feel like we kind of have a jump on being close brothers, of sorts. The four of us have grown to be fairly tight. I expect that this mentor group will help us bond together more," Caden answered.

"Yes, I recall having a conversation with Wes about something like that last semester. I believe that you boys are bonding, or in the vernacular of the day it's called . . . bro-mance, if I recall," Dr. Ashe responded. "Nonetheless most guys can *bond* over a televised ballgame at the local sports bar. What will this experience give you that, let's say . . . being in a fraternity can't?" Once again, Dr. Ashe raised a serious question and left it unresolved.

"What about you Wes? You have been most aggressive about making this happen. What do you expect?" Dr. Ashe questioned.

"Umm, you've mentored some great men, Doc," Wes offered. "We want you to mold us into men who impact our world like those other guys."

"Well I wish I could take the credit for the quality of the men who preceded you, but alas I can't. So if you expect that a mentor will make you a great man, then you may be grossly disappointed," Dr. Ashe returned.

Wes remembered his former RA, Dave's words. *Doc doesn't make men great, but great men may immerge from this experience.* Wes was puzzled about how he should respond. He looked at each of his friends. They appeared to be as confused as he was but it was obvious that each guy was ravaging through the corners of his mind to come up with an answer. They hadn't really thought about what *they specifically wanted* from these meetings. All they had for answers were clichés.

Dr. Ashe directed the conversation to Ian. "And Ian, what are you expecting from this mentoring group?"

The guys knew that Ian's mind was racing to come up with the *correct* answer but they were surprised to hear the words that came from his mouth. "I expect we will be called upon to be raw and real with each other in a way that will bring out the very best, and possibly the worst, of our character."

Doc smiled, "That you will, my son," he proclaimed with a gleam in his eye. "You will embark on a great adventure where each will hone the other to live at the top of his game."

"So we *will* be learning and acquiring wisdom," Josiah asked, trying to make his question sound like a statement.

"Of sorts," Dr. Ashe explained. "Many people see mentoring more like a didactic experience, but the mentoring relationship is much more than a hierarchical cognitive experience or tutorial. Acquiring knowledge or developing a set of skills is not the primary task of mentoring. Learning, that redefines one's self and brings about transformational growth, is. I expect that this experience will be a life-involved, lifelong synergogic experience."

"Synergogic?" Josiah asked. "Don't you mean synergistic?"

"No, this will not be pedagogic but a two way character sharpening experience; a synergogic experience. It is a two way street. Real strength of character comes when the mentor and protégées contextualize teachable moments that redefine who they *both* are. I will never be the same once you have joined me in this journey. I hope we all emerge better men," Doc said with a tone of expectation.

"Wow," Wes exclaimed, "I suddenly feel like the bar was just raised." Groping for words he continued, "I guess I'm realizing that there is a sense of responsibility that I have to you and these guys . . . but I don't know what I have, or even if I have much to offer."

"You speak of being a close knit band of brothers, Wes. Well, make your brothers succeed, at any cost. If each of you selflessly commits to bring out the best in each other, then you will have a truly uncommon bond. Your hearts will be bound together," Doc replied.

"But, Doc when Ian mentioned being real, you indicated that we will see each other's flaws. Shouldn't we help each other overcome the weaknesses we have? I thought integrity involved eliminating character flaws. Shouldn't we call each other out on things? Isn't that what accountability is?" Caden stated, expecting Doc to resonate in agreement with his observation. The guys expected as much from Caden.

Caden Boyd believed that *he* had a handle on truth and rightness almost to a stubborn fault. It wasn't that Caden thought that he was right all the time, as some would count arrogance. It's just that he believed that there were absolute values that should govern life. He usually was quick to notice when others deviated from those values that *he* deemed *absolute*. He was equally quick to confront his friends, believing that it was his moral responsibility to champion truth. Caden often came across as a judgmental and hostile person because of his aggressive, confrontational tones. As the result, some people had little to do with him. But Caden believed that that was the price one should be willing to pay, to take a stand for what is right.

"Caden, is there ever a possibility that the values to which you hold, may be flawed?" Doc asked.

"Well, I think that if a man takes a strong moral stand then he can't go wrong," Caden returned.

"But is there a possibility that in taking a stand and pointing out another person's flaws, *you* may be wrong?" Doc prodded again.

"I would be a fool to think that I'm right every time – and for the record, I really don't think I'm right all the time, Doc" Caden confessed.

"Well then it would make sense to redefine accountability. True accountability doesn't look to identify and eliminate the flaws that a brother has but rather allows him to so exercise the best traits that he possesses. In doing this, the flaw pales and is starved out of a man's character," Doc explained.

The best analogy for those types of mentor groups is that they shape men to be navel gazing; where a guy fixes his eyes so intently on his navel that he, along with his brothers, fail to see that there are more amazing feats that he can accomplish besides collecting lint in one dimple.

Dr. Ashe faced Caden and said, "My friend, don't misunderstand. Standing for truth and correcting a brother is in fact a noble characteristic, but you can do more good by *calling out* that which is great in your brothers than that which is flawed."

"Touché Doc, I'll work on that," Caden remarked.

"No, *we'll* work on that Caden," Doc continued. "Men of truly great character are never *self-made*. They are not rugged individuals who learn to be fully independent; rather they have come to a deep understanding of what it means to be inter-dependent. Our society points to many powerful men who have become symbols of character and success. Often these men boast of being self made and they practice this ideology by wielding their power, professionally distancing themselves from those they are in authority over and deliberately staying outside the community of others so that they can inform, lead and control the community. This is a skewed and perverted view of a man of character. Men of great character know the value of the statement, Where we go one, we go all. He understands the profound truth that life change happens in intentionally loving and caring relationships. This keeps great men in the tension of not making more of their own personal accomplishments, but applauds the strengths and accomplishments of a community. It also makes men more gracious, less judgmental, more optimistic and hopeful. It serves to create a sixth sense in a man, affording him to see the incredible value of, and the best in others."

As he spoke, the four young men hung on every word. Dr. Ashe looked at his watch. They had little time before the convocation would begin.

"Well since I would be a part of this group too, I would like to tell you my expectations," Dr. Ashe proclaimed.

Each guy shifted his weight and leaned in closer to the source of these next words.

CHAPTER
NINE

The brothers had wondered if Doc would share his expectations, since each of them were called upon to give their account. He had often said that he would be as much a part of the group as they would be.

"I expect three things from this experience and you," Dr. Ashe stated. "First, I expect that each of you will engage this process with your entire being; intellectually, emotionally, physically and spiritually. There will be times when each of you will encounter a physical challenge only to discover that it may have a spiritual outcome. Or you might wrestle through an intellectual question, only to find that it brings deep emotional release. You will come to know that the process is as important, if not more important than the end result. Mentoring is more about the journey than the destination. You need to decide if you can meet this first expectation," Doc said. Before the guys could give any gesture or voice of affirmation, Doc was on to the second expectation.

"Secondly, I expect each of you to intentionally *commit*. Mentoring involves commitment; commitment to meet weekly without failure and commitment to take the challenges set before each of you. You must commit to trust your mentor and each other, even when you don't understand or see the final outcome. You must commit to bring out the best in each other and finally, commit to become the man that you hope and desire to be. If you do this you will discover amazing things."

He looked each guy squarely in the eyes and said, "You need to decide if you can and will do that." Nobody moved. They hardly breathed waiting for his last expectation.

"Finally, I expect that you would be willing to die for each man in this group." Dr. Ashe paused to let his words sink in then he continued, "If you would be willing to die for each other, then you certainly will be real with each other. If you know that the men around you would give their life for you, then this will be a safe place for each of you to wrestle through and develop the characteristics that will make you, beyond a shadow of a doubt, great men of integrity. If you would truly give your life for your brother then you will really work to ensure that he becomes all that he can be," Dr. Ashe leaned in toward his intently focused friends and soberly said, ". . . and I don't mean this metaphorically. You boys have entered into an arena where the stakes are high. Becoming the man you hope to be, is costly and involves the commitment of each of us to the other. In this arena truly great men are made."

The old professor raised his coffee mug to his lips and sat back against the sofa. "Throughout the remainder of this day consider the cost and if you decide that you are in, meet me next Monday evening at half past eight o'clock, at the Mystery Brews Coffee Shoppe. If you are there, I will know that you have counted the cost and you are making this commitment. I hope I will see each of you there Monday night, gentlemen."

Dr. Ashe stood up and the guys immediately rose to their feet as if respect snatched the back of their collars and yanked them upright. Nobody spoke as Doc opened his office door. The guys all filed out and almost robotically headed toward the President's Convocation. They didn't say a word until they passed Mrs. Welton's desk.

"Have a nice day, boys," she said. Her words seemed to bring them back to reality as they each smiled and acknowledged her.

"Whoa, that was intense!" Caden stated.

"Guys, this is serious stuff. Doc doesn't play games. We have to do this together. I'm in; are you guys in?" Wes said. He was so excited he could hardly contain himself.

CHAPTER NINE

"I'm in," Caden said, without hesitation.

"Me too!" added Josiah, in quick form. "Doc has wisdom like my grandfather – this is going to rock our worlds."

Ian didn't say anything. He looked like he was just hit by a truck. "What about you Ian? You're in, aren't you?" Wes asked.

"I need to think about this more, just like Doc suggested," Ian replied. "The level of commitment is really high and I need to do well academically this year, plus there is . . ."

"You were so pumped up about this last semester. You never mentioned any concerns," Caden interrupted. He seemed disgusted by Ian's hesitation.

"I don't know. All that talk about committing and dying for each other – *not metaphorically* - that's intense stuff. I didn't know about that last semester. I've got to really do well this semester or I'll lose my scholarship," Ian proclaimed.

"This is more important than any course we'll take. I have a feeling that there will be more learning and life change that comes out of this hour each week than a month of class time," Josiah added in an attempt to give Ian some insightful perspective. He placed a reassuring hand on Ian's shoulder. Not looking for consolation, Ian just shrugged it off and began to walk at a more brisk pace ahead of his friends.

Ian's response only served to fuel what Caden thought to be unjust and selfish. He quickly stepped from behind Ian and butted his shoulder into Ian's as he passed. Then Caden reeled around to face him head on. Pointing his finger in Ian's face, he stated, "Dude, you're in," as if he had made Ian's decision for him. Wes glared in Caden's direction as if to say, *"Can you be any more of a jerk than you're being now?"*

Caden acknowledged the glare by saying, "What! - If Ian's out, then we're out too because Doc will only meet with a group that has four or more. It won't be fair to the rest of us."

Wes just shook his head at Caden's impudence. "C'mon, where we go one, we go all," he recited with a smile and he threw his arm around Ian's neck. "Besides we're committed to make you succeed," Wes whispered as the four guys stepped into the assembly hall where the convocation had already begun.

CHAPTER
TEN

Ian Bound had grown up in the Bible-belt of the south, the eldest son in a strict, blue collar family. His parents worked hard and sacrificed much to help him get to Mason University. Ian was raised under the assumption that one lived by a strict set of well defined, conservative, life rules and never questioned authority.

Of all the guys in the band of brothers, Ian would be pegged as the one who was most disciplined, and he was. He had a set time when he would study each day; he never missed a workout routine; he called home at 7:45pm every Sunday night because he knew his family would be home from Sunday night church service. He would even get bent out of shape if he missed brushing his teeth three times a day. Josiah often joked that you could set your watch by Ian's *bathroom* routines.

This talk of deep commitment and radical transformation made Ian very uncomfortable. It sounded so . . . messy. Ian sat through the President's Convocation and never heard a word of it. His mind bantered like a violent tennis match; *What if I commit and don't get straight A's? Do I really need straight A's? What if I disappoint my parents, by doing this? Then I'll be forced to quit the group after this year or at the end of the semester, or worse in the middle of the semester. What if I don't commit to this? I could miss the most amazing experience of a lifetime. Doc has a great track record. What if Doc really doesn't like me, after he gets to know me better? He asks questions and doesn't answer them – What if he never tells us what to do to become the men we want to be? I can't handle that – He should tell us what to do. He should answer the questions. If I back out the guys will hate me. This is all really scary to me. I think I should be out but I really want to be in.*

When the convocation ended, Ian picked up his books and started rapidly for the exit.

"Ian?" Wes yelled.

"Later guys, I have a class," Ian called back.

"Yeah, in an hour – I'm in the same class," Caden yelled, but it was too late Ian was gone.

"Just leave him alone. You know that he really hates change," Wes reminded Caden.

Throughout the week, Ian seemed to be in tortured thought. He immersed himself in his studies and hardly talked with the guys. Whenever Caden brought up the subject, Ian would physically leave the room or say that he didn't want to talk about it.

Monday morning came. This was the day of reckoning. Caden's alarm clock went off at 6:30am. He rolled over and shut it off then looked to see if Ian was awake. He remembered going to bed before Ian came in, which was unusual since Ian was so meticulous about getting the proper amount of required sleep. He must have been out cold because he never heard Ian come in. Ian had been distant all week and it was beginning to put a strain on the healthy relationship roommates should have, let alone two guys who considered themselves *brothers*. Across the room, he saw that Ian's bed was made and everything was neatly put in its place. He scanned the room – Ian was gone, or maybe he never came in last night.

CHAPTER
ELEVEN

The crisp Monday evening air seemed unseasonably cooler. Autumn was rapidly approaching. Mason University's campus would soon explode with color, making it an enchanting place. The sun began setting sooner hastening autumn's arrival. Although the night had come, the campus at Mason University was still very active.

With the completion of the first week of classes, students were settling into the routine of the semester but the reality of their newly acquired syllabi hadn't fully set in. The campus still lacked the serious scholarly ambiance that it would develop as the semester progressed and autumn came into its fullness. Groups of students sat in various places on the campus commons and garden walks enjoying the great camaraderie of their college friendships. They were very aware that these stress-free, fair weather evenings would quickly disappear in short time, to be replaced by mid-term exams.

Wes, Caden and Josiah sat in Caden and Ian's room ready to go. They were scheduled to meet with Dr. Ashe at the Mystery Brews coffee shop in thirty minutes.

"I don't think that Ian is going to show up" Josiah said. "All week long he's made comments about having too much homework. I think he's afraid to commit. Caden, do you think he's backing out"?

"How should I know?" Caden frustratingly replied. "He hasn't said a word about it all week; as a matter of fact he's hardly talked to me all week. I haven't seen him since dinner last night. I don't think he came home, or if he did, he was gone before 6:30 this morning. He's so worried about everything that it would be just like him to leave us high and dry. I bet he's sitting in the corner of the library convincing himself that he's doing the right thing – he *does* have to worry about his *scholarships*, you know."

Wes looked at his watch. It would take about fifteen minutes to get from the dorm on the northeast corner of campus to the Mystery Brews Coffee Shop just across Marble Street outside the University South Gate. Wes felt uneasy as each minute encroached upon their travel time but he wanted to give Ian the benefit of the doubt.

"Give the guy a break; you know that if he loses his scholarships he can't come back to Mason," Wes said.

"You know as well as I do that that's not the issue," Caden bit back. "He's freakin-smart and hardly cracked a book all last semester, but he still made the Dean's list. Ian is afraid of anything that gets him out of his comfort zone. He fears doing the wrong thing, disappointing or making people mad at him, breaking the rule or violating what *THEY* say – Those mythical authorities that make people like Ian live constipated lives. *THEY* say you should change your car oil every three month, and Ian freaks out if it's been three months and one day. *THEY* say you shouldn't go swimming for and hour after you eat, so Ian counts the seconds to exactly one hour. Truthfully, I think the idea of this mentor group scares the hell out of him."

Wes looked at his watch again; "We still have plenty of time. He'll be here."

"That doesn't sound very reassuring. Were you saying that for our benefit or are you trying to convince yourself," Caden asked.

"I'm going to call him. We're going to be late if he doesn't get here soon," Josiah stated.

"Go ahead, but he's not answering!" Caden returned. "I've already left about four messages. He didn't return my texts either. He's deliberately avoiding us or he's dead, which I highly doubt".

Josiah's cell phone rang Ian's number. Ian's phone went right to voice mail. Josiah rolled his eyes, shook his head and loudly clicked his cell phone shut. "He's not coming. Wes, I agree with Caden, Ian's out! He's not going to show."

"He's in!" Wes replied.

"Keep dreaming dude," Caden said under his breath.

"How can you be so sure he'll come?" Josiah asked.

"Just a feeling I have. You guys know Ian; he's probably weighing out the pros and cons of this. He gets so stressed about making big decisions. He probably needed to be alone to process. We'll wait five more minutes. If he's not here, we'll leave without him. I'm sure that he'll catch up with us at the coffee shop – at least I hope he will."

Caden chuckled, "There you go again – you just keep right on reassuring yourself. Ian is wound up tighter than an expensive Swiss watch. He experiences anxiety over having to choose an entrée in the cafeteria. He's always so worried that he's making or going to make a wrong decision – like he's committing some mortal sin. The guy lives in an invisible psychological straight jacket. He's not weighing out pros and cons bro; he's just *NOT* going to join us and he's too much of a whimp to tell us straight out."

"Remember last year when we were all hanging out in Josiah's room?" Wes asked. "We started to talk about how freeing it was to be away from home. We didn't have to report to parents or live by their house rules anymore. Caden you had just broken up with your girlfriend back home and you were feeling like a burden was lifted from you. We all talked about doing things that we dreamed of doing but hadn't been able to for some reason or another."

Caden seemed to get caught in the nostalgia of that memory and some of his anger was replaced with amusement. His eyes sparkled and he got this grin on his face, "Yeah! We declared that day our Independence Day," Caden reminisced.

"Exactly; but it was Ian that made it real. The next morning he left campus and got that tattoo of the eagle with its wings spread wide across the back of his shoulders. He said his parents probably wouldn't like it, but he was independent. And as the result of that, the four of us committed to be the *band of brothers*. Later that day we each got our own tats. We called it our . . ."

"Rite of Passage," Josiah said in concert with Wes.

"That's right, our *rite of passage*, sealing the deal. Remember?" Wes asked as he pulled up the sleeve on his left arm revealing a heart wrapped in barbed wire and impaled through the top by a sword.

Josiah smiled, flexed his right bicep and revealed the Japanese script that he had tattooed on the inside of his arm across the bicep. "I think it means knowledge without wisdom is like a load of books on the back of an ass – I'm not sure. It just looked really cool." Josiah added.

"I know – I have mine too," Caden said as he hiked up his pant leg revealing a sword, wrapped in a banner in scripted with the word *veritas*, burned into his calf.

"So what? Ian inspired us to claim our independence from parental control and band together. That has nothing to do with the fact that he's dumping us now."

"That wasn't my point," Wes said. "He went out and got the tattoo. Haven't you noticed that Ian has this rebellious streak in him? He's like a libertarian desperately attempting to break free from the bondage that enslaved him. Ian is wired up for revolution, but his fear of being a disappointment to others shuts down the free-spirit within him. I think he knows that this mentor group is the best thing for him and wants it to happen. He won't let us down."

Caden took a deep breath, laid on his bed and looked at the ceiling. "He's got three more minutes," he said.

Josiah sat on the edge of the desk reading the text messages on his phone – nobody said a word. Wes paced the floor and kept stepping into the hall expecting to see Ian running toward their rendezvous point. Every time he stepped back into the room, he looked at his watch. Another minute passed. Five minutes passed. Wes realized that they had waited as long as they could. If they didn't leave now, they wouldn't make it to the meeting on time.

"Let's go," Wes sighed as he grabbed his jacket and headed out the door. If Wes' thoughts had been audible, his friends would have heard him say, *"C'mon Ian – be at the coffee shop when we get there . . . where we go one, we go all"*.

CHAPTER
TWELVE

Wes, Josiah and Caden started their long walk across campus. They had less than fifteen minutes to get to the coffee shop on time. In order to save some time, they would pass the commons and cut across the athletic field. The lights of the field were on because at this early point in the academic year, many of the athletic teams extended their practices into the evening. The bright lights highlighted the three travelers as they hastened to get to their destination.

With every step, Caden became more aggravated. In his mind, he processed Ian's withdrawal and absence as an egregious act of injustice. He replayed Ian's excitement of last year and the countless conversations that he and Ian had about the possibilities of this mentoring venture. He thought of how much Wes and Josiah looked forward to this. If Ian backed out, they would all lose the opportunity. Caden quickly lost any sympathy over the fear that Ian might be feeling, and was increasingly convinced that Ian's actions were a flagrant act of selfishness.

"This is bullshit!" Caden exclaimed, as he stopped dead in his tracks in between the pitcher's mound and third base of the well-lit baseball field. "We aren't going to do this without Ian. I'm pissed that he's flaking out. He was the guy that was so pumped up all summer to make this happen. Doc isn't going to take us on; he told us that there had to be at least four guys in the group. I'm going to find him and he will join us if I have to drag his sorry ass into the coffee shop."

CHAPTER TWELVE

Caden's warrior mentality was emerging. He often had a short-sighted sense of *right-ness*, like most people do, when they believe that their decisions are always supported by truth. His ruddy face usually lost its handsome charm, when he went into warrior mode.

Caden's dad was a military lawyer in the Judge Advocate General Corp of the US Army. Colonel Mark Boyd believed that truth and justice were the highest virtues that a man could embody. This belief was passed on to his only son. While Caden didn't want a military career, he had adopted a black-or-white, almost militant approach to attacking issues, and a four star general's demeanor to leadership. He had been taught that a warrior champions truth and that truth leads to a just, or right response. Like so many people who become warriors of truth, Caden believed that his perspective and conclusions were infallible because they were based on what he believed was the absolute truth. He failed to see that his militant actions often left a wake of innocent people destroyed by right-ness.

Caden started to march into conquest back in the other direction, when Wes grabbed hold of his arm.

"Wait a minute G.I. Joe," Wes stated, just short of coming unglued himself. "When you go into military mode, someone always gets killed."

Josiah chimed in, "Caden, It's better for us to stick together and meet with Doc without Ian right now. We can talk to Ian later. Maybe Doc will reconsider and just take on the three of us. But he won't do that if we don't go in united. If we don't get there Doc will think that we decided not to follow through."

"If you go on a crusade we become even less united" Wes added, then his tone softened, "Besides, I know Ian will come. Don't ask me how I know; I just know deep in my heart that he will be there. *Trust me.*"

Caden had a hard time calming down but agreed that it was probably more advantageous that they stay the course and walk into the meeting united. The guys broke into a quick jog to make the meeting on time.

CHAPTER
THIRTEEN

The trio jogged across the athletic field, past the Spellman Science Complex and Planetarium and out the South Campus Gate. They could see the Mystery Brews Coffee Shoppe across the street. The well-lit large old world *Mystery Brews* sign with its bubbling apothecary beaker and Bunsen burner logo was set above the door of the establishment. The boys waited for the South Gate light to turn green, then resumed their jog to their meeting point. They didn't break their stride until they reached the brass polished wand-shaped handle of the shop's door.

Mystery Brews was a favorite spot for students and other patrons from the surrounding community. Situated right across the street from the University gates, it served as a pseudo-getaway for students who wanted to just, get off campus for a while. The environment was warm and inviting. A long saloon type bar flanked the establishment's red brick wall. This allowed patrons to sit and have conversations with the baristas, many of whom were MU students engaged in part time employment. Throughout the rest of the establishment the oversized chairs, sofas, bistro tables and soft lighting, all orchestrated perfect conversation spaces that easily doubled as study spots percolating the rich grounds of learning, yielding a robust blend of new thought. In the middle of the venue was a small stage that was used on various evenings to showcase local area talent. It wasn't unusual to find MU student musicians and thespians in artistic performance. The walls of the coffee shop became a gallery, exhibiting local artist's paintings and sculptures. The brushed maroon, etched tin plated ceiling, thick crown molding and soft wall spotlights added an antiquated touch of class, which gave the art clad walls a museum finish. At the far back of the shop, was a loft that was home to many overstuffed sofas. The walls under the loft were bookcase lined. Throughout the years, students traditionally left old textbooks that they didn't want or couldn't sell. Occasionally patrons would come across a book that they saw as a treasure. The sign on the book shelve read, *Knowledge is free to all who want it and shared by those who value it. Take a book if you need it - Leave a book if you've used it and pay it forward!* Long velvet red curtains hung in front of the loft opening. Normally they were tied back, but occasionally they could be drawn to allow patrons under the loft a private party. The ambiance was additionally enhanced by the aroma of the rich libations that gave the shop its fame. Many blends of coffees and teas from around the world gave the quaint establishment its international flair and its name, *Mystery Brews.*

The boys walked through the doors into the warm coffee shop. Throughout the establishment, students and community patrons sipped coffee and tea as they engaged in conversations or got lost in the homework before them. The boys stood for a moment at the door to peruse the patrons, identifying Dr. Ashe sitting alone at a table in the back under the loft. He was deeply engrossed in a book and was oblivious to the time and his surroundings, let alone the fact that the guys had arrived. Wes noted where Dr. Ashe was seated and then his eyes began to read the venue for any sign of Ian.

"He's not here. I told you he wasn't coming," Caden whispered in Wes' right ear. "I am so going to kick the crap out of him when he gets back to the room tonight - if he comes back."

"Calm down, Caden. Let's just go meet with Doc," Wes said with a semi-defeated tone. *I thought he would surely be here. Maybe Caden is right!*

The boys approached the table, but Dr. Ashe was too engaged in his literature to see them coming. It wasn't until they stepped up to the table that they startled him from his task.

"Oh gentlemen, I guess I lost track of the time; is it 8:30 already? Only three of you - where's your fourth brother?" he said.

Wes replied, "Well Doc, I guess . . ."

". . . He's coming in the door right now," Josiah interrupted, finishing Wes' sentence as he pushed his shoulder into Wes' back. They all turned to see Ian standing at the door to locate where his friends were and then coming their direction.

"Good, then take a seat and let's begin," Doc commanded.

Wes locked eyes with Caden and smiled. Caden just shook his head and gave a grin.

As they sat down, Ian quickly found his seat in the group. "Sorry I'm late; I had a difficult time finding a parking spot. The weather is getting a bit misty," he said. The guys each exchanged glances and smiles of relief. They all knew that Ian owed them some explanation, but they would have to wait until their meeting with Doc was over.

Doc began the conversation in his usual way, with another question. "What kind of man do you want to be?"

The boys looked puzzled so Doc re-phrased his question. "When you are dead and gone, how do you want people to talk about you? What words will they use to describe you? Why don't you think about it as you get something to drink? I noticed you didn't order. Besides, I need a refill."

Each of the young men suddenly became contemplative as they took assessment of their life, desires, reputation, goals and dreams, and personal characteristics. This usually isn't a question asked of a late adolescent guy, and it certainly isn't one that they would give much thought. Dying and being remembered is not even in the repertoire of a young guy who is still having difficulty selecting a college major.

The guys followed Dr. Ashe up to the bar to order their coffee concoctions.

"I can't even decide what I want to order – How am I supposed to decide what kind of man I want to be," Josiah said as they stood in line.

"Yeah," said Wes, "I guess I've never even thought of myself as being a man yet."

They each got their brew and returned to the table to answer the question that seemed to linger in the space under the loft.

When they sat down each guy began responding. *Great athlete; loving father; good doctor; successful man;* the list went on. Doc let them talk. Their conversation tended to stimulate the thinking of the others and the list grew larger. The boys took pride in their responses, until Dr. Ashe added his observations to the discussion.

"Each of you has defined himself by the roles that he hopes he will play, or by the things that he will accomplish. You have come to learn well that *being* is equivocal to *doing* – as in a role you engage or career you choose. Since you were little boys, you were asked what you wanted to be when you grew up. You answered by naming a role: Fireman, cowboy, doctor, teacher and so on. You each have learned to let what you *do* define *who you are* rather than letting who you are define what you do."

"I don't understand that," Josiah said. "Isn't being remembered as a *good father*, a great quality?"

"No, it's a successful role – albeit a great one. Rather you should come to identify the qualities or virtues that would *make* you a good father. Do you understand?" Doc asked.

Each guy nodded affirming that he was closer in his understanding of the question than he had been minutes ago.

"If people were to only ascribe single words about you, - words which described who you are; what would those words or characteristics be?" Doc clarified.

"Funny", Caden blurted.

"That's right" Doc affirmed. "Funny is a characteristic of *being*. The list of characteristics can be positive or negative. Think about it . . . *who you are* may be funny, optimistic, kind, *OR* ignorant, arrogant, and so on. Do you get the picture?"

The light started to go on as each guy began to take character inventory. While they were engrossed in the process, they didn't understand where this whole thing was going. Nonetheless, nobody wanted to ask if there was a point to this exercise, so they just waited in hope that Doc would bring them into some sense of enlightenment.

"Now follow this line of logic boys. Because you *are* these characteristics; *ARE* - meaning the essence of being; you will do things that are driven by that characteristic."

The guys looked lost in a sea of rhetoric once more, so Dr. Ashe tried again, "Let me illustrate it. Caden, if you *are* funny your conversation will be witty and people may ascribe the role or label of comedian to you." Doc went on, "similarly because a person *is* kind-hearted he will *do* humanitarian things and may, someday find himself in the role of executive director of a great non-profit organization. You see, doing humanitarian things does not make you kind-hearted; being kind-hearted drives your actions. Who you *are* should define what you *do* rather than what you do defining who you are."

"That's cool Doc," Josiah said, finally enlightened. "That can also mean I'm not a *screw-up* if I make mistakes, because my actions won't be the defining mark of my character."

"Keep going," Doc encouraged.

"But if I am, oh let's say . . . loyal; then I will stick by my bros even if they do things that I find annoying."

"You've got it, Josiah," Doc acknowledged. "Loyalty is the characteristic that makes you a good friend," Doc paused for a moment then said, "So then gentlemen, this begs the question: What characteristics define you, and better, what characteristics do you *want* to define you?"

Doc opened up a door that started to make the guy's heads spin. Personal characteristics aren't always innate; many of them could also be chosen and cultivated. The guys began to realize that each of them could determine the type of man that he wanted to be. They didn't have to wear any label of the past and they could cultivate the best traits that each possessed. This was so incredibly promising, and yet so dauntingly overwhelming at the same time. You could see each guy deep in process. One by one, each began to understand that he could *be* whatever type of man he wanted to be.

Wes' heart started beating fast as he thought about the possibilities. He felt as if he had so many questions but still didn't know what those questions were. He just knew that he and his friends were standing at the threshold of a great unknown adventure that seemed more exhilarating than he had thought would be.

CHAPTER
FOURTEEN

Mystery Brews was beginning to get more crowded as many more students found their place to study that evening. The small mentor group in the back under the loft was so engrossed in their conversation that they hadn't noticed that the venue was nearly filled to capacity.

"Many young men don't think about these things until they become older," Doc said. "As a result they are shaped by outside forces and messages, instead of intentionally developing and exercising who they are or want to be. You need to cultivate and internalize great and noble characteristics now, not when you are too old. That way you can live the majority of your life doing great and noble things that leave a legacy for your sons who follow you. I believe that mentoring is the vehicle through which those characteristics can be developed."

Caden thought about the characteristic he mentioned earlier, "I like being funny" he proclaimed. "But I hope that that's not the characteristic that defines me. I don't want to be remembered as being comical when I can be remembered as being . . . just."

"Caden, you don't have to worry about being remembered as being funny 'cuz, you're really not," Josiah quipped, getting chuckles from Ian and Wes.

Josiah continued, "But I understand what you mean Caden. I want to be known for deeply profound character qualities that impact people . . . like my ojichan. I would describe him as - wise. I will always remember him for his wisdom. That's how I want to be known."

"Josiah, I believe that you are beginning to understand," Dr. Ashe said. "Now let me take this to another level. The reason that each of you committed to this mentoring venture was because you wanted to become great men. Well, the men of profound character that I have encountered throughout my life time have all been marked by four character virtues. People say these men are: loving, good, wise and free. While one of those characteristics is more dominant, all men of integrity have these four characteristics in common".

Doc's words suddenly stirred Wes' memory. "Doc, I saw those words inscribed on the sword in your office. The inscription read, *Hearts bound: Men of love, goodness, wisdom and freedom.* Does the sword have anything to do with what you are talking about? And what about the crest on the sword – tell us about that too," Wes pressed him as if he was a twelve year old who believed that he had discovered a hidden treasure.

"Oh you saw that, did you? I can only hope that you will come to understand the meaning of that in due time," Dr. Ashe continued. "But for now, if you truly want to become a *real man,* and what's more, a real man of integrity and influence, then you must choose to be marked by these traits. One of the four will be your hallmark but all must define who you really are."

"Wait a minute Doc," Wes interjected. "I don't know too many men who are described as *loving*, especially college guys. Compassion sort of runs counter to the tough guy persona. If a guy is known as being a loving guy, he's considered more of a sissy than a man. Love is sort of viewed more as a weakness rather than a manly strength."

"Yes, I know, Wes, that is why it is so rare and why there are so few truly great men. Compassion is viewed as a compromising trait to a man's power," Dr. Ashe clarified. "It's acceptable for a man to be deemed *loving* if the term is used to describe his sex life, or if he loves and cares for his family. But a truly compassionate man is someone whose love extends as a powerful force to all people. When you encounter a man with a heart of compassion you feel like you have been in the presence of greatness."

There was silence for a few moments, and then Caden spoke up. "Doc, we are also told that *good* guys finish last. If you're a good guy then you get walked all over. Not only that, but chicks dig *bad* boys, and as much as we want to ignore it, it's true. Girls think a guy is a push over if he doesn't muscle up and develop a bad boy attitude. If a guy gets labeled a *good* guy, he can kiss dating good-bye, along with any chance of getting a hot woman!"

"Ah, but you may miss any chance of getting a *quality* woman if you are *not* known for goodness. I believe that you can have a woman of character who is also . . . what word did you use . . . *HOT*. Besides, goodness isn't just about getting *chicks*, as you so eloquently put it, Caden. People know a good man because at the core of his being, his soul exudes goodness. A good man lives in the tension of being merciful and just at the same time. One feels safe when they are around a *good* man. He is virtuous, fair, honorable, dependable, gracious and . . . just."

Caden took a deep breath. He hadn't ever thought about goodness in such a profound way.

"Doc, what about wisdom?" Josiah asked. "I want to be a wise man but I never thought that a man could just decide to be a wise man and cultivate it. How would you cultivate wisdom? Do you look for controversial situations to address or seek answers to complex life questions? Do you climb a mountain and sit under the tutelage of a guru, hoping that some wisdom will rub off? If wisdom just rubs off on someone, then I should be very wise, because of my grandfather. Besides, he once told me that as soon as a wise man thinks he is wise, he becomes a fool."

"Josiah it sounds like you have the makings of a wise man. A wise man must constantly and intentionally *seek* wisdom. It is a lifelong venture because wisdom can dissipate like a vapor. There are many men who possess, what I would call, *situational wisdom,* or wisdom concerning specific issues or decisions. These men seek wisdom only when they need it. This doesn't make a man wise in character. It is rare to find a man who is *characterized* by wisdom. A wise man realizes that his mind is constantly being renewed. And your grandfather is right; the only way a wise man knows when he is wise is when the people around him affirm that characteristic. So wisdom is cultivated in a relentless lifelong pursuit for it."

Again, the group got quiet. Dr. Ashe noticed that Ian was unusually quiet and appeared to be a bit withdrawn. "What about you Ian, you're very quiet, what are you thinking?"

"I – I want to be a free man, but I just don't know how that can be developed and I guess I'm not even sure I know what it means," Ian sadly stated.

"I see!" Doc affirmed with the raise of his eyebrow. "Some would lead you to believe that buying power or wealth makes you free because your life will be lacking nothing. To these people, freedom means having whatever they want or never living in the fear of need. Others would tell you it comes with being top dog; absolute power brings freedom, meaning they can do whatever they want. But a man truly marked by freedom lives without fear. He doesn't worry because he knows and embraces his limitations. He is free because he trusts, rests in, and relies on something greater than himself. He has learned to rest in a greater power that he doesn't control, cannot manipulate, or cannot hinder. A free man has a contagious spirit of faith that liberates himself and others."

"What does that mean Doc?" Ian asked. "Are you talking about fate or some energy force or the gods?"

"Something like that – but much more powerful, personal and real. A man who is characterized by freedom includes a reckless abandon of all that he would hold dear, to make life secure, only to embrace something more powerful and permanent. This kind of faith or *rest*, as it were, makes a man of freedom - a wildman," Doc replied.

A spark glimmered in Ian's eyes as if someone had given him an infusion of hope. "I want to be a wildman", he said with a twinge of excitement. "How do I get *that* freedom?"

"As I have said, you will acquire it as you exercise faith, by letting go of everything to which you hold dear and grabbing hold of, something greater." Doc resounded.

"Doc you're talking in riddles, this is hard to understand and even harder to make real. Can't you just tell me the right answer or give me some steps to follow?" Ian asked.

"Ian, it is a riddle that you will discern only as you quit relying on your own power."

Then Doc addressed the group again, "Ponder these thoughts, boys. You are told, good guys finish last; loving men are weak and often viewed as sissies; wise men are old, outdated and many times not pragmatic; and freedom is defined by having and doing whatever you want. All lies! Therefore, acquiring these traits will not be an easy journey because, in their truest sense, they run counter to the messages which constantly bombard you regarding what it means to be a great man."

Once again, the four guys sat captivated. Dr. Ashe continued, "You just ventured into battle ground that has been defined for you, gentlemen . . ." Before he could finish his thought their intense group conversation was interrupted by a very beautiful young girl.

"Excuse me! I'm so sorry for interrupting but are you Josiah Nestor?"

Josiah was caught off guard. He had forgotten that they were sitting in a very busy coffee shop. The place was bustling with students and as the noise level increased, it unconsciously made the mentor group more focused and intent. Doc just mentioned a battle ground and each guy was waiting for combat instructions, instead they were brought back to the ambiance of an artsy American coffee shop.

"Are you Josiah?" she asked again. "My roommate, Natalie Sanchez knows you. She told me that you were great at Algebra and could possibly be a really, great tutor. I need to pass the class and I suck at algebra. I'm very sorry for interrupting your conversation and I won't take your time, but I really need some help this semester."

While she spoke, she fumbled through a notebook to find a piece of paper. She started to scribble something. "My name is Rachel. Here's my phone number. Call me." She smiled, handed Josiah the piece of paper with her number on it then turned to address the rest of the group.

"I'm really sorry that I interrupted," she apologized, and as she walked away, she put her hand up to the side of her head as if she had a telephone and mouthed the words *"Call me"*, in Josiah's direction.

"What was that?" Caden said with an intrigued smile. "You have beautiful women handing you their phone numbers?"

The rest of the guys stared at Josiah, waiting for a response. He could feel the rush of an embarrassing blush overtake him. Doc looked over his eyeglasses, the corners of his mouth turned up in an impish grin and he didn't say a word. As a matter of fact, nobody said a word. Josiah kept his head down and then looked up at Caden and said, "I guess hot chicks don't dig bad boys, they dig *Asian* boys."

The humor of the moment seemed to encroach upon any attempt to regain the intensity of the conversation. Even Doc got a chuckle out of Josiah's conclusion. But Josiah grinned, looked at Doc, and then regained the seriousness of their conversation by saying, "You were saying something about a battleground, Doc."

"Oh yes," Doc recalled as he gathered his thoughts again. He quickly recapped, "Each of you will have to challenge the messages, influences . . .", then he slowed down and deliberately stated, ". . . and dark forces that would keep you from becoming a *man* first, and then a man of *integrity*, secondly. These powerful forces are sometimes overtly identifiable and audible, but many times they are subversively and unconsciously, spiritual or mystical. They will seek to infiltrate your heart, soul and mind to keep you common, and if you are intent on becoming uncommon men, they will seek to take your very life. Come closer men and heed my words. This is not a virtual game for boys, but a life or death challenge that you are about to engage. The forces of which I speak are strong and individually you cannot see them, but together you can identify them and battle against them. Pray that you become aware of what lies ahead." The tone in Doc's voice was so intense that it gave the conversation a sobering, dark, eerie twist.

Dr. Ashe continued, "And now you must commit. The future of generations to come rests in you four . . . but alas it is 10pm and I must get home. Mrs. Ashe will be waiting up for me!" Doc gathered his books, donned his jacket and put his hat on his head. "I can't wait to hear of the adventure, next week when we meet," he said in parting. The boys stood up as the old gent began to walk away. "Hot chicks dig Asian guys – that's rich. You know, Mrs. Ashe is a pretty *hot* chick too!" he said and began to chuckle again as he headed out of the coffee shop. The band of brothers remained standing, stupefied as he shuffled toward the door, occasionally pausing to engage a student or two on his way out.

CHAPTER
FIFTEEN

"That was creepy- intense," Ian said as he watched Doc leave the Mystery Brews Coffee Shoppe.

"Yeah! Who says, *'the future of generations to come rest on you,'* and then just, up and leaves on a jovial note. I don't get it!" Josiah added.

The guys sat back down and looked mystified. There was a long silence where each guy began to say something but silenced it before it left his mouth.

"That sounded like something out of a comic book," Caden said, finally breaking the silence. Then in a deep phony game show announcer voice he said, "The fate of the world rests in your hands boy wonder, but for now I'm going home to my hot seventy-five year old wife!"

They guys burst into laughter, not so much because Caden's comment was so funny but because they needed to break the tension of the sobering awareness that they were feeling.

"We gotta talk about this boys, but first I'm getting more coffee," Wes said. Each guy got up to place his order. While they waited for their coffee, they chatted with other MU friends who were kicking back or studying. They refreshed their brews and made their way back to their conversation spot. When they regrouped, the mood was much less intense, yet so much of the conversation still raged in each guy's head.

"Doc said we have to commit! What do we have to commit to? I thought we already did that by showing up here. What more are we committing to?" Caden asked.

"To becoming great men; to each other; to seeing and battling dark forces; to being real and safe for each other . . . to die for each other – all of it, I guess!" Wes proclaimed.

"Which brings us to another issue," Josiah said as he directed his attention to Ian. "Are you in or not, because we can't do this without you, and we don't want to either."

Caden had almost forgotten, but Josiah's question brought him back to the rage he felt on the baseball field. "Bro, I need to hear you commit to being a part of this group. No lame excuses! No frickin' scholarship cop-out! AND, committing means that this is priority over anything else including . . . women. I want to hear you tell us that you're in. Are you or aren't you?"

"Yeah bro, back off, I'm in and I apologize for being late. I went over to the University Chapel last night to think. It's quiet and contemplative there. I fell asleep. When I woke up, I had missed two classes so I just rushed right to my third class. Anyway, I went back there after class and spent most of the day over there thinking. I made lists of pros and cons about this mentoring thing and concluded that I logically *shouldn't* do this, but deep in my gut, I wanted to. At about 8pm it suddenly dawned on me that the real reason why I was so indecisive was because I was afraid. This stuff is way intense . . . and the idea of defining or redefining oneself, and then letting others into the process is scary. Fear was manipulating my decision and I really didn't want it to be the motivator. So I quickly left the Chapel and got here as fast as I could drive. I'm still afraid but I'm here – and definitely in!"

The hour got later as the fire of their conversation grew. They rehashed all that Doc said, while the patronage of the coffee shop diminished.

CHAPTER FIFTEEN

"What do you think all that dark-forces; infiltrate-your-soul-mind-and-heart; life-or-death-battle stuff was, that Doc mentioned? He was speaking metaphorically, right? I never can tell. He's such a mystery. Was it another Doc-riddle?" Ian asked.

"I'm not sure, but he made it a point to tell us that we need to be able to see those forces," said Josiah. "Maybe there is more of a spiritual or mystical element to this process than we understand. I want to be a wise man and now I understand that it won't come easy and probably not without a price. I will fight to be that man. And I imagine, from all that Doc said, it won't happen unless I commit to do the same so that you guys can be the men you were created to be too."

As Josiah finished his sentence, one of the baristas began wiping down the tables near the place where the guys comfortably sat. "Sorry guys, but we're closing up now," he said.

"Whoa, it's about ten minutes till midnight, I've got an eight o'clock class in the morning," Josiah said as he caught a glimpse of the large clock hanging on the wall behind the bar.

"Me too," said Wes. As they gathered up their belongings he continued, "Right before he left, Doc gave us warning about the dark forces that are subversive, mystical and spiritual. He said that we couldn't see them alone but that together we will overcome them. Remember the sword in Doc's office; it had the words *Hearts Bound* on it, along with the four character virtues that we talked about."

Wes kept talking as they started to walk out. When they got to the door, Wes blocked their exit. He turned to face the guys and said, "We're in this together right? Hearts bound – band of brothers. No turning back, no backing out from this point on, to the death if we must, right?"

Each guy excitedly nodded his commitment. Then Wes extended his hand and said. "Where we go one, we go all!"

Josiah grabbed Wes' hand and said, "Where we go one, we go all!"

Caden enthusiastically made his pledge, "Where we go one, we go all!"

They all looked at Ian. "Guys, this is so corny . . . but truthfully, I've never been more serious about any other commitment before." With that, he grabbed their hands with both of his hands, "Where we go one, we go all," he said with a smile and passion that gave the other guys a deep sense of surety.

CHAPTER
SIXTEEN

Wes, Caden, Josiah and Ian stepped outside the Mystery Brews Coffee Shoppe. They were the last patrons to leave the venue. The coffee shop baristas began turning off lights as someone locked the door behind the boys. The night had changed dramatically. A dense fog had rolled in during the short hours that they were in their conversation. The fog was so thick that they couldn't see the street or the University across the way. While buildings and structures weren't visible, the University lights dimly broke through the mist creating tiny haloed orbs suspended in the mist.

The guys stood under the light of the Mystery Brews Coffee Shoppe sign that hung above the door, attempting to get their bearings as they assessed the density of the fog and the chill of the midnight air. They weren't standing there long, before the coffee house staff extinguished the outdoor sign lights, leaving the guys in the dark.

"My car is over there somewhere," Ian announced as he pointed in a general direction. They could barely see the lights of the parking lot let alone Ian's car.

"Follow me," Ian said. They each stepped away from the coffee shop door and off the curb into the fog. The only thing that was visible was the asphalt beneath them and about three feet of space in front of them. Even if they found Ian's car, it would be difficult to drive it back to the parking lot of Adams Hall.

"I think it's over here" Ian called.

The guys stepped cautiously in Ian's direction, groping their way through the dense mist. As they walked, the asphalt beneath them suddenly lost the hardness that is indicative of a paved parking lot and felt much softer and unsure.

"Ian, you've led us into the grass," Caden exclaimed.

"Let's turn around and go back toward the shop," Josiah suggested. "We don't want to be walking around blindly. We might end up on the road. If someone were driving by they wouldn't see us until it was too late to stop."

The boys turned around but couldn't even see the coffee shop or the University lights. "How far did we walk and where are we?" Wes stated.

Just as he finished his sentence, a gentle brisk wind stirred. The breeze began to blow apart the fog and the boys found themselves in unfamiliar territory. They were no longer in the coffee shop parking lot, nor were they on the Mason University campus. They were standing on the side of a long unpaved country road. The darkness of night was broken by a few faintly lit cottage lights far off to the left, in the distance. Only the expanse of bright stars and the brilliance of a full moon lit the unfamiliar countryside. In front of them was a rolling glen. The moonlight casting off the wind tossed field grass made it look like a dark emerald sea. They could smell the green moss and dew drenched foliage of the landscape. The starry night cast the silhouette of a great deep purple mountain range that broke the horizon against the midnight blue sky. Behind them was the dense edge of a dark forest. They had just walked from that direction but there had been no trees, and now there was no asphalt parking lot, coffee shop or university.

The guys stood by the roadside stunned and confused. "I have an eerie feeling about this," Caden said. They all felt a chill come over them as if a great evil lurked in the woods behind them.

"You're right, something very wicked is nearby. I hadn't counted on *dark forces* being this real," Josiah said.

CHAPTER SIXTEEN

As he spoke, their attention was diverted by a thunderous sound. Up the road, coming toward them was a large open wooden, horse-drawn wagon. The wagon was charging right toward them at lightning speed and with such force that the boys couldn't think fast enough as to what they should do. They also realized that the wagon was not being drawn by a horse but by a large and powerful stag. They could hear the carriage driver yell, "Quickly, there they are Cervus."

"RUN! Hide back in the woods," Caden yelled. The boys instinctively ran to take cover in the dense forest behind them but they were abruptly stopped in their tracks. The vines that made up the groundcover beneath their feet suddenly sprang up around their ankles and their shins all the way to their knees. The force of the guy's sudden momentum, along with the strangulation of the vines resulted in each of them falling to the ground, helplessly immobile on his back.

At that moment, the powerful stag drawn wagon stopped in front of them. The massive animal reared his head high as the driver rose to his feet from the carriage seat and in a swift single motion armed himself with a golden bow and arrows.

The large stag towered over the four guys. It's massive muscular frame and enormous twelve point antler rack was bigger than that of any genius of deer they had ever seen. Breathing heavily from its swift run, the beast's exhale in the brisk air created short bursts of steam from its nostrils that only made it look more ferocious. The stag seemed agitated and kept glancing back and forth as if it were being hunted. Its eyes were wide and black, but when the moonlight caught them, they glistened a blood red center.

The archer's stance at the helm of the wagon created an ominous silhouette in the bright light of a full moon. The slim stature and fine features indicated the archer to be an adolescent boy of about seventeen years of age. He wore a large fur hat that covered his head. The lining on the collar of his olive drab cloak was the same dark fur as his hat. Under the coat, he wore leather pants and high buckled boots. The great golden bow in the archer's skilled hand was drawn and a sharp arrow was awaiting its orders to hit the mark that its master desired. One could gather that this archer was a marksman from his cat-like reflex in how he quickly grabbed his bow, pulled the arrow from its quiver, drew the bowstring to its anchor point just beside his right ear and took his stance. From their helpless position on the ground, the four guys feared that something dreadful was about to happen. When the archer pulled back the taunt bow string, the guys gasped and held their breath in fear.

Ian closed his eyes and grabbed two fists full of grass and dirt as if to brace himself. Out of reflex, Josiah tried to roll on his side and curl himself up, making himself a smaller target to hit. Caden began thrashing in an attempt to free himself, thinking that they could take the archer out before he got off a second shot. He wasn't going to go down without a fight. Wes' body tensed up and he just held his breath keeping his eyes locked onto the archer. Wes could feel his heart pounding within his chest with such great force that he feared it would become a challenging visible, moving target for the archer.

CHAPTER SEVENTEEN

The band of brothers lay helplessly on their backs, entangled in the clutches of the forest flora that somehow was in concert with their attacking archer. The stag reared his head, lifted his front hooves high above the ground and let out a deep low snort. This didn't shake the archer who was still intent on sending his arrow to ravage its target. But the arrow never left the bow.

"Quickly, get into the wagon and hide yourselves beneath the straw," the archer commanded in a forced whisper. "We have little time to waste, lest we be discovered. It's very dangerous for you to be here."

As he spoke, the vines that held the guys in place retracted back into their positions on the forest floor. Relief poured over the guys like a waterfall. Each quickly rose to his feet while the archer remained alert. They realized that his bow and arrow were trained, not on them but on the forest behind them. Could it be that they were being saved from the evil that they sensed? Looking to see what the archer's arrow was aimed at only revealed a darkness so ominous, that it chilled the guys to the core.

"Move quickly," the archer commanded again. As the guys stood up, they could feel the evil of the forest licking the back of their necks. This was all the motivation they needed. They climbed into the back of the wagon and covered themselves with straw as the archer lowered his bow and assumed his place as the coachman.

"Fly Cervus; take us away from the wickedness that lurks here!" The great stag looked behind as if to make sure that everyone was secured in their place, then he broke into a full gallop with unnatural speed. The wagon bolted down the road and around a bend away from the dark forest tree line.

The only thing that the guys could hear was the loud beating of Cervus' hooves as they pounded the red clay of the road beneath them. When the wagon was clear of imminent danger, the archer spoke with a voice that was calmer and more friendly. His stern forced whisper was replaced by a clear audible tone. "I'm sorry to have startled you, but too many Otherlanders are destroyed on that road before they could even make it to the King."

"Who are you? What is this place and where are we going?" Wes asked as he and the others began to immerge from under the pile of straw that covered them.

"Stay hidden!" the archer barked. The youthful voice carried such power and authority that it startled the boys back beneath the straw. "You are not out of danger until I have you safe in Eindhoven Glen." The guys each resumed their position beneath the hay as the archer drove on and gave them more information.

"Wes, Caden, Josiah and Ian, I am glad to meet each one of you, although I wish it could have been in more pleasant manner. My name is Clarion. King Elyon told me of your coming and commanded Cervus and me to find you and serve as your guide. We're sorry about not getting the exact location correct but it's often difficult to predict where Otherlanders will emerge from the woods."

Wes restated his question more emphatically, "Where are we"?

"You are in Salamgard, the Kingdom ruled by King Elyon. You have been chosen to become Ambassador-Knights of his realm. The king has brought you here to bestow upon you great virtues that will allow you to be representatives of his kingdom back in Otherland, where you live. Few are chosen for this great honor and of those chosen; fewer survive the dark forces and principalities whose mission it is to keep them from completing their task."

"We're not from Otherland," Caden stated. "We're from . . ."

Clarion quickly interjected, "Everywhere outside of Salamgard is Otherland. You are from Otherland."

"What task? You said we were brought here to complete a task?" Josiah asked, from under his covering.

"The King has decided to honor your desire to be a wise man, Josiah. He will give you unusual wisdom which will mark you for the rest of your life", Clarion proclaimed without ever looking behind. The archer remained steadfast to his task of safe passage for his charges.

"How do you know who we are, and how do you know that I desired to be a wise man?" asked Josiah.

"King Elyon informed me. He will also make you, Caden, a man marked by goodness. People will see your good works as just and merciful. It will be a reflection of how good Elyon and his kingdom are. And Ian, you will be given incredible freedom – your faith will be a strong reminder to all men that they too can live unhindered. You will live free from worry, fear and anxiety because you will come to trust the power and greatness of the King. And Wes you will receive the most powerful virtue of all – Love. You will come to know the powerful force that love is. But each of you must understand that acquiring these characteristics requires that you journey to King Elyon's palace. That is your task."

Clarion continued talking as Cervus charged ahead unimpeded. "Your journey will not be easy. You will encounter great tests and the evil powers of the Dark Lord, Ubilaz. He will stop at nothing to destroy you. If you succeed in acquiring these virtues your impact will be great and Elyon's kingdom will advance. To our knowledge, Ubilaz has yet to discover that you are here in Salamgard."

"Hold on," Ian said sternly as he sat up in defiance to the Clarion's warning, "We never signed up for this. I don't know any King

Elyon and I'm certainly not going to battle some Dark Lord over his political agendas. You need to take us back to . . . *Otherland*, or whatever the hell you call it, and point me in the direction where I left my car. We've all got classes in the morning."

"This is what Doc was talking about, don't you see?" Wes said emphatically as he pulled Ian back down to a prone position in the wagon. "King Elyon will make us the men that we desire to become. It's not a political agenda. It's about the forces that would keep men from being great."

"Ian, you have the makings of a great man. That doesn't come easy nor is it attained without cost. You *did* commit to this – *where you go one you go all,"* Clarion reminded.

CHAPTER
EIGHTEEN

Cervus began to slow down and then came to a stop. "You're safe for the time being. You can disembark the wagon," Clarion stated. The guys pushed their way out from under the straw and jumped from the back of the wagon.

"Move inside quickly and be welcomed to my home." Clarion invited. The archer opened the door of the cottage and perused the property around the house for anything evil that lurked. "I know that you have many other questions and I have much more to tell you in preparation for your journey. Please, go inside now".

Then Clarion addressed Cervus, "Take the wagon away. Tell the young bucks of your clan to scout the forest to see if our guests' presence has been discovered."

The great stag gave a low and noble nod of affirmation then disappeared around the side of Clarion's cottage.

As they followed Clarion into the dimly lit cottage, Wes questioned, "That stag, um . . . Cervus? It understands every word you said?"

"Yes, the animals of Salamgard are as much citizens of Elyon's kingdom as any other creature. While they cannot speak, they have profound intellect. They can communicate through their gesture, if you ask direct questions or communicate in a direct manner to them. But you must be careful; some of the animals have given their allegiance to Lord Ubilaz. They serve him and will not think twice to betray you, or kill you. Cervus, the Great Stag is the lord of all hoofed creatures in Salamgard. He is a faithful Knight in the Realm of King Elyon."

Clarion gave one more look for anything suspicious before closing the cottage door. Clarion's cottage was rustic and earthy. The furniture throughout the place was hand carved from the trees of the surrounding forest. A glow from a warm fire in the hearth of a grand fireplace provided the central light and heat for the great room. Clarion lit candles as the brothers positioned themselves close to the fireplace to get warm. It was a much colder autumn in Salamgard and the T-shirts and jeans that the guys wore really didn't serve as adequate attire for the climate.

"Warm yourselves." Clarion stated while continuing to illuminate the corners of the cottage with newly lit candles. "You will be given proper garments in the morning for your journey to the King. The clothes you wear now would only serve to give your presence away."

"I guess wearing Mason University Athletics on my chest would make me an obvious target" Ian stated with profound awareness as he looked at his T-shirt.

Clarion finished lighting all the candles that now bathed the cottage in a soft amber ambiance. The archer came to join the boys near the warmth of the fireplace. The glow of the firelight revealed Clarion's face more clearly. The soft adolescent-like features robbed this hardened archer of a once intimidating presence. Clarion shed the long cloak and hung it on a stand near the fireplace. Then the archer removed the fur hat and as it was lifted, tresses of long dark black hair fell shoulder length. As Clarion turned to face the guys they were amazed once again.

"You're . . . you're a woman!" Josiah said with surprise. Standing in the fire's radiance without the concealing cloak and fur hat revealed the form of a young woman, not a teenage boy.

CHAPTER EIGHTEEN

"You are very discerning, Josiah! Does being a woman make me any less an appropriate protector and guide? I assure you that the King has every confidence in my abilities. I am the King's Master Archer," Clarion stated with a humble bow.

"No . . . we just . . . I mean, I," Josiah stumbled. "I just thought you were a teenage guy."

Clarion smiled and said, "In Salamgard, things aren't always as they seem to be, so be alert." She pushed her way between Josiah and Wes to cross the room for a luminator.

"Excuse me boys," she said. "Josiah, you look like you've never seen a woman before – Welcome to Salamgard," she continued as she placed her hand under his chin and closed his mouth. They hadn't noticed the aroma of her perfume until she got close. Then both guys were ushered into their memory of the girl at freshman orientation.

"You're the girl!" Wes said, "The girl in the athletic center that day Josiah and I met."

"I looked for you all year and could never find you," Josiah added.

"King Elyon sent me to make sure that you gentlemen connected with each other. He has always been intricately involved in your lives. He has a great purpose for each of you."

"And what about the elevator where 'Siah and I really became friends and Caden and Ian being on the same floor and in the same classes . . . was that all coincidence?" Wes asked.

"King Elyon is very powerful. He has many resourceful knights in his realm, who orchestrate events that carry out his will. There are no coincidences. Come now and sit, I have much to tell you in preparation for the journey that we embark upon tomorrow morning."

Caden caught Wes' eye and silently mouthed the word, "WOW" as the guys each found a chair around a low table near the fire. They all were ready and eager to hear what Clarion had to say.

"You are here because the King has selected you. Elyon's kingdom is far reaching and, unbeknownst to you, Otherland, the land where you live, is also part of his realm. The king has appointed many men and women in Otherland as his Ambassador-Knights. They are people who profoundly impact the lives of those around them by exercising the characteristics that indicatively represent Elyon's kingdom. As people encounter love, goodness, wisdom and freedom, they experience Elyon and his sovereign monarchy. You have been selected to be among those men," Clarion proclaimed.

You could almost see the wave of encouragement, pride and delight sweep over the four guys. Clarion noticed it too, so she quickly continued, "Lest you become too enamored with that thought, you should heed the warning I gave earlier. There are few chosen, but even fewer survive Dark Lord Ubilaz."

"Who is Ubilaz?" Wes asked.

"He is a very powerful Lord who has also established his kingdom in Salamgard. His kingdom is Eikondor," Clarion answered.

"Where is Eikondor?" Caden asked.

"You are in it," Clarion replied.

"But I thought you said we were in Salamgard," Caden responded in rebuttal.

"You are," Clarion nodded affirmatively.

"So there are two kingdoms that occupy the same place, each ruled by a King," Josiah interjected.

"Yes, to some extent you can say that." Clarion affirmed. "Listen and you will understand better. Your lives may depend on your grasp of what I am about to tell you."

CHAPTER
NINETEEN

Cervus walked slowly into the woods of Somberbos Forest. He dared not give the impression that anything was out of the ordinary. Just into the midst of the trees, he could see a small herd of deer. Three young bucks quickly lifted their heads and gazed in Cervus' direction when they detected his presence. Cervus ambled gently into the center of the herd.

The young bucks gathered close to him then after a few moments, one by one, they quietly left the herd and darted into different sections of the dense forest.

One buck was sent to rally Eleus and Virtus, two mighty stallions who were captains of Cervus' hosts. Cervus wisely concluded that they would need to be close at hand should Ubilaz wage an assault against the newly arrived guests. Eleus and Virtus would serve as undercover escorts, so as not to draw attention to the travelers. They would be charged to guard and protect the band of brothers at any cost.

Ubilaz had many fierce and devoted creatures living in the forests and throughout Salamgard, which comprised his army. The animals of Salamgard, like all other living creatures discerned good from evil. They each could choose to either follow King Elyon or succumb to the wiles of Lord Ubilaz. If Ubilaz were to mobilize his forces against the new visitors, no foe could stand a chance unless reinforcements were readied.

The second messenger was sent to other commanders in Cervus' dominion. Their top secret mission was to establish a protective hedge along the route that would take Clarion and her friends from Eindhoven Glen to the fortified city of Aanda. Cervus was particularly concerned that the mightiest warriors be available to fight at a moment's notice, yet remain undetected. The presence of the four visitors needed to remain hidden from Ubilaz as long as possible. This would put them closer to successfully and safely accomplishing their mission. Many of the cat warriors would position themselves in the trees as if lounging lazily on a brisk autumn morning. Some of the mighty grizzlies would give the impression that they were in search for food among the flora, near the travel route. Wolves, snakes, hawks, hyenas, rhinos, horses, badgers and stags were all put on alert.

The third messenger was to establish the lines of communications. The intelligence network of the forest was charged to intercept and send communications, should the visitors be discovered. The birds, squirrels, chipmunks, dragon flies, skunks and a host of others kept a keen vigil on the pulse of the forest. As soon as they became aware that Ubilaz had knowledge of the guys' presence in Salamgard, they were to notify Cervus and Clarion immediately.

Throughout the peaceful dark of night, Cervus' secret mission began to unfold quietly. By morning, the forest would appear to be locked in its normative pattern but deep undercover, a silent army would be ready to spring into action at a single word from its supreme commander. All was being made ready.

CHAPTER
TWENTY

Clarion placed a polished brass bowl of water in the center of the table.

"This luminator will help you understand what I am about to tell you."

"What is a luminator?" Ian asked.

"It is a sacred vessel, with power of revelation. It will bring you into the mystical truth of Salamgard," she said.

Clarion turned and selected a wick from a container near the fireplace. She touched the wick to the blazing fire then passed it over the water in the brass bowl. The fire danced on top of the water, until it filled the bowl. The hypnotic effect of the luminator enwrapped the guys until they found themselves standing on a glassy floor of water surrounded by flames. The brothers were amazed at the colorful fiery wall encasing them. Blue, yellow, orange, green and red flames gracefully revealed the visual panorama of the story. The guys listened and watched as Clarion started her story.

"Long ago King Elyon established a wonderful kingdom where everything was pure, good and lived in harmony without any fear of evil."

Her soft tone and the enchantment of the luminator transported the guys into the story as if it were happening in real time.

She continued . . .

There was no pain, death, hatred or sorrow in this kingdom. Goodness and Love marked the citizens of this kingdom, which came to be known as Salamgard. Elyon ruled in glory and power and so great was his power that the citizens of Salamgard could not comprehend the breadth or depth of it. This great power provoked fearful awe in the hearts of all citizens, yet this sobering fear was offset by the mighty and gentle love that the king so freely lavished on every citizen. All of Salamgard lived securely in peace and prosperity because of their powerful and glorious King, Elyon.

The Kingdom of Salamgard flourished. Every creature, from the smallest borrowing insect under the earth, to the creatures that walked the earth and those that graced its skies and seas, lived securely. So vast was the king's sovereign reign that he appointed Balic, as Lord of all his hosts. He gave Balic powers that superseded any other power in Salamgard except the King's own. Of all the members of Elyon's kingdom, Balic was the most amazing and powerful, holding the highest post that any being in Salamgard could aspire.

Over time, Balic began to harbor envy and hate in his heart. Even though everything in Elyon's kingdom was his to enjoy, Balic cultivated an insatiable hunger for power. He began to plot the overthrow of King Elyon and claim Salamgard as his own. Because Balic was so renowned among Salamgard's citizens, he became a master of disguise and deception. Over time, he also mastered the ability to counterfeit the King's power. Balic led the citizens of Salamgard to believe that he was Elyon's equal.

Many of Elyon's loyal subjects forgot how real and raw the King's power and love was, and became dazzled by Balic's magic. He deceived them to follow him by doing miraculous deeds, making those deeds appear greater than they actually were and promising those who pledged allegiance to him a portion of his power and glory. Many citizens tasted that power and became intoxicated by it.

Balic also generated malicious rumors that Elyon's power was degenerating and his love was suspect. This caused the citizens of Salamgard to harbor doubt and rebellion in their hearts against the King.

Citizens great and small pledged their loyalty and devotion to Balic. He began acquiring subjects, slowly and steadily like a cancerous growth that infests an organism. He believed that he could ultimately deceive the entire kingdom to follow him. Elyon could have forcibly stopped Balic by controlling the will of every citizen, but his love allowed them to choose who they would serve.

The King's wisdom thwarted Balic's schemes when he freely gave any citizen who so desired, the insight to see Balic's true character. Numerous followers of King Elyon, even some who had pledged their allegiance to the wicked Lord, acquired this discernment and saw Balic's wicked ways, resulting in their repudiation of the Dark Lord and unwavering loyalty to King Elyon. Still many willfully followed Balic. This broke the King's heart but he allowed them to make their choice and he relentlessly continued to pursue them with his loving kindness in an attempt to woo them from Balic's grip.

Elyon's goodness prevailed and Balic began to lose his stronghold. Balic became more obsessed with overthrowing the Kingdom. His wicked scheme turned lethal when he discovered how to manipulate the necrophim into doing his bidding.

The necrophim were once beautiful musical spirits who were loyal to Elyon. Balic allowed the necrophim to taste a new and more diabolical power. They abandoned King Elyon to assist Balic in his quest to overthrow the kingdom. Balic gave them the power to take life by breathing their poisonous spirit essence into a being. All the necrophim had to do was whisper deception into their victims. This played on their victim's vulnerabilities, insecurities, worries and fears. The inhaled essence of the necrophim quickly corrupted the soul, heart and body, destroying the victim. Death was torturous, painful and sure. Having acquired this dark talent, the character of each necrophim radically changed from a peaceable creation to a fierce warrior spirit whose sole purpose became one of deception, destruction and death. Once beautiful to behold, the appearance of these creatures deteriorated with their character. They became dark, grotesque, hideous, blood red creatures who rarely manifest themselves in their repulsive spirit form. Now, the necrophim deceptively disguise themselves in the physical forms of other creatures in Salamgard. Often they appear as the most beautiful of all creation, attracting their prey. But when they administer their lethal breath, they can only do so in their true, visible grotesque form. The spontaneous transformation from a creature of beauty to their fiendish reality, in the face of their victim, wreaks terror. Most of the time the necrophim remain invisible, except to few who have been given special sight to see and discern the disguised necrophim from other creatures.

Under Balic's bidding, the necrophim brought death to Salamgard, something that the citizen had never known or experienced. Death created a new and overwhelming dread in Salamgard, giving Balic the appearance of omnipotence. Knowing that Balic and his necrophim army were not omnipotent, as they presented themselves to be; King Elyon armed his subjects with the assurance that no harm including death, would come to them. The king had equipped them to live forever, if they trusted his love and goodness.

Elyon continued to lavish good things on Salamgard. But Balic twisted things that were evil and made them look equally good to deceive Elyon's followers. He also took the things that Elyon deemed good and made them appear to be evil, causing the deceived to become afraid and reject the goodness of the King. Balic and the necrophim terrorized the citizens of Salamgard until the faithful cried out for King Elyon to deliver them.

Elyon heard the cries of his people and issued a battle challenge to Balic. The great day came when Elyon declared that he would defeat Balic in an ultimate battle on the Mountain of the North called Aphesis. King Elyon's Palace, Asilo, was positioned in a valley flanked by Mt. Aphesis the majestic mountain of the North, and Mt. Kratos to the South. In front of Asilo and the two enormous mountain ranges, lie the plain of Dura. The King chose to have his battle on Mt. Aphesis so that all of Salamgard could gather on the Plains of Dura to see the defeat of Balic and his hosts.

Balic assembled his army, comprised of the fiercest and deadliest necrophim, the strongest warriors and the most ferocious animals who declared their allegiance to him. They gathered on Mt Aphesis, in their battle array, armed with weapons of death. All of Salamgard could see Balic's great army. Their armor glistened in the sunlight and their banners were unfurled to indicate their undying loyalty to Balic. The hours passed and there was no sign of King Elyon or his army anywhere in Salamgard. The citizens of Salamgard thought that he would surely burst onto the scene in spectacular form. They spoke of imagined visions that King Elyon and his army would arrive from the sky on thunderbolts, or that they might spontaneously generate in ambush around Balic's forces with such great power and might, that Balic's soldiers would surrender without ever lifting a weapon. Time passed and none of these things occurred.

Balic's army grew restless. They wondered if the speculations of the people might be true and began to fear the element of surprise. They began to lose their focus and ravaging appetite for the battle. Balic recognized the agitation of his warriors and from his post upon his great steed at the apex of Mt. Aphesis, he began to mock King Elyon. He taunted, saying that an impotent king had abandoned his citizens. The citizens of Salamgard began to embrace the toxic deception that Balic so vehemently orchestrated. A sense of fear and defeat started to suffocate Salamgard. Balic also issued an ultimatum for Salamgard's citizens to either join his ranks or suffer death at the hands of his army. His blasphemous speech fueled his hosts. Balic's army joined in a great fiendish chorus, mocking King Elyon.

Just when the scoffing had reached a fever pitch and hope seemed to be gone, the drawbridge of Asilo began to lower. A silence spread swiftly across the kingdom. The darkened mouth of the archway in the great wall of Asilo showed no movement. Finally, a single warrior on a majestic white Stallion followed closely behind by two magnificent albino lions emerged with great speed, like a bat out of a cave. The warrior wore the King's silver armor and royal robe, the train of which flew in full array behind the rider from the immense force of the wind generated by the speed of the stallion. On the riders head was the King's silver jeweled diadem.

It wasn't long before someone recognized that the rider was King Elyon. The citizens of Salamgard cheered as their King and his escorts didn't break stride but swiftly scaled the mountain slope. Everyone waited for an army to appear but there was none.

Balic's forces stood with anticipation awaiting an ambush but none came. Once at the top of Mt. Aphesis, King Elyon's steed stood nose to nose with Balic's steed. A hush came across everyone in the land. The short conversation was not heard by all, but those within the sound of the King's voice penned the words for all to remember.

Balic said, "Elyon, you must underestimate my power, that you would come alone."

"You are deceived Balic in thinking that you have any power at all, that has not been given to you. And indeed, I come alone."

"Then you make it easy for me to take your life from you, rendering you an insignificant memory," Balic roared.

"There is nothing that you can take that has not already been freely given," Elyon replied. The strong truth and calming way in which Elyon spoke those words just enraged Balic all the more. Balic drew his sword. The sound of metal against metal as it exited the sheath, echoed from the mountain top. The sharp blade in the vile warrior's hand glistened for all to see. Elyon kept his sword sheathed.

"You shall not fight me?" Balic mocked. "Then die, impotent fool. Death shall swallow you up and all Salamgard will see that I have the power of death," Balic cried.

"You may strike me, Balic, and even kill me, but it will become known that your weapon, your *only* weapon, is death," King Elyon boasted.

When Balic heard those words, he wielded his sword high above his head and with a single, powerful motion cut the King down. With audible gasps of horror, all of Salamgard watched the good king fall from his stead. Balic dismounted and stood over the motionless body of his opponent. From their places throughout Salamgard, the citizens heard Balic's petrifying echoing bellow.

"King Elyon is dead, Salamgard has a new king," and with that he raised his sword again, both hands around the hilt, and thrust it downward into the lifeless body of the king so that it passed through Elyon and securely pinned him to the ground.

Leaving the sword in its mark, Balic raised his hands in victory and his followers and army erupted into vicious shouts hailing *King Balic*. Some of Elyon's faithful, so gripped by fear, fled to hide as Balic and his hosts celebrated. With glee, the necrophim manifested themselves in their revolting demonic form and painted the heavens with praise to Balic. Horror gripped Salamgard.

Balic ordered the albino lions to take up the king's dead body. His first decree was that every citizen of Salamgard look on the fallen form of the slain King, Elyon. He wanted every citizen to know that Elyon was gone and that he had the power of death. The lifeless, bloodied body of the dead king was draped across the back of the two great lions. They were to be followed by the rider-less stead in a dismal royal funeral procession. The three animals attended to the task before them in royal fashion without any sign of emotion. They remained unmoved by the death of so great a King. One would have believed that they were in alliance with Balic, until the lions gave a great snarling roar when Balic attempted to draw near again to Elyon's body.

Elyon's albino attendants carried the King's remains from the northern most part of the kingdom to the southernmost region. Two days passed insuring that every citizen, man and animal would come in obedience to Balic's decree.

As the funeral procession made its way through Salamgard, the animals of the forest and the people of the cities and villages lined the trails, byways and streets to view their fallen monarch. While many hid their grief in fear of Balic, he and his followers celebrated ceaselessly for two nights and two days. The celebration brought the worse debauchery the kingdom had ever seen. The ominous glow of Balic's celebration fires, against the dark of the night, made the forests and plains look like they were ablaze. The orange fire's luminescence danced atop the black silhouetted mountain range where they met the ebony sky, making it look as if a ribbon of fire was suspended in the air. An abominable black veil of evil covered the land creating darkness, unlike any that Salamgard had ever experienced.

When the sun began to set at the end of the second day, the funeral entourage crossed the vast Dura Plain en-route to Asilo, the final internment of King Elyon. The citizens of Salamgard followed the entourage in a grand procession as their concluding act of remembrance to their king. Balic and his hosts intercepted them at Dura. He ordered the mighty cats to enter Asilo alone and to lay the kings body in the palace courtyard. The large white lions slowly walked across the downed drawbridge then disappeared through the great arched entrance behind the walls of the Asilo. A short time later, the lions emerged without the king.

Balic questioned the lions for assurance that they had completed their task. They responded with a deep nod of affirmation, but not trusting them, he looked to the sky where a raven flew. His spy affirmed that the task was complete. Elyon's remains lay on a stone alter in the courtyard of Asilo. The palace that once brought life to the land of Salamgard now served as a sepulcher.

Then in a final attempt to rid Salamgard of any hope or memory of King Elyon, Balic gave orders for Asilo to be burned to the ground. Everything was to be reduced to ash including the king's body. A company of archers stood prepared and at Balic's orders, they set their arrows afire and launched them over the walls of the palace.

The citizens of Salamgard once again experienced the terror that would become the hallmark of Balic's reign as smoke billowed from behind Asilo's walls. Everyone, including the bravest of Salamgard's citizens watched helplessly, because King Elyon, their hope, was dead. Salamgard mourned as Balic reveled in his victory.

As the horrified citizens watched flames rise above the walls of Asilo and black smoke billow from the center of the royal structure, the wind began to stir. The black smoke began to gray and then turn white, as it rose higher and higher around the palace spires. It looked as if a mysterious fog had settled on Asilo. Smoke swirled in the opened gate of the palace, throwing shadows that looked as if someone was walking in the midst of the flames. The shadows became more defined, revealing the familiar figure of a man. Slowly it became clear that the man was clad in the King's royal robes. He walked briskly, dispelling the smoke in his path, emerging from the darkened smoke filled arched entry way.

"King Elyon! He lives!" came a cry from the crowd. The citizens of Salamgard looked more intensely. Their dread was turned to rejoicing as they cheered at the sight of their approaching king!

The King's step was sure and vibrant as he emerged from Asilo and walked across the drawbridge to address the myriads of citizens gathered on Dura. His crown and armor glistened. The bloody marks of defeat that once stained the king's breastplate were gone as if they had never been there. The train of his majestic robe caressed the ground behind him with pomp befitting a conquering Sovereign.

"Elyon has defeated death, and Balic," cheered the citizens.

Upon seeing the victorious risen King, Balic's army fled into the woods with great dread. The necrophim let out horrific screams of defeat as they cloaked themselves in invisibility and dissipated into the night. Balic could not believe what he saw and in trepidation, fled in a flurry of mystical sulfuric smoke.

When the king reached the edge of the great crowd, everyone bowed low in awe and adoration. Elyon bid them, "Rise," and then he addressed his subjects.

"Anyone who trusts the king need not fear anything, including death. I have shown you that I alone hold the power over death. I have defeated what you fear most; Balic and death," King Elyon proclaimed.

The hope and light had returned to Salamgard. The citizens and their King celebrated the ultimate victory. From that day forward, Salamgard celebrated *Victorium Morte*, the Day of Death's Defeat.

Elyon also announced that he would give Balic a kingdom so that the citizens of Salamgard could chose to live in the security of the King or join Balic's ranks. So sure was the King's victory and so great was his grace and love for Salamgard that he desired for every creature to choose to trust his power. Elyon decreed that Balic would be given the new name of Ubilaz and that his kingdom would be called Eikondor.

CHAPTER
TWENTY-ONE

Clarion's voice became more pronounced in the guy's hearing and the glow of the flames that held them spellbound in the clutches of Salamgard's lore, returned them to their prior state; seated around the table with its luminator centerpiece.

"Where is Ubilaz now?" Wes asked.

"Over time, Ubilaz and his host inhabited the caves in the Woods of Ataroth. They continue to scheme, acquiring citizens for Eikondor through intimidation, fear, and deception. Ubilaz has come to understand that the vastness of Elyon's reign includes other realms beyond Salamgard. He is active in infiltrating the far reaches of Elyon's kingdom and establishing his own realm. It is rumored that he plans to wage another great war someday," Clarion answered.

"So what does all this have to do with us?" Ian asked.

"Elyon's kingdom is lived out in men who are marked by the ideals of his kingdom; love, goodness, wisdom and freedom all generated in a deep rooted trust in their Mighty King. Ubilaz believes that the only way for Eikondor to advance is to destroy those chosen by, or devoted to King Elyon. Many men and women have been summoned by the King to become Ambassador–Knights of his kingdom. Elyon equips them with great character and then gives them a broad sphere of influence in Otherland where they become representatives for his kingdom and its ideals."

As Clarion spoke those words, the luminator's fire blazed higher revealing the faces of different people who passed through Salamgard. They quickly recognized the face of Dr. Ashe and then their former resident advisor, Dave Madison.

"There is something more that you need to know," Clarion stated. "Ubilaz has also counterfeited Elyon's plans by calling and empowering his own ambassador knights in Salamgard and in Otherland. He has also given the necrophim greater power for destruction by releasing them in both realms."

"Wait, you mean that there are necrophim floating around where we live?" Caden asked.

"Yes, you have come to know them as dark forces."

"So these necro-whatevers are trying to kill people back home – in Otherland?" Ian asked.

"They have been ordered to keep a subversive profile and confound Otherlanders. By keeping them in darkness, they will never taste the glory of Salamgard. Their primary objective is still to destroy, and in some cases death still comes."

"I really don't understand. If King Elyon defeated death then why do Ubilaz and his necrophim still have the ability to kill?" Ian asked.

"At that first celebration of Victorium Morte, King Elyon informed the citizens of Salamgard that they would continue to experience pain, suffering and even physical death. These would serve to remind Salamgard to trust the goodness of the King, even in the face of dreaded onslaughts. It would also serve as an opportunity for Salamgard to understand how their King suffered so that he could deliver his people. Like you, we didn't understand how we could experience pain and death if the King defeated death. Elyon proclaimed that death, to those who trust the king, was only a temporary experience that held no threat, just as he had proved. For a true citizen of the Kingdom of Salamgard, the power of death is broken."

"And that's where King Elyon's Ambassador-Knights come in," Wes said. "Those great men bring Salamgard to . . . Otherland."

"Yes. The Ambassador-Knights become a destructive force against the power of Ubilaz," Clarion said.

"So what happens to those who don't, as you said, taste the glory of Salamgard," Josiah asked.

"They become part of the kingdom of Eikondor. Ubilaz believes that he will acquire a greater host than Elyon, once again allowing him the opportunity to overthrow the King. His numbers have increased greatly, but nobody is sure just how strong Eikondor is. He keeps his myriads hidden until the opportune moment arises when he can wage his battle. In the mean time his forces will stop at nothing to destroy any Otherlander who comes into Salamgard."

"You mean us, don't you?" Josiah stated.

"Yes. As soon as Ubilaz discovers that you are in Salamgard he will be hell bent on destroying you", Clarion continued. "He knows that if you reach King Elyon, then you will take your ranks among the most influential men and women in your world." The four brothers saw their own faces briefly appear in the candle fire glow, then disappear in a flurry of smoke.

"The outcome is not yet decided," Clarion stated soberly.

"Can we fight or are we just sitting ducks who have to scurry through the woods?" Caden asked.

"For now, our best defense is your anonymity. But if we are discovered, you *will* fight against Ubilaz's soldiers. His warriors are comprised of the mightiest citizens of Eikondor. You will be made ready for those battles. I will tell you more of that in the morning. The battle will be fiercest against his necrophim. It is against the necrophim that many Otherlanders fall."

"Is there any way that we can overcome the necrophim?" Wes asked.

"They can do you no harm when you are bound together. You must, all four, always stand together in the face of the necrophim until you have been equipped for battle. If the necrophim can separate you, they can destroy you. Even after you are battle ready, it is important that there is strength in your bond," Clarion stated.

"Where we go one, we go all," Wes said with a deep pensive sigh, realizing the sobering truth of their mantra. The awareness that this warm-fuzzy, team spirited saying really was a prophetic mandate that could determine their life or death, changed its meaning.

"Yes Wes, but you also need to know that *you* will be the primary target because you have been chosen to be marked by Elyon's most powerful trait - love. If Ubilaz can destroy you he can weaken the bond that unites your brotherhood," Clarion warned.

Wes sat back in his chair dazed by this dour news. A certain dread came over his brothers, as they looked speechless at Wes. Clarion's voice broke the silence.

"King Elyon has great plans for you four gentlemen. You each will need to learn to trust him. He has dispatched his finest to equip you. For now, we have a great journey ahead of us, which starts tomorrow. You must be rested and alert come morning so I advise you get proper sleep. We will continue this conversation when you are fully alert.

Come, I will take you to your bed chambers," Clarion announced.

The young men were lead by their host to a grand bedroom that had four huge beds. The curtains that lined the bedposts were drawn open in anticipation of their guests.

"I will call on you in the morning. We must make the day's journey to the city of Aanda. The King's trusted advisor and Knight, Lemuel will be awaiting our arrival. We will stay in his palace through the holiday," Clarion said.

"Holiday?" Caden replied.

As Clarion began to close the door behind her, she smiled and said, "It's two eves before *Victorium Morte*."

CHAPTER
TWENTY-TWO

The next morning the sun burst through the window beside Wes' bed. He rolled onto his back and stretched as he allowed his eyes to adjust to the sunlit room. Although Wes remembered that the room was quite large, the round shaped bedroom looked much bigger in the daylight than it did before he fell asleep. There was a large fireplace to the right of his bed next to the huge wood-carved oak bedroom door. Smoldering embers filled the fireplace, the remnant of the fire that burned through the night to keep them warm. Three windows filled the walls of the unusually shaped bedroom, each between the four beds in the room. The massive domed ceiling with its rough cedar support beams accentuated the other-world look of the room.

As Wes got his bearings, he became much more aware of how comfortable the oversized bed was. The massive wooden bed posts were carved to look as if a serpent was winding its way up a pillar of ivy. Positioned beside each bed was a candle stand, which matched the bed posts. The large candles that donned the top of the stands looked like they could light the room for ages. It also looked as if each candle had burned for many hours judging from the wax spillover that ran down the side of the stands and had accumulated into the round wooden basin at the bottom of the stand.

A wooden canopy was set on top of the four-pillared bedposts of each bed. The ornately embroidered drapery that covered the canopy matched the privacy curtains of the bed and each bed's adornments were unique. The curtains and canopy of the bed Wes slept in, were a rich hunter green. Ian was still asleep in the maize clad bed to the left of him. Next to Ian, in the midnight blue bed was Josiah who was just beginning to stir from the bright morning light. The bed directly across from Wes was dressed in a deep wine colored drape. In it, Caden was sleeping soundly with his head buried under the pillows.

After Clarion left the room the previous night, the guys stripped off their clothes for a comfortable night's sleep. In common form for college guys, wherever their T-shirts and jeans hit the floor, they usually stayed. But now their clothes were gone and a new set of garments, fashionable to citizens of Salamgard, had been neatly set at the foot of each bed. The color scheme of the clothes matched each of the beds on which they had been laid.

"Siah, are you awake," Wes forced a loud whisper to Josiah. Josiah stirred again. "Siah, wake up!"

"Oh man what time is it?" Josiah scratched his head with both hands arousing his hair follicles from a deep hibernation.

"Morning time! I don't know, I usually use my cell phone to get the time, but somehow I don't get reception here," Wes returned sarcastically.

"Not only are you an annoying *morning* person but you're a smart ass too," Josiah mumbled as he sat up and rubbed the sleep from his eyes. Drinking in the full ambiance of the room he exclaimed, "This place is amazing. I love this bed; it's the best I've ever slept in. I wonder if I can bring it back to school with me. Of course we'll have to move *your* stuff into the hall to make enough room for my new bed," Josiah said as he raised his eyebrows and smiled.

"Who's the smart ass?" Wes returned.

"I slept well in this bed, once I fell asleep. I had a difficult time falling asleep last night. My mind was racing."

"What were you thinking about?"

"Everything! I'm still processing it all – I guess I'm coming to some conclusion about . . . the man that I am and that I want to be. That sounds weird. I need more time to think it through. We'll talk about it more another time," Josiah said.

Their talking woke Ian who sat up abruptly in a disoriented frenzy, yelling, "What the . . . where the HELL are we?" It was obvious that Ian's disrupted slumber was less of an annoyance than the panic he was experiencing in an attempt to get his bearings on his unfamiliar surroundings. The outburst startled Wes and Josiah at first but they quickly were amused and humored by their friend's perplexity. Josiah pulled his pillow up to his face to muffle his laughter so as not to awaken Caden or anyone else in the house. Ian sat with a glazed look on his face, not quite fully awake and still taking inventory of this foreign domicile.

"Ian, you're not in hell, you're in Salamgard. Don't you remember . . . Clarion . . . her house . . . King Elyon and Dark Lord Ubilaz?" Wes kept dropping cues as Ian began to come into the fullness of the present.

"You mean all that was real?" Ian quickly lost the befuddlement that glazed over him. He plopped back down onto his pillow, "That means I'm going to miss my Intro to Philosophy class this morning."

"And that's a problem because . . .?" Wes sarcastically refrained, waiting for Ian to complete the sentence.

Ian pulled the covers over his head as he sheepishly, in a barely audible tone said, "because, I don't want to get behind." Then in a sudden burst of energy beneath the maize colored bedcover he belted out, *"Where we go one, we go all! I know, I know!"* as if he were circumventing a motherly lecture. This sent Wes and Josiah back into hysterics. It wasn't long before Ian joined them, being amused himself by the quick progression he made from a dazed stupor to a full recall of his commitment. All the while, the three friends were laughing, Caden's sleep appeared to be unfazed.

"We really should wake him," Wes said.

"Some cold water would raise him from the dead," Ian replied.

From under the blanket on Caden's bed came a clear voice, "Don't even think about it! You guys seem pretty bright and cheery considering that we are about to face a journey that could lead to our *DESTRUCTION*." Caden rolled over, threw the bed covers back and slid out of bed. "Wes, did you forget Clarion's warning? You're a target. *'Where we go one we go all'* retranslated means, *You fall, We fall,"* his words juxtaposed a mocking antithesis to Ian's realization, which suddenly darkened the spirit of the room.

Caden stood at the side of his bed in his boxers looking at the floor for the clothes that he knew he left there the night before. "I hardly slept last night too, thinking about this . . . *journey*. Wes, I'm concerned for you, bro! I don't know what's going to happen or what it will look like but I came to one conclusion in the middle of the night; If I have to fight for you or even die for you, *I will* . . . and that goes for you guys too."

Each guy sat in his bed without saying a word. Caden's words made them experience a quaking that shook the core of their soul. His verbal promise and vulnerability was out of the ordinary for him but certainly not out of character. Wes, Josiah and Ian just sat in their beds a bit overwhelmed and speechless.

Caden felt that he had dropped an emotional bomb in the room so he quickly lightened the mood. "Now I really have to go to the bathroom. What did you guys do with my clothes? This isn't funny! I'll die for you, but I'll also kick the crap out you before I leave this room in my boxer-briefs!" he stated.

"They are on the other side of the bed, on the floor. They slid off the bed when you got up," Wes replied as he also got out of bed to dress. "We got new clothes, just as Clarion said we would."

Caden walked around the foot of the big wooden bed and picked up the clothes. "These look really cool," he said.

The other guys quickly got up to dress too. Each had a pair of suede pants and high buckled and strapped boots. Caden quickly put on the wine colored linen and leather shirt left for him. The front of the shirt looked like a padded breastplate. He pulled it across his chest and buttoned the large front flap under his left arm. Then he laced the leather straps through the buckles across the corresponding shoulder. He looked like a swordsman ready for battle. On the upper left corner of the breastplate was the embroidered emblem of a strong man's arm and fist, holding a snow white lily. After Caden dressed, he held out his arms and turned around to show off his outfit.

"So how do I look?" he asked. The others all acknowledged his attire, "Nice," "Cool," "Great," but each were too busy getting dressed themselves, to admire him as he wished they would.

Wes buttoned up his silken blousy white shirt that looked like it was designed for a buccaneer. He quickly tucked it into the suede pants and then donned an open hunter green vest. On the left chest side of his vest was an embroidered Chalice with an ornately engraved heart on it. He also had a tan colored sash that wrapped around his waist and tied on the side of his hip.

Josiah was given a long midnight blue jacket that went the full length of his body and stopped at his shins. Silver filigree buttons ran down the front, from the collar to his waist and down the sleeves from the elbow to the wrist cuff. There was also an emblem, which adorned his jacket. A blazing torch set through the middle of a gold crown, resting over an open book was embroidered on both sides of the jacket chest panels.

Ian quickly jumped into the suede pants. The belt for his pants was a long leather strap that widened about four inches in the middle then tapered to the ends. He placed the wide part of the strap against the small of his back, then tied the loose ends of the strap together in front. His outfit came equipped with a hooded cloak. He was a bit excited to put that on. He picked up the cloak, looking for a shirt but found only a maize-colored button up vest.

"Do you guys see a shirt lying around?" Ian asked, as he shuffled through the bed linen. There was no shirt to be found.

"Maybe you're not supposed to wear one," Josiah said.

Ian shrugged it off and put on the vest. Each button made the vest fit more snugly as if it were designed by a tailor who knew his exact waist and chest dimensions. As the final touch, he flung the brown flannel cloak over his shoulder. The broach that fastened the cape securely around his neck was fashioned in the shape of an ornate crest. In the crest was a soaring eagle. Ian flung the cloak off his shoulders like it was a cape.

"That cloak is very cool, Ian" Josiah commented as he buttoned up the last of the silver filigrees on his coat.

"Yeah, it's a good thing I have it. It's really the only thing that gives my clothing character," Ian replied.

"Do you think that we'll pass as Salamgard-ites or Salamgard-ians or whatever you call a person from Salamgard?" Caden said.

Wes gave Caden a quick up and down assessing look, "I guess. You would to me, but I haven't seen anyone from Salamgard except Clarion . . . and remember, things aren't always as you would expect them to be in Salamgard."

Caden gave an "OooHa" of agreement and high fived Wes.

"At least we *don't* look like Otherlanders, if that's what they call us here", Josiah replied as he strained to pull on his leather boots.

The band of brothers were clad in their tailor fitted clothing ready to face the journey that lay before them. What would this day hold? Would they come into new joys and excitement or would this day be the last day of their young lives?

CHAPTER TWENTY-THREE

After the four young men finished tucking, fastening and buttoning their clothes they exited the door of the bedroom and stepped into the grand room they left the night before. Clarion was there to greet them. She looked less like a teenage boy and more like a beautiful woman now. Her black hair was pulled back behind her head, loosely braided and adorned with pearls. She wore a deep burgundy velvet vestment, which accented her feminine form. The velvet skirt panels hung loosely from her waist to the floor. It looked as if she was wearing a dress when she was standing still but when she walked, one could see that she was wearing pants and boots, allowing her the freedom to ride and fight as a proper archer, should the situation arise. Clarion's beauty caught the guys off guard. They all stopped and just stared.

"You're absolutely beautiful," Wes reverently remarked with awe.

"Thank you Wes. And you gentlemen look like proper *Citizens of Salamgard*," she said as she gave a modest nod in Caden's direction.

"Ah, that's what they call the Salamgard-ese," Caden quipped under his breath.

"Thanks for the cool clothes," Ian replied, "We really like them. It's remarkable how well they fit."

"What do these symbols mean?" Wes asked as he pointed to the embroidered chalice on his vest. "I've seen them before. They were in the crest that was on a sword in Dr. Ashe's office."

"They are very significant. They are the symbols that adorn the crests of four of the Kings greatest Knights. You will come to know their meaning more fully before you reach Asilo. But for now, you should eat. We must leave within the hour if we expect to make it to the City of Aanda before nightfall."

The mention of food redirected the guy's attention and made them lose all interest in clothes, crests and even traveling. Filling their bellies was now the primary objective and driving force of their existence.

At the opposite end of the grand room, Clarion had set a table and prepared breakfast. The boys sat down and began to devour the rich breakfast cakes, meats and fruits set before them. They had never tasted food so rich in flavor.

"These cakes are awesome," Caden remarked. "I've never had anything like it. It kind of tastes like . . . Christmas." There was a sense of agreement manifested by indistinguishable grunts from each guy as he slid deeper and deeper into a gastronomic catatonia.

"The food in Salamgard is unlike that in Otherland because here your senses are undistorted. You will hear things more acutely, see things in more vivid color and taste things with greater flavor," Clarion said.

True to the form of late adolescent males, the brothers just kept chowing down without acknowledging Clarion's comment. It was as if they were caught in an enchanted spell, which forced their stomachs to overtake their intellectual capacities. Clarion began to wonder if she had lost the opportunity and earnestness that she needed, to prepare her charges for their impending journey.

"I hope you can divert your attention away from the meal and listen to my instruction while you eat," she said.

The tone in Clarion's voice and the directness of her statement struck the mothering-nerve in each guy and in one accord, they abruptly stopped and looked in her direction like a pack of trained dogs who had just heard their master's whistle. They all realized that they weren't being very accommodating so they slowed down the intake and directed their attention to the conversation.

"Pay close attention to what I have to tell you," Clarion began. "Before we reach Asilo and King Elyon, each of you will encounter a mentor, one of the four Knights of which I spoke last evening. He will reveal to you more of the King's plan for you. You must heed the instruction of your mentor. He will *mark* you and give you a weapon that will assist you in battling Ubilaz's forces."

"Mark us?" Josiah asked. He had just taken a big bite out of a succulent piece of fruit. Not meaning to talk with his mouth full but intrigued by Clarion's words he continued, "What does that mean? Are we being branded like cattle?"

"While you are in Salamgard, the defining characteristic given to you by the King will be visible and tangible in some way. It will set you apart and distinguish you as an Ambassador-Knight," Clarion answered. "Once you see King Elyon, he will embed those characteristics deep within each of you permanently, by official-ly knighting you. When you re-enter Otherland you will remain marked men, but there will no longer be any visible or tangible icon to define you as an Ambassador-Knight. Your mentor will also give you a weapon and instruct you in its use. Your weapon will equip you in battle against any of the Dark lord's warriors. It will *not* help you against the necrophim unless you learn to complete-ly trust Elyon and allow his power to flow through your weapon. When that occurs, your weapons will be a destructive force against the necrophim."

"Will we know our mentor by the crest that we wear?" Josiah asked. "You said that Lord Ubilaz is a master of disguise and de-ception, won't he try to pose as a mentor?"

"Your mentors know *you*," Clarion reassured. "And you will know them because your spirit will resonate with their spirit. It will feel as if two pieces of a puzzle have mysteriously come together. Ubilaz may attempt to pose as a mentor but he cannot knit hearts together as Elyon can; besides Ubilaz does not yet know that you are in Salamgard. The longer it takes for him to discover your presence, the easier it is for your mentors to equip you for a possible battle. You must remember that his subjects are all throughout Salamgard, or as they say, Eikondor. He will stop at nothing to keep you from reaching King Elyon. So guard your conversations and your behaviors lest you be discovered."

Clarion rose from her place at the table, "We can continue this conversation as we travel. Keep your tone quiet and do not say anything that would give away your identities as Otherlanders. Remember the forest is watching and listening." She positioned the quiver of arrows over her shoulder and flung the golden bow onto her back as if she were putting on a coat. As she lead the guys out the front door she slipped her arms through the leather arm guards and began to fastened them securely, readying herself for any possible battle.

Just outside Clarion's front door, the morning was glorious. The green rolling hills of Eindhoven Glen along with the smell of the dew that graced them, created a memorable picture in the minds of each young man. Never had they seen color so glorious. They could not have even imagined the beauty of this place from the glimpses they had amidst the straw and in the darkness of the prior evening's traverse through the countryside. The brothers stood peacefully for a moment in front of Clarion's cottage to drink in the wonder called *Salamgard*.

Clarion finished lacing the armguards and then raised a small silver charm to her lips that was secured to a chain around her neck. She took a deep breath and blew into the charm but no sound came forth. Content with the result of her actions, she dropped the charm to its graceful position around her neck and waited expectantly.

"Is that a whistle or something?" Wes asked.

"It is a *calling charm*," Clarion explained. "I have been given *understanding* by King Elyon. This gift allows me to understand and communicate with those who others find difficult to understand."

CHAPTER TWENTY-THREE

"But I didn't hear anything when you blew into the charm."

"You weren't being called."

Before she completed her sentence, Cervus thundered from around the side of the cottage. The cart that served as the chariot for their midnight ride was still following the muscle defined stag. As he paraded before them, the guys were reminded once again of how overwhelmingly huge and spectacular this magnificent animal was. He stood about twelve feet tall from the ground to the top of his great antlers. His mane was a full rich golden brown and his form was chiseled, indicating that he possessed the strength of a hundred men.

"Cervus, my dear friend!" Clarion said. The fond affection in Clarion's voice evidenced that there was a very special bond between her and the great forest lord. She stroked Cervus' beautiful mane, "The morning is always more majestic when you come into view." Cervus bowed his head very low as if to acknowledge her compliment in full humility.

"Has the presence of our friends been detected?" Clarion asked.

Cervus looked at Clarion and then away, returning his gaze once again to her. Clarion smiled, "That's good news!" She turned to her four bewildered friends and translated, "Cervus' clan kept vigil all throughout the night and listened intently to the conversations of the trees. They are certain that Lord Ubilaz is unaware of your presence in Salamgard."

Cervus lifted his head high, having more to say. The massive rack atop his head came so low that it almost rested on his strong back. Clarion directed her attention to the enormous animal. He lowered his head to fix his dark brown eyes to her crystal silver blues. A moment passed and Clarion spoke, "You are so wise and brave, Lord Cervus. King Elyon is glorified to have so grand a Knight the likes of you in his realm." Cervus again humbly acknowledged her compliment as she embraced the commanding creature and pressed her cheek against his powerful neck.

Clarion turned once again to translate, "Throughout the night, Cervus set a series of events in motion to secure your safe passage to Aanda. If your presence is detected, Ubilaz will surely mobilize his forces. The less time he has to do that, the better it is for our safety. Many of the forest creatures have strategically taken post between here and the gates of the Aanda. At Cervus' command the forest is prepared to interfere with the delivery of any message that would compromise your anonymity and, if necessary, fight so that you may flee to the safety of the fortified City. There are many who would gladly die so that you can reach King Elyon."

Wes timidly extended his hand to reach toward Cervus. The animal was so large and intimidating that Wes almost felt unworthy to touch so majestic a creature. Cervus appeared to understand and leaned his head in to meet Wes' hand.

"Thank you, Lord Cervus," Wes announced with a deep heart-felt gratitude and sincerity. "You are surely a magnificent servant and powerful knight." Wes didn't know if he was saying the right thing. He felt like a tourist attempting to try out his foreign language skills. His heart truly meant what he said, but it just seemed awkward coming out of his mouth. Cervus accepted his remarks and his sincerity by bowing so low that his antlers graced the ground in front of him.

"We must be on our journey now," Clarion stated as she positioned herself in the back of the wagon.

CHAPTER TWENTY-FOUR

Clarion climbed aboard and was making herself comfortable in the back of the wagon. Wes smiled, as if Clarion was playing with them, "Aren't you the driver?"

"No you are, Wes. It will be less suspicious and give a perception of normality if you hold the reigns. I am recognizable to many in Salamgard. If I sit in that seat it will appear as if I am transporting visitors."

This appeared to visibly, unnerve Wes. Clarion reassured, "You need not worry. Cervus needs no directing. He is very much in control of your safe passage."

Wes assumed his position behind the reigns. Caden mounted the coach seat beside him as Josiah and Ian jumped into the back alongside Clarion. With everyone in place, Cervus broke into a steady gait down the red clay road toward Somberbos Forest. It would be about a mile's journey before they reached the edge of the forest. Cervus was not yet into a full gallop when suddenly out of nowhere two young stallions, one black as night, the other a deep roan, charged the wagon in full stride off the right side of the wagon. The sight startled Ian and Josiah who could see the pair barreling down on them.

"We have company," Josiah yelled. "I didn't think we would be detected so quickly!" Everyone turned to see the horses coming closer at a mounting speed.

Clarion called, "Eleus and Virtus glad you are joining us." Then she turned to the guys, "Be at ease, these stallions are captains under Cervus command. They will escort us until we reach the forest line, and while they will be with us throughout our entire journey, unless trouble arises, you will not see them again after we enter Somberbos."

The boys directed their attention to the two captains and saluted their gratefulness to the escorts, who never once broke stride. Both nodded their head in recognition. Then Eleus broke away from the traveling pack, sprinting well in front of Cervus, to serve as the party's scout. Moments later, he reached the tree line and in a single bound disappeared into the forest. That was the cue for the black stallion, Virtus to break rank and position himself just to the front right side of Cervus. As they reached the forest, Virtus took a great leap forward then quickly became invisible in the dense flora of Somberbos. Cervus slowed his pace to a steady leisurely trot as he passed the tree line into the shaded tundra of Somberbos. Clarion saw a leopard, high above lounging in a tree. She smiled and gave a slight affirming nod. The leopard tilted his head and raised his brow slightly to acknowledge her and yet keeping his mission concealed.

Wes held the reigns that hung from the bridal on Cervus' head, staying true to the façade of being the one in control. Cervus stayed a course on a well-worn forest trail always watching and aware that there were eyes in Somberbos that were protective as well as destructive.

The hours passed without any disruption of the pleasantness of the journey. The conversation was delightful as Clarion retold the story of Salamgard, King Elyon and Lord Ubilaz, this time in more detail. Once again, the boys were caught up in the mystery and magic of the great epic. When she had finished the story, she looked around to assess their location. "We are a little more than an hour from Aanda," she said as she leaned back in a comfortable and relaxed position on the hay.

"That's great," Ian exclaimed. "I guess we're pretty good Ambassador-Knights by pulling one over on Lord Ubilaz." His words rang clear enough for Cervus to give a concerned glance behind and come to an abrupt halt. His eyes darted from side to side revealing that similar "hunted" look that he had the first time they saw him. Clarion also rapidly moved from her relaxed position to one that would allow her to spring into action at a moment's notice. She looked all around anticipating the befalling of some unknown fate.

"What's going on?" Wes asked as he let the reigns fall from his hand and quickly turned his body around to get some sense of security from Clarion. Caden sensed Clarion's panic and rose to his feet from the seat next to Wes looking as if he were readying himself for a fight.

"The forest listens to our conversations," Clarion whispered with a concerned caution. Ian slumped back in his seat fearing that he betrayed his friends. As he sunk into the side of the wagon, Clarion sprang to her feet and armed her bow. She lifted the arrow high above her head as a large raven lifted itself in flight from the tree limbs. Clarion pulled the bow and released the arrow, "*Altivolus*," she said as the let go. The string of the bow sung as the arrow flew and cut through the black winged informant. Caden quickly jumped from his carriage seat and grabbed a fallen tree branch on the road side to serve as a club just in case a battle broke out. Cervus' eyes darted all round attempting to assess if other trouble lurked. He knew that it was no longer good for them to be in Somberbos. There may be other spies, with greater speed and cunning, who may have witnessed this event.

"Caden, get back into the wagon," Clarion ordered. "We may still be safe. Ubilaz's spy may have been working alone. I don't see any other creatures." Caden vaulted back up onto his seat still clutching his pacifying weapon. Everyone stood in silence for a few seconds listening and watching for any other movement. The forest remained peaceful and still. None of Cervus' hidden sentries emerged, indicating that there seemed to be no threat of battle.

"How did you know that that raven was an informant of Eikondor?" Josiah whispered, quietly breaking the forest silence.

"The King's mark was missing from under his wing," Clarion reported. "Every animal declares its allegiance to Elyon or Ubilaz. If they are loyal to Elyon, they are boldly and visibly marked by the King's red fleury cross."

Cervus turned his head and lifted his chin high. There on his neck, stained in the white of his under-mane was the fleury cross. The guys hadn't noticed it before but now it was so distinct that they wondered how they could have missed it.

"Why didn't we see that before?" Josiah asked.

"Maybe your sense of sight has become keener. Most creatures bare the mark on their neck, shoulder or back. The birds bare the mark under their left wing. If you are attentive, you can see the mark when they take flight. That raven did not bare the king's mark," Clarion replied.

"So all the ravens are part of Lord Ubilaz's kingdom," Wes stated.

"No! Every individual creature can choose who they will pledge their allegiance. Just as families and friends influence your choices, the clans of animals influence their own," Clarion answered.

"What does that mean?" Wes returned.

"It means that there may be many more ravens who side with Ubilaz but only a fool would believe that all ravens are part of the Kingdom of Eikondor; just as it would be foolish to think that all deer follow King Elyon because lord Cervus does. You must look for the fleury cross marking."

"But that would be so easy to counterfeit. Doesn't Ubilaz mark his spies so that they can deceptively lurk about?" Josiah questioned.

"There are some mysteries in Salamgard that generate from King Elyon. We do not know why nor can we explain how it works, but if a creature falsely bears the mark of the King without pledging allegiance to him, a painful death consumes it. Ubilaz cannot counterfeit loyalty to King Elyon."

"Is that also why we will be *marked* as you said earlier? Are all those loyal to King Elyon *marked*? It would kind-of be good to know who we're fighting, don't you think?" asked Caden.

"There is no mark on the human citizens of Salamgard or Eikondor. The only way that you know their loyalty is by their actions, attitudes and behaviors. That's why you must beware, because *those* attributes can be counterfeited. You are marked as Ambassador Knights, indicating that you have received a higher calling and mission by King Elyon," Clarion returned.

"What is *Altivolus*? You said *altivolus* when you shot that bird. Is it a magic spell?" Caden asked.

"Not a spell but an invocation of blessing from King Elyon to empower and make my arrow fly swiftly to hit its mark."

Clarion quickly got back to business, "It looks like there is no immediate danger which means this was not a trap. But we can't be sure that there are no other spies. Ubilaz may soon know that four new Ambassador-Knights have been recruited for Elyon's Kingdom. Cervus we must hasten our pace to Aanda. I fear that we have been compromised."

Cervus had the same agenda. Eleus and Virtus emerged into sight this time flanking both sides of the wagon. The powerful trio rose on their hind legs and exploded into full gallop sending the riders rolling back into their seats. They could reach Aanda in a little more than an hour if they kept a rapid pace.

Ian felt the acid in his stomach rising up to burn the back of his throat. Riddled with guilt, he threw the hood of his cape over his head and cocooned himself from the wind. He lay motionless in the back of the wagon, thinking that it would have been better for his brothers if he hadn't committed to join them.

The travelers left a flurry of dust and leaves as they disappeared down the trail. As the upheaval settled, returning the forest to a quiet peace, it revealed the carcass of the dead raven lying just off the trail, still pierced through with Clarion's red feathered arrow. Close to the carcass a large unmarked centipede, watching the events, quickly scurried out from the underbrush. As it climbed the closest tree, it morphed from its disguised form back into its natural state as a necrophim and flew into the darkness of Somberbos.

CHAPTER
TWENTY-FIVE

Venem swiftly flew from Somberbos Forest carrying the news of the four intruders. His flight took him over the Nera Mountain ridge and through Ataroth Woods leaving a blood red misty trail hanging in the air. Ataroth's dense trees created a canopy that let in little sunlight. The eerie effect of the darkness, even during midday, was accentuated by the felt evil that lurked in the Ataroth caves and underground caverns. The forest creatures loyal to Elyon had long abandoned their homes in Ataroth, giving the woods over to the wickedness that inhabited it. Venem sneered with confidence knowing that he had escaped interception from Cervus' sentries. He dodged and maneuvered between trees, over rills and around the rugged rocky terrain with such great precision and speed that it was difficult for anyone to see him, except for the red polluted trail that he left to quickly dissipate in the atmosphere.

Surely, Lord Ubilaz will reward me for bringing such important news so swiftly, he thought. The necrophim rocketed straight for a large oak tree positioned in the middle of the woods. The ancient tree's massive roots broke above and below Ataroth's floor like the far-reaching arms of a giant squid. Venem sped straight for the base of the tree where the roots had created an opening to an underground passageway.

Whoosh, a large suction of sound was created by the vacuum that broke as Venem flew into the passage. The orange glow from the flaming torches that lined the walls of the passageway made it travelable. Venem glided swiftly along until he could see the opening of a great cavern far ahead. He slowed his flight and approached the cavern with a sense of fear, awe and great respect. He dared not come rushing into this sacrosanct chamber with irreverence.

There was already much activity taking place in Ubilaz's throne room. The great cavernous room was filled with warriors, necrophim and elite citizens of Eikondor. All had assembled to pay homage or give report to their king. Venem slipped into the crowd and listen as three of Ubilaz's necrophim captains gave report. The throne room glowed an eerie yellow from torches that illuminated and heated it, just enough to make it noticeably uncomfortable. The air was stale, warm and thick with a dank smell of sulfur. The ceiling far above the crowd was adorned with thousands of icicle like stalactites that taunted the subjects below with their iconic impressions of cooler temperatures.

Venem pushed his way slowly and deliberately through the cordon of spectators until he could see the drama unfolding in the center of this cavernous throne room. Ubilaz's magnificent throne was carved in the stone wall on the other side of the great cavern. Six ascending black slate platforms served as steps that led up to the sovereign chair. Twelve of the mightiest necrophim warriors stood century, six to the left and six to the right of the throne. Their black armor, capes and draped vestments matched the slate floor making them appear to be pillars that accented the ascending avenue to the throne. Each necrophim warrior kept vigilant watch over the proceedings while awaiting Ubilaz's battle orders at a moment's notice.

The back of the ornately carved rock throne towered fifteen feet above the seated monarch. Venem inched his way to the front edge of the crowd. He wanted to situate himself for the perfect moment when he would deliver his news to the Dark Lord. *I wonder if anyone else has arrived with such welcoming news?* He thought.

His eyes darted throughout the horde of worshippers to catch a glimpse of anyone who evidenced a sense of urgency.

Venem plotted his strategy and rehearsed his lines in his head. *If I am right at the edge of the crowd, I can quickly speak up if I think anyone is attempting to bring urgent news to my Lord. I can quickly say, "My Lord, I have some news you must hear." No, no, no, I will say, "My glorious king, your humble servant brings you urgent news." Yes, that's it.* Then his concern turned again to glee as he scanned the many onlookers. *Lord Ubilaz will surely make me a captain right here in front of all these citizens of Eikondor. I may become famous. One moment I was a scout the next a captain.* He was so enthralled in the fabrication of his own exaltation that he didn't notice that the proceedings had begun.

"I always take great delight to hear of the advancement of my kingdom, Eikondor. I trust that each of you have something substantial to report?" Ubilaz said as he rose to address the three captains who stood before him. The sight of the Dark Lord took Venem's breath away. In that moment, he knew that the legendary depiction of Ubilaz was true. It had been said that of all the creation in Salamgard, Ubilaz was the most beautiful.

Ubilaz's stature was tall and commanding. He appeared to have no defect in him. His perfectly chiseled features, towering form and his agelessness gave him the look of a young and powerful ruler. His long black vestments had threads of ruby running through it, giving him a luminous crimson glow with every movement of his body. On his head, he wore an onyx diadem that was inlaid with rubies and diamonds. The crown held his jet black hair in place. A lock of deep red began at his right temple and continued over his head, cascading with the tresses of his black mane against his shoulders. His silver eyes pierced through the darkness of his character. Their dark pupils reflected a glint of the ruby thread's luminescence, in his clothing. This frequently gave the illusion that his eyes emitted a flash of scarlet lightening. They appeared as if they could cut through the very soul of the person upon whom he transfixed his gaze. Ubilaz also donned what appeared to be a royal stole intricately adorned with row upon row of ebony feathers. The high collar of this mantle framed the back of his head and the train filled the floor with a black satin softness.

"Gath you presided over the city necrophim, what have you to report?"

"My Lord, the citizens of Aanda prepare for that dreadful. . . *Victorium Morte* holiday," Gath reported. The distain in his voice echoed his loyalty to the Dark Lord. The long dramatic pause after the statement almost provoked a response.

"Is that the extent of your report? You dare waste my time with information that is common knowledge as well as being benign?" Ubilaz barked at the captain standing before him.

"No, your Greatness," Gath gloated as he humbly bowed. The smugness of his countenance indicated his delight in being asked that question. One could have gathered that Gath was hoping that Dark Lord would require more. "This year many of Elyon's loyal followers in Aanda plan to assemble for a great feast at Lemuel's castle. I have taken the liberty in preparing *my* legion to over-throw the festival in one single attack. We will destroy most of the population of Aanda in a single evening. King Elyon will not be attending the gala, so there will be no interference from him. The attack will be swift and deadly. It will mark a great victory for you, my lord."

Gath again grinned smugly and lowered his head in a nod of contrived humility as he slowly finished the last words of his sentence. He waited, wallowing in his self-induced glory, for the Dark Lord to lavish praise on his responsible actions.

"You must have put a lot of thought into this, Gath," Ubilaz said. "Did you presume to think that I would agree to such a misdirected and impetuous scheme? If your legion attacks, you will prematurely alert the citizens of Salamgard to the power that we have and continue to acquire. Your foolish actions will make them *run* to Elyon. They must believe that we are an impotent force, growing weaker daily. We must lull them into a complacency that displaces their trust in what they cannot see with a comfortable trust in what they can see. They must believe that the victory, which they so gullibly celebrate in this upcoming holiday, rendered us powerless. Our tactics must be deceptive, subversive and disguised," Ubilaz growled through clenched teeth as he fixed his silver-eyed stare at Gath. Gath's ill acquired confidence melted into a calculated fear.

"My deepest apologies, my king," Gath cowered as he looked at the floor while backing away from the throne. "We shall let them celebrate unhindered".

Ubilaz didn't break his gaze from Gath. "You shall not," he said in a soft, deliberate, hollow tone. The power in his voice sent chills down the spines of all within the sound of his voice. "Your legion shall take on the form of the citizens of Salamgard and attend the gala. Surely your necrophim remember that they can morph to appear as any being they so desired?" Ubilaz questioned.

Gath didn't utter a word. His face still directed toward the floor, he only lifted his eyes toward the ominous ruler and nodded.

"Good, then your primary tactic as before, and shall be until *I* otherwise direct, is to interfere in the affairs of Salamgard's populace without detection. You must lead those loyal to Elyon into the bondage of doubt and denial. Most certainly, your legion can whisper their spirit essence slowly into the souls of Elyon's followers, gradually taking their lives. They should doubt that Elyon deeply loves and cares for them and have misgivings about his goodness. The citizens of Salamgard must deny that Elyon is powerful and learn to trust in their own power, more and more. Deceive them into thinking that their power *is* Elyon's power. You have one day to reconvene your legion and ready them, I suggest you do it quickly".

"Yes, my lord," Gath replied and in the blink of an eye, he vanished, leaving only a dissipating red misty vapor where he once stood.

Avah, captain of the woodland necrophim stood next to give report. Unmoved by the incident that he just witnessed; he waited for Ubilaz to acknowledge him.

"Avah, I trust that you have a more appealing report," Ubilaz said as he directed his attention to the captain standing before him.

"Lord Ubilaz, we have come to find out that the *Kalos Sapphire* is out in the open," Avah replied.

There was a gasp of awe in the throne room and whispering conversations broke out like a ripple among the congregants. Ubilaz's countenance changed, exposing his great delight. "Then it is out of Elyon's possession!" he stated.

"My Lord, Elyon does not *hold* the gem but it is still claimed as his possession. It has been given to Tobijah the Great Warrior Knight of Elyon's realm. Elyon has charged Tobijah to *protect that, which belongs to the king*. The sapphire has been fashioned into an amulet. The great warrior wears it around his neck, my Lord."

"That precious stone has the ability to increase its owner's powers seven-fold. Do everything within your power, Avah to insure that it becomes my possession," Ubilaz stated.

"The only way to get it from Tobijah is with a show of force, Lord Ubilaz. He and his men are very powerful warriors. We would have to overpower them and then torture the Great Warrior to, willfully give it up. But alas, you just reminded us that we should avoid battles."

"NO, I said we should avoid the blood bath of battle that would rally the citizens of Salamgard," Ubilaz said.

Ubilaz continued to speak as if he were thinking out loud, "Some battles are inevitable. This battle would only involve Tobijah and his warriors, but alas Avah you are right, he and his men are very powerful. We could run the risk of losing that precious gem altogether. We should use force as a last resort. It will take a cunning spirit to steal it away from one such as Tobijah." Ubilaz shifted his attention and addressed the crowd, "Raith, step forward," he commanded.

Venem, now standing at the front edge of the crowd, looked to his right and left down the line of devoted followers who called themselves citizens of Eikondor. There was no movement. Then from the corner of his left eye, he saw the crowd begin to part. He turned his attention to the frontline of spectators who were moving out of the way allowing someone to pass. He couldn't see the creature because too many citizens shielded his view. Then from the gap in the crowd emerged a fierce looking hyena. His hideous perpetual smile bared his razor sharp teeth. It was difficult to discern if his expression was one of wicked delight or just sheer ferocity. Everyone resumed their places closing the gap and leaving the hyena standing alone a few feet in front of an audience of onlookers.

Ubilaz smiled and gazed fondly at the hyena positioned between the place where Avah stood and the crowd of spectators.

"Raith, you have been a faithful servant to me," Ubilaz stated.

With that, the hyena bowed in gratitude.

Ubilaz continued, "You are also among the most cunning of any citizen in Eikondor. It would please me if you would join forces with Avah to bring the Kalos Sapphire into my possession."

The hyena let out a hideous laugh indicating his acceptance of the task and then bowed low as if to pledge his service to his lord. Avah turned back to look at the hyena. His glance indicated that he was not happy with this partnership. But Avah feared Ubilaz so he quickly concealed his aversion to being aligned with such a vile creature. He turned to face the Dark Lord, also bowing in allegiance and commitment to the task given him. The hyena stepped up to Avah's side.

"I want that gem. Mobilize necrophim, animals and men, if you must, but get that gem. Remember that the Kalos sapphire is only powerful when it willfully changes ownership. If Elyon has entrusted it to Tobijah then he becomes the King's proxy. Trick him, torture him and kill him if you must, but get him to give the gem to me. What Elyon possesses must be mine. His power will decrease as mine increases."

Avah and Raith genuflected and slowly stepped back into the crowd, leaving Daemonicus, the last reporting minion captain standing alone.

CHAPTER
TWENTY-SIX

Daemonicus commanded the necrophim of the air, whose job it was to serve as sentries and scouts over the whole land. The legions of necrophim under his command even extended their work into Otherland in an attempt to thwart and destroy the increase, influence and establishment of Elyon's kingdom. Daemonicus' soldiers were powerful and swift. They were the fiercest and most destructive of all necrophim.

There was a silence as Ubilaz attempted to regain himself from the drunken state of covetousness brought on by his passion to acquire so great a prize, the Kalos Sapphire. Venem stood agitated in the front of the crowd.

Now . . . no wait . . . yes now. I should just take one step forward and say, "My dear Darkness I also have news that will make you overjoyed." Yes, he is already in good spirit, he will receive the news with delight and maybe crown me prince over a host of necrophim. Just as he was about to take his step forward and speak up, Daemonicus calmly spoke.

"Lord Ubilaz, Serik is on the move. Our eagles first spotted him coming from the east, when he was far off beyond the City of Toleth."

Ubilaz seemed jolted back to reality. "What did you say, Dae-monicus?"

The stately necrophim captain stood tall with his hands clasped firmly behind his back and tranquilly said, "Serik has come back to Salamgard. The most powerful Knight in Elyon's realm and most powerful being in all Salamgard . . . present company excluded my Lord . . . has returned."

"SERIK! I despise him. He has compelled many from the far reaches of the universe to become Elyon's Ambassador-Knights. Fortunately, we have intercepted and reprogrammed scores of those ambassador-knights for the glory of Eikondor. We have also de-stroyed equally as many who refused to shift their loyalty away from Salamgard. Elyon's kingdom is expanding because of Serik. Why is he here now"?

"My hosts are keeping watch. He did not stop at Asilo but con-tinued on, making his way toward the city of Aanda," Daemonicus said. "He may have just returned at the request of Lord Lemuel to attend the holiday celebration in Aanda."

"I think not; something of greater proportion is brewing. Surely he did not return just to attend that ridiculous, *death-victory holi-day,*" Ubilaz contemplated aloud as he pulled the feathered mantle, positioning it in a way that would allow him to sit majestically on his throne.

Daemonicus replied, "My Lord, nothing out of the ordinary stirs in Salamgard, short of the preparation for their holiday. Elyon re-mains at Asilo. Serik did not even stop to pay homage to his King. We have no reason to believe that Serik has returned but for this celebration feast."

"There must be more. If the most beloved son of Elyon's realm doesn't even stop to let his king know that he has returned home, he must have an urgent agenda. He is making haste to that city but he doesn't want to appear to be in too much of a hurry. He and Lemuel are using the holiday celebration as a cover. Something is going to happen in Aanda that is greater than this forth-coming miserable holiday."

"I have my shrewdest scouts positioned in Aanda. Naturally, they are well disguised and have infiltrated the fabric of Aanda's community. They share my lord's distain for Serik and will stop at nothing to assure that his plans are thwarted. We are keeping a high vigilance and a low profile."

"You have done well Daemonicus. It is imperative that we learn of Serik's mission. There is a variable that is still beyond our detection and it seems that time is of the essence," Ubilaz proclaimed.

At that point, Venem knew that he needed to speak up. He hadn't thought that news he carried was as critically urgent as it now appeared to be. He found the right moment and cleared his throat loudly as he took a step forward from the crowd. The attention dramatically shifted in Venem's direction.

"Pardon my disturbance, your royal highness. I trust that you will graciously tolerate the interruption by your humble servant who carries some important news," Venem said.

The Dark Lord stood and took a step forward to look beyond Daemonicus who was blocking his view of the necrophim who was addressing him.

"Who are you and what news is so important that you would disturb my proceedings?" Ubilaz questioned.

"My name is Venem; I am assigned to keep watch in Somberbos. I am so delighted to be in your presence my lord. I knew how important it was to come reverently into this sacred place so I made as little disturbance as possible. I am overwhelmed to be in the same place as my sovereign liege," Venem rambled.

"Yes, yes." Ubilaz tolerated his obsequiousness with disgust. "What news is so urgent?" Ubilaz demanded.

"My Lord, I said the news was important, not urgent. Well maybe it's a little bit urgent now. At least I didn't think it was urgent until a few minutes ago," Venem proclaimed. "I came from Somberbos, Clarion killed one of your ravens who was most likely en-route to tell you of the news."

"What news?" Ubilaz voiced with slow impatient distinction.

"The Master Archer was accompanying four young men. One of them spoke loud enough for us to figure out that they were Otherlanders on their way to becoming Ambassador-Knights. Well, one young man actually *said* that they were going to be Ambassador-Knights. That's how we knew. We really didn't figure it out, but I digress! They were on the trail which exits at the Gilbreath Plains."

As those words fell on Ubilaz's ears, he became alarmed. "FOUR? Are you sure there were four of them?"

"Yes, your holy darkness. I saw them with my own eyes. One had blond hair and the other was a bit more muscular with kind of reddish or maybe brownish red . . ."

"Shut up you fool," Ubilaz growled. "They are headed for Aanda. Serik has been sent to rendezvous with them. These boys are of significant importance to Elyon and his kingdom."

Ubilaz's voice became more thunderous with each word he spoke. "Those four boys are destined to do great damage to Eikondor. They will be acquiring extraordinary powers if Serik is involved. We must stop them from reaching Aanda. How long ago did you have this encounter?"

Venem looked to the stalactites in the ceiling as he calculated aloud, "It must have been just more than one half of an hour past."

"And how long of a journey's travel time do you estimate it would take them if they were headed for Aanda?" Ubilaz urgently inquired, attempting to keep his composure.

"At a good pace, they could arrive at Aanda in less than one full hour. Cervus carried the travelers and I would well say that he could make the trip easily in that time," Venem replied.

"If they reach Aanda they will be protected by Lemuel and Serik," Ubilaz shouted. He grabbed the hem of the great black feathered cape and flung it away from his body. What appeared to be a cape, transformed into a pair of massive black wings that expanded four times the length of his arms. His voice thundered, "That must not happen. I want all forces marshaled to intercept those boys. Kill them, along with Clarion and Cervus," he raged.

The throne room fell into utter chaos as necrophim and soldiers quickly formed ranks, readied themselves for battle and departed in obedience to their king. Eight of the twelve necrophim who guarded the throne swiftly departed. The other four moved in close to Ubilaz as body guards maneuvering protective measures. Daemonicus turned and barked orders to his officers who immediately took flight from the throne room.

Venem became aware of the gravity of the incident. *I shall not be a prince or a captain today! If I don't leave now, I may not even remain alive,* he thought. With that, he attempted to get lost in the chaos and followed the myriads of those on the mission of stopping the travelers from completing their journey.

As Daemonicus prepared to leave, Ubilaz called, "Daemonicus, come here for a moment. I wish to speak with you privately." The great necrophim warrior stood composed and at attention in the final moments as the throne room emptied. The Dark Lord dismissed the remaining necrophim guards leaving him and Daemonicus alone in the great cavern.

"If our immediate attempts to kill them fail and they successfully arrive in Aanda, you must keep them from reaching Elyon, as has been the success of so many Otherlanders. If these four boys band together, and are then empowered by Elyon, they will become untouchable by our dark forces. No doubt, once they reach Aanda, they will be amply assisted in their mission, by the citizens of Salamgard and a host of others, loyal to Elyon. Daemonicus, if they make safe passage to Aanda, remain calm and order our forces not to interfere until they leave the refuge city and are vulnerably in the open again. Keep a strong watch on every move those boys make. Our first strategic offensive maneuver should be the subtle conversion of one of them to join ranks with us. This will break their bond and render them impotent. It could also give us a strategic ambassador in Otherland. If this strategy doesn't work, then separate them and return to our original plan, which is to destroy them. Remind our forces to avoid any encounter with Serik or Lemuel. We don't want to ignite a premature battle causing the four Knights of Elyon's realm to unite. Serik, Lemuel, Tobijah and Kesh can mobilize forces that can set us back millenniums," Ubilaz said. His words echoed in the great cavernous room, now that there were no longer bodies present to absorb the sound.

"I understand, Lord Ubilaz. Your orders will be carried out as you wish," Daemonicus replied.

"Are you confident that your soldiers can get close enough to these boys without their detection or the detection of Serik?" Ubilaz asked.

"My lord, there are none more deceptive and diabolical among all who serve you, than me and my legion. I will personally take an active role in making sure that your wishes are carried out without detection," Daemonicus answered.

"You have my confidence, loyal Daemonicus," Ubilaz stated. "Now go quickly and bring back a report that those young men have failed to arrive in Aanda."

CHAPTER
TWENTY-SEVEN

The great stag burst from the Somberbos Forest tree line on to the Gilbreath Plain. The five riders gripped the sides of the wagon, holding on with all their might. The road in front of Cervus widened from the traffic that had trodden up to the fortified city. Cervus increased his speed. His grand hooves beat the dirt road like a timpani roll and the stag's strong audible exhales syncopated the journey in a frenzied counterpoint.

Eleus and Virtus faithfully remained, flanking either side of the wagon with thunderous speed. A large eagle with a red fleury cross emblazoned beneath his wing made a swooping circle in front of the wagon. Clarion lifted her head and fixed her attention on the majestic bird.

"Lord Logos!" she whispered. She held tightly to the wagon and listened intently. After a few moments, she turned back and shouted to the guys, "Ubilaz knows of your presence. He has unleashed his necrophim. They are ordered to destroy us before we reach Aanda. Lord Logos has come to inform us that the hosts of the Dark Lord have reached the edge of Somberbos. They are moving quickly."

CHAPTER
TWENTY-EIGHT

In a house on the upper northeastern edge of the city of Aanda, a servant girl knocked on the chamber door of her mistress.

"My Lady you have a message," she called through the closed door.

The door opened to reveal a beautiful young woman. Her beauty was renowned throughout the city of Aanda. Her long gently curled auburn hair and deep green eyes made her immediately conspicuous. Her beauty was also enhanced by her perfect form and soft, glowing skin. "Of what message do you speak, Hannah?"

"A hawk just flew to the window with this." Hannah stretched out her hand and gave the woman an envelope. On the envelope was written, *Sabedoria*.

Sabedoria quickly opened the letter and read it silently. She turned with delight to her chambermaid, "Hannah, it is from our lord. He has a task for me. There may be a young man making his way to Aanda right now for the upcoming holiday. If he arrives, he will be traveling with companions. It is important that I meet with him . . . alone."

"What is your business with this young man?"

"He must choose to align himself with our lord or he will die. Our king has called upon my persuasive powers."

"How will you convince him?"

"I will call to him in song. I will sing from the highest point in the city. My song will flow through the streets. I will beckon him to come to me. He will hear it and be drawn to respond!"

"My lady the sweetness of your voice can enchant any living creature. But this order is from our powerful ruler. What if the young man hears it but doesn't listen?"

Sabedoria smiled and said slyly, "Then I will pursue him and seduce him!"

CHAPTER
TWENTY-NINE

Cervus thundered ahead. The wagon he was pulling shook violently from the powerful force that was bearing upon it. The fortified city of Aanda was in view. The great white metropolis was constructed into the side of the Sargo Mountain range. Each city dwelling towered above the other against the incline of the mountain. At the apex of the city, high above the dwellings stood Lemuel's castle. It looked as if it was positioned there to keep watch over the city. The closer the travelers got to Aanda, the more defined the city became. Aanda's fortified walls offered a deep sense of safety that beckoned refuge to the charging convoy.

"Quickly Cervus, we are most vulnerable on these plains" Clarion pleaded. The short five mile stretch of road from edge of the Somberbos forest, across Gilbreath, to Aanda's entrance seemed to be the longest and most frightening leg of the journey. Wes and Caden sat in the coachman's seat monitoring their forward momentum closer and closer to Aanda. Clarion was now standing in the back of the wagon, having a firm grip on the back of the coachman's seat. She had situated herself between Wes and Caden so she too could keep an eye on their progress.

Ian sat about midway to the back of the wagon on the left side of Clarion. He kept his head lowered, not wanting to look forward. He feared that they would not make it to Aanda and that he and his friends would suffer a terrible fate as the result of his foolish mistake. He pulled the hood of his cloak forward over his head to shield himself from the straw that was being kicked up by torrent of winds that rushed past the wagon.

Josiah sat in the front corner of the wagon behind Wes, to the right of Clarion. He stretched his arms across the side and back-boards, holding on with all his might. From his seat, Josiah was the only one who could see Somberbos moving farther away as they drew closer to Aanda.

Josiah began to see something unusual happening behind them. He pulled himself up to look more intently at the expanse of trees. "Ohooo guys," he yelled. "I'm afraid we're in serious trouble!"

Everyone turn to look back. A red mist, like a rolling blanket of fog, hovered above the tops of the trees midway through the forest. The mist was moving rapidly in their direction.

"What is that?" Wes shouted over the noise of the wagon.

"Necrophim! They are moving very fast," Clarion yelled. She turned forward again to assess the distance to their safe zone. "The necrophim will certainly overtake us before we can reach the safety of Aanda. More speed, dear Cervus; run with the power of the King."

Cervus lowered his head in a charging fury but could not muster up any more speed. The red billowing mist was moving closer to the lip of the forest, just before it broke to the plains. Ian pulled himself forward into the safety of the front left side corner of the wagon. As he pushed his way through the hay scattered on the wagon floor, he uncovered a coil of rope.

Josiah spied the rope. "I've got an idea," he yelled as he grabbed the coil. "We can harness the power of Eleus and Virtus."

Clarion sprang quickly into action. She pressed the calling charm to her lips summoning the two captains closer to the wagon.

CHAPTER TWENTY-NINE

"Wes you must now take the reins and help to guide Cervus," she said. Wes quickly grabbed the reins and wrapped them around his hands. He slid to the center of the coachman's seat, pushing Caden closer to the outside edge of the wagon.

Eleus and Virtus were now moving closer to the wagon's edge, still charging at blazing speed. Clarion tied the end of one rope around her waist and handed the end of a second rope to Caden.

"Secure this around your waist. When Virtus gets close enough you'll have to jump onto his back then tie that end of the rope around his neck. I will do the same with Eleus on this side," she yelled over the thunderous noise of Cervus' pounding gait and the noises of the swift moving wagon.

"Ian and Josiah, hold fast to the other ends of these ropes. When we have mounted the stallions, tie off the ends of the rope securely to the metal side rails of the wagon," Clarion ordered.

Ian found the end of Caden's rope and stood by to complete his task as soon as Caden jumped. Caden was standing, rope around his waist, judging the distance between himself and Virtus as the stallion drew closer. Clarion also readied herself opposite Caden, one foot on the side rail of the wagon in preparation for making the leap at the appropriate time.

Eleus and Virtus moved as close as they could to the wagon. Wes held the reins tight against Cervus neck. He knew that the great stag could no longer see the charging captains who were now behind Cervus' peripheral view. If the wagon veered even a centimeter from its course, it could take out one or both stallions and mean the certain death of his friends. Wes needed to parlay Cervus' vision and timing, keeping the great animal straight and steady, so as to alleviate some of the risk for Caden and Clarion's leap.

Virtus moved close and slowed his pace slightly. Caden waited a moment gauging the rhythm of the animal's movement. His heart pounded in his chest as he calculated his actions. If his jump wasn't timed accurately, he could end up being trampled by the stallion or under the wheels of the wagon. Just then, he heard Clarion yell,

"NOW" as she leapt onto Eleus' back. Without thinking, Caden jumped from the wagon onto Virtus' back. He held the muscular horse's neck with all his might, trying not to slide off the side of the charging stead. As soon as he got his balance, Caden untied the rope from his waist and secured it around Virtus' neck.

Josiah and Ian both sprang into action when Caden and Clarion took their flight. Now with room enough to hang over the sides of the wagon, they tied the ropes securely. By the time they were done, both riders had their ends of the rope fastened as a harness around their charger's necks.

"GO!" Josiah yelled indicating that the ropes were secure to the wagon, and in a burst of speed, the two captains bolted forward. Their pull on the wagon reduced the drag that Cervus carried, giving him a renewed energy and greater speed.

Josiah looked to the back of the wagon. The necrophim had passed the forest edge but the increased speed of the wagon pulled them away faster. He turned forward to see Aanda looming closer.

"We're going to make it . . . WE'RE GOING TO MAKE IT," he yelled. Wes and Ian joined in the cheering as they were now moments away from the sanctuary of Aanda's walls.

CHAPTER
THIRTY

The massive ornately carved wooden gates of the city of Aanda were overlaid with silver and bronze. Each gate towered high, dwarfing those who would pass through. Cervus, Eleus and Virtus did not slow their pace until they crossed the threshold of the gates.

Josiah looked back once again to see if the enemy was still encroaching. "They're retreating," he called.

Everyone turned around to see the red mist fractioning apart and dispersing in every direction. A wave of relief came over the travelers. "We have sanctuary here," Clarion said. "And it looks like the Dark Lord will not pursue us now, but we must still remain vigilant because he will stalk us like a lion stalks its prey. Then when he feels the moment is right, he will pounce."

Cervus and his captains turned a sharp left beyond the great gates and began to slow their pace until they came to a stop. They rested just outside the city's inner walls. The space between the outer walls with their great gates and the inner walls of Aanda served as a resting area where vagabonds and peddlers could set up shop and sell their wares. Refugee wagons with colorful banners, streamers and bells lined the stone laid street. Many of the wagon dwellers had already transformed the thoroughfare into a market bazaar ladened with handcrafted treasures and the fruits of their talents. Children ran happily among the street vendors and traveling troubadours filled the air with less than refined music.

The smell of meats and nuts roasting on the open fires, along with the scurry of the people, created a festive mood that solidified the sense of peace that the guys were now experiencing. The Otherland gentlemen found themselves in the middle of a renaissance faire. While it was nothing like Mason University's Campus Job Fair, it felt as safe as home.

"We will rest a while before going on to Lemuel's Fortress," Clarion called to Cervus. The three great animals reared their heads in affirmation and allowed their riders to dismount. Wes jumped from the wagon as Ian and Josiah untied the ropes from the metal side rails to free Eleus and Virtus. Wes quickly threw his arm around Caden's neck, "You were amazing, bro," he announced.

"That was such a rush! Did you see my flying leap onto Virtus' back? "Caden asked. Then striking a superhero pose, he said in his broadcast announcer voice. "Able to leap tall stallions in a single bound."

Wes chuckled, "I guess that you proved you were a super-man today!"

"I haven't felt power like that before. It was amazing what an adrenaline rush can do. We kicked necrophim booty. I'm so amped I feel like I could kick the crap out of a thousand necrophim," Caden boasted.

Wes and Caden continued to flaunt their bravado as they basked in the celebration of their victory. Clarion heard the exchange as she passed by to give homage to Lord Cervus and his captains, the more deserving heroes, for carrying them to salvation. A bit put off by their grandiosity, she said, "Beware my friends, power can be intoxicating and can color your view of what is good and noble. You fail to realize that you are most susceptible to attack when you revel in victory. The entire state of affairs has changed. Ubilaz knows that you are in Salamgard."

Her stern tone challenged Caden's daring, who saw this as the next hill to take. "Ok, we get it, but for now we're safe. Just chill, remember we're the good guys," he barked.

Clarion quickly squared off with Caden. "Just Chill? You really don't understand. As a matter of fact, you are clueless. Danger lurks all around you and Asilo is still many days away." Clarion pushed her bow in Caden's direction as if she were pointing her finger in his face.

"Even now Ubilaz has his necrophim plotting and scheming to overtake you. You have lost any hope of anonymity. All of Eikondor will be bent on separating your band of brothers and then unmercifully destroying you. Those evil forces have probably been alerted, so you best watch your back. Look around you – what do you see?"

"High fortified walls and a festive mood. It looks like a carnival. Everyone looks happy as if they were getting ready for . . . oh let me think . . . a *holiday*" Caden said glibly.

"That's right, you only see what is on the surface – But things in Salamgard aren't always as they may appear to be. Ubilaz will make that which is evil, appear to be good and that which is good to appear evil. What you cannot see are the necrophim that are probably watching our every move and listening to our conversation. And you cannot see the hearts of the people. There are many who are loyal to Ubilaz". Clarion pushed past the guys to gratefully thank Cervus, Eleus and Virtus. She turned and said, "And as for you being the *good* guys, that will only be true when King Elyon affirms it by knighting you."

Josiah walked over to the place where Caden and Wes were standing. "What was all that about?" he asked.

Caden shrugged it off, "Female drama!" he said and quickly changed the subject, directing attention toward the colorful surroundings and merriment of the market. He and Josiah beckoned Ian to join them as they began exploring the market. Wes was uneasy leaving the conversation with Clarion unresolved. As he approached her, he overheard her conversation with Cervus.

"You are so right Cervus; his lust for power may be his downfall. I believe that Caden may never know the power of the King. He trusts his own power," she said.

Cervus raised his head in conversation with her. Clarion replied, "Absolutely, the King's power did bring us to safety. It coursed through you and it was made even stronger when you were in unity with Eleus and Virtus. These young men must learn to trust the King. They have yet to discern the limitations of where their power ends and where the King's power begins."

Wes stepped closer and Cervus caught a glimpse of the approaching young man. Clarion turned to face Wes. She still looked quite perturbed.

"I'm so sorry for the way we responded. Lord Cervus, Virtus and Eleus I wanted to thank you for bringing us to safety. If not for you, a terrible fate would have befallen us," Wes said.

Cervus flicked his head and snorted. Clarion turned to face him then returned her attention to Wes.

"Cervus wants you to understand that he did not save you but rather the King saved all of us" Clarion replied. "We have come to know that even our most powerful efforts are weak by comparison to the power of Elyon. It is only in our weakness that the power of Asilo is made strong. When we come to the place where we give up our own power, that is when the King empowers us".

"That's really hard for us to grasp because in Otherland we are taught that we can only be *men* if and when we seize our personal power."

"That's no different than here. It is one of the most pervasive lies of the Dark Lord. The greatest power you can muster; even the greatest power of the Dark Lord, which is exponentially greater than our power, is dwarfed by comparison to King Elyon's unfathomable power. That is why King Elyon must increase while we decrease. His power is evident most in your weakness not your power."

"I'm beginning to understand more of the wonder of this great King. I now know that the only way we will be able to have victory over Ubilaz is to rely on Elyon. I'm also realizing that if we are going to become great men we must completely trust the King. We will need your help with that because it is so hard for us to trust the king when we have never met or seen him," Wes admitted.

CHAPTER
THIRTY-ONE

Daemonicus stood tall with his hands clasped behind his back, on the inner wall high above the noise and bustle of the city. The wind blasted around him but he stood unaffected, firmly planted, keeping his eye on the travelers far below. He watched as Clarion and her friends walked through the marketplace toward the inner gates of the city. He was soon joined by Gath who sat on the edge of the City wall.

"There is a strong power in these young men. I cannot figure it out. They are unlike any other potential ambassador-knights who have ventured this way," Daemonicus quietly stated. "The Dark Lord is also more unnerved by these four. I fear that we will not be able to turn them, so we must divide their ranks and destroy them."

"What do you propose?" Gath asked.

"We should use their powers against them."

"You mean intoxicate them with . . . love . . . and wisdom . . . and. . ." Gath grimaced with the mention of each word.

"Yes, yes that's exactly what I mean". Daemonicus' impatience began to show.

CHAPTER THIRTY-ONE

"How do you plan to do that"?

"We only have to get one of them away from the others, before they reach Elyon. That will make the entire group vulnerable. If we destroy one, we can destroy them all. We must lure one away by making him believe that his lone, unassisted actions are virtuous." Daemonicus was thinking more out loud than sharing a strategy with a comrade.

The air stirred a blood red mist and the two necrophim were suddenly joined by Avah who had heard Daemonicus' assessment. Avah crouched on the top of the city wall like a vulture ready to swoop on its prey. "So this is the rabble that is raising such a stir in Eikondor," he said. He cocked his head to listen to the conversation below.

"While there is a strong force with them, they have vulnerabilities that they think are virtues. One can often be turned from a true path if that one believes that he is rightly justified in his direction. Yes, there is one that can be turned." Avah said.

The three necrophim captains remained quietly unmoved like stone gargoyles set upon a fortress. They watched every move their new enemy made and they listened intently to their conversations. The wind kicked up, causing their long garments to unfurl about them.

Avah arose from his crouched position. "I have a more important task to be concerned about than four pitiful Otherlanders. There is a gem that I must acquire for our Lord Ubilaz." Then as quickly as he arrived, he vanished leaving only his residue to swirl about his other two comrades.

"I have reassembled my legion and they are dispersed throughout the city. They will be heavily represented at Lemuel's celebration," Gath remarked.

Daemonicus didn't respond he just remained lost in his surveillance. Gath decided not to engage a conversation and joined Daemonicus in his task of attempting to identify the weakness or point of vulnerability in the Otherlanders. Both necrophim remained silent, watching the band of brothers' fascination with the marketplace.

In a proclamation of enlightenment, Gath pointed and said, "Before the wretched holiday is completed, that one will be dead. I will follow my Lord's instructions and the boy will be deceived into trusting his own power. That will be the last thing he will do." Gath let out an evil laugh that would have been audible had they not been so high above the city. He pushed himself from his seated position off the wall into a free fall. Then the still laughing necrophim flew off to set his plan in motion.

Unamused, Daemonicus said under his breath, "Always, you make the wrong choices." He lingered steadfast on the wall to watch his prey. They were being entertained by the Vitatha gypsies and the activity of the market. *Mere mortals,* he thought. *Elyon's power may be strong on you, but you will never trust him.* As he watched, one of the guys seemed to lag behind. *It would be so easy to drive a wedge between you and the others. In one swift motion, I could have you in my clutches then exhale so that you breathe in my death.* His thoughts and thirst for death seemed to intoxicate him. And as if coming to his senses, he directed his attention to Wes Litchfield and thought, *I must be patient, there is a far better way. Lord Ubilaz would be more pleased if you die. You have just shown me the way to make that possible.*

The red mist floated in the air. Daemonicus was gone.

CHAPTER
THIRTY-TWO

The market place between the city walls of Aanda was bustling with festivity. Clarion and Wes caught up with Caden, Josiah and Ian who were already being amused by an entertainer who was juggling flaming torches.

"Is all of Aanda one big street party like this?" asked Josiah.

"No, these are Vitatha merchants. They travel between the cities of refuge in Salamgard setting up camp and selling their wares. Their homes are the wagons, tents and shelters you see behind their merchant tables. While they find asylum in Aanda's walls, they are not welcomed beyond the inner walls of the city," Clarion explained.

"Why can't they go into the city?" Wes asked.

"There is no law that forbids them from going into the city, but they don't because they can be persecuted and even experience violent retribution from some of the city's citizens. The Vitatha are not trustworthy people. They vacillate between their loyalty to King Elyon and Ubilaz. Their allegiance often depends on what serves them best. As a result they are not held in high regard," Clarion stated.

"So are they citizens of Salamgard or are they citizens of Eikondor?" Caden asked.

"Neither!" Clarion responded. "The citizens of Eikondor despise them because they only declare their loyalty to Ubilaz at their convenience. And the citizens of Salamgard reject them because they are quick to compromise their loyalty to Elyon. Both kingdoms know them as traitors who would sell out true followers at a moment's notice. As the result they are hated vagabonds forced to live outside of the cities."

"That's unfortunate, but it does seem like they are reaping the consequences of their behaviors and heritage," Caden commented.

"What does that mean?" Josiah asked Caden.

"Don't get me wrong, I'm sorry that they are destined to live the life of refugees but it just follows that justice is being served. If a person lives hypocritically, compromising when they know the right thing to do, then they suffer the consequences of their actions. After all, what goes around comes around – You know – What ever you sow you reap," Caden replied.

Considering the source, Wes rolled his eyes and ignored Caden's righteous grandstanding. "I thought that the citizens of Salamgard reflected the virtues of King Elyon," Wes said. "Shouldn't they be more gracious to the Vitatha?"

"Many of the citizens of Salamgard have suffered the pain of betrayal at the hand of the Vitatha and are not able to get beyond their pain to be compassionate. Others often forget their virtues and stand in judgment of the Vitatha for rejecting King Elyon. These citizens forget the benevolence that Elyon shows all people."

"Are they safe in the space between the walls of the city?" Josiah asked.

"Yes, quite safe. They find safety and security just inside the outer walls of all cities of refuge; Wreingor, Eldon, Toleth and Aanda, by decree of King Elyon. However, if the Vitatha venture beyond the inner walls of those cities, they may often suffer violent persecution."

"Well they seem happy enough," Wes chuckled as a group of laughing children swirled around the guys. The children's laughter turned to dancing as a group of musicians began to play.

A little girl with colored ribbons in her hair grabbed Clarion's hand and beckoned her to dance. Clarion smiled and twirled with the child to the bright cadence of the music. Soon Wes and Josiah were pulled into the dance. Caden sat on a wooden box next to one of the musicians who quickly placed a drum in front of him. He rapidly picked up the beat, joining the jovial spirit of the festivities.

Wes was dancing and laughing when he spied Ian off to the side leaning against a wagon. Ian was still withdrawn in the hood of his cape. The whirlwind of having entered into Aanda and the Vitatha market left the guys unaware that Ian was lagging behind, not engaging with them.

Wes exited the dance unnoticed and walked over to Ian. He crossed his arms and rested against the wagon next to his brother. After a moment of silence, he leaned into Ian and quietly said, "You're not very festive."

Ian turned his back on the dance and faced the wagon. Wes realized that there was something dramatically wrong. He turned to face Ian, putting his hand on Ian's shoulder. Ian pulled away. "It's my fault," he said.

"Dude, what are you talking about?" Wes returned, as he grabbed Ian's arm and pulled him so he could look square into his face.

Ian's lip quivered as he fought back tears. "I almost got us all killed," he said. "I just wasn't thinking. I'm so sorry. I should have kept my mouth shut back in the woods. Ubilaz knows we're here because I'm such a screw-up." Ian clenched his fist and cocked it back to hit the side of the wagon. He restrained himself and instead pressed it against his lips. A single tear streamed down his cheek.

Wes suddenly felt the weight of the burden that his brother was carrying. "Ian, it's not your fault. None of us were thinking. We were all caught in the moment and in the wonder of this place. Anyone of us could have said something revealing."

"Yeah, but you guys didn't and I did, now we are open targets. I've jeopardized our lives."

Wes was silent for a moment then said, "Ian I learned something today. I learned that we need to trust King Elyon. He brought us here. King Elyon is the one who will make us great men and I know that he is going to guard us. We need to trust that."

"Well it would have been nice if he would have shown up today."

Wes smiled, "He did. We're not dead yet! Ian, you have to let it go – it was an innocent mistake. Nobody faults you, and anyone who wants to take a shot at you will have to go through me . . . that includes you, if you're bent on beating yourself up. I really believe that our hearts have been mysteriously and powerfully bound."

Those words were soothing to Ian. "I guess you're right. I'm still skeptical about King Elyon and all the power that Clarion keeps ascribing to him. I may not trust him yet, but I trust you Wes. If our hearts are bound then you must trust King Elyon for both of us because I'm too weak."

"I will. I'm told his power is more evident when we are weak." Wes put his arm around Ian's back and quickly pulled the hood off his head. "You don't have to hide in shame. You're with brothers who love you."

Ian smiled, "Thanks bro."

"No problem, buddy. You want to dance now?" Wes asked.

Ian grimaced, "I'll pass - You're really not my type!"

CHAPTER
THIRTY-THREE

The troubadours began another jig and two little girls each grabbed one of Josiah's arms. They danced around him as if they were turning around a Maypole. Josiah held tightly to their small hands and spun with the music. Wes and Ian watched from their comfortable leans against the side wagon. They laughed at the sight of Josiah being pulled in two directions.

"Chicks dig Asian guys, 'Siah", Ian shouted.

"Right," he returned. "I'm getting a little dizzy, so I better stop."

He graciously bowed to his little partners and stumbled over to Ian and Wes. The children moved on to other adventures and eventually the music wound down. The three young men were reunited by Caden and Clarion.

"The smell of the food in the air is making me hungry," Caden proclaimed.

"Just inside the inner gates of the city, a few paces up King's Cross Lane is the Rose and Raven Pub. We can stop there before we travel through the city to Lemuel's Fortress," Clarion commented.

"We don't have any money for food," Wes exclaimed.

"You have been well provided for," Clarion replied as she withdrew a red velvet pouch from her quiver and handed it to Wes. The weight and feel of the pouch indicated that it contained a substantial fill of gold coins.

"This should serve you well while you are in Salamgard," she continued.

"Wow, thanks – I guess we're eating," Wes said directing his comment to Caden.

As they conferred about their journey to the Rose and Raven, a young boy of thirteen years of age came around the side of the wagon. He looked weathered and worn. His pant legs were torn off at the knees and his jacket was tattered and fraying at the seams. He wore the coat over his shirtless form, which was badly in need of bathing. The boy's shoes looked as if they were too large for his feet and were coming apart at the seams. On his head, he wore a cap that resembled a rag more than any of the hats seen in Salamgard.

"Please sir, buy my wares," the boy sheepishly said to Wes. His face was dirty and his large brown eyes pled for assistance. The lad reached into his pocket and produced a number of brightly braided wrist bands. He displayed them in the dirty palms of his hands.

"Did you make these?" Wes asked.

"Yes my lord," the boy replied.

"What's your name, kid?" Caden asked.

"It is Maayin," the boy replied.

Feeling compassion for the boy, Wes said, "Well Maayin, we will buy five of your finely crafted bands."

Maayin's countenance lit up as each of the guys and Clarion selected their band and secured it around their wrist.

"These bands will serve to remind us that we are bound together to accomplish a certain mission," Wes said, reached into the pouch that Clarion just handed him and produced a gold coin.

CHAPTER THIRTY-THREE

"Thank you, my lord you are very generous," Maayin said.

Wes smiled and began to follow Clarion and his brothers through the market place toward the inner gates of Aanda. Maayin waited a moment then he began to follow. Wes sensed that the boy was behind him, so he hesitated, allowing the boy to catch up to him.

"I can't buy any more of your wares, Maayin," Wes stated.

"Oh - No my lord! I thought that maybe I could serve you," Maayin returned.

Wes chuckled, "I don't need a servant, Maayin, besides we are on a journey and I'm sure that your family would not want you to leave them."

"I have no family, my lord."

"What do you mean? Where are your parents?"

Maayin looked at the ground. The melancholy returned to the boy as the question stirred something deep within him. "Dead sir," he replied. "My mother died in childbirth. I lived with my father, and an aunt and uncle and their son who was my age. My aunt and uncle and cousin were killed by the Dark Lord."

"And what about your father?" Wes asked.

"He was the leader of our Vitatha tribe. We were traveling from the Eldon to Aanda when Lord Ubilaz attacked our Vitatha caravan. My father quickly hid me in the hollow of a tree during the commotion of the battle. I watched as the soldiers of Eikondor seized and bound my father. They carried my father away. Then they executed everyone in the caravan including my uncle, aunt and cousin. Later I was told that my father was executed by Lord Ubilaz."

Wes' heart became heavy. "How long ago was that?"

"It was more than four years past," the boy said.

"So who watches over you? Where do you sleep and eat?"

"Nobody in my tribe was left alive so I watch over myself, my lord. I have a few clothes and a blanket. When the troubadours move to other cities of refuge, I travel with them. Some of them are kind to me but most cannot be bothered so I just remain quiet and hidden in the caravan. But I mostly just stay near the Vitatha market here in Aanda. I can sleep under the wagons without the wagon master knowing. The warmth inside the wagon often comes through the floor boards enough to keep me through the colder nights. I sell my craft to eat and when I have no coins I can find food in the . . ." A prang of shame stopped him in mid sentence then continued. "I manage, sir. But my lord, you need not worry I shall not eat much if I serve you and I am perfectly fine with sleeping on a floor so I shall not take up much space."

"Maayin, please don't call me lord because I am not your lord and as much as I would like too, I cannot take you with me on this journey," Wes wished that the words he spoke were not as true and realistic as they sounded. He could feel the sadness welling up inside him as he faced the Vitatha lad at the inner gates of the city. Maayin stopped as Wes crossed the threshold of the beautifully embellished inner city gates.

I feel like my heart is being ripped out of my chest. This is the girl in the cafeteria all over again. I just need to walk away, Wes thought as he stepped backward down King's Cross Lane looking at the disheartened boy.

"My lord, I am hungry!" the boy shouted as he began to cry.

The words pierced Wes chest like a dagger. He knew that he could not face the boy without becoming emotionally undone. "Wait there. I'll bring you some food, I promise!" he called as he turned and quickened his pace to meet his friends who were nearing the Rose and Raven Pub.

CHAPTER
THIRTY-
FOUR

The gates in the inner wall of Aanda were wide open. The city welcomed the band of brothers. Wes had lagged behind talking with Maayin, the Vitatha boy that he had met in the market place. Ian, Josiah and Caden were drinking in the sights and sounds of the city. As they passed the opened gates, they admired the ornate carving in the white wood. Each gate bore the crest of a torch that had been passed through a diadem and set resting upon an open book.

"That is the crest that's on your jacket," Ian pointed out to Josiah.

It was hard to tell because the crest lacked the deep blue and gold color that Josiah had become accustomed to.

"Hey! Yeah, you're right!" Josiah exclaimed. "Clarion, that crest is the same as the crest on my vestment. Tell me about it."

Clarion stopped in the middle of King's Cross. "That is the crest of Aanda," she said.

"Why is a city crest on my jacket?" Josiah asked.

"It is also the crest of Lord Lemuel."

Josiah thought for a second. "Then Lemuel is . . . my mentor," Josiah stated with lack of certainty.

"Yes. He is the Sage Knight of Salamgard. The torch represents the luminous light of wisdom. It is set above the book of all wisdom," she stated.

"And what about the crown, what significance does it have?" Josiah asked.

"That you will come to know when you meet Lord Lemuel," she returned as she resumed walking up the street to the pub.

The villagers in Aanda were hustling in and out of the shops that lined the brick stone lane. The city was as busy as the Vitatha market place outside the walls. Everyone was busy preparing for the holidays. The young men kept their eyes on Clarion who guided the entourage. They walked up King's Cross Lane, which gradually ascended through the heart of the city. The street meandered all the way from the inner wall gates to the top of the mountain where it ended at the gates of Lemuel's Fortress. From where the guys stood, they could only see the main thoroughfare where the shops were situated, to the top of the incline where King's Cross turned out of sight.

"What was that?" Josiah said as he stopped suddenly and looked all around.

"What was . . . WHAT?" Caden asked.

"Someone called my name," Josiah said.

"Dude, you're in the middle of the crowded street. There is noise all around you. You must have heard something that sounded like your name," Caden said.

They resumed their trek up the street to the pub. "There it is again. Didn't you hear that?" Josiah said, stopping again in the center of the street in an attempt to locate the person calling him.

"I didn't hear anything," Caden replied. They looked to Ian and Clarion. Both indicated that they too had heard nothing. Caden looked down the street where Wes was still talking to Maayin near the gates. Wes' back was to them. "I don't think it was Wes; he's not even looking this way," Caden deduced.

CHAPTER THIRTY-FOUR

"You need to rest and eat," Clarion remarked. "Some people see things when they are tired and hungry, but maybe you hear things."

"I can't believe that you didn't hear that. It was a woman's voice. It was as if she were . . . singing. I know that sounds crazy but I'm not making this up. I heard a woman call, Josiah Nestor," Josiah stated.

"You heard her call your first and last name?" Ian asked.

"She called Josiah Nestor more than once," Josiah returned.

They all stood still outside the door of the Rose and Raven Pub waiting to see if they could hear any singing woman. They waited a minute or two, but there was only the sound of the bustle in the streets.

"I don't hear anything now. It seemed so clear a moment ago," Josiah said. "I guess I *was* hearing things."

Clarion pushed open the door of the pub and the guys followed her in. Wes caught up to them just before the pub door shut closed.

CHAPTER
THIRTY-FIVE

The Rose and Raven Pub on King's Cross Lane, was known to many a weary traveler. It was the first venue where one could find refreshment upon passing through the gates of Aanda. The aged cedar beams, brick and mortar, and stucco plaster on the old building reflected eras of trade. The wood carved coat of arms suspended over the Pub's entrance, adorned with a black raven holding a red rose in its beak, served as the emblem for the venue.

Clarion and the guys stepped into the dark craggy pub. The thick bluish-green bottle glass windows let very little light in. The low cedar beamed ceiling, dark stone walls and black slate floors gave the impression that one just stepped into a medieval dungeon. Smoke from the patron's pipes, along with the musty smell of ale hung in the air. It took a few seconds for the five new customer's eyes to adjust before they could clearly see the interior of the pub and the clientele who had already assembled. In the center of the establishment was a large square bar. The barkeep stood in the middle keeping customers on four sides well supplied with the Rose and Raven's finest brew.

The Pub was already full of activity, as many had already taken their tables in anticipation of the approaching dinner hour. The barmaids were lighting the lanterns on the four corner pillars of the bar and along the walls. The lantern's glow revealed the surly, noisy clientele that decided to get a start on the holiday eve celebration.

Clarion scouted out a table against the wall. As she pointed her friends to their resting place, the bar keep called, "Food and Ale?" His voice was harsh and rough.

"Yes, both!" she replied.

"We only serve a meat and wild barley pie this eve'nin," he returned.

"Excellent, four, please and pints as well," she returned.

"Don't you mean five? There are five of us," Caden responded.

"No I am going to leave you here to eat while I go tend to Cervus, Eleus and Virtus. Cervus must still carry us to Lemuel's Fortress before the evening wears on. You gentlemen are safe here, so rest and enjoy. The Rose and Raven serves the most excellent meat and wild barley pies in this part of Salamgard."

The guys remembered breakfast and the amazing flavors they encountered. They hadn't eaten since and realized how sustaining the morning meal had been. But now their appetites were fueled at the remembrance of their morning feast. The thought of more such food made their mouths water and their stomachs growl.

Seeing that the guys were cared for, Clarion exited the way she came in and the four brothers rushed the table to await their meal. As they repositioned the chairs and began to jostle into their places around the table, Wes accidentally bumped into a big burly man who was walking past.

"I'm sorry, pardon me," Wes said.

"Bastard Otherlanders, always clumsily pushin your way into everything," the man raged.

"I'm very sorry, I didn't mean . . ." Wes was interrupted by the agitator, who commenced to press in on him.

"I dislikes you Otherlanders just about as much as I dislikes the Vitatha vermin that camps outside me city gates," he barked.

Immediately Caden positioned himself between Wes and the brute. Almost nose to nose with the nemesis, Caden clinched his teeth and said, "He said he was sorry, mate!"

The thug grabbed two fists full of Caden's shirt to throw him out of the way. As fast as that happened Caden grabbed the guy by the neck with one hand and with the other, drew his fist back to leverage enough momentum to at least take out a few of the thug's teeth.

Just then, the door of the Rose and Raven flew open revealing the darkened silhouette of a tall man. A silence fell over the establishment as the man stepped out of the street and into the dim light of the pub.

The burly thug immediately loosened his grip on Caden. "Serik the Conciliator!" he muttered under his breath.

Serik was a commanding figure. His lean, towering frame filled the doorway. As he stepped out of the shadow of the night into the light of the pub, the soft light revealed a strong but kind and compassionate face with finely chiseled features. His hair was white as snow, not because of age since Serik appeared to be a middle aged man. His hair was white from birth and was slicked back on his head. His eyes caught the reflection of the lanterns making them look like two orbs of burning orange fire. Serik wore vestments and a cloak that were white like wool and across his back, he wore a battle shield. The shield was not very large because it also served as a weapon. The perfectly round burnished bronze shield was designed to be worn on the conciliator's forearm. The edge of the shield was razor sharp and could cut through an enemy with a single pass. On the face of the shield was Serik's crest, a gold chalice on which was emblazoned a heart, set against a forest green backdrop.

The door closed behind Serik and he stood just inside the entrance perusing the room as he removed the riding gloves from his hands. His presence had a transformational effect on the pub.

Arguments stopped and people began speaking kindly. The aura of seediness changed to a more gracious ambiance. Even the countenances of the patrons changed from a stressed and hardened look to one that was gentle and more inviting.

The thug released Caden and brushed the wrinkles out of his vestment. "I'm beggin' your pardon for offendin you. Please lets me buy dinner for the lot of you, to alleviates the distress thats I put you and your mates through," he said.

Caden and Wes looked dumbfounded. *What is this power that changes the hearts of men when they are in its presence? Wes thought.*

Serik began to make his way toward their table. As he passed other patrons they smiled and greeted him, not out of fear but because they were genuinely gracious. As he neared their table, the brothers felt a profound warmth washing over them.

The thug stepped into Serik's path to greet him. "Lord Serik, it's so great to have you back in Salamgard again," he said as he hugged the great conciliator.

"Haven't we talked before about loving kindness being a quicker and more powerful solution than brawling, Bartomay?" Serik asked.

"Yes m'lord, but I often forgets and reverts back to me old ways," Bartomay replied.

Serik looked into the burly man's eyes, smiled and patted him on the shoulder. The man turned and shook Wes and Caden's hand then went to the bar where he paid their dinner tab and exited the pub, a forgiven and gracious man.

The boys sat at the table looking up at the large figure that towered over them. "Wes you will come with me," Serik said. "The rest of you can stay and enjoy your meal. You needn't worry about Ubilaz and his necrophim. When one of you is separated to engage with his mentor, the mentor will unleash a *protectus* blessing that will confound the forces that would come against you." Serik removed a ring from his finger and set it on the table. *"Presidium Electus,"* he said. The crystal stone in the golden prongs of the ring began to glow, releasing a lazar like beam that shot upward toward the ceiling. It exploded in an umbrella of light that engulfed the guys.

"The protectus blessing is only visible to you. Those who do not have evil intentions may enter its scope but you must remember never to leave its perimeter. Now Wes we have much work to do. Come, follow me."

As Wes walked away with Serik, Caden leaned in toward Josiah. "What's a Conciliator," he asked.

"It's a person who is an agent of compassion, benevolence or good will. He's kind of like a pastoral caregiver. He reconciles relationships or makes things . . . right," Josiah replied.

CHAPTER
THIRTY-
SIX

In the upper part of the City of Aanda, Sabedoria emerged from her home and stepped into the middle of King's Cross Lane. She could see the rooftops of the homes that made up the vast city far below. She could also see the boundaries of the inner and outer walls with their massive gates as they defined the boarders of Aanda.

Sabedoria centered herself in the middle of the street, closed her eyes and began to sing,

"*JEROCH NESTUM. AIEROCH TU AE VISHLO VEC.
UBEL LIST TRA GORBU CORDUM. SAESA VERDU ILRAN
QUEL. OOMAT KAI DOLETH BELDORUM.*"

She stood silently and listened. There was only the sounds of a cool autumn night; the slight whistle of a refreshing breeze, the chirp of some courageous crickets that ventured to sing before the sun fully set and an occasional call from the songbirds that graced the trees before retiring.

After a few seconds in her contemplative state, she opened her eyes. Some of the homes below began to light the evening lanterns.

Their glow added to the air of repose. *I will continue to call. He will hear and I will have him*, she thought. She smiled and returned to the comfort of her cottage.

Far below in the Rose and Raven Pub a barmaid set four pints of ale on the table. Josiah sat relaxed on a bench with his back against the wall. Ian sat to his right with his elbows on the table soaking in the merriment of the pub. Caden sat in a chair next to Ian. He lifted the pint of ale to his lips and blew the foam from the top of the glass.

"Did you hear that? There it was again," Josiah said. He pushed himself up from the table without fully standing to look over the crowd in the pub.

"Are you hearing your lady, serenade again?" Caden remarked. "I didn't hear anything, did you Ian?"

"No," Ian replied.

"'Siah, nobody is calling or singing to you," Caden continued.

"That time it was stronger and much clearer. I feel like I'm being drawn by that voice," Josiah remarked.

A sober look came over Ian. Without saying a word, he got up from his seat, pushed past Caden, and walked around to sit on the other side of Josiah, sandwiching him between himself and Caden.

"You're not leaving the perimeter of this protectus blessing. I'm not taking any chances. If you're going to be pulled anywhere you'll have to be pulled past us," he stated. He reached across Josiah for his pint of ale, took a large gulp and forcefully set the glass down in front of him with a thud against the wooden tabletop.

"I'll drink to that," Caden said as he lifted his glass. Ian followed suit, as did Josiah, clanging their glasses together. They just finished their toast as the barmaid appeared with their savory golden brown meat pies.

CHAPTER
THIRTY-SEVEN

Wes was looking straight into the center of the crest that decorated Serik's shield. He walked a few steps behind the large figure of the Conciliator. Serik led Wes through a short hallway into an adjacent room off the Rose and Raven pub. There was a table reserved for him in an alcove cut into the corner of the room. The cove was accented by a long vertical bottle glass window. Two benches barely fit at forty-five degree angles in the corner against the wall. Serik removed the shield from his back and hung it on the hook outside the alcove. He swept back his white coat to remove a long leather sheathed dagger from his belt, and set it on the table. The handle of the dagger was wrapped with a hunter green suede grip. A metal replica of the crest, which graced Serik's shield, also adorned the dagger's grip.

Serik slid into place on the bench. "Join me lad," he said to Wes as he motioned for him to slip behind the table onto the other bench.

Serik began, "My son, *LOVE* is the power that changes the hearts of men when they are in its presence."

Wes took a deep breath surprised at what he heard. When he saw the effect Serik had on the Pub's patrons a few minutes earlier, he had asked himself, *What is this power that changes people?* Suddenly feeling very exposed, Wes thought, *Can he read my mind?*

"Judging from your facial expression, you are probably wondering if I can read you're your thoughts. I assure you that I cannot, Wes. I just know that everyone is confronted with the exact same question when they first reckon the powerful force by which love is characterized. And you have been given that strong force, Wes. The greatest of men are the ones marked by love. A man can build fortified cities, and make speeches to motivate masses, and understand the magic and mysteries of the universe, but if love is not the first thing that people identify when his name is mentioned, then he is a worthless verbose shell of a person. Nothing is more hollow, than a man with accolades who has accomplished great things, yet is void of love."

Wes listened intensely. "I don't know if I really understand what love is," he said.

"It is that burning sensation that you feel in your chest, that deep passion that you suffer for your brothers, the sensation that you fight to keep inside you when you are moved by the plight of others."

"Ha, yeah, well I hate that," Wes said boldly.

"Because your father told you it was not manly?" Serik asked.

Wes was caught off guard again, *How did he know about my father?* "Yeah. Well, he was right. I needed to toughen up. I tried all my life to push those feelings away. I wanted him to see that I was strong," Wes said.

"Ignorance and denial are never a form of strength, but accepting and living into your emotion makes one a strong man. Wes, you don't know the power of love because you have always looked to your dad for a definition and example of love. But his words just cut deep wounds into your spirit."

Wes got quiet. He felt something welling up deep within him. His heart started to accelerate, he suddenly felt cold and clammy and found his breathing becoming more labored. *I don't want to talk about my dad. He has nothing to do with the way I am or how I feel. I'm not going to go there. I'm not playing this psychobabble bullshit game – Think of something to talk about, change the subject, think of anything, hurry,* Wes' mind raced.

"That's not the only wound that you suffered by your father, was it Wes?" Serik asked.

Wes forced a smile, "What do you mean?"

"Wes, I have talked long with King Elyon. He has given me the insight into your life and circumstance, you know what I mean."

Wes put up a stoic facade, but he could feel unbearable pain building in his chest, "Are you referring to the time when my dad left? A lot of kids go through divorce. That happened when I was thirteen, almost six years ago. I'm over it - time heals all wounds."

"Time heals all wounds, Wes?" Serik asked rhetorically. He directed his attention away from Wes and looked into the room, which was now filled with additional patrons of the pub. This also prompted Wes to look in the same direction. People were talking and laughing. One barmaid entered the room carrying a tray of meat and barley pies. The other was trying to juggle six pints of ale, one of which just dropped from her hands and was about to shatter on the floor when Serik raised his hand and passed it over as if to cover the room.

"Subsisto Vicis," he said in a low deliberate voice. Everything in the room stopped. The patrons were suspended in mid sentence. The glass of ale hung in the air as did the ale that spilled out from it. Wes looked into the adjacent room and everyone was suspended in time. There was no longer any noise or movement.

"You froze everyone," Wes exclaimed.

"No, I stopped time for you," Serik said. "Now tell me how your heart is feeling? Your parents didn't divorce. Your father walked out of your life in a drunken rage six years ago leaving you and your mother to struggle alone. The last thing he said to you was that you were a worthless cry baby faggot. Your mother began drinking to escape the pain, and a result, checked out on you too. Tell me; what does a thirteen year old boy feel when there is nobody to watch over him?"

Wes could hardly bear the pain. *"Who watches over you?"* His own words to Maayin came back to haunt his brain. Wes immediately recalled the conversation. Those words, "My lord, I'm hungry" and the picture of that boy weeping by the city gate busted the dam that Wes had so strongly bolstered over the years. He began to weep.

"I'm hungry," Wes said. "I've been starving for something that I never can have. I have never seen my dad since he left. I don't know if he is dead or alive. I have worked hard to resolve life without the love and affirmation of a father."

"And as a result you have missed *the love of a father,* Wes. King Elyon has had his hand on you since birth. The mighty King loved you so much that he adopted you as his own son. You belong to him, Wes. He has poured his love over you by raising up men in your life, all throughout your life, to demonstrate that love to you. Even I have been honored to step in and love you as a father loves a son. Do you remember a lacrosse game in your high school freshman year when you were body checked by the Union high school defenseman and took a slash to the head?"

"Yes, the official never called it. I ended up flat on my back with the wind knocked out of me. I hurt so bad that I went behind the bleachers and started to cry. I didn't want anyone to see how much of a sissy I was. I prayed that my dad would somehow miraculously show up and tell me that it was alright – that I was alright."

"What happened then?"

"An old man who was at the game turned and saw me through

the openings in the back of the bleachers. He got up and came under the bleachers. He told me that he thought I was amazing out on the field and that he didn't think that he could have survived a blow like the one I took. He told me that I . . ."

". . . was a great man and that he was adopting you for the rest of the game as his son. He said that he only had daughters, but if he had a son he would want him to be just like you," Serik finished Wes' sentence.

Wes held his breath and stared into Serik's eyes. Serik smiled and his eyes glint the same twinkle he remembered seeing in that old man's eyes.

"And then I told you that I was proud to have such a fine son as you. Throughout the rest of the game, you kept looking to see if I was there. I cheered for the man I saw you becoming. Wes, if you're hungry all you have to do is eat, son."

Wes exhaled and began to sob. He folded his arms on the table and buried his face in them. "*Son*" – that word was so satisfying. Serik lovingly reached over and put his hand on Wes' head, stroking his hair like Wes had often imagined a caring father would do. He felt as if Serik was passing on his power or some mantle of blessing by putting his hand on his head.

"Wes, time does not heal wounds – the king's powerful love does. And the king chooses to pour that love through people. No single man could ever fulfill the love that Elyon wants to lavish on you. It takes many to do that. You have just wanted it so desperately to come from one man, who cannot give it to you, that you missed all the others who did."

"I thought that if I was a better kid, I would be loved," Wes sobbed.

"Wes the king loves you without condition. So great is his love, that you cannot even begin to wrap your mind around it. There is no human measurement for it. It is the most love there is. The only way for you to understand, is to say his love is . . . the *most*. Wes, he loves you *the most*, my son. There is nothing that you could ever do, to lose his love. You get it all without condition. He will always love you *the most*. Conversely, there is nothing that you can do, to gain more of that love – He loves you *the most*. You get it ALL without condition."

Wes continued to weep but now from joy rather than pain. He began to feel on fire. A new energy surged through him. Wes lifted his head and looked into the warm eyes of the powerful Conciliator. "For the first time in my life I'm not . . . hungry," he said.

Serik smiled and put his strong hand on Wes' shoulder, "That's because you have come to taste love; a powerful love that reconciles wrongs done; heals the pain of deep relational wounds; satisfies you with a sense of belonging, and floods you with the confidence that you are highly prized and most valuable. Some men experience a father wound, but all experience a *father hunger*. The hunger is driven by love and makes you constantly seek out many fathers, who will serve as mentors in your life. The father hunger will also make you seek out those who are fatherless so that you will pour love into that boy's life. In doing so, you then reflect the king. Father hunger makes the circle complete; a father pours into a son, who then becomes a father who pours into his son. My son, the love that Elyon pours on you, is the same love that he plans to pour through you. You will be like the chalice that adorns my crest. Elyon will pour his love on you, in you, and through you."

"Then I will go off and pour it into others", Wes joyfully exclaimed.

"No, you will get close to other chalices and let that love brim over until it is overflowing in them. In that way you will come to know that you are only the vessel and the power of the king is made strong in your weakness."

"So I will never become empty?"

"Never, but you should know that love isn't always a joyful feeling. Sometimes love will compel you to sacrifice and suffer. In that way, you will feel poured out. If you look closely at the crest you will make another discovery". Serik pushed the dagger in front of Wes.

Wes picked it up and examined the crest carefully. "The chalice is . . . cracked," he said.

"That's right. Love may require you to be broken. But love bears and endures all things. Love also generates hope in King Elyon."

"I'm ready. I want Elyon to love through me," Wes said.

"Then you must receive the king's mark," Serik said. Wes sat up straight. The sleeves of his shirt were wet with tears. Wes wiped his eyes and took a deep breath again.

As soon as Wes was settled, Serik reached over and pressed the palm of his hand against the bare flesh of Wes' chest. The design of Wes' shirt allowed the Conciliator to position his large hand fully over the young man's heart. Serik pushed hard against Wes' chest causing him to be pinned against the wall of the alcove.

Although Serik's palm was warm, Wes gasped as if an icy cold blade had been pressed against him. Immediately Wes felt Serik's hand heating up, warmer and warmer. The warmth was deeply penetrating. Wes could actually feel his heart becoming emblazoned.

"The mark that you wear will be the imprint of the king on your heart. As a Knight of Elyon's Realm, I have been charged to act in the king's stay. From this day forward, you will be defined no longer as a boy who is too sensitive, but as a man whose heart is owned by the king. You will be one of Elyon's conciliators. The king holds your heart in his hand to use it in any way he deems fit. This mark will serve as a banner of his love over you. Everyone in Salamgard will see that King Elyon has written his name upon your heart."

Serik removed his hand. On Wes' chest, there appeared an artistically designed tattoo of the swirling print of Serik's palm. "Your mark is sealed and now you must have a weapon so that you can fight Ubilaz's forces and the necrophim."

Serik stood up and beckoned Wes to do the same. He lifted his shield from where it hung. "My shield now becomes yours. It is primarily used as a defensive weapon but its sharp edges can cut through any necrophim that venture in its path." Serik slipped his arm through the straps that secured the shield on his forearm. He held it up to demonstrate for Wes how to use it as a blade. Then he removed it and encouraged Wes to wear it the same way.

Wes slipped his arm through the leather straps and brandished the shield as he had seen Serik do. After Wes took a few passes through the air, Serik took a firm hold of Wes' arm and moved it so that the shield became situated in front of Wes' chest.

"The shield was created to protect your heart. This is its primary purpose. Wes, be vigilant. Heed my words. You are Ubilaz's primary target. He knows that you will impact Otherland in a very powerful way if you are knighted by King Elyon. Keep your heart covered with this shield and you will thwart any attack or power that seeks to destroy you."

Serik reached over to the table and snatched the dagger. He handed it to Wes. "I also give you my dagger. This weapon will serve you in battle. The blade was forged in Asilo by Elyon's gifted blacksmiths. Your weapon is infused with the power of the king. When you use your shield to slice through the necrophim or when your dagger pierces them, they will be disintegrated. This dagger and shield hold a powerful blessing for the bearer, which works as an obliteration curse only against necrophim."

Wes stood with the shield on his left arm and the dagger in his right hand. He moved the dagger to slice through the air, practicing what it would feel like to wield the sharp blade.

"Now a note of caution," Serik said. "You must not use your weapon against the necrophim until all your brothers have been armed by their mentors. The power of few weapons alone will render those who are unarmed easy prey to the necrophim. When you each are equipped, the battlefield will be leveled and you may use them against the necrophim."

CHAPTER THIRTY-SEVEN

"But what if we're confronted by the necrophim before we're all armed?"

"Then stand together firm in a close bond. Your brotherly love is a powerful force that becomes impenetrable to the necrophim."

After Serik finished his instruction, he helped Wes strap the shield on back. Wes placed the dagger in its hilt and slid it through the sash he wore around his waist. It fit snug and secure against his side.

"Wes there is one more very important instruction that I must give you regarding love's highest power. I will tell you about it as we return to your friends. It is the most crucial of any instruction that I will give you. But first, we must enter back into the reality of the good citizens in this pub. Just remember that time doesn't heal wounds –It's the King's love poured through his ambassadors that brings healing." Serik again raised his hand, *"Restituo Vicis,"* he proclaimed. Immediately the noise level returned to a blaring decibel. The glass of ale shattered on the floor and the patrons of the Rose and Raven never missed a second of time.

CHAPTER
THIRTY-
EIGHT

Clarion finished pulling the toggle pins from Cervus' harness, releasing the great animal from the wagon. A few minutes earlier, she had left the band of brothers in the security of the Rose and Raven Pub to make sure that Cervus, Eleus and Virtus were properly cared for before they made the final leg of their journey to Lemuel's Fortress.

A hawk flew in circles high above, in the dusk of the twilight sky. With each pass, he screeched and called. The hawk flew lower and screeched again. This time he had Clarion's attention. Clarion looked skyward to see the silhouetted hawk against the amber, orange and purple streaked sky. As the hawk swooped in closer, she could see the fleury cross that marked the underside of the bird's wing. Cervus raised his head to listen to the winged scout.

"He is certainly excited about something, but I cannot hear him over the noise of this market place," Clarion said.

Cervus grunted an order and the obedient hawk flew in closer.

"He says that there is trouble in Somberbos Forest", Clarion said. They listened intently as the hawk made a couple more circular passes.

Cervus grunted and the hawk swiftly soared high making looping circles as if it were in a flight path holding pattern. He turned to communicate with Clarion.

"Yes Cervus, I agree you should go. The news that the scouting party holds may be essential to our mission and if there has been loss of life as we suspect, then you must attend to it personally. I will ride with you. If we leave now we can be back before the hour gets too late."

Cervus lowered his huge antlers. As soon as Clarion had a hold on them, the great stag bolted into a full gallop. The forward thrust coupled with the flick of Cervus' head sent Clarion into an aerial leap onto the animal's strong back. She grabbed the strap of the harness across Cervus' back and leaned low and close to him, cutting the drag and wind resistance. Cervus charged out through the outer gates of Aanda with Eleus and Virtus following on his heels. The hawk flew just a furlong ahead of them.

They crossed the plain in good time and with less stress than their previous journey over this same stretch. The hawk flew in closer as Lord Cervus passed into the forest line. He led the way to the place where the scouting party was resting. After a few minutes, Cervus knew exactly where they were heading. He bounded into a clearing where a small gathering of squirrels, raccoons, birds, field mice and a few other small woodland creatures had assembled.

Two squirrels high above in the branches of a tree began to chatter hysterically at the sight of Cervus. "Slow down and talk one at a time," Clarion scolded. Both squirrels stopped then one began to chatter again.

"Lord Ubilaz has ordered many of the loyal animal citizens of Eikondor to take up the search for an object?" Clarion asked.

The squirrel chattered again.

"And he has empowered a host of necrophim to join them? This object must be very precious to him," she stated.

Cervus gave out a grunt of inquiry as to what the object was.

The squirrels began to chatter again.

"One at a time please," Clarion reminded.

The second squirrel seized the opportunity and chattered away.

"You could not find out exactly what the object was?"

The squirrel chattered again. "I understand you were flustered and afraid. You have done well," she said. Then she directed her words to Cervus, "We must find out what this treasure is and why it is so precious to Ubilaz."

Cervus grunted in agreement then continued to communicate.

Clarion replied, "Ah yes!" and turning to the squirrels she said, "The hawk told us that there was bloodshed."

The chatter rose again as the squirrels gave directions to another nearby hollow in the woods. Clarion, Cervus, Virtus and Eleus followed the squirrels and found a gathering of forest animals huddled in a circle.

The creatures parted to allow the newcomers a view of the carcass of a raccoon. The squirrel continued to tell how a fierce hyena had cornered the raccoon. The hyena believed that the raccoon had information regarding the sought after treasure and was being uncooperative. The raccoon didn't even know what the hyena was talking about. The fierce hyena bared his razor sharp teeth as he became more and more perturbed with the coon's perceived impertinence. At a frustrated breaking point, the hyena pounced and in one swift second the raccoon was wounded beyond recovery. The raccoon managed to crawl back to the clearing where his wounds took their fatal toll.

Clarion felt the grief that her woodland friends were feeling. She also felt a rage of injustice well up inside her. "So, Ubilaz's hosts will kill anyone who gets in the way of the recovery of this object. This object is obviously of great importance. If Ubilaz desires to acquire it at the cost of lives, then it must have some power he plans to use against Salamgard. We must find out what the object is and its importance. The best way to avenge this scout's death is to acquire it before Ubilaz does."

Cervus grunted again and had the attention of the small wood-land creatures. They listened to the great stag and then swiftly scampered off.

"It was very wise of you to order them to spread the word to gather information without interfering with Ubilaz's mission. The timing of Ubilaz's obsession may have a positive outcome. If he is looking for this object, he may not be aware of the importance of our four young Ambassador-Knights and thus not so intent upon destroying them. Lord Cervus we must return now to Aanda and Lemuel's fortress. Our primary mission is the safe passage of our four friends. They are a great hope for our kingdom."

CHAPTER
THIRTY-NINE

Josiah broke the golden crust that topped his meat and barley pie at the Rose and Raven Pub. The slice of his knife allowed the aroma of the savory dish to escape into an intoxicating swirl of steam.

"Oooooh, this smells so amazing," he said.

"Wait till you taste it," Caden said as he raised a second fork full of the succulent meat to his mouth. Ian was blowing over his pie in an attempt to cool it down. He could hardly wait to partake in the flavors that tempted his taste buds. Within minutes, the three guys were lost in a culinary time cocoon where the sights and sounds of the room vanished. Nobody engaged in conversation. They didn't even notice Serik and Wes standing in front of the table.

"Hey guys," Wes said, but there was no response.

"GUYS," he said again louder than before as he knocked on the table the same way he had knocked at their dorm room door to awaken them for class, so many early mornings. In unison, the three stopped eating and looked up at the two men who had broken their concentration.

CHAPTER THIRTY-NINE

"That must be some meat pie," Wes said.

"Oh brother, you can't even begin to know," Caden responded with his mouth full of the savory dish.

"Wow you're back already? You weren't even gone ten minutes," Josiah commented.

"Yeah well it was longer than you think. I now understand more about how things *really* aren't always as they seem in Salamgard," Wes said.

"Well Wes, it's good that you're back because your pie just arrived," Ian said as he pushed the hot dish in front of the opened chair. "I'm sorry we didn't get one for you, Lord Serik but I'm sure the barkeeper could bring one out quickly. Should I tell the servers that you will be joining us?"

"That's very kind of you Ian, but I really must take my leave. I must attend to some important matters before the holiday celebration tomorrow night. I will see you all tomorrow," Serik stated. "Wes, remember my words and warnings."

Serik picked his ring up off the table and placed it on his finger. As he did the light of the protectus blessing vanished. "You are back to being a band of brothers once again. Be on guard because Ubilaz is very aware of your presence in Salamgard."

Serik turned and walked for the door as Wes slipped the shield off his back and set it on the floor next to the chair he then sat in. He could feel the enthralling draw of the meat pie.

"So what happened?" Ian asked.

"It's amazing, I feel like there is a fire in my bones that is ready to blaze from my fingers and eyes and mouth and . . . my entire being," Wes answered. By now, Wes was in full front of the meat pie and had less of a desire to share his experience than he did to dive into the dish. He pulled the pie closer to the edge of the table and leaned over it to inhale its quintessence. As he did, his shirt opened slightly.

"Whoa! Wait, do you have a tattoo on your chest?" Ian asked as he pulled Wes's shirt to get a better view. That jolted Josiah and Caden's attention.

"That's got to be the mark, Clarion was talking about," Josiah stated.

"Yes, but it's not the mark that you guys will get. This mark uniquely defines me as a protégée of Serik. It is the mark of a conciliator," Wes said.

Ian pulled Wes' shirt opened to see more of the tattoo, but also to pull Wes closer. He intently stared at the mark.

"At first glance, it looks like the print of the palm of a hand, but when you look closely, it definitely isn't a hand print," Ian proclaimed.

"Let's see," said Josiah as he leaned in so close over Ian that he was practically on top of him, pushing him to the edge of the bench. Caden quickly left his chair and came around the other side of Wes to get a good look too.

"Dang, you're right. It says 'ELYON', it's the King's name," said Josiah. The elaborate and intricate swirls of the palm print were actually the artistically rendered signature of the king.

Wes looked down at his chest in an attempt to see what they saw but it was too difficult since he was looking at it upside down. Then he became very aware that his friends were making a scene by scoping out his chest in a public place. He quickly pulled his shirt closed.

"Fellas, I don't think we should do this in the middle of the pub. I'll have to find a mirror later to see what you guys see."

They agreed. It did look rather strange for the three of them to bare Wes' chest and gawk at it. They returned to their meals, content to wait to examine the mark later when there weren't so many spectators.

Patrons continued to come and go through the Pub's front entrance as the streets of Aanda grew darker. The ambiance and spirit of the pub grew darker with the exit of Serik. Once again, the Rose and Raven became the establishment that it was when the brothers first entered.

Suddenly a commotion rose near the front door, grabbing the guys' attention and interrupting the meal.

"What are you doing in here?" shouted the gruff voiced barkeep as he pulled a cane from behind his work station and approached the unwelcomed guest.

"Vitatha filth, you dare to be so arrogant as to come into my fine establishment. You deserve the beating you are about to get," he barked.

Wes looked over to see the angry man raise his cane and charge toward Maayin, who was near the door cowering and covering his head to protect himself from the impending blow. Wes quickly rose to intervene on behalf of the boy. He hadn't thought that the young Vitatha lad would follow him into the city.

As the barkeep started to bring down his cane in full force, Wes stepped between him and Maayin and caught the enraged proprietor's wrist with one hand. He stood there looking into the angry man's eyes, staying his arm with the cane, high above his head.

Wes began to feel a strange sense of compassion for the hardened man. "I know that deep within, you are probably a very kind hearted citizen of Salamgard," Wes said calmly but authoritatively. The young conciliator could feel a force beginning to surge within his chest and ascend, up his arm. It continued to his hand that held the proprietor's wrist and then seemed to pass into the man.

"I believe that you would much rather leave an impression on the young boy's life than on his hide," Wes quietly spoke into the depth of the man's soul.

The man looked at Wes' hand gripping his wrist and followed it downward until he saw into Wes' eyes; then his gaze traveled down to his chest where the tattooed mark was in clear view. The man quickly looked back with wonder into Wes' eyes, and humbly said,

"I beg your pardon sir," as he lowered his arm. The entire pub was looking at Wes. Some began to whisper, "He bears the mark of the king" and others whispered, "Elyon's name is written upon him".

Wes became conscious that he had become the focus of the venue. He was suddenly aware that there was a buzz stirring among the Rose and Raven's constituents. *Why are all these people looking at me?* Wes thought. Then he realized that the loose fit of his shirt had revealed his mark for all to see.

Wes pulled the shirt closed and resumed his business. "I'm sure that you won't mind if my guest joins me for dinner," Wes said to the barkeep.

"No my lord, I didn't realize that the lad was your guest," he returned. "I shall have another pie brought to your table immediately."

Wes put his arm around Maayin's shoulders and escorted him back to the table. "Why did you come in here, Maayin?"

"I was hungry and you promised to bring food, but you never came back to me. It was getting dark. I have had beatings before and I thought it would be worth the lashes if I could eat, my lord."

Wes smiled, "You will eat, buddy, and without the lashes. Then you will come with us to Lemuel's fortress. I will see if I can get you some clothes, a hot bath and a warm bed for the night. But be clear about this - You cannot follow me after I leave Aanda. It would be far too dangerous. Lord Lemuel will know what to do with you."

Wes could feel a deep compassion pouring through him. He felt a fondness for the boy similar to his feelings he had for Josiah, Caden and Ian. He felt that his heart was being bound to the boy's. Maayin smiled as he took his place at the table with the brothers. He ate his full without a care in the world. Wes knew that the boy was experiencing a new sense of belonging that had been absent in his life since the loss of his father. He sat back with his arms folded, watching Maayin enjoy the loving company of the brothers and the meat pie. The young conciliator felt overwhelmed with the realization that the boy was finally no longer hungry. King Elyon would not let the boy be deprived of a father's protection and care.

CHAPTER
FOURTY

The band of brothers, along with Maayin had finished their meat and barley meals. They were patiently awaiting Clarion's return in anticipation of taking their refuge in Lemuel's fortress for the evening. The Rose and Raven Pub was still cycling through its mealtime clientele. Although the night was still young, Ian was growing anxious.

"Where is she?" he asked. "Clarion should be back by now. She was just going to care for Cervus, Eleus and Virtus. She certainly should have been done by now. Do you think something has happened?"

The guys could sense Ian's growing uneasiness even before he voiced his concern. Ian's mind played through many scenarios. *What if something happened to her? What if we are stranded here all night? What if we are being set up for a necrophim ambush? What if . . .? What if . . .?* His mind began a downward spiral of worry.

"Don't get your boxers in a bundle, Ian", Josiah answered. "I'm sure she hasn't forgotten about us. I would assume that we are safe here or she wouldn't have left us in the first place. Besides, we have nothing better to do so let's just make the most of it".

"Ian we're alright", Wes assured. "We're together and that makes us immune to the attack of the necrophim. Besides we are trusting Elyon to bring us to Asilo safely". Wes gave a nod and a smile in Ian's direction as a reminder that he was trusting King Elyon for the both of them.

The conversation came to a quick end when a small group of musicians began to play in the corner of the pub. The guys looked at each other with pleasant amusement.

"I guess it won't be hard to make the most of it now", Josiah added above the swell of the music.

The mood of the Pub became a bit more cheerful. People were clapping to the music as the barmaids began to entice a dance. One of them pulled Caden from his chair and he willingly obliged. The guys got a good laugh out of watching him bumble through the dance steps. What was supposed to be a Gaelic looking jig ended up looking like salsa meets jumping jacks. The brother's laughter just fueled Caden's desire to be more out of control.

"Why don't you guys get out here and try this," he taunted.

Maayin jumped up and joined the dance like a pro. "It's not fair – he has the hometown advantage," Caden stated through labored breathing as he kept dancing. "I want to see all you guys do this. Wes, get up here," he continued.

The barmaids picked up on Caden's invitation and soon were pulling the rest of the brothers onto the floor. Wes went with enthusiasm. Ian was reluctant, but joined in because he was being coaxed by the prettiest young barmaid in the pub. Josiah was also invited but he graciously declined.

"'Siah, get out here," Caden yelled.

"I think I'm going to pass. I'm still recuperating from the earlier dance in the market," Josiah replied as he raised his glass to salute his brother's frivolity.

The music played and the boys danced. Josiah sat back and watched the fun. He looked over the patrons in the Rose and Raven, enjoying the joy that filled the establishment. He surmised that this being the eve of a holiday also added to the celebratory mood. As he looked around the small gathering of celebrants, he noticed a young woman across the room staring at him. He looked away, and then his eyes returned to the place where she was sitting. She was still looking at him. Josiah smiled and nodded at her. The young woman smiled back then got up and walked over to the table.

"May I join you?" she asked.

"Umm, sure," Josiah said.

From their huddle on the dance floor, the guys watched the scenario unfold. "What is it about him that makes girls flock to him?" Caden remarked.

"No idea", Wes replied.

"What if that's the girl who's been calling to him?" Ian questioned with suspicion. Ian started to leave the dance, "I'm going to sit down, just in case . . ."

Wes grabbed him by the arm. "You're not leaving yet, Michael Jackson – we want to see your moon walk," he said. As he pulled Ian closer, he reminded him that they had a good view from where they were and that all was safe. If Josiah got up to leave with the girl, they certainly were close enough to intervene.

"My name is Puerilis," the girl said as she sat beside Josiah. She had a subtle but stunning beauty. Her short black hair framed her Mediterranean face. Her girl-next-door features and small frame gave her the look of a sweet innocent young woman.

"I'm Jos. . ."

". . . Josiah, I know," Puerilis said. "You are an Otherlander – I knew that you were coming."

"How did you know that?"

"I was sent to give you aid by my king."

"Puerilis! So it was you calling my name earlier."

"No, that wasn't me. The voice you heard calling you belongs to Sabedoria. I also heard her call you that is why I am here."

"You heard her? How could you? My friends didn't hear her. Nobody in the streets or in the Pub reacted when she sang. They all were deaf to her voice."

"She sings in a mystic ancient language. Only the one being called and those who understand the language can hear her words."

"Puerilis, her song was so beautiful. I didn't understand what she said but I specifically heard her call my name. It was like a magnetic pull on me."

One of the young barmaids approached the table to collect the empty dishes. The conversation stopped abruptly, but she over-heard part of Josiah's statement. The barmaid begged forgiveness for intruding, stacked the dishes on her tray and lifted the heavy tray to her shoulder. As she walked away, she heard Puerilis con-tinue the conversation. She slowed her pace, set her tray on an ad-jacent table, and began retrieving the plates from that table. She wanted to stay within hearing range so that she could be certain of what was being said.

"You must resist her! Sabedoria's words are powerfully allur-ing, as is Sabedoria," Puerilis continued. "You must be careful. She is a deceiver just like the one she serves. Sabedoria will attempt to draw you into her clutches. Please take heed and listen to me; she will destroy you. Her draw on you is alluring and will become greater, but she can do nothing unless you willingly give in to her."

"So if I choose to reject her, she has no power over me?"

"Yes, but rejecting her is not enough. You must choose some-thing or someone else in her place. That is why my lord has sent me to you," Puerilis said as she moved closer to Josiah. "I have been given a very special potion that will give you the ability to see the necrophim when they cloak themselves in invisibility. You must reject Sabedoria and choose me in order to see the necrophim."

The barmaid unobtrusively left the tray of used soiled dishes on the table and walked over to the bar. She took off her apron as she engaged the barkeep in a short conversation, then she covertly exited the Pub. Puerilis and Josiah were still unaware that someone had overheard their discussion.

Puerilis pressed in against Josiah's side. The mood shifted from a cautionary admonition and more sultry intimacy. Josiah didn't back away, nor did he encourage Puerilis' advances. Puerilis put her arm around Josiah's neck and whispered in his ear.

"Tomorrow I will bring the potion to the Grand Ball. Keep this to yourself lest your friends fall victim to Sabedoria's seduction too. I'm sure you will make the right choice," she said. She ran her hand through Josiah's hair, "I know that you are the wise one. I can tell that you are the strongest; your brothers tend to be naïve." She pressed her lips close to his ear. He could feel the warmth of her breath caressing the side of his face. Josiah closed his eyes and inhaled the sweet aroma of her femininity.

"A wise man is difficult to find and is very much sought after by women of virtuous character," she remarked as she kissed him on the cheek. "I know you will make the right choice. I must leave now," Puerilis said. As she stood up, Josiah rose to his feet.

"I'll see you tomorrow," she said.

As Puerilis walked toward the door, she looked back and gave a smile. Josiah remained standing as she exited the Pub. Just as Puerilis exited, Clarion walked in. She had a determined look on her face. She walked briskly to the table. Caden, Wes and Ian saw her enter and determined that it was time to give up the dancing. They arrived at the table the same time that Clarion did.

"Cervus is ready to escort us to Lord Lemuel's fortress. Shall we go?" Clarion asked.

"Yes! We are ready to leave now," Wes said as he picked up the shield and situated it on his back.

"I see that Serik was here. He did warn you against using your weapon prematurely?" she asked.

Wes nodded as he adjusted the leather straps that crossed in front of his chest.

"We started to wonder if you were coming back," Ian said.

"*Ian* started to wonder if you were coming back," Caden corrected.

"I do apologize for not returning in a timely manner but Lord Cervus and I needed to return to Somberbos. It appears that Ubilaz has his loyal animal citizens and a host of necrophim busy looking for some lost object. The scouts were not sure what the object was, but it may be the diversion that we need to secure safe passage to Asilo for you gentlemen."

"Then let's hope it takes him a long time to find, whatever it is he is looking for," Ian announced.

"He is ferocious about finding it. The forest buzzes that he will kill whoever possesses the object and handsomely reward the one who finds it. We shall know tomorrow what this object is. Our small scouts are very cunning in their abilities. But now we must leave and take our rest."

As she turned to lead them out of the Rose and Raven, she saw Maayin standing on the periphery of their conversation.

"My sweet boy, how did you come to find your way in here?" she said.

Wes stepped behind the boy and put both his hands square on Maayin's shoulders. "Umm, long story. He's my guest and he will accompany us to Lord Lemuel's where he can be properly cared for," Wes said. The tender loving, yet authoritative tone with which Wes spoke, made Clarion smile with delight.

"Yes, my lord," she said, with a polite curtsy. She knew that a late adolescent guy had been transformed into a compassionate man.

CHAPTER
FOURTY-ONE

The evening at the Rose and Raven had certainly been eventful. King's Cross was dramatically quieter than it had been hours earlier. The night air was brisk and the lights from the expanse of the night sky, along with the lanterns' glow breaking through the windows of the cottages bordering the lane, cast a soft light on the dark cobblestone street. As the tired travelers climbed into the wagon behind Cervus, they were anticipating a good night's sleep, but their minds were also rapidly debriefing the events of the day.

Wes was still reeling from his meeting with his mentor Serik and the revelations about the power of his compassionate heart. He touched the mark emblazoned on his chest, smiled and felt the strong emotion welling up inside him. He was given the mark of a conciliator, King Elyon's name written upon his heart. Wes felt a powerful love and affection growing for his new king. He was overwhelmed with a new sense of belonging and acceptance from a loving king who claim an average teenage guy as his own. Not only did he wear the king's name, he wore Serik's shield and he kept the dagger close to his side. He thought about the day coming when he would need to use them, but he knew he dared not, until his brothers were also armed.

Wes pulled Maayin into the wagon. The young Vitatha boy stayed close to Wes. He had found protection and care in Wes, his new hero. The young conciliator felt deeply about the boy. To Wes, Maayin had become a little brother. He had a very strong sense that he was now the mentor to a young protégée.

Josiah also contemplated the evening. He wondered if he would hear Sabedoria call him again. His mind raced through the conversation with Puerilis. She had warned him that Sabedoria was a deceiver and planned to destroy him. He knew that he would have to reject Sabedoria's advances and choose Puerilis' offer to give him the ability to see the necrophim. He wanted to talk with his brothers about the entire conversation, but refrained, fearing that Sabedoria would attempt to go after them.

Caden and Ian only thought of getting a good night's sleep. The entire day had become physically and emotionally draining. Ian was feeling much more secure knowing that Josiah was within the fold of their group. He had been worried when Josiah described the effect of Sabedoria's song, which nobody else had heard. Ian was just afraid that Josiah would feel so compelled to find the source of the one calling his name that he would wander off, leaving himself and the group vulnerable to attack. At any rate, he was glad that the incident seemed to be over and was looking forward to being in the walls of Lemuel's Fortress.

Ian and Josiah both lent a hand to hoist Caden into the back of the wagon. Caden was still wondering how Josiah managed to attract these beautiful girls. He wanted to know what interests the girl in the bar had with Josiah. Josiah had passed it off as *"just a young girl wanting to know about Otherland."* Caden wasn't very satisfied with that answer, but didn't pursue it further. For now, he was satisfied that he had experienced the adrenaline rush of a lifetime in fleeing and defeating the necrophim earlier that morning, followed by a delicious meal and celebratory dancing with pretty barmaids. The one who came to the sobering conclusion that *"Where we go one - We go all"* also meant *"You fall - We fall"*, didn't have a care in the world at the moment.

Clarion climbed into the coachman's seat behind Cervus. She looked to see if her passengers were settled. The guys sat in the soft hay leaning against the sideboards of the wagon. Sleep was creeping up on them. They quietly settled in for a peaceful trip. Nobody had said a word from the time they walked out of the Pub.

"The ride up the mountain side will only take short time," she said. "I hope you gentlemen can stay awake long enough." She turned to Cervus, "Our guests are falling asleep; let's get them to the warmth and comfort of their beds."

Cervus lifted his head in acknowledgement and playfully bolted into a swift start sending the boys rolling around in the back of the wagon. He gave a loud grunt and then slowed down to a gentle gait.

"Lord Cervus *deeply* apologizes for such an abrupt start," Clarion said with a chuckle.

"Very funny, VERY FUNNY, Lord Cervus", Wes yelled. "We haven't had enough adventure today." Then he turned to his friends, "Everyone's a comedian – And we get stuck with a *big reindeer that has a sense of humor.*" He said that loud enough for Cervus to hear. The stag nodded and continued his pace.

Cervus steadied his gait and ambled upward along King's Cross Lane. The road meandered throughout the city past rows of thatched roof bungalows and small lantern lit cottages. Some of the homes had small gardens in the front and others looked as if the had been built into the slope of the great mountainside. As they rounded each curve and climbed higher, they could see the tops of the homes they passed. The guys could hear music and laughter emanating from some of the homes and smell the wonderful aromas of baked goods wafting from others. There was a peaceful anticipation that reminded the young travelers of the atmosphere they experienced every Christmas Eve.

Cervus reached the gate of Lemuel's Fortress. Lemuel's crest adorned the lintel of a great arched entry gate. The white stoned road from the front gate to the fortress doors reflected the moonlight giving it an iridescent glow. The wagon came to a stop in front of the great edifice of the castle fortress. The large entryway with its massive white doors resembled a European Basilica that commanded awe and reverence as one ascended the white marble steps.

The guys jumped from the back of the wagon. They all stared at the massive structure with its fortified walls towering over them.

"This is home for the next two nights, my friends," Clarion said. She began to walk up the stairs to the front entry. The guys naturally followed as Cervus strode away. As they climbed the steps, Josiah hesitated. He could hear loud and clear the beautiful song once again.

"*Josiah Nestor. Aieroch tu ae vishlo vec. Ubel list tra gorbu cordum. Saesa verdu ilran quel. Oomat kai doleth beldorum.*"

This time his name was distinctly clear. Sabedoria's pull was even greater on Josiah. She was being relentless in her pursuit.

From the lack of response on his brother's part, Josiah knew once again that they didn't hear the song. He didn't want to alert them, so he just kept walking up the stairs as he slowly perused the grounds trying to catch a glimpse of the songstress. *Her song sounds so close and so clear. She must be very near. Sabedoria is calling me even late into the night. It is very hard to resist something so beautiful. Puerilis said that she is as alluring as her voice. I must see this girl. I will reject her call, but I need to see her,* he thought.

As soon as he reached the top landing in front of the white doors, Sabedoria's song stopped, bringing Josiah back to the present. As if on cue, the great white doors opened for the guests. The group was met by a stately old woman, dressed in a fine white linen robe with a midnight blue sash that draped from her waist to the floor.

"We have been expecting you. Please come in. I'm sorry that Lord Lemuel is not here to attend to you personally, but he has been called away. He asked that I show you his full hospitality and assure you that he will be here to greet you in the morning. My name is Daesis; I am the head of the household."

"Thank you Lady Daesis. It is always good to see you," Clarion said as she kissed Daesis on both cheeks. It was evident that she had a warm relationship with the woman.

"And the same to you, my sweet darling girl. We don't get to see enough of you Clarion. We'll catch up tomorrow, but right now, I must attend to these dear young men. Please come in, boys."

The entourage followed Lady Daesis into the grand hall of the fortress. The guys were immediately captivated by the awe and grandeur of the hall. The high vaulted arches of the ceiling and the white stone colonnades reflected the orange glow of the torches that were strategically mounted to the castle walls and columns. Twin walk-in fireplaces were cut into opposite walls on either side of the enormous room. Befitting the old world architecture, each fireplace had a sitting area right inside the fireplace where guests could stay for awhile to warm themselves.

A grand marble staircase ascended from the expanse of the pallid marble floor directly across from the entranceway. In the center of the staircase where it split to give access to the wings on either side of the great hall, was a stained glass window. It was difficult to see the beauty of the glass because darkness that had already fallen, but the magnificent window displayed a burning touch, a diadem and a great opened book. The decorative luminary held Lemuel's crest.

"I can't wait to see that in the morning," Caden whispered to Josiah.

Lady Daesis stopped the processional in the center of the grand room. "You gentlemen must be tired. I see we have an additional guest. Lord Serik came by and mentioned that you might be joining us, young master Maayin," Daesis said.

Maayin tried to hide himself behind Wes. But Lady Daesis' soft smile and gracious welcome made the Vitatha lad feel secure. He smiled and bow his head in humble appreciation.

"Lord Serik saw you enter the Rose and Raven. He had a notion that Master Wes would respond as lovingly as he expected he should". Maayin looked up at Wes, who just smiled and winked at him. The lad's eyes expressed his grateful appreciation to Wes.

"Now if you will all follow me to your bed chambers, we will quickly get you to your rest." Daesis walked across the immense marble floor and began to ascend the stairs. The six travelers walked close behind. At the top of the staircase, they entered a long corridor that had six carved arched doors. At the far end of the corridor was a wooden table with a lamp set in the center of the table top. A bright white light shot straight up from the top of the lantern and bounced off the ceiling to illuminate the entire corridor.

"Protectus blessing!" Clarion said.

"Yes, Lord Lemuel invoked this before he departed. It covers all the rooms in this corridor. He just thought that this would be an added protection for the evening. Although Aanda and this fortress are safe places, they are not impenetrable. Only the protectus blessing can assure your safe keeping when you are separated. You boys are very precious to King Elyon; we will not take any risk in your safety."

They stopped in front of the first door on the right side of the corridor.

"Lady Clarion this is your chamber, as usual," she said.

"Thank you dear Daesis. Gentlemen I'll see you in the morning. Sleep soundly," she said as she entered the chamber closing the huge door behind her.

"Master Wes Litchfield, you shall have the chamber directly across the corridor from Lady Clarion."

As Wes started to open the door, he saw a look of worry come over Maayin. He immediately sensed the lad's fear of being alone this far into the city. Before he could say anything, Daesis spoke again.

"Master Maayin, you shall have the room next to Master Litch-field. There is a door that opens between the two chambers."

"Great, I know I'll sleep easier with those doors opened," Wes said to Maayin.

"There is also a bath drawn inside for you, Master Maayin . . . and a change of clothes awaits," Daesis continued.

Maayin shyly caught Daesis' eye, "Thank you, gracious Lady," he said quietly.

She caressed his cheek with her soft warm hand. "You are quite welcome, dear child. You are a very special boy and we are honored to have you here." Daesis then turned her attention back to her task. "Master Caden Boyd, you are across the hall from Master Maayin."

"OOHA," Caden said, extending his fist in Maayin's direction for him to pound. The gesture caught Maayin off guard, frightening him. He quickly took a step back against the wall. Josiah saw the boy's sudden fear and realized that this gesture was foreign to Salamgard.

"Whoa buddy, its good; go like this," Josiah jumped in and returned the pound with a smile. "It's simply a gesture of approval or . . . brotherhood."

Caden smiled, cocked his head, raised his eyebrows and again extended his fist to the boy. This time Maayin smiled and pounded back. "You got it, buddy!" Caden said as he rubbed Maayin's head messing up his hair even more than it already was.

"Master Ian Bound your chamber is on the right next to Master Boyd's and Master Josiah Nestor you are directly across the corridor from Master Bound."

The guys bid each other good night and went to their respected chambers. Lady Daesis picked up the lantern that emulated the protectus blessing and set it in the center of the floor midway down the corridor.

"Sleep well, young Knights," she whispered as she walked away.

CHAPTER
FOURTY-
TWO

Josiah entered his bed chamber. He delighted in seeing a large bed set upon a raised platform. The bed was similar to the one he slept in the night before at Clarion's cottage. It was so inviting and he was so exhausted that he knew that he would fall asleep as soon as he lay down. Directly across from the bed were five long leaded glass windows, which looked out on the vast gardens of the castle grounds. A warm fire crackled in the fireplace on one wall and directly across from it was a mirror that towered upward toward the chamber ceiling. The mirror filled the stone wall that it was propped against.

Josiah had never seen a mirror so large. It was bordered by an artistically crafted, wide ebony frame. Josiah stood before the mirror, admiring it. He could see the reversed image of the bed chamber behind him. He stared at the fire in the fireplace behind him; its fire-dance reflected in the mirrored glass. As he stood there, he also began to admire the blue coat he wore, particularly the crests on each breast panel.

I wonder what the crown in the crest, symbolizes. I suppose I'll get to talk to Lemuel tomorrow when he returns. I wonder what that will be like. I'm kind of excited but I'm also a little . . . intimidated. "Humm," Josiah said out loud, to his reflection in the mirror, "That's the same way I felt about our meeting with Doc."

Josiah turned away from the mirror and plodded up the two steps of the raised platform to the bed. He took off his jacket then sat down on the side of the bed and began pulling off his boots. As he undressed, he looked again at the mirror and something caught his eye. The ornate frame had words carved into it. He spied the word, *wisdom* on the right side of the frame about two-thirds of the way down the side. At the top, he saw the word *beyond* and then he saw the words *darkness* and *glass*. Josiah sat and stared. The words were so random that it didn't make sense to him. He stepped down from the bed platform and walked back to stand in front of the mirror to study the frame more closely. He could clearly see a line of words encompassing the entire frame. His eye followed from one word to the next as he tried to determine what they meant. As he kept reading, a continuous sentence began to immerge. The large ebony frame read:

"Beyond the haze and reflective glass fix one's gaze in darkness past; wisdom comes to those who see, that things are not always as they seem to be"

Josiah read it again. *I wonder what that means. Maybe it's a proverb. Maybe it doesn't mean anything at all. I'll be sure to ask Lemuel about it when I see him tomorrow. Right now, I need a good night's sleep.*

Josiah walked back to the bed. He sat down then lay back still staring at the massive mirror, pondering the proverb. He could feel the warmth of the fireplace and the softness of the bed. He knew he shouldn't lay there long or he would fall asleep. His eyes grew heavier until he quickly dozed off.

CHAPTER
FOURTY-THREE

A dark figure silently walked up King's Cross Lane. The darkness and the velvet cape's hood hid the nightwalker's face, while the crisp bright moonlight cast the walker's portentous shadow down the center of the thoroughfare. The chill of the night prompted the woman to return quickly to her home. When Sabedoria entered the front door of her cottage, she was greeted by her handmaid, Hannah.

"You've been calling him; have you not, my Lady?" Hannah asked. She helped Sabedoria remove her cloak and bade her to sit near the warmth of the fire place.

"Yes I called, but I feel that he is setting his volition against my overtures. I went into the streets and called to him a number of times. I even called into the town square. I know that he hears me because I feel a strong connection when I sing his name. He cannot have missed the attraction of my song. His will may be strong, but mine is stronger."

"My Lady, it is not just his will that is in resistance to you. Josiah Nestor is being . . . courted."

"What do you mean Hannah? How do you know this?"

"My father was short staffed and in need of help at the Pub today. I went down before the dinner hour to lend him service. The Otherlanders came in. I watched a young woman lurking in the pub waiting to catch the young man alone. When his friends joined in the dance, she accompanied him at the table."

"Who was this woman? Do you know her?"

"No, my Lady, I have never seen her in Aanda. The young gentleman Josiah called her Puerilis. I inquired about her identity among some of the more worldly patrons and pub staff. I had imagined that she would have been known by at least one, but she was unknown to everyone. She is very attractive, my Lady. Her beauty would have made her memorable to anyone who previously met her."

"Our opposition has intensified their efforts to acquire the young man."

"Yes, my Lady, I believe so. They counterfeit everything our lord has designed, including you. Puerilis is beautiful and alluring. I sensed that she too has great persuasive power. She has put young Josiah to a choice, warning him to choose her over you and your deceptive wiles, as she put it."

Sabedoria laughed, "No woman can have a more powerful sway on a young man than I."

Hannah stood silently. When Sabedoria caught her eye, she looked away quickly. "There is something more. What haven't you told me Hannah?"

"Puerilis has promised the young man vision . . . vision to see . . . necrophim."

"Then she knows!" Sabedoria stood bolt upright from her seat in front of the fire's warmth. "I must not let her get a stronghold on the young sage. My lord entrusted an important task to me and I will faithfully deliver gentleman into his hands. If Josiah Nestor is to make a choice, then I will raise the stakes and become more alluring. He must know that this is a life or death decision. He will then be drawn in by the sweet nectar of my song."

"You must go to him. He will surely not resist your beauty, Lady Sabedoria."

"No Hannah, he is in the safety of Lemuel's fortress. I cannot go to him, but I will call to him all through the night while he sleeps. My voice will enter into his dreams and into his subconscious. By tomorrow, he will want me. I will also tell him that I alone can give him power to see the necrophim. I will fill his mind with warning that Puerilis is a murderer who is attempting to lure him away from his brothers so that she can slaughter him like a fatling . . . and his brothers as well. I will tell him how her lips drip with honey, but her tongue is a viper's shard, sharp as a double edged sword. Tomorrow you will make ready my finest gown. I will meet Josiah at the gala. He will hear me and see me, and then I will have him."

Hannah smiled. Her fears of failure in this dire task were dispelled by the resolve and confidence that Sabedoria displayed. She knew the power of her mistress.

"But for now Hannah, fetch my cloak again and ready my coach. I will go near the gates of Lemuel's fortress and begin a long night-song."

CHAPTER
FOURTY-FOUR

Josiah jolted awake. He had dosed off on the big comfortable bed in the bed chamber of Lemuel's fortress. *That was a weird dream. I think Salamgard is getting to me . . . or into me.* Josiah took inventory of his surroundings. The fire in the fireplace still crackled in a full blaze. The windows still framed the blackness of the night. Josiah looked down the length of his body. He was still half dressed lying on top of the covers at the foot of his bed. *I must have dozed off for a few minutes. I need to get into bed and get a really good night's sleep.*

Josiah rose from the bed to finish getting undressed. He anticipated the feeling of his body melding into the cushiony mattress and being sandwiched in by the weight of the covers. He grabbed his coat from the side of the bed and walked over to hang it on a hook next to the mirror. He stopped again and read the proverb carved into the ornate ebony frame of the mirror.

"Beyond the haze and reflective glass fix one's gaze in darkness past; wisdom comes to those who see, that things are not always as they seem to be."

"I have no idea what that means," he said aloud once again to his reflection in the mirror. As he spoke to his reflection, he noticed a smudge mark on the glass that blurred the image of his face. Josiah looked around for something to clean the glass. He found a cloth on a table near the windows. He returned and rubbed the glass in a circular motion in front of his face. The smudge didn't go away. Josiah looked again and the glass looked more blurred. *There must be something on this rag.*

He opened the rag, but it was clean. Then he rubbed his finger across the mirror to determine what was making the smudge. Nothing, the smudge remained unaffected. The blur was growing into a smoky blind inside the glass of the mirror. Josiah peered closely at the smudge then he remembered the words, *"Beyond the haze and reflective glass fix one's gaze in darkness past".* That's it! It's a wise mystical proverb. The smudge is the haze that I must look past.

Josiah suddenly didn't feel so sleepy. He squared off in front of the mirror and attempted to stare through the hazy smudge at his face. He tried to see something but couldn't. He looked back at the proverb, *"fix your gaze in darkness past".* He stared in the mirror again – *darkness past, that must be an era of time. Maybe I'm supposed to look at myself through the blurred smudge and think about a dark time in my life.* His mind ravaged through his nineteen years of life and hit upon the sad dark moments when his grandmother passed away. He stared pensively in front of the mirror, looking into his own eyes, thinking of his grandmother's death, but nothing happened. Then he noticed the reflection of the fireplace with its dark sooty black wall behind him. He turned to face it. He could see the blackness of the soot stained brick beyond the flames; this was darkness past the light.

Maybe that's it. I need to look in the mirror, past my reflection at the darkness of the fireplace wall. Darkness past may not mean a bygone era; it might refer to the location of the darkness. He turned to face the mirror again. He trained his eye on the hazy spot and then he let his eyes focus beyond the haze of his own reflection to the mirrored image of the blackness of the fireplace wall.

Josiah stood quietly staring into the blackness. His intense concentration came to a crashing halt when the blackness turned into the movement of a black shadow. It startled him taking his breath away. He quickly turned to see what lurked behind him. There was nothing. He looked around the bed chamber but nobody was there and there was nothing in the room, which could have caused the shadow. Josiah's breathing was short and rapid. Adrenaline began to flow like a mighty current through his body. He could feel his heart beating in the veins of his neck and temple.

NECROPHIM, he thought as the violent wave of fear rushed over him. *They must be here, in this room; cloaked in invisibility. I need the potion that Puerilis was going to give me so that I could see them.* He wanted to run for the door to get to the bond of his brothers but he felt frozen by fear. He looked over to the chamber door for an exit strategy. Beneath the opening at the bottom of the chamber door Josiah could see the glow of the protectus blessing.

As fast as he had been overcome by fear was as fast as he was relieved at the sight of the sparkling blue glowing light. *There can't be any necrophim here. This wing of the fortress is doubly protected. The Protectus blessing is more powerful than the community of my brothers. It is the protecting power of King Elyon.* He felt secure and convinced that there were no necrophim but his mind returned to the notion that he definitely saw something move in the reflection of the mirror. *If there are no necrophim here then the shadow must have been caused by something or someone else. Maybe that is what I'm supposed to see. Maybe I must get past the darkness of my fears. I must face the mirror again.*

Josiah took a deep breath and turned into the full reflection of the mirror once again. He found the darkness as before. Once again, the shadow more vividly returned. Josiah's heart began to beat loudly in his chest. He could feel his breathing becoming more pronounced and rapid. He wanted to turn to confront the image that he thought might be looming behind him, but he kept his eyes fixed on the shadow in the mirror.

Slowly a figure began to immerge. Josiah could feel his body start to tremble. Then there was a bit of light in the darkness as if the shadow was beginning to transform into a clearer image. The light carried a new hope that vanquished Josiah's fear like the bursting of a balloon. As Josiah watched, the haze grew larger like a fog overtaking the entire mirror. Then the fog cleared to reveal blackness. It appeared as if the fog was a veil, opening to a dark cavern. The entire mirror was now black as coal. Josiah remained staring into the darkness and saw the shadow transform into the figure of an old man with a long silvery-white beard. Josiah turned around to see if the man was in his room but he wasn't. He redirected his attention to the mirror as a scene began to unfold.

The darkness gave way to another room. It looked as if the mirror reflected a short dark vaulted corridor, which opened to a very brightly lit secret chamber. It soon became clear that the chamber was a library. Dark wood bookcases lined the stone walls. Josiah could also see a staircase, which led to another level where more books and glass cases filled with mystical relics decorated the walls. There were tables with maps and other artifacts. An oversized leather chair was positioned in the library beyond the dark vaulted corridor, directly in front of Josiah's line of vision. The chair actually looked more like a throne than any chair Josiah had seen. A round leather ottoman was set beside the chair.

The corridor and chamber looked so real. Josiah glanced behind himself, to see if the fireplace had opened into a corridor. But he was still in his bed chamber, nothing had transformed. Then he walked to the side of the mirror. *An entrance to a secret room must have opened behind the mirror glass*, he thought. The mirror still angled upright against the wall. Josiah put his face against the wall and looked across the back width of the mirror. There was no corridor only the cold stone of the wall on which his face was pressed and the hard back of the ebony casing in which the mirror set.

Josiah returned to the front of the mirror. The corridor and library were still there, only now the old gentleman was stirring about the library. His hair was long and silver, as was his beard.

He wore a long deep blue robe with silver filigrees and there was a deep blue turban-like hat upon his head. In one hand, he held a staff crafted of fine silver. The top of the staff held a crystal orb enclosed in a swirling platinum encasement. The old man held a book in his other hand, in which he was engrossed as he paced the floor.

Josiah knocked on the glass. "Hey mister, can you hear me. Hey what's going on here; who are you?"

The man was deaf to Josiah's calls. He remained engrossed in his book and soon tired of pacing so he set the staff against the side of the leather throne then sat down. The old man remained undeterred from reading his book. Josiah again remembered the proverb, "Beyond the haze and reflective glass fix one's gaze in darkness past; *wisdom comes to those who see . . ."*

Josiah leaned against the glass of the mirror with both hands. He hung his head and looked at the ground to concentrate. *Wisdom comes . . .,* Josiah thought. *A shadow came . . . then the old man came from the shadow and now I just saw the man come into the library – wisdom comes. The shadow is wisdom. No, the man is wisdom.* Then it dawned on him, *the man is Lemuel. I'm seeing Lemuel in that room. But he must not be real. He didn't respond to my calling. Lemuel is not even here tonight. Maybe I'm seeing a shadow of where Lemuel is and what he is doing.*

Josiah lifted his head to look back into the mirror. The man had stopped reading and now sat looking directly at Josiah.

"Lord Lemuel," Josiah said. The old sage didn't say a word, he gestured for Josiah to come. "Lord Lemuel, you want me to come to you? Where are you? How do I get to you?" Josiah seemed perplexed. *I'm talking to a freakin television set or some magical 3D hologram in a window.*

Josiah looked again to Lord Lemuel. Again, he gestured for Josiah to come. "You want me to come to you," Josiah said. "But I don't know where that library is located. Is the library located somewhere in the palace or in a distant remote place?"

There was no response from Lemuel. The old sage just sat patiently waiting for Josiah to join him. Josiah began to think out loud.

"The library must be in this building. Maybe the library is on the other side of this wall? No that can't be, Maayin's bed chamber is on the other side of the wall. I watched him enter the chamber myself. But then again maybe the library is only an extension of this room and the corridor between them is the only way to get to the library." Josiah looked back at Lemuel and noticed that the man was nodding his head in affirmation.

"That's it, isn't it? The room is an extension of this bed chamber," Josiah said to the man in the mirror. Josiah looked at his hands still pressed against the glass. He eyed the full frame of the mirror and didn't see any opening. He ran his hands across the glass trying to find a seam or latch to open the window that blocked his entrance.

The wise old sage closed his book and looked over the top of his half-lunar shaped spectacles. He waited silently and patiently watching. Josiah stood up straight and looked again at the frame, *"wisdom comes to those who see that things aren't always as they seem to be"*. Josiah took a few steps away from the mirror and began to pace as he talked aloud.

"The proverb doesn't say that I see wisdom. Wisdom comes to those who see *things . . . !* It says wisdom comes to the person *who sees that things aren't the way they seem to be.* What isn't the way it seems to be?" Josiah turned full faced in front of the mirror.

"The mirror isn't a mirror it's a portal. It is only a mirror with glass when I think it is. Wisdom waits for me in that room and I must walk through the portal to get it," he said.

Josiah looked at the large frame and then looked directly at Lemuel who was seated with an amused grin of affirmation. "Things aren't always as they seem to be," Josiah whispered with a new air of enlightenment.

I'm just going to walk straight into that corridor because there is nothing that will keep me from wisdom. With a confident brisk pace, Josiah walked toward the mirror and then stepped over the ebony frame into the vaulted corridor.

Josiah stood in the dark vaulted corridor somewhat dazed that his plan had worked. The glass of the mirror behind him hazed over once again and then returned to its reflective state. Josiah could no longer see the bed chamber. The closed portal also made the corridor darker, putting more demand on the small candle-burning wall lanterns to light the passage.

The old sage rose from his throne. "I fain to think having passed the haze and darkness of the mirrored frame that foolishness, now ushered in, would render you standing idle in a corridor of darkness," he said. Lemuel's voice was deep and low and rumbled with force even though he spoke softly. It sounded like the thunderous basso overtones of a waterfall when it plunges into a bottomless pool. The voice shook Josiah, who hadn't expected to be engulfed in so large a sound.

Through darkness pass, Josiah thought as he walked through the dark corridor and stepped into the light of the magnificent library.

"You have thus, passed through the corridor of reason so dimly lit, to arrive in the hallowed chamber of wisdom," Lemuel said. The old sage sat back down in his chair. "Sit, my son," he said, inviting Josiah to take a seat on the ottoman next to the throne. "The night hours race on like a great hart across the Gilbreath Plains and there is much for us to discuss."

CHAPTER
FOURTY-
FIVE

Josiah sat on the edge of the leather ottoman beside the throne in which Lemuel was seated. The library captivated Josiah's attention. There were swords, bows, armor and other weapons of warfare mounted on the wall between the bookcases. Tapestries and crests hung from the rafters. Lemuel's crest hung on the wall above the corridor that Josiah had just passed through.

"This is amazing," Josiah said as his eyes wandered around the room.

Lemuel sat silently watching Josiah. After a few minutes, amidst his perusal of the room, Josiah came to the realization that the old sage was staring at him. Like a schoolboy who just got caught cheating on an exam, Josiah sat up straight and focused on his mentor. Lemuel didn't break his trance. He just leaned in uncomfortably closer and stared into Josiah's eyes like an optometrist who was examining his patient. Josiah felt as if the old Sage was looking into his mind.

Josiah began to feel very uncomfortable with the old sage's muteness, intense gaze and violation of personal space. "Uh, nice place you have here," Josiah said as he nervously smiled.

Lemuel didn't respond nor did he blink an eye. "The eyes are portal orbs of a young man's innermost being. Deep within the recesses of your being I sense a man of wisdom awaits in repose, like a slumbering giant dormant, made ready for awakening from lifelong sleep," Lemuel spoke. Then coming out of his eye-gazing trance he continued, "You seek wisdom, do you?"

"Yes I do Lord Lemuel. I want to be a wise man."

"I should say so. There is prudence, understanding, discernment and wisdom within. Yet there is much more of wisdom to acquire in your knowing. Mind you this, that a man wise in his own estimation, slowly plods the road to foolishness like an aged oxen being lead to slaughter."

Josiah listened to Lemuel but still became distracted by all the artifacts in the room. At times, he found himself looking past the old sage sizing up the swords on the opposite wall or the apothecary jars filled with potions on a side table. The place looked like a wizard's lair.

Lemuel realized that he still did not have his protégée's undivided attention. He turned his body to face Josiah. They were now knees to knees and face to face with nothing between them. The old sage leaned in again and with one hand grabbed Josiah's face at his chin and directed the young man's gaze to look straight into the face of wisdom.

"Your curiosity turns your head about like blades upon a windmill, twisted in slow wisps of a gentle breeze. With all intensity of spirit, I propose you listen to my words. Write them duly upon your brow, visible for all to read," Lemuel said as he ran his long spindly finger across Josiah's forehead as if it were a quill penning a parchment.

Still holding Josiah's chin steady so that he could only look into the sage's eyes, Lemuel clenched the hand of his free arm around Josiah's bicep and squeezed. "Bind these wise words as strength around your arm. . ." he said.

Then he put his fist square against Josiah's chest, ". . . and wed them to your heart. For if you but stray from the path of wisdom set before you, surely you shall revel in the folly of a fool and taste the bitter gall of destruction."

Lemuel released his grip from Josiah's chin and sat back in his throne. Josiah didn't move. He had forgotten his surroundings and was transfixed by the wise old sage. Lemuel's eyes were still intently locked in an unflinching stare with Josiah's.

"Lest while your gaze is fixed but still your attention fleeting, hear these words in knowledge full, that before the hallowed Victorium Morte's eve has crest, wisdom shall be put to ordeal which shall render life so rich and sweet, or result in the tragic dire of death," Lemuel said.

"Lord Lemuel, I'm so sorry for failing to give you my attention. I do want wisdom to guide my thoughts, actions and desires. Please tell me how to be a wise man."

"If it is wisdom you seek, then a lifelong search you must begin. As most men desire the wantonness of women, so should be your lust for the sweet woman, wisdom. Seek her intently till the passion to acquire her becomes the obsession of your life's calling. More than silver, gold or precious jewels should her value exceed, thus tantalizing your longing and drive to gain hold of her all the more. Never shall you be aptly satisfied, for at the onset you believe that you have her in your grasp she slips away like water through a sieve or dissipates like smoke caught in the wind."

"So you are telling me that a man of wisdom is defined by his intentional continuous life long search to become wise. If that is true then how will I know when I am a wise man?"

"The quest to answer such a question vexed begins the right and proper journey toward becoming that so desired man. Knowing, is the mire on the road that impedes the journey. But far be it from any lad who ventures on that road from naivety to discernment, only blindly to fumble along without affirmation of navigating his rightful course. The king shall give his leading and from the boy of simple thinking shall spring forth a man of wisdom."

"I must trust that King Elyon is giving me his wisdom and he will affirm when I am acting wisely."

"Tis rightly spoken and be in awe of the King, you must. For from him alone, emanates the light of wisdom like a blazing beacon atop a high held torch."

"Just like your crest!" Josiah exclaimed. "The torch is set through the diadem of the King to remind me that wisdom only comes from Elyon. But how will I know when I have the king's wisdom and affirmation?"

"Elyon has marked you with wisdom, thus," Lemuel said as he removed the blue turban from his head. On his brow was a platinum diadem that looked like a solid glimmering sliver headband. It was plain and smooth, without blemish, etching or precious gems. Its sliver finish reflected the full circle of the room around Lemuel's head. At mid-brow right above Lemuel's nose, the diadem peaked forming a diamond shape in the center of his forehead. Lemuel removed the diadem and placed it on Josiah's brow. The band morphed to fit his head tightly as if becoming part of Josiah's body. Josiah felt a surge of power shoot through him from the top of his head to the bottom of his feet as Lemuel pressed the diadem upon him.

"Henceforth, you shall be marked as a sage in the realm of King Elyon according to the authority with which the king has so richly bestowed upon me. Never shall the diadem be removed. This shall be a sign to all, and more to you, of the affirmation of wisdom pursued and bestowed by so great and wise a king. You shall come to know the power that gracefully crowns your brow."

Josiah couldn't see the diadem but he could feel it. He reached up to his forehead and felt the platinum as slick as glass. His finger ran against the edge revealing the hardness of the metal juxtaposed against the softness of the skin of his forehead and his jet black hair. *This is the diadem of Lemuel's crest. It is wisdom, the crown on the head of a wise man,* Josiah thought.

Lemuel stood up and walked over to the wall to retrieve something from behind a bookcase. He revealed a staff carved out of ivory. At the top of the staff, two platinum hands held a deep blue crystal sphere.

"Wisdom from your lips alone shall not quell the dangers of Ubilaz nor necrophim, wielding impetuous death. Arm yourself with this staff, from which the force of Elyon flows, in lightning flashes. Extend your strong arm at your foe and speak words thus, *Excessum Neco*."

Lemuel extended the staff toward a suit of armor at the opposite end of the library. When the words *Excessum Neco* left his lips a bolt of blue lightning flashed from the crystal sphere, disintegrating the armor into a heap of ash.

"Until your brothers bear their arms, this staff carried shall be impotent at your side." Lemuel stated.

"Yes, Wes told us of the warning when Serik bestowed upon him his shield and dagger."

Lord Lemuel handed Josiah the staff. The young sage gripped the ivory and could feel its power. Josiah thought about using the staff in a future life and death battle which triggered him back to the present life or death encounter that he was about to face.

"Lord Lemuel you did say something about a life or death decision before tomorrow evenings celebration is over. I know that your warning is in regards to Puerilis and Sabedoria. Puerilis warned me that Sabedoria is a murderer who is luring me away from my brothers so that she can kill us all. Puerilis also promised to give me a potion, which would allow me to see the necrophim in their invisible state. On the other hand, I had a vivid dream where I met Sabedoria. She told me that Puerilis is a deceiver who weaves an elaborate web of lies in an attempt to separate me from my brothers then destroy us all. She too promised to give me sight over the necrophim by providing me with a pair of eyeglasses equipped with that power. If Puerilis is telling the truth that Sabedoria is a murderer then she is delivering us from the clutches of evil and death. But if Puerilis is a liar as Sabedoria claims, then Sabedoria is forewarning us and circumventing our destruction. Both are beautiful and alluring. Both promise the same power to see the necrophim. But choosing one over the other will mean life or death. Lord Lemuel, please help me discern the proper and wise choice."

"You speak fair in earnest and honesty, but I am unable to succor you through this brutal test. Like wisdom and foolishness, both are alluring and promise great power but one has a destructive path. My words alone implore you but to trust the giver of wisdom, listen intently and remember my teaching. Now my son the night grows short and sweet respite calls from your bed chamber."

Josiah turned and looked down the dark corridor. The mirrored portal was open and he could clearly see the inviting glow of his bed chamber. "But Lord Lemuel," Josiah began as he turned back to gain more clarity. But the old sage was gone and the blazing torches that lit the vaulted ceilings of the library began to go dark. The library was beginning to vanish. Josiah quickly grabbed his staff and ran down the corridor one step ahead of the blackness that was closing in on him. He bounded through the frame and turned to see the mirrored portal close up and his reflection standing once again in front of the large mirror.

CHAPTER

FORTY-SIX

A red mist wisped through the trees in the Valley of Ithcar. The sun had just begun to rise over the Sargo mountain range ushering in a crisp new morning for Salamgard. As the brilliant morning star slowly washed the tree tops and flora floor, the tenants of Ithcar began about their business chirping in the trees, scurrying through the underbrush or searching for a delectable breakfast. The increasingly growing timbre of the valley drowned out Venem's conversation with himself.

"This is ridiculous; I've covered every inch of Ataroth and have been up one side and down the other side of the Sargo range. Now I'm told that I must scout out this wretched valley."

Venem stopped for a moment to get his bearings. He perched himself on a rock and looked all around.

"This valley is so large. How, in the name of our Dark Lord can Avah expect me to do this alone? I suspect that he is jealous that I brought valuable information to Lord Ubilaz about the Otherlanders' presence in Eikondor. He is jealous so he consigns me to this tedious task."

Venem set his sights to the west and began his search again. He cut through the air at a slower pace so that he could get a careful look.

"Lord Ubilaz has all of his scouts out looking for Tobijah and that gem. Tobijah is too smart; he continues to elude any of our scouts. How am I to find him if the scouts cannot? This is all Avah's doing. When I am a captain, I will make Avah and that hideous hyena pay. I will assign them to sentry duty at the top of Mt. Aphesis."

Venem stopped again this time to collect his thoughts. "But first I must become a captain. I need to do something spectacular. What can I do . . . kill the Otherlanders! No, that wouldn't work especially if Lord Ubilaz has plans to convert them. What shall I do?"

As he sat deep in thought, his contemplation was disturbed by the rapid gallop of a warrior on a charging steed, far off in the woods. The warrior was riding away from Venem. The crest on his shield was familiar to the necrophim.

"He is one of Tobijah's warriors! He doesn't see me nor shall he. I shall follow that foolish warrior right to Tobijah's camp. That's it! I will be captain if I can get the gem for my king, Lord Ubilaz," Venem muttered.

Venem swiftly fell into pursuit. He kept sufficient distance so that the warrior could not detect his misty presence. Yet he stayed close enough to keep the warrior in his sights.

The beating of the charging steed's hooves against the forest trail set a powerful rhythm. The warrior rode on without breaking stride. He knew this forest terrain well, cutting through the dense trees and hedges. He glided over ridges and around rocky passes that blocked the trail. Venem stayed in pursuit picking up the pace slightly when the rider momentarily disappeared from view because the terrain concealed him.

The rider took a sharp left turn off the trail and bounded over a ridge. Venem stayed close but slowed to peer over the ridge before he burst into view of the warrior. When he looked over the ridge,

THE CREST

the rider was nowhere to be seen. The ridge opened to a valley clearing in the forest. Venem frantically flew over the ridge to see if he could spot the rider. He was nowhere to be seen.

The necrophim scout hovered in the middle of the clearing, turning in every direction to see if he could spot some evidence of the rider. There was nothing. No dust being kicked up by the horse's gait. No flash of the silver armor in the distant woods. No prints from the animal's hooves any direction beyond the clearing. Then Venem remained silent.

Maybe I can hear them, he thought. But there was no noise of the gallop or no chatter of the woodland creatures hailing a hero.

"Tobijah's warriors be damned," Venem screamed his curse out loud. "I shall never be captain. I shall not be consigned to menial tasks. I will find you warrior . . . and Lord Tobijah. I am still a necrophim with power greater than your sword. I will acquire that sapphire for my Lord." Venem wisped away to resume his search.

High above in the trees sat one of Elyon's squirrel scouts. He quickly scurried off with the news. Ubilaz knows that Tobijah has the Kalos sapphire. That is the object, which he so desperately wants to acquire.

CHAPTER
FORTY-SEVEN

Wes stepped from his bed chamber in Lemuel's fortress, into the corridor where the protectus blessing was still burning bright from the lantern on the floor where Lady Daesis had placed it the night before. He noticed that Clarion's chamber door was open and the room was vacant. He stood waiting and after a few minutes, the door to Maayin's bed chamber opened. Maayin was wearing brown suede knickers, a silken shirt and a new warm jacket and shoes. The lad had bathed and his hair was combed except for a cowlick tuft on the right front side of his forehead that stubbornly refused to rest uniformly on his head. Wes hadn't noticed the cowlick for the disarray the lad's hair was in when they met.

"You look great buddy. Did you sleep well?" Wes asked.

"Yes my lord. I didn't want to leave the bath last night and then I didn't want to leave the bed this morning. I had come to forget such peace that is found between a soft mattress and mountains of covers."

Wes smiled and put his arm around the boy. "I think a few other people didn't want to leave the bed either. We need to wake up the sleepers in the other rooms. You bang on Josiah's door and I will pound on Ian and Caden's doors."

They both took their places and in concert began pounding. Ian stepped into the hall immediately. "Morning gents," he said bright and engaging. "Last night's sleep was the best I've had since I arrived in Salamgard. I think the dancing and the ale at the Rose and Raven might have helped."

Shortly after, a different picture emerged from Caden's bed chamber. "No matter where we are, morning always comes too early," Caden said. He was still securing the straps on his shoulder that held the front panel of his shirt in place. "Where's 'Siah?" he asked.

Maayin stepped away from Josiah's door as Wes stepped in to give it a few raps. He tried to open the chamber door but it seemed to be locked. "Josiah are you awake?" he said loud and close to the chamber door. He leaned his ear in to listen for some stirring, but there was none.

"The singing voice got him," Ian said. You could begin to see his countenance of contentment turning into one of consternation.

"OR . . . he's already down at breakfast," Wes added. "Let's check that option before we kick the door in." Caden laughed but Ian wasn't amused at all.

They left the corridor and descended the grand staircase. The sun backlit the magnificent stained glass window with Lemuel's crest sending color cascading all across the white marble stairs and floor. Clarion entered the great hall from a side hallway as the guys descended the stairs. She waited for them at the base of the staircase.

"Joyous Victorium Morte," she greeted.

"Oh yeah, today is the holiday; and a joyous Victorium Morte to you too, Lady Clarion." Wes said as he kissed her hand and gracefully bowed.

"We all must have slept very well", she said.

"I think we did but we haven't seen Josiah yet. Have you seen him," Wes replied.

"I see him right now," Clarion answered pointing to the top of the staircase.

The guys turned to see Josiah at the top of the stairs ready to descend. He was carrying his staff and the diadem was on his brow.

"You were with your mentor last night," Caden remarked as Josiah joined them.

"Yep! I met with Lord Lemuel. It was quite a night but surprisingly I feel like I slept better and deeper than I have in a long time. And I had the most vivid, amazing dreams, if you know what I mean."

Caden raised his eyebrows and smiled, waiting to see if Josiah would elaborate. Wes quickly intervened.

"So I take it the mark you've been given is the silver headband," Wes commented. He could see his image mirrored in the smooth polished platinum finish of the diadem.

"Yes, it is to remind me to bind wisdom to my head and to seek her more than any precious metal or riches."

"And the staff – is that your weapon?" Ian asked.

"Yes. Lord Lemuel instructed me with a powerful demonstration of its capabilities. I feel ready and equipped to battle the necrophim."

"Then Lord Lemuel must have returned during the night. When will we meet him?" Caden asked.

"You shall meet him forthright," sounded the booming voice from behind the guys. They all turned to see the Sage standing behind Clarion.

"It is the great honor of Aanda to have so distinguished a gathering of fine young men, on which to bestow our hospitality. My friend and comrade of many years, Lord Serik joins, to break the long fast of evening. Even now awaits the patient knight, like a sentinel anticipating leave of his post. Let us join him directly. Follow me to the sweet and savory table where you shall taste gracious hospitality," Lemuel said.

The Sage of Aanda and Knight of Elyon's realm, turned to lead the group into an enormous dining hall where a table was prepared with the choicest foods Aanda could prepare.

As the guys followed Lemuel, Caden whispered to Josiah, "Where did he come from? I didn't hear or see him come in."

"Beats me, it's all a mystery. He leaves the same way he enters," Josiah commented.

CHAPTER FORTY-EIGHT

Lady Daesis was content that her able bodied staff could more than adequately serve breakfast to this small group of guests. She needed to attend to more pressing matters. Tonight was the grand gala celebration of Victorium Morte. They expected thousands of guests and there were still so many preparations.

Daesis opened the leaded glass doors that led to the garden terrace behind the fortress. The grounds were immaculately manicured as gardeners buzzed like bees about the maze of shrubbery and multi-colored flora, snipping and pruning to insure that every plant held its perfect form. Many other workers were arranging tables on the open patio and lawn. Daesis gazed across the terrace to a large pavilion. The chefs were already preparing tables and food stations under the great structure. Her eyes rose to the top of the pavilion. She could see another crew busily at work making ready the space that would hold about a thousand more guests. The hanging gardens that cascaded from the top of the pavilion to the ground below were in full bloom, creating waterfalls of color.

Everything is right on schedule, she thought. *I must make sure that there is sufficient lighting. I hope we have enough lanterns and we should probably elicit the help of our friends the fireflies. They could add a beautiful touch that would make the evening sparkle.*

Her thoughts were quickly interrupted. "Lady Daesis, the concertmaster has arrived with his orchestra and chorus. They are awaiting instruction as to where you would like them to set their stage," one of the butlers said.

Daesis looked over the grounds. The far end of the garden abruptly ended against a cliff that rose behind the fortress, capping the mountain in which the city of Aanda was built. "There!" she said as she pointed. "The foliage of the cliff wall and the gentle streaming waterfalls will make a very nice backdrop."

"Very good my Lady, I will inform the concertmaster directly."

The butler turned and proceeded to attend to his task. Lady Daesis produced a calling charm from around her neck and blew into it. No sound was heard, but moments later, a beautiful basset hound and a cheetah came bounding across the lawn.

"My dear friends, will you please scurry to the woodlands and solicit the assistance of the fireflies. Tell them we are counting on them to make this event sparklingly brilliant."

The two messengers bounded off, obediently carrying out the command of their mistress. Lady Daesis again took assessment of the work being done. *Things are moving along well here. I should check the preparations in the kitchen,* she thought as she turned and exited the terrace.

The butler led a procession of musicians who made their way across the terrace grounds. They carried an assortment of stringed and wind instruments. One by one, they filed into the garden and made ready their place for the performance. Among the musicians were Sabedoria and Hannah.

"You're trembling Hannah, what is wrong with you," Sabedoria said.

"We are on the grounds of Lord Lemuel's fortress. It is so big and foreboding. It intimidates me so."

"You have nothing to fear. We shall take our place among the musicians and wait."

"My lady your confidence always gives me strength. Will you call to him now?"

"Not until the appropriate time. We must be patient."

From the point where the musicians were to perform, Sabedoria quickly assessed that she had full view of the garden and terrace grounds. She looked to see if she could spy Josiah. He was nowhere to be seen.

"This is a perfect vantage point for us. We can see all the guests from this spot. When the timing is right I will call to him and he will come to me."

"Are you sure my Lady? He seemed to be easily pulled by Puerilis. He never resisted her in the least when they were in the Pub."

"Hannah, all throughout the night I spoke to him. I let my words seep deep into the crevasses of his mind and soul. Before the night ended, he had very sweet dreams of being locked in my embrace. He became drunk with desire for me. I am very confident that I have swayed him. I felt a very strong connection to him. We just need to wait patiently. Before the night is out, he will be mine or he will taste death."

CHAPTER
FORTY-NINE

The guys ate their full of breakfast then devoured the sweet conversation and fellowship around Lemuel's table, as time gobbled through hours like they were savory moments. The conversation ranged from a jovial and free spirited focus on the customs and traditions of the holiday, to a more strategic perspective on their upcoming travels. Wes leaned forward, propped his elbows on the table, prayerfully folded his hands and used them as a support for his chin. He couldn't help but drink in the satisfaction of the moment. His eyes slowly scanned the circumference of the table. His best friends and brothers Josiah, Caden and Ian were laughing, joking and passionately locked into the conversation. His new friend Clarion sat nearby offering her insight and Lord Lemuel offered his whimsical contribution and tactical wisdom. Wes' eyes moved to Maayin who was entrenched in the whole experience. The boy was at home; eating his full, poking fun at the brothers when they teased him, and resting secure in the love of his hero and older brother, Wes.

Wes looked directly across the table. His mentor Serik was as mesmerized with Wes as much as Wes was with the passionate ambient circle before him. He and Wes locked eyes and smiled. Without saying a word, they knew each other's thoughts. *It doesn't get better than this; being surrounded by the people, you love. This is the dynamic of hearts bound.* Wes stared for a moment at Serik who winked back at him. *This is what it feels like to have a loving dad, who would go to the wall for you,* Wes thought. He could still feel that fire burning deep within his being.

"What do *you* think, Wes?" Caden asked.

"What?" Wes replied, being jolted out of his dreamy inventory.

"Don't you think we should leave as early as possible? Clarion thinks that it may be difficult to connect with Tobijah, so we might do well to get off as early as possible."

"Um sure – I guess! Who is Tobijah and why will it be hard to connect with him?" Wes asked.

"Dude stay with the program!" Caden teased.

"Tobijah is King Elyon's mighty Warrior Knight. He and his company of warriors will provide safe passage for us through the Valley of Ithcar. We have come to understand that Elyon's Kalos sapphire is in the protective care of the Great Warrior. The sapphire is the object, which Ubilaz desperately seeks. Although Ubilaz is unaware that we need to make contact with Tobijah, his search for the mighty Warrior Knight and the Kalos gem will put us at greater risk," Clarion said.

"If I know Tobijah, it will be difficult for you to locate him. He has probably invoked a cloaking blessing over his camp," Serik added.

"Cloaking blessing?" Caden asked.

"A cloaking blessing makes the entire camp invisible and muffles any sound that occurs in the camp. It allows the camp to function undetected. It can only be invoked when the company of warriors is stationary. Tobijah will attempt to find you because you will never find him. He knows to be looking for you, after all, he is Caden's mentor," Serik said.

"My mentor – Tobijah, the mighty Warrior Knight is my mentor?" Caden asked. "That's amazing. I'm going to be a warrior!" He extended his fist to Maayin who smiled and pounded it without hesitation.

"If Tobijah is going to be looking for us we should get as early a start as possible. I suggest that we leave before dawn breaks," Clarion said bringing the conversation full circle.

"I agree," Wes commented. "Lord Serik and Lord Lemuel, will you both be accompanying us tomorrow as we travel to Asilo?"

"No, I'm afraid that neither of us will accompany you gentlemen. We will be about some important business for King Elyon. You will be in good hands with Clarion," Serik replied. He looked in Clarion's direction and caught her eye. There was a long pause as the two stayed focused on each other. Serik had the same look that Clarion usually had when she was communicating to Cervus. Then he smiled and she smiled back giving an affirming nod. Clarion rose abruptly from the table.

"If you boys will excuse me, I think you gents should be alone to chat," she said. "Maayin, I happen to know that there are archery targets along the west side of the garden near the forest edge. That is where King Elyon's archers are trained to be master archers. Why don't you join me and I will teach you to shoot like a master archer."

Maayin's face lit up with delight. He quickly rose from his seat and followed Clarion out the garden doors. When they exited the building, Serik began the conversation.

"I asked Clarion to take the boy out of the room so that we can freely speak. I don't want him to become alarmed. Lord Lemuel and I have become very aware that Ubilaz is plotting another attempt to overthrow King Elyon. I'm afraid that he has gained more power and force than the citizens of Salamgard realize. He would like for us to believe that he is just acquiring citizens to his kingdom when he is actually raising up an army," Serik commented.

"Evil fleshed, is the Dark Lord, and knowing of bound hearts' presence in Salamgard affixed with strength of character that each of you desire, has set with putrid loathing spite that evil flesh aflamed. I do not know, but wisdom prods me to surmise that the wicked lord's mind is vexed with barbarous thorns of contemplation over destructive wiles that shall be leveled against Eikondor by such a band of brothers as you. His mission hence, is a relentless obsession to unbind those hearts and kill the ones in whose breast's they beat," Lemuel said.

"That's why it doesn't seem fair that we cannot use our weapons. I don't understand. It seems unwise to carry weapons and not be able to use them if we are attacked. We are helpless targets," Josiah commented.

"You are not helpless targets, my son. Already you trust more in the weapon you hold for protection, than the King who guarantees your protection. If you are attacked by Ubilaz's flesh and blood warriors, you may use your weapons and fight to defend yourself. But the weapon will be useless against the necrophim until you each have your weapon and you understand the power that flows through you and your weapons. For now, you have a greater defensive means of protection against the necrophim," Serik said.

"Community – hearts bound. We need to stay together," Ian answered.

"Your bonded brotherhood creates an impermeable barrier of which the vile spirits cannot pass. When you stand in unity you are intertwined like a three stranded rope, difficult to be broken," Lemuel replied.

"Why? What makes our brotherhood so magical?" Ian asked.

"Not magical – mighty," Serik answered. "The question you should ask is; what is it that makes your brotherhood strong?"

"Love!" Wes replied with a new sense of awareness. "We love each other to the extent that we will die for each other. I've never said that before even though deep down, I knew it. To say it sounded so un-manly and felt like a threat to my sexuality. But now I know that love is a powerful force and declaring it seems wholly true and profoundly right. Our brotherhood is strong and our hearts are bonded together, not just because we have made a commitment to each other but because we *love* each other."

"And it is that very love that threatens the necrophim's existence", Serik said. "The necrophim fall powerless against your love because it was love that brought them into existence."

"Wait, you mean to say that they were created out of love?" Josiah asked.

"Yes. Long ago King Elyon had a very special garden. This garden yielded the most beautiful flowers, foliage and fruits. There was one tree in the center of the garden, which yielded a special fruit. The tree was called the Birthing Tree. King Elyon would draw blood from his finger and place a droplet on the center of the leaves of the Birthing Tree. Each leaf would curl around the drop of blood to form a protective pod. After three days, the pod opened to release an amazingly beautiful winged creature known as Venustas. This tiny creature transforms into full maturity moments after their pod opens. The Venustas were born out of the deeply loving act of the King, who sacrificially yielded over his life blood so that they could exist. This powerful love enabled the Venustas to bring healing to the heart, body and soul of the person over which they sang. The breath from the Venustas on which their song was carried, when breathed in by the individual, generated new life. Ubilaz's rise to power began when he discovered a way to corrupt the Venustas. He learned that these spirits were created with minimal volition that could be bent to do the bidding of another master. The affect was avalanching and the entire host of Venustas fell under Lord Ubilaz's reign. When their volition changed, so did their power and beauty. The Venustas became the necrophim of today. Love brought them into existence and love threatens their existence. Unbeknown to the necrophim and Lord Ubilaz, these spirits became vulnerable to death and defeat by the single loving death act on the part of King Elyon."

"Victorium Morte!" Josiah said.

"That's correct, Josiah," Serik returned.

"But where is the Birthing Tree? Can more Venustas be created?" Josiah continued.

"Rumors like horses escaping a stable enflamed, run in frenzied panic, that the vile lord, in foxed intuition has learned secrets to generate necrophim in full form from the Birthing Tree. But he knows not where to find said tree, for the wise king has concealed the garden's location and has set a fierce guardian with flaming swords before the tree. Long has been the debate among the citizens of Salamgard and Eikondor regarding the whereabouts of good King Elyon's garden. These citizens wile away precious time fretting and plotting to find the flora treasure which never shall be found. The dilemma yielded from such mental frenzy is that the necrophim's origins and the birthing tree are but mere mythical legends," Lemuel added.

"This is also why Lord Ubilaz wants the Kalos Sapphire. With the increase of his power seven-fold, he may be able to ascertain the location of the garden. Sobering days lie ahead of Salamgard. It is crucial for you gentlemen to get to Asilo as quickly as possible to receive your commission as Ambassador Knights. Your role in the ensuing battle and the hope of Salamgard is crucial," Serik said.

As Serik finished his sentence, Lady Daesis entered the dining hall. "I dislike breaking up this intimate conversation but I must. Gentlemen, you need to dress for the gala celebration. I have seen to it that dress robes have been put in your rooms. Guests will begin to arrive in less than two hours."

The guys exited the great hall leaving Serik, Lemuel and Lady Daesis. The three watched as the four brothers ascended the stairs and disappeared into the hallway.

"Never has Salamgard seen four who exemplified the King's virtues so strongly and whose hearts were bound so closely, since the four of you," Lady Daesis said to Lemuel and Serik. "The bond that you two share with Lord Tobijah and Lord Kesh has been a promise of Salamgard's security."

"That is why these four young men are so important to the King. They will carry on the legacy," Serik said.

"Their knighthood alone is not the threat that the vile one fears," Lemuel responded. "These gents of virtue strong, with hearts entwined, shall serve the King and Salamgard beyond the role of Ambassador-Knights of King Elyon's realm."

"Their hearts are not just bound by love, they are bound by a unified intent purpose, of which will be revealed to them when they reach the King. They will learn that they will be their mentor's successors and the next great Knights of the Realm. Ubilaz has probably deduced this. He has always been aware that one day four young men each possessing one of the four high virtues would come into Salamgard to this end. He has watched many become great Ambassador knights but never four whose hearts were bound by the King in such a way as these. Lord Darash, Salamgard's faithful gatekeeper has been patiently watching and waiting for these four. Ubilaz will do all in his power to crush them, for where they go one, they go all," Serik responded.

CHAPTER
FIFTY

Guests from every part of Salamgard began to assemble on the garden grounds at Lord Lemuel's fortress high atop the City of Aanda. Victorium Morte was Salamgard's High Holiday. The band of brothers convened in the hallway outside of their bed chambers. Each donned the dress robes that had been prepared for them.

"These robes are pretty fine," Caden said. "They look like old world tuxedos."

"I think they look more like academic regalia with bow ties," Josiah replied as he pulled his collar to loosen it a bit.

"They still look really cool. I can't believe that they even have our crests embroidered on the front panels," Wes said.

"Well boys, I think we ought to join the party. Remember, have fun but stick close. I don't think that there will be any protectus blessing over us during the gala," Caden said.

"I'm so nervous. I think I'm going to throw up," Ian said as he took a deep breath and exhaled audibly. "There are probably a couple thousand people down there and we don't know if they are friend or foe. Half of them could be necrophim in disguise for all we know."

"I doubt that the necrophim would risk coming to a gala here in a fortress so heavily guarded," Wes said. "Just hang close buddy. Let's all agree that we won't ever be more than ten feet away from each other. And let's not forget that Serik, Lemuel and Clarion will be here too. Oh yeah, Clarion already went down with Maayin – she was looking smokin' hot."

"Okay, let do this," Caden said as he walked toward the staircase. He deliberately bumped into Ian with his shoulder, "You're looking - *smoking hot* – too," he said as he smiled and raised his eyebrows. Then he threw his arm around Ian's shoulder, "Don't worry bro, I've got your back."

He turned and faced his brothers, running his hands down the front of his lapel panels to smooth them, "My mentor is a freakin' war-yor." Caden mimicked in his best rap beat and gangsta moves, as he made his claim.

Caden's comic relief lightened the mood. The guys descended the stairs and before then reached the last step Ian had regained his confidence and was ready for a party.

Outside, the gala was in full swell. The sun began to set sending hues of red, orange and purple light across the sky and painting the wall of the cliff behind the orchestra. The ethereal glow of sunset was made more poetic by the countless fire flies that anticipated this moment to begin firing up. The patio and garden were filled with guests and dignitaries. All were dressed in fine holiday array. There were also many animals; beast and fowl alike, that regally mingled among the many guest.

The band of brothers stepped in synchronized cadence, out the leaded glass doors onto the patio. Their presence was immediately and visibly acknowledged by the ripple of whispers that went through the crowd. The Otherlanders had come into view and many guests positioned themselves to catch a glimpse or to ready themselves for a friendly conversation. As the guys walked across the terrace, they were met by Clarion and Lemuel.

"Ah, my distinguished guests, fill your bellies with our choice food. Eat and drink. Dance and be merry for this is the celebration of death's dark hold, broken and vanquished from our fears," Lemuel said. "There are many who would press in to meet you. Be at home." Lemuel didn't linger with them very long. He was ushered into another conversation with other guests.

"As you can see there are many here who are curious to engage with the *famed* Otherlanders, who have entered Salamgard just as Lemuel said," Clarion remarked. "If you become overwhelmed just catch my attention and I'll do my best to rescue you."

Clarion wore a deep purple gown. The top of the gown looked like it was laced with diamonds. The gown's hue and the sparkle of the diamond embroidery made her eyes shimmer a shade of violet. Her black hair fell in graceful curls against her white porcelain shoulders. Diamonds were mystically scattered all throughout her hair like stars against a black sky. It wasn't difficult for the guys to get lost in her beauty.

"I will be expecting a dance with each of you boys before the night is over." Clarion commanded as she pointed her motherly finger at each of them.

"Before the night is over" that phrase jolted Josiah's memory to the important task that faced him this evening. He remembered that he would have to make a life or death choice before the evening's celebration ended. Puerilis says that Sabedoria is a murderer and Sabedoria says that Puerilis is a liar intent on destroying them. Josiah's body suddenly went into alert as if an internal radar switch had been turned on. *She must be here I can feel her presence*, he thought. He panned the crowd looking for her, keeping a vigil watch.

The guys began to walk deeper into the crowd. As they did, many of the Citizens of Salamgard warmly escorted them into conversation. Josiah looked over to the terrace where the chefs had prepared the food tables. It was then that he saw Puerilis. She was coming in his direction. He felt a knot tighten in his stomach. He had hoped he wouldn't see either woman.

Like Clarion, Puerilis looked amazing. Josiah hadn't remembered her looking so beautiful, but instantly he was captivated by her beauty. As she came toward him, her red gown flowed behind, looking as if she were on fire. She met Josiah and before words could be exchanged, she seized him and kissed him as if they were long parted lovers.

"My only thoughts were of you, since our last meeting. Today is a holiday that is filled with love. This has made my heart long for you all the more," she said.

Josiah backed away, more out of the awkwardness of who may have been watching this exchange, than out of a desire to avoid her advances. Her red dress seemed to be alive as the color continuously changed from red to orange to yellow and back again. It actually looked like she was wearing fire. Around her neck was a crystal vile that had a reddish iridescent glow.

"Puerilis you are so very beautiful," Josiah said.

"You make me blush. You are so sweet to notice," she remarked.

"Uh-hem," Caden coughed loudly as if to get Josiah's attention. The three brothers stood behind Puerilis waiting to be introduced.

"Oh sorry, Puerilis these are my brothers, Caden, Ian and Wes," he said.

Each of the guys extended their hand in greeting. "Nice to meet you fine young men. I wish we could have met in the Pub but I had to leave rather urgently. Each of you looks so dashing this evening. I'm sure the women of Salamgard will be battling over you," Puerilis said. "I hope to get to know all of you very well, but right now I believe that Josiah owes me a dance." She turned and took Josiah's arm almost forcefully whisking him away from his friends and off to the dance floor.

"Why can't women back at MU battle over us?" Caden whispered. The boys laughed and grabbed goblets of Salamgard's finest libations as a server passed.

Josiah turned Puerilis around the dance floor. "You haven't told them about Sabedoria," Puerilis said to Josiah as they waltzed to the music.

"No, I would never put my brothers at risk. But I can feel Sabedoria's presence. She is here I know it."

"Then you must make your choice and take this," Puerilis said as she touched the iridescent crystal vile around her neck. "It contains a very powerful potion that will give you the ability to see invisible necrophim. You must listen to me and heed my words," she said as she grabbed his chin directing his attention forcibly into her eyes. "If Sabedoria is here, there are probably many necrophim all around us. She will murder you."

Josiah's mind rushed with the recall of Lord Lemuel doing the same thing to him. *Puerilis must be the right choice*, he thought.

Before Josiah could make any decision there was a tap on his shoulder. "May I cut into this dance," came a woman's voice behind him. He turned quickly, relieved to see Clarion. "I would love to dance with you Lord Nestor."

Josiah excused himself from the conversation with Puerilis and stepped into the music with his new dance partner. "She's very beautiful. I've never seen her in Salamgard, who is she?" Clarion asked.

"Just a girl that I met in the Pub when we came into Aanda," Josiah replied. He looked over Clarion's shoulder to see his brothers standing nearby chatting with Puerilis. Then he watched as Ian offered his arm to escort Puerilis onto the dance floor.

Josiah spun Clarion to the cadence. As he did he saw the full circumference of the dance floor. Maayin just rendezvoused with the guys holding a huge plate of food. On the next turn, Josiah realized that Wes was attempting to flag him over. "I think that the guys want to go get some food," Josiah said. "We promised each other that we would stay close, you know, just in case something was to happen."

"I think that is a very wise decision," Clarion commented as they exited the floor. Ian and Puerilis also returned to the group. Clarion quickly intervened on behalf of the brothers again.

"Come, my dear let's get something refreshing to drink. I'd love to get to know you," Clarion said to Puerilis.

"That would be wonderful," Puerilis returned as the two women walked away.

Maayin led the guys to the food tables, excited to be making a return trip. "That was some kiss Puerilis gave you," Wes said to Josiah as they walked through the crowd.

"Yeah, I can't say that I didn't enjoy it but it was a bit uncomfortable with everyone watching."

"Well you looked like you were having fun. She's a hottie!" Caden chimed in.

"Yeah, I guess," Josiah returned. The tone in his voice made Wes very aware that something was not right. He remembered hearing the same tone once before when Josiah's grandfather became ill. Josiah was worried that his grandfather would not be able to recover from his sickness or live through that night. The stress and worry in his voice sounded the same as it did now.

"Siah, something is not right with you," Wes said.

"Why, what makes you think that?" Josiah asked.

"Just this feeling I have deep in my heart. You're my brother and roommate, I think I know you well enough to sense when something is bothering you."

"What could be so wrong when a guy has two beautiful women who want him", Josiah returned, putting on his best smile. He couldn't hide the dimness of his fallen countenance, which replaced the joyful glimmer that earlier shown in his eyes.

"Two beautiful women? Which two beautiful women want you?" Caden asked.

Josiah was a bit caught off guard. He didn't want them to know about Sabedoria.

"You don't mean Puerilis and . . . Clarion, do you? You think Clarion is into you too?" Caden quickly questioned.

"Um, yeah! Exactly!" Josiah responded.

"Dude I don't think Clarion is interested in any of us. She's kind of become a sister to us," Ian returned. "I also think you should watch out for this Puerilis woman. I don't think she can go back home with you, like, if you became an item or something. You know what I mean. This could be an impossible long distance relationship so you better guard your heart."

"You're so right bro," Josiah said, hoping to end the probing conversation. "Let's eat. I don't know why, but I'm hungry again."

The guys sat and ate their meal, danced more and were delighted by the conversations and new friendships they were making. The festive mood was contagious and the fireflies kept the night twinkling.

The orchestra returned to the stage to begin the next set of dance music. The brothers were immediately mobbed by the women of Salamgard, each awaiting their turn to dance with the distinguished Otherlanders. One by one, the guys stepped on to the dance floor with a beautiful woman. Wes was the first to be invited to the dance by one of the Salamgard women. He was quickly joined by Ian and Caden, both of whom had new dance partners. Even Maayin gleaned from the attention that the guys were getting because he too was invited to dance by a young lady. Josiah smiled at his brothers as they each spun briskly on the floor. A few other women pressed in to have their chance to dance with the last Otherlander not on the floor. Josiah looked into the faces of the women, and then he saw her.

Sabedoria walked slowly through the group of women who willingly parted for her. Her beauty far excelled the women at the gala. She wore a deep blue gown, the same blue as Josiah's coat and Lemuel's crest. She was heavily adorned with necklaces and bracelets of silver and gold that glistened with every step she took. The breeze of the evening caught her auburn hair as she now stood face to face with Josiah.

Josiah immediately knew who this woman was because he so vividly saw her in his dream. He felt that he had known her very well. As much as Josiah thought he could battle her strong sway; he succumbed and was completely drawn in by her. "Sabedoria!" he said.

"I think this is our dance," she said. Without saying a word, Josiah graciously held out his hand mesmerized by her beauty. She coyly accepted and they both stepped onto the dance floor.

CHAPTER
FIFTY-ONE

Serik stood in the middle of a group of guests on the patio of the gala. From his point of view, he could see the four brothers on the dance floor. They looked like they were having a great evening. Serik sipped a bit of the cordial from the goblet in his hand. *These young men should enjoy the evening because troubled times lie ahead,* he thought.

As he resumed the conversation with the guests, Lemuel stepped into the circle and interrupted.

"A word, mighty Conciliator," he said. Serik bade his guests leave, and followed the Sage who was clutching his staff and walking at a brisk pace. He followed Lord Lemuel to the rooftop terrace. The aroma of the food below, mixed with the scent of honeysuckle from the hanging floral garden gave a sweet ambiance to the bitter intensity that would shape this meeting. From the top corner of the rooftop terrace, Serik and Lemuel could see the entire gala.

"I fear that the trouble may have already begun," Lemuel said as he pointed to the scene below. "The young sage is entangled in her arms like a python around a boar's belly. He must make his choice within the next hour."

From the other side of the garden they could see Puerilis began moving through the crowd toward the dance floor. She grabbed Maayin who stood on the side watching the dance. The lad was surprised and delighted as they both stepped onto the dance floor and followed the flow of the stream of dancers. Puerilis stepped quicker attempting to move closer to Josiah and Sabedoria. She knew that she needed to get to Josiah as quickly as possible without drawing any attention to the situation.

Clarion also stood at the side of the dance. She saw Puerilis making her move and turned to see the stately figures of Lord Lemuel and Lord Serik standing sentry above the celebration. Serik whispered something, his lips moving at times without an utterance of sound. He was speaking to Clarion. She watched intently, nodded and quickly walked to the side hedges where she retrieved her hidden bow and quiver. Serik slowly withdrew his dagger from his side scabbard and held it concealed in his cape.

"I fear that blood may again flow rich and red on this hallowed day", Lemuel said. "Our response shall require split second timing and precision". Then the Sage exited the rooftop to take his place strategically, in the garden below.

CHAPTER
FIFTY-TWO

Josiah held this beautiful creature in his arms. Dancing with Sabedoria felt so natural. He could see his band of brothers dancing with their partners, all around him. They were close enough in proximity that they felt safe from any danger.

"Josiah I have longed to be in your embrace," she said as she pressed her body against his. Josiah pushed away, leaving room between him and her like two teens who had been scolded by nuns at a catholic school dance. It was so difficult to do because the allure of this beautiful woman was intoxicating and Josiah never wanted any woman more than he wanted her right now.

"I alone can give you sight," she whispered. "Puerilis is a liar who plans to destroy you. If you choose me, I will give you a pair of spectacles that when worn will allow you to see the necrophim. Choose now and you will have sight. If you do not choose me, death is inevitable."

Her words cut through him but he couldn't help but desire her more. The turning of the dance and the sweet fragrance of Sabedoria's hair continued to break down Josiah's defenses.

Puerilis was moving in as fast as she could without drawing attention. She knew that she needed to intervene before Sabedoria persuaded Josiah's choice. Maayin, oblivious to what was happening enjoyed the adventure of the rapid pace at which Puerilis took the dance.

Out of the corner of her eye, Sabedoria could see Puerilis moving closer. She spun Josiah so that his back was now to the pursuant maiden. Sabedoria pulled Josiah close again. This time he didn't resist but rather embraced her boldly causing her to exhale with a groan.

Sabedoria pressed her warm soft cheek against his face. Josiah closed his eyes and inhaled the sweet perfume of this woman as he buried his face in her hair. Her ruby lips pressed softly against his ear. "You shall never resist me, it is I whom you seek," she said. Then in the middle of the dance floor, she seized him and kissed him as passionately as Puerilis had when the evening began.

As she did this the music of the dance ended and the guests applauded as the dance floor became a sea of individuals blocking Puerilis' trajectory. Sabedoria quickly exited leaving Josiah standing alone in the center of the floor with his eyes closed.

Puerilis headed toward Josiah but she was suddenly intercepted by Ian. "Hey Puerilis I'd really like to dance with you again. Can I have the next dance?" he said.

As Ian talked with her, she noticed that Caden and Wes were now at Josiah's side. It became clear to her that Josiah had not made his choice. The music began to swell again as Wes and Caden walked off the dance floor with Josiah. Puerilis looked at Ian for a moment and then smiled. "Sure Ian, I'd love to dance with you," she said as they fell into step with the others who were joining the new dance.

"What the heck is going on Siah? Women are passionately kissing you and yet you look demoralized," Caden said.

"I am," Josiah returned. "I can't do this alone. You guys have to help me." The dread in his voice made Caden and Wes alert that something terrible was happening.

"Bro, tell us what's happening?" Wes said and both he and Caden stepped in inexplicably close. Each supported Josiah's arms because he looked as if he would fall over.

"I was told not to say anything by Puerilis because it would put you in great danger."

Caden tightened his grip on Josiah's arm and said, "Where we go one, we go all. I'm getting Ian over here." He started to walk away to pull Ian from the dance when Josiah grabbed his arm.

"Wait, I'm ok," Josiah said.

"What is it that you have to do; that you think you need to do alone?" Wes asked.

Josiah told Wes and Caden about the decision that he needed to make. "If I choose wrong, I will die tonight," he said.

"Then don't choose," Wes stated frantically.

"I don't have the luxury to not choose. Even Lord Lemuel told me that I must make this deadly choice before the evening ends and that's about to happen in ten minutes."

"Then we fight," Caden stated.

"Caden, when we first started this journey you said that you would die for us. Well I would do the same. And my life to save you three is far better than all of us dying. Besides, nobody needs to die at all. I can end this by making the wisest choice."

Lemuel moved close to the guys. Josiah saw him and immediately called him into their huddle for advice.

"Lord Lemuel I need Elyon's wisdom. Tell me what choice to make."

The dance and gaiety of the celebration swirled all around the guys. Suddenly a beautiful song broke out. Sabedoria was on stage with the orchestra, singing her magnetic song. Josiah raised his hand to his temple as if he was nursing a migraine headache. The words were bouncing wildly in his head.

" *JEROCH NESTUM. AIEROCH TU AE VISHLO VEC. UBEL LIST TRA GORBU CORDUM. SAESA VERDU ILRAN QUEL. OOMAT KAI DOLETH BELDORUM.*"

Lemuel grabbed Josiah's chin again making him focus his attention away from the music.

"Your choice is clear as the crystal. Take heed and listen. Trust that your brow has been crowned by so great a King, with discernment and wisdom," the old Sage Knight replied.

Josiah stood up straight. "I have to do this now, guys," he said.

"We're staying right here next to you," Wes assured.

Josiah closed his eyes and began to think out loud. "Lord Lemuel said to listen. He told me the same thing when I was with him last night. Puerilis also told me to listen," his voice pitched and his words became rapid. "She even grabbed my face to remind me to focus on her, like Lord Lemuel did– she must be the right choice."

Sabedoria's song swelled a little louder. Josiah opened his eyes to see her in all her beauty singing on the stage. The lure was powerful. He closed his eyes again.

"Sabedoria told me that I have been *seeking* her – but she was the one seeking me." Josiah stopped as if he had a new revelation. "Lord Lemuel told me to seek wisdom like I would a desirous woman. He also said that both wisdom and foolishness would be like alluring women who would try to seduce me. One will lead to life the other destruction. Listen . . . listen," Josiah reminded himself attempting to solve the life threatening riddle that faced him.

Josiah took a deep breath and bowed his head. "I will trust that King Elyon will give me his wisdom," he said. Then he exhaled in peaceful repose. He could hear Sabedoria's beautiful song. He listened intently. Then, over the melody, he began to hear a whisper of the ancient song being translated in his ears. It was the soft sweet voice of Sabedoria.

CHAPTER FIFTY-TWO

*"JOSIAH NESTOR. I AM WISDOM WHOM YOU SEEK.
I'LL DELIVER YOU FROM STRIFE. CHOOSE ME NOW ERE
EVENING PEAKS. YOU SHALL SEE AND RESCUE LIFE."*

Wes and Caden stood silent and close, looking absorbedly into Josiah's face. He was still and they could see the full action of the dance floor clearly mirrored in his metallic headband. The dancing guests twirled across Josiah's head. The panorama on Josiah's brow was interpreted when the guys saw a reflection of Josiah standing in the center of the dance floor. *How could this be since he was right in front of them?*

Wes glanced over at Caden who affirmed that he was seeing the same thing. They watched the scenario continue to unfold in the reflected headband. Josiah began to walk off the dance floor where he extended his hand to Sabedoria. She graciously accepted and they embraced in a sweet kiss.

Josiah opened his eyes to look into the concerned faces of Wes and Caden. "Its Sabedoria! I must choose Sabedoria. I hope that's the wise decision?"

Wes and Caden's eyes grew large with wonder. "It is, Sabedoria!" Wes exclaimed.

"Yeah, that's right," said Caden. "The headband, we saw it in the headband – it's glowing now!"

"There is an inscription that's beginning to appear," Wes said.

"Hurry, tell me what it says. We only have a few minutes," Josiah stated.

"It says – *Only when others affirm a man's wisdom will that man know he is wise*", Wes read out loud. "Buddy, Sabedoria is the right choice!"

Josiah smiled, "Lord Lemuel told me that I will know when Elyon gives me wisdom. I guess now I know how that will happen."

Josiah briskly walked to the stage as Sabedoria finished her song. "I choose wisdom – I choose you," Josiah said. Sabedoria threw her arms around Josiah and hugged him. "I thought you were evil," he said.

"Things aren't always as they seem. That is why wisdom must guide you," she replied.

Wes and Caden came walking in their direction. "I guess he made the right choice, she didn't kill him; he's still alive," Caden joked.

Sabedoria handed Josiah a pair of glasses. "Quickly, put these on you will need them to avert death."

"I thought I averted my death when I chose you."

"No, your wise choice allowed you to discern or see things that others cannot so that you could avert death. You assumed it to be your own death."

Josiah put the glasses on then gasped and quickly pulled them off his face.

"What did you see?" Caden asked.

"The place is crawling with necrophim. About a third of the guests here are really necrophim in disguise." Then he became panicked. "Where's Ian. Ian isn't with us."

The guys frantically looked through the crowd. Ian was nowhere to be seen but Josiah spotted Puerilis. She lowered her head, bared her teeth in a wicked smile and leered at him as she backed away through the crowd. Josiah quickly put the glasses on. Puerilis' beauty immediately gave way to her true form: a grotesque necrophim. Puerilis was Gath in disguise. He laughed at Josiah and then disappeared into the crowd of celebrants and necrophim.

"Ian!" Josiah yelled.

"Where is he?" Caden called frantically as he pushed his way through the crowd who were more of a deterrent than help.

Lemuel looked up to Serik and then over to Clarion. Everyone was ready. He raised his staff and then pummeled it in a single blow against the earth. As he did his booming voice yelled, *"Visum Fidelis"*. That sent a visible shock wave of blue light rippling away from his staff. The waved passed through everyone giving the faithful citizens of Salamgard and the band of brothers the ability to see the invisible necrophim. Caden and Wes stood abruptly halted in their tracks at the grotesque sight.

As soon as the necrophim were visible, Serik brandished his sword. Clarion quickly armed her bow and about two hundred of the other guests who were knights of Elyon's realm, bared their arms. The sight of this show of force made the necrophim, in one accord, dissipate in an explosion of red mist. Gath was the only one who stood defiantly next to Ian who sat slumped against a garden wall of the patio across the grounds from Wes, Caden and Josiah. Gath laughed and then disappeared in a cloud of red mist.

The band of brothers rushed to Ian who sat still, his eyes glazed over in shock. In Ian's hand was the vile that hung around Puerilis' neck. It was empty. Clarion pried the vile from Ian's hand as Josiah yelled, "Did you drink that? Ian talk to me, did you drink that potion?"

Clarion raised the vile to her nose and sniffed. "This is raxin venom, a deadly poison. There is no antidote."

Josiah grabbed Ian's robes, "Ian look at me, LOOK AT ME. Did you drink that potion?"

Ian still remained catatonic. He began to drool as his eyes dimmed and started to slowly, close. Caden plopped down on the ground in disbelief and helplessness. Wes' eyes began to well up with the thought that they may watch their brother slowly and pain-fully die.

Then Josiah in a fit of frustration, still holding two fists full of Ian's robe, punched his hands into Ian's chest, "Come on Ian, an-swer me!" Ian blinked and started to regain his composure.

"Ian, Ian, tell me you didn't drink that potion," Josiah said with a new hope in his voice. Caden quickly turned to see Ian coming out of his stupor. Wes knelt down and placed his hand on Ian's shoulder to steady him. Ian looked at his brothers one by one as if trying to remember who they were. Then he shook his head as his memory began to return.

Ian wiped his mouth with his sleeve, "No, I didn't drink it. Puerilis handed it to me and promised I would see the necrophim. As I raised the vile to my lips, I was hit with a blue light and Puerilis transformed into a repulsive necrophim. I remembered that the necrophim had to transform into their natural state before they killed. The horror of that creature made me spill the vile all over the ground, and then I don't remember anything else after that."

"Your fear caused you to black out," Serik said.

The guys helped Ian to his feet. Caden laughed with joy and hugged Ian so hard lifting him off the ground. The four guys embraced in relief and joy. Clarion sighed and Maayin brushed tears from his face as sorrow was replaced by joy.

"I think the night has ended well," Serik said.

"That it has dear friend," said Lemuel as he produced a lantern. *"Presidium Electus,"* he said and the lantern glowed with the protectus blessing. "We shall retire well."

CHAPTER
FIFTY-THREE

Early the next morning before the sun started its ascent across the skies of Salamgard, the band of brothers began to assemble in the great entrance hall of Lemuel's fortress.

Clarion was the first to descend the grand staircase. Her bow was slung across her back next to a quiver full of arrows. She was lacing on her leather arm guards in final preparation for the journey. Caden was right behind her, which was unusual since mornings were so difficult for him.

"I didn't expect you to be the first down this morning," Clarion commented. "You appear to be bright and cheery - an odd early morning surprise."

"I'm going to meet my mentor today and I'm pretty amped about that," he replied with a smile and a spring in his step.

Ian and Josiah were already descending the stairs and overheard Caden's remarks. "You'll meet your mentor today . . . if we can find him," Josiah remarked.

"Serik said that Tobijah will find us! Besides, I'm a very determined guy. I'm confident that we'll connect today."

Josiah had his staff in hand. The silver headband was still on his head and the discerning glasses were in his pocket. He looked ready for the journey but Ian on the other hand looked like he had a rough night.

"Ian, are you well?" Clarion asked. "You still look a bit distraught."

"I didn't sleep very well. I had nightmares of that hideous creature staring in my face. Necrophim are vile ugly things. I kept waking up to that memory and I guess I'm just worried about the journey too," he replied.

"You needn't worry. There is enough faith all around you, to carry you through this experience," Clarion replied.

Lady Daesis entered the hall. She was carrying two large backpacks. "These are filled sufficiently with enough food to sustain you until you get to Lord Tobijah's camp," she said as she handed the packs to Ian and Caden. They both secured them across their backs. Serik and Lemuel joined them from an entrance off the grand hall as Wes and Maayin came down the stairs. Wes had his dagger strapped to his side and his shield was positioned across his back, framing the young man in a metallic halo.

"Today you will embark on a dangerous journey," Serik said. "Ubilaz most likely has the news of Gath's failed attempt to destroy you. He most likely will have already put into motion other schemes to insure your destruction. My inclination is that he probably alerted every ferocious beast loyal to him, with orders to kill you on sight."

"Ferocious beasts are flesh and blood so we can fight against them, right?" Ian inquired with a bit of tremble. The events of the previous evening lingered in his memory. He was still visibly unnerved by the entire experience.

"That's correct, my son," Serik said. "But I'm afraid that it will not be as easy a task as you think. The beasts of the woods are combat trained. They stalk in a far more purposeful way then just hunting prey. Given your weapons and Clarion's expert archery skills, you may be able to hold your ground. But unless Tobijah's forces intervene in any battle, the outcome shall not fall favorably for you."

"That's comforting to know," Ian said looking a bit pale from the news.

"Your primary objective is to get over the Sargo Mountain range and head straight northeast through Ithcar as quickly as you can. The cover of darkness until the morning sun breaks will be in your favor. You should be able to get far if you keep a good pace. Tobijah will intercept you in Ithcar. He knows to be watching for you. Move as quickly and alertly as possible, until you connect with Tobijah's warriors."

"How was it that the necrophim could get so close to us last night? Will the necrophim be after us too? I thought that they were powerless when we were in community?" Ian asked.

"Powerless are the spirits rendered when they enter love encircled, but enter they still may. They weave a cloak of deception by their daring to taunt so great, that love. Gath did prove the lengths that wickedness will go to relish your destruction. Had you not been in delimited love, Gath's emergence from Puerilis fair, like the quick turn of a coin, would have scored the intent to snatch your soul with deadly breath," Lemuel replied.

"I think I'm going to be sick again," Ian said under his breath.

"I'm still trusting that Elyon will protect us," Wes said.

"So do I," Josiah chimed in.

Serik looked at Maayin who was desperately trying not to be noticed by standing behind Wes, slightly peering around his shield. Maayin knew that he wasn't allowed to embark on this journey with his new friends but he came dressed and ready to go, in the off chance that the opportunity presented itself.

"My boy, I am afraid that you must stay here," Serik said.

"Please my Lord, I can fight," Maayin cried as he boldly stepped into view. His thirteen year old frame looked a bit more adult-like from the confidence that he had gained by being in this loving community. Far different from when they first met him.

Wes still had to bend down slightly to look the lad directly in the eyes. "Maayin, we talked about this already. I know that you are afraid that you will be abandoned but Lord Lemuel and Lady Daesis will care for you. They will be your new family and this will be your new house. And if it is possible I will return to you."

Maayin grabbed hold of Wes' wrist. "I want to go with you," his lip quivered as he fought back tears. "I will be your armor bearer. I will fight and die for you. Please my lord, don't bid me stay here." Maayin's eyes welled up and his voice broke as he spoke. He began to feel the same overwhelming grief that he experienced when Ubilaz murdered his family.

"You must stay with Lord Lemuel. I would never be able to forgive myself if something happened to you," Wes replied.

Lady Daesis stepped over to Maayin and placed her hands on his shoulders to reassure him of her loving support. "You will not return," he cried to Wes as he pulled away from Daesis' embrace and bounded up the stairs to return to his bed chamber.

"Maayin . . ." Wes yelled and he began to follow, when Serik stopped him.

"Let the boy grieve. He has tasted the richness of your love. Its absence is an indication that your care is powerfully impacting. He will taste the same again with an understanding that you Wes, created the standard by which he will measure love," Serik said.

"It's best a Vitatha lad return to peddling his wares in Aanda's city walls than to venture into harm's way in Ithcar. He shall come to know safe abode here," Lemuel added. "But now you must take your leave in haste. It is more prudent and shall save you steps to pass over the Sargo range from the back garden."

The entourage followed Lemuel out the terrace doors. At the top of the stairs, Maayin sat weeping having heard their final words and watched his friends leave. "I shall not stay here," he said to himself as he wiped his nose on his silken sleeve. "I shall join up with my master Wes and his brothers on the other side of the mountain." Maayin quickly and quietly bounded down the stairs and exited through the massive front doors of Lemuel's fortress.

CHAPTER
FIFTY-
FOUR

The sun reached its apex high above the towering trees over Ithcar Valley. The band of brothers and Clarion had been hiking for over six hours. Clarion kept them at a brisk pace with an understanding that the guys looked able bodied enough to handle the rigors of this trek. She knew that it was crucial for them to get as far into Ithcar as their legs could carry them so that if a battle incurred, Tobijah could be close at hand.

Despite the tree cover, the warm sun still did its job to raise the guys' body temperatures and impair their pace. They came upon a stream that cascaded in rapid falls as it ran from the mountainous slopes above them.

"We must find a place to cross," Clarion said. "And if my memory serves me correctly, there is a place just up the way where the stream shallows and the rocks in the center of the running water can serve as a cool resting place as well as a place to pass. Let's press on to that point and we will stop to enjoy the refreshment that Lady Daesis prepared for us."

Ian and Caden had forgotten that there was food in the backpacks that they carried, although they hadn't forgotten the backpacks. The weight of the packs reminded them of the burden that clung to their shoulders. But now the thought of food, rest and the dipping in the refreshing cool water of the rushing stream gave them new energy.

Clarion blazed the trail along the flowing waters. As they walked to the point of crossing, the water's flow became louder and louder. The sight of the crystal running water taunted the guys to stop and plop in while it poured over their bodies. They finally got to the place where they could cross. Clarion looked around, then pressed her calling charm to her lips and blew. Within minutes, a number of sparrows, finches, squirrels, chipmunks, skunks and a small spider monkey appeared. Clarion smiled and began her mystically skilled communication. As fast as the creatures appeared, was as fast as they departed. The guys looked on in wonder.

"I asked them to scatter and keep watch while we rested. They will let us know if danger approaches. We can rest peacefully," she said.

"Great!" Caden said as he slipped the backpack from his back. "I'm starving but before I eat, I'm getting cooled down by this stream." He removed his boots and socks, then peeled off his clothes down to his pewter gray boxer briefs. He figured that his boxers were adequate swim wear for Salamgard and didn't mind if Clarion was present. It didn't take an invitation to get the brothers to lose their inhibitions and all follow his example. Half naked the guys waded carefully into the center of the cold water as it rushed around their legs. The force of the current was more powerful than they anticipated it would be, only making this experience more tantalizing. Caden stopped in the middle of the stream where a large boulder created a waterfall above him. He pushed his head under the fall and gave out a loud gasping shriek as the icy water hit his head and spilled down his back.

Clarion unpacked the lunch while the guys became rejuvenated by the life giving current of the stream. Wes stood in the middle of the stream and looked up the mountain to where the stream began its journey. The waters seemed to come out of nowhere as it cut through the brilliant green tints of the trees leaving a gap for the bright blue hued sky to be seen.

"I'm grabbing my lunch and I'm going to sit on that rock up there," Wes said as he pointed to a place where he could comfortably rest and let the water cascade over his waist. One by one, the guys found a place where they could do the same and enjoy the delicious meal that Daesis prepared for them.

Clarion removed her boots and waded in to let her feet be refreshed. She dared not remove her bow and quiver lest her scouts alert her and the company in her care, fell prey to an ambush or some other evil that threatened to overtake them. Wes and Josiah on the other hand, not being versed in the art of warfare, left their weapons setting on the side of the stream next to their clothes.

Wes was highest upstream from his brothers. He could look down and see Caden, sprawled on his back across a rock, his fair skin already starting to turn lobster red from the sun. Caden lay with his arm across his face to shield his eyes from the sunlight. Josiah sat just below Caden with his back to Wes. The young sage was straddling a rock, with both legs, up to his knees in the flowing water. Ian stood a short distance downstream from Josiah. He splashed water against his chest and face then amused himself by casting stones into a pool created by a waterfall below him. Clarion stood on the opposite bank of the stream from Ian, having waded into the water up to her shins. The guy's clothes and contents of the backpacks littered the stream side behind her. She ate a piece of fruit while she stood listening to the forest's conversations.

"This is the life!" Wes said.

"What?" Caden yelled as he peeked from under his forearm up at Wes who was slightly hidden in the blinding sunlight. He squinted enough to adequately see Wes and the distinct mark Serik left on his chest. Caden sat up to get a clearer view without being blinded by the light. As his eyes focused, he became fearful of what he thought he was seeing.

"I said, this is the life," Wes yelled. Caden quickly rose to his feet as horror was written over his face.

"What's wrong with you," Wes said now feeling a bit panicked. Caden quickly glanced to see Wes' shield and dagger over on the side of the stream, well out of his reach. His mind strategically calculated how he could lay hold of them. Caden promptly held his finger to his lips indicating for Wes to be still and quiet. On the rocks above Wes stood a six hundred pound, ten foot long, white tiger.

Not heeding Caden's directive, in one rapid motion, Wes instinctively stood upright and turned to see what was behind him. The tiger let out a great roar and pounced. Wes fell backwards into the water and the tiger landed a paw on his bare chest, powerfully pinning him down. The sound of the tiger's roar made Josiah and Ian turn in panic. It also sent Clarion into action. In a single motion with both hands, she grabbed her bow in one and an arrow from her back in another and then spun to take aim at their foe.

"Themba!" Clarion shrieked with delight as she lowered her bow. Wes lay under the cat's strong paw unhurt but he could feel his heart beating at a precarious rate. The shallow cold water from the stream still pelted his body. From this vantage point on his back in the water, Wes could see King Elyon's fleury cross on the breast of the snow white cat.

"Themba, the young man under your paw is Wes Litchfield and this is Caden Boyd, Josiah Nestor and Ian Bound," Clarion stated.

"Gentlemen, this is Lord Themba. He is a commander in Tobijah's company and a Knight of King Elyon's realm."

The tiger snarled at Wes then bowed graciously releasing him from under his powerful clutches. Wes stood up quickly but didn't know where to go or what to do, as he tried to steady himself against the streams current.

"You needn't be afraid, Wes," Clarion called. "Tobijah sent Themba ahead of the company to scout us out. He will escort us to the Warrior Knight's camp which is in the thick of the forest, an hour's journey that direction." Themba motioned with his head in the direction of the camp as Clarion pointed in the same direction beyond Ian.

"You boys should get dressed and we should quickly get to camp," she commanded.

The guys immediately obliged her but Wes still stood unmoved next to the great cat. His heart rate was deescalating and his breathing was coming back to normal.

"You really know how to scare a guy," he said to the tiger.

Themba purred and rubbed his face against Wes' belly just as a house cat would, against its owner's leg when it wanted to be lovingly caressed. Gingerly, Wes reached down and buried his hand in the white fur behind Themba's ear, to affectionately scratch. The cat gave out a little grunt of glee and pushed his face more pronouncedly into Wes' abdomen causing him to laugh and become a bit unbalanced.

"Tobijah is waiting for us. We'll resume the loving when we get to camp," Wes said as he exited the stream. The band of brothers quickly dressed and got back on the trail. The white tiger walked by Wes' side. Wes kept his hand on his new friend's head occasionally giving him an affectionate scratch.

CHAPTER
FIFTY-FIVE

Maayin pushed his way through the trail. He had been following his new brothers at an undetectable pace. But he had begun to tire about an hour earlier and lost sight of the group. His thigh muscles burned from the hike and he began to feel the effects of having no food and water. Sweat beaded on his brow as he determined to catch his friends. He looked ahead into the trees but could no longer see where his friends were. His lips were parched and dry and the humidity of the forest bed along with the rising heat began to make him feel faint. He pulled his shirt off and tied the silk sleeves around his forehead to serve as a bandana. The body of the shirt covered the back of his neck and shoulders to shield him from sun. Since he could no longer see his friends, he began to fret. The shadows of the woods became more menacing in his mind. He picked up a large stick, *this shall serve as a very good weapon,* he thought.

As Maayin stood among the trees attempting to get his bearing, he heard the thunderous roar of a tiger in the distance. So great was the roar, that it shook him. He didn't know if he should run toward it in a rescuing attempt to save his friends who may be in peril or if he should run away from it in fear that he may become the main course of some wild beast's lunch menu. Instead, he stood frozen in his tracks. Then he faintly heard Clarion's voice and laughter. He couldn't quite make out what she was saying but he knew that she didn't sound like she was in danger.

I shall follow her voice, he concluded. The lad was happy that he regained his sense of direction. He headed toward Clarion's voice but after a short while, he could no longer hear anything. He stood still on the trail, attempting to relocate her conversation. Nothing! Yet, undeterred he decided to follow the trail he was on in the direction that he assumed Clarion and his friends had traveled. He could hear the rushing water of the stream and knew that they may have stopped to be refreshed.

Maayin pulled the knot in the silken sleeves of his bandanna tighter and mustered up a new surge of energy to plod forward. *They can't be too much farther ahead. Any moment now, I will see them.* His mind assessed the day long journey he had already made. *I will not be afraid. I have come a long way by myself without a caravan. Surely, I am a man, for only a man could do such a thing,* he thought. His new sense of invincibility made him naive of the danger that lurked close by.

Perched high above the boy in a tall tree sat Venem, watching Maayin's every move. The necrophim had only been there a few short seconds having just arrived from making another pass through Ithcar. He had arrived too late to hear the tiger's roar and was unaware that the band of brothers was very well within his grasp. He also didn't realize that Tobijah was closer than he imagined.

What brings a Vitatha boy way out to the middle of the Ithcar Valley? He is a long way from any of the refuge cities, Venem thought keeping his watchful eye on the boy. *Maybe he has strayed from a troubadour caravan.* Venem looked around but could not see any signs or traces of any other life, let alone a caravan.

This is odd . . . but significant. He must have strayed from Tobijah's camp. That seemed to be the only logical conclusion, which made Venem shiver with glee. *I must quickly alert Avah.*

The necrophim scout flew away almost at the speed of sound, stirring the leaves of the trees and leaving his red mist high above Maayin's head. Maayin heard the rustle of the trees, but felt no wind. He looked around but didn't see anything. The lad was too young and unskilled to think of looking overhead for the residual of the necrophim. Convinced that there was nothing to be alarmed about, Maayin continued to follow the trail right to the place where the guys had entered the stream.

Before departing for Tobijah's camp, Clarion had emptied the backpack leaving a remnant of fruit for her woodland scout friends to feast on. Maayin happened to get to it first. *They were here. I know they are close by,* he thought. He was overcome with excitement, first to have food and secondly that he was back on the trail of his friends. He sat on the bank of the stream eating and scoping out his travel options. He identified the place in the stream where he could easily cross and where the trail picked up on the other bank.

They must have gone across, he thought. He strained to see if he could catch a glimpse of them but they were out of sight. *They cannot be far. I will catch them. Wes will be glad to see me. I know he will.*

Maayin stood up to resume his pursuit when a cramp violently seized his leg. He let out a cry as the pain pushed him back to the ground. The lad rubbed his leg in an attempt to massage out the knot. *I cannot go on, I must rest for a while. After I rest, I will be able to run to catch them.*

Many miles away, at the top of the Sargo mountain range, Venem met up with Avah and Raith who were interrogating some of the forest inhabitants.

"Your presence annoys me, Venem", Avah disclosed as he held a terrified badger in his clutches. "So unless you have some pertinent news you should leave."

Venem was as disgusted to be in Avah's presence as Avah was in his. Venem had a moment of bliss again thinking of the necrophim and hyena sitting in the frigid air on top of Mount Aphesis as sentries. "I believe that my discovery is pertinent," he said.

"You *believe* it to be pertinent? Well is it or isn't it?" Avah shouted.

"I have spotted a Vitatha boy roaming the Ithcar Valley. I think he lost his way from Tobijah's camp."

Venem suddenly had Avah's attention. "Raith I believe we have found the break we were looking for," Avah said. The hyena let out a spine chilling cackle indicating that he thought the lead wasn't worth pursuing.

"It is worth pursuing my ugly friend. Two days ago, I stood atop of the City walls of Aanda and watched the Otherlanders befriend a Vitatha boy. Gath also told Daemonicus and I that a Vitatha boy accompanied the Otherlanders to Lemuel's gala. I believe that Gath *danced* with the boy", Avah said with a disgusting tone. "I would bet my rank as one of Lord Ubilaz's captains that the boy Venem located is the same boy."

You'll bet your rank as captain? If only . . . Venem lustfully thought.

"If we find the boy we will find the Otherlanders and the Warrior Knight Tobijah. That means the Kalos gem may not be too far away," Avah commented. Again, the hyena laughed his evil laugh.

"That's right, Raith this is important enough to stop what we are doing and investigate. Take us to him quickly," Avah barked as he threw the badger aside. The badger scurried away quickly in the underbrush.

Venem led Avah in flight down the mountain range into the Valley of Ithcar faster than Raith could run. The necrophim knew that they needed to find and keep watch on the lad until Raith could meet up with them.

They came to the exact location where Venem had left Maayin. "He was right here when I left, less than half an hour past. He was walking the trail so if we follow that path we will come on him. He should not have gotten far," Venem stated.

"He should not have gotten far?" Avah mocked. "He should not have gotten far unless Tobijah found him first and brought him under that cursed cloaking blessing you dimwitted necro-phim. Didn't you think to alert one of our scouts to keep watch?" Avah scolded.

Venem was feeling like he had failed. He could see his dream of becoming captain slipping into the darkness of his wicked mind again. Then he spotted the glisten of the boy's silk shirt through the trees.

"He is down there," Venem said with an air of assurance as his dreams came rushing back in along with his confidence.

The two necrophim perched in the tree above and watched as the young lad slept. The rigor of the six hour hike had taken its toll on the young teen's body. He couldn't help but fall asleep from sheer exhaustion.

Avah signaled directions to Raith who arrived as quickly as his hyena legs could carry him. As the lad lay sleeping against a rock, Avah and Venem transfigured into their visible forms and quietly crouched on the rock above Maayin's head. Raith came into the clearing and slinked close to the sleeping boy.

The peaceful slumber of the lad juxtaposed against the violent horror that crept up against him made Venem shiver with excite-ment to be a part of such a vile momentous encounter.

The hyena slowly pushed his snout millimeters from Maayin's face. Raith's razor sharp teeth were bared. The blacken tartar on his gums glistened with slobbering saliva that began to accumu-late from his appetite for malevolence. His hot rank breath and wet nose began to make the boy stir. Raith gave out a deep bellied monstrous laugh that jolted Maayin awake.

The boy screamed at the sight of the hyena's incisors inched from his face. He threw is head back to escape the hyena's snarl only to catch sight of the two grotesque necrophim hovering overhead. The horror that surrounded the boy caused him to faint in utter fear.

"Curses, we shall have to wait until he recovers to question him," Avah said.

"You think that was a bit over the top?" Venem asked.

"Must you always be so heinously sensational, Raith?" Avah scolded, passing the blame.

Raith backed away and Avah jumped down to rouse the boy by slapping his cheek. Slowly Maayin regained consciousness to discover that the horror he experienced was a reality.

"Where is the Kalos sapphire?" Avah yelled.

"I don't know what you are talking about," Maayin cried.

"Then tell us where Tobijah's camp is, or I will let my friend the hyena eat you alive; starting with your arms and legs."

"I . . . don't know . . . any Tobijah. I was . . . looking . . . for my friends," the boy heaved with fear as he sobbed out his statement.

"Your friends? You are friends with the Otherlanders, aren't you?"

"No! I was separated from a caravan of troubadours," Maayin hoped that his lie was convincing.

"LIAR!" Venem yelled. The intensity of his reprimand was painful and made Maayin cower.

"Patience, my dear Venem," said Avah. "You shall tell the truth, Vitatha boy." Then Avah turned to Venem, "Grab the boy's arm we shall take him to Lord Ubilaz."

Maayin shook violently with fear as he let out a blood curdling scream of panic. The last time he was in Ubilaz's presence, he witnessed the abduction of his father and the slaughter of the Vitatha caravan. The two necrophim lifted the boy and flew off to Ataroth Woods with their prize. Raith rolled on his back on the forest floor in evil hysterics.

CHAPTER
FIFTY-SIX

Wes grabbed his chest and stopped suddenly on the trail in the Ithcar Valley. He was flanked by Themba who hadn't left his side since they crossed the stream about fourth-five minutes earlier.

"What's wrong, why are you stopping?" Clarion asked. "Themba tells me that Tobijah's camp is just ahead."

"Something is dreadfully wrong," Wes said. "I felt a terrible pain shoot through my heart. I believe that King Elyon is forewarning me of impending doom."

"Then we should quicken our pace and get to the safety of Tobijah's camp," Josiah said.

Before Josiah finished his sentence, Clarion interrupted, "Be quiet, I hear something." They stood silently and then everyone began to hear the bark of an approaching dog.

"That is Venn, Lady Daesis's basset hound. He is trying to alert us," Clarion said. The guys could hear the barking coming closer and louder but couldn't tell from which direction it came.

"There!" Caden yelled, pointing off into the distance. They looked to see the hound with its flopping ears running through the forest, weaving between trees and shrubs as he charged to his destination. The dog continued to bark his message.

"Something is not right. Lady Daesis has sent Venn," Clarion said as she strained to listen. "I can't quite make out what he is saying, he is still too far." She listened again. "Something is lost . . . or cannot be found."

Venn stopped barking and focused his attention on getting to the travelers. When he arrived, he waited for a moment to catch his breath, panting heavily.

"What merits so urgent a message? Something must be terribly wrong if you have been sent on so long a journey. What cannot be found, Venn?" Clarion asked as she massaged the dog's neck and back.

Venn barked out his message again. Clarion listened, stood up straight, and turned to face Wes. "Maayin cannot be found. He left Lemuel's fortress. Lady Daesis sent out scouts who canvassed the city of Aanda. They couldn't find the boy. Nobody in the Vitatha village has seen the lad either. Lady Daesis believes that he may be heading toward us."

"He's in trouble. That's what I felt. We have to go back," Wes said.

"Themba, go and alert Tobijah. We'll double back over our tracks and find the boy. We will need the assistance of Lord Tobijah's warriors," Clarion ordered.

Themba sprang ahead. Venn followed the mighty cat. Clarion and the guys doubled back in a quick sprint. It took them about twenty minutes to reach the crossing point at the stream. They slowed their pace as they stepped carefully across the smooth slippery stones.

Clarion was the first to reach the solid ground of the bank on the other side of the stream. She scanned the streamside and inspected the trees. Her scouts were nowhere to be seen but the food she left was gone, short of the uneaten cores and rinds of the fruit. She squatted down and placed her hand against the ground where Maayin had slept, as if some force was beckoning her. Wes could see Clarion's alerted concern.

"What is it?" he asked.

"There may have been tragedy here but I'm not sure I can identify it," she returned. By now, all the brothers had crossed the stream. From her kneeling position on the ground, Clarion looked off in the direction of the trail. "We should keep looking in that direction. Let's go," she said. The five resumed their run down the trail once again. They looked in every direction as they ran, stopping occasionally when they thought they had spotted something unusual. Nobody dared to yell for Maayin, out of fear of drawing more attention to their presence in Ithcar.

The search party slowed their pace, each feeling a bit winded. The trail began a steep ascent that crested into a clearing on the other side of the ridge. Large boulders jutted from the forest floor and the trail became a bit more rock hewn, causing it to lose its definition and become more difficult to navigate.

Clarion stopped. "I thought I heard something. It sounded like a muffled cry." They all stood again listening but there was no sound except the wind rustling in the leaves overhead. "We need to stay vigilant; the forest vibrates with the presence of evil. Conversation in the trees is deafeningly silent," Clarion said as she pealed the bow from her back and readied it in her hand.

The group trudged up the rocky slope to the top of the ridge and stood at the edge of the forest glade. They were exhausted, feeling the painful toll that the workout was taking on their bodies.

"I need to rest here for a minute," Ian said holding his side in pain. Josiah panted heavily and nodded in agreement.

"I don't like this." Clarion spoke, looking down the rocky hill behind her. Her words were still winded from the run, "Evil lurks here. We need Lord Tobijah's help."

The forest and the glade in front of them were darkening. The early evening dusk caused the sun to throw eerie dark shadows of the trees, across the boulders and onto the forest floor. An air of macabre hovered in the space.

"We should resume our search before it gets too dark," Caden said as he began to lead the party through the clearing.

"Wait!" Clarion said grabbing his arm. Everyone stood alerted at Clarion's command as she starred ahead into the clearing.

"What do you see," Ian whispered.

"Shadows . . . I'm not sure but something is there," she said soft and slow.

"There's nothing there, it's only shadows," Caden said as he leered intently into the opening in the forest.

"Things aren't always as they seem to be," Clarion whispered. The four brothers looked ahead, waiting, but there was only the movement of shadows as the wind shook the tree branches. Still nobody moved for what seemed to be an uncomfortably long time.

"We can't stand here all day playing chicken with shadows," Caden stated impatiently and he brashly stepped into the clearing.

WHOOSH, came the sound of rushing wind that violently parted the air in the forest glade. Big black wings unfurled from a dark shadow on a boulder at the opposite side of the clearing. They stretched from one side of the forest glade to the other, blocking anyway to pass.

"I knew you could not be so patient, young Lord Caden," boomed Ubilaz's voice.

CHAPTER
FIFTY-SEVEN

Ubilaz stood before the band of brothers in an intimidating show of force. At the sight of the Dark Lord, Clarion instinctively pushed Josiah and Wes behind a large rock. She spun to see Ian grab the back of Caden's shirt and pull him into safe cover behind another large boulder. Clarion then darted alone behind a tree between the two rocky shelters. The tree served to shield her well and gave her the ability to snatch an arrow from her quiver and set it in her bow. Seeing this, Wes pulled the dagger from his side and brought his shield into position in front of his chest. An icy wave rolled over the guys making the hair on their arms and necks stand straight up.

Standing on top of a large rock at the other end of the forest glade, was Lord Ubilaz. His position above the guys gave him a daunting advantage. The band of brothers had a clear view of him from behind their battle lines. They were mesmerized and terrified by their first sight of the Dark Lord whose slender black clad frame shimmered in the twilight. Ubilaz stood with both hands behind his back and his silken ebony wings extended. He was beautifully vile. His cold piercing eyes looked down at the guys as if he could rain the fires of retribution upon them or command the stones to swallow them whole.

"I have not come to do battle. I have come in good will to offer a treaty," Ubilaz said softly. The sound of evil dripped sweet from his deceptive lips.

"How can one so evil, profess to know of *good* will?" Clarion called back.

"My dear Clarion, you underestimate my heart . . . and my power. I could have destroyed all of you while you stood there playing guessing games with the shadows. Instead, I am graciously extending an invitation to this amazing band of brothers to join ranks with me. King Elyon offers you shallow rhetoric, filled with intangibles like *quality of character* and *integrity*. I can give you so much more – enough for you to redefine *character* for your world, as I have done with so many who have preceded you. My offer is simple, join me . . . or die."

"We will never join you," Wes yelled.

"Wes Litchfield, I long most for *you* to join my ranks. I can promise to make you and your brothers, great men. Join me and I will give you power, wealth and fame. Anything that you could ever want or desire will be yours. You will accomplish great and mighty things. Choose, and I will personally mentor you and allow you to return to Otherland as my ambassador."

"Nobody in their right mind would choose your offer!" Josiah called.

Ubilaz laughed, "Josiah Nestor, my boy this is no longer a pitiful dance selection between two weak titillating women. I am offering you power and influence beyond your wildest imagination. There have been many who have ventured this way before you. They chose to join ranks with me and live in the fullness of my promise. I'm sure that you have had contact with some of them – I am aware that you know one very well. Still others have chosen not to take my offer. I willingly accommodated their choice and they too died, right where you now stand."

CHAPTER FIFTY-SEVEN

"We'll die before we become ambassadors of Eikondor," Caden called out.

"Ah, young Mr. Boyd, all I can say to you is that I know you will do the *right* thing. There are always two sides to justice, depending on which side you align. I will make you a powerful warrior, whose judgment will be feared; not some impotent pawn in the hands of a King who is mercifully indecisive. And what of you, Ian Bound? You remain silent cowering behind that rock. I take it you are wishing that you never came to know Dr. Darren Ashe who opened the gates for this frightening death encounter that you now face. My son, I can make it so that you are never afraid again but rather feared by others. I can give you confidence and authority. What worry could you have if you are powerful and wealthy?" The Dark Lord's detailed knowledge of their lives and personalities was overwhelmingly paralyzing. As Ubilaz spoke, he drew his right hand from his back. In it, he clenched a long glistening curved blade dagger.

"I will sweeten my deal and give you a few moments to consider this . . ." as Ubilaz spoke, he revealed something else from behind his back. Maayin was pulled into sight. His hands were bound and a shredded piece of his shirt served to gag him. His naked dirty chest and dirty face were streaked by his tears. He moaned in horror and pain as Ubilaz tightened his grip around the boy's throat.

". . . you will join me or the boy will die." Ubilaz raised the dagger high above his head, as Maayin's eyes grew bigger with trepidation. The band of brothers was frozen with fear.

"You have three seconds," Ubilaz called.

"Wait," Wes said as he moved out from behind the rock with his shield held in front of him for protection. "Take me instead". Wes had no intention of joining Ubilaz but he had hoped that if he stalled long enough, Tobijah and his warriors would soon come on the scene and provide full deliverance.

"Take you instead? Your savior complex may appear to be valiant to Otherlanders but it will not change my course of action. The entire band of brothers joins my ranks or the Vitatha boy tastes death," Ubilaz said.

"Please let my brothers and the boy go. Take me and kill me if you must," Wes returned.

Ubilaz scowled. His countenance looked more evil than it had moments before. "You try my patience and insult my intelligence. Did you really think that you could stall to give Lord Tobijah time enough to come to your aid? You feeble minded infidel. You serve the wrong king. You have no idea who you are dealing with." With that, he plunged the blade into Maayin's breast. The boy's eyes enlarged and glazed over in desperate horror. Maayin's muffled cry was caught by his silken gag. He gasped in pain and then went limp.

The band of brothers watched in horror as if time suddenly slowed to a fraction of its pace. Maayin's knees buckled but Ubilaz still held him up by the neck, like a rag doll held in the clutches of a vicious bully. As Maayin's eyes rolled white in his head, the Dark Lord retracted his blade from his chest and flung him into the center of the clearing to die.

Wes cried out in terror, "NO!", as he dropped his dagger and shield and bolted into the opening to catch and assist the dying boy. Josiah couldn't react fast enough to hold Wes back because, as Wes made his fast break for Maayin, Josiah remembered his discerning glasses and was putting them on.

Josiah now could see Daemonicus, Avah and Gath poised to attack. They were each accompanied by a small company of necrophim warriors, in the trees around the forest glade. As Wes ran to Maayin, Ubilaz gave the attack order. At the same time Josiah yelled, "Necrophim!" and burst in full gait after Wes realizing that their circle of community had been broken making them vulnerable. Seeing Josiah chase after Wes made Caden and Ian also spring into action. They instinctively dashed from their protective place to the center of the clearing toward Maayin's dying body. Clarion also broke cover and went running.

Wes slid into the center of the glade and snatched Maayin in his arms. He was overcome with grief. Caden, Ian and Josiah arrived simultaneously a second after Wes, making their circle invincible to necrophim attack. The necrophim scattered in fearful disgust by the powerful bond of community that halted their ensuing attack. The guys huddled on the ground allowing enough room for Clarion to make a running leap into the center of their bonded circle. She stood immovable with her bow drawn and arrow trained on Ubilaz.

"You dare draw your bow against me, Clarion," Ubilaz said. "I can snuff out your life with the wave of my hand."

Clarion pulled the bow string more taunt making it creak with tension. "Your necrophim are powerless against me because I stand in the center of a ring forged by a force with which to be reckoned. So this leaves the standoff between you and me. You may slay me but not before I get my arrow off. And be assured, my arrow is carried and infused with the power of Elyon, making it swift and sure. The King who I serve has conquered death but you Lord Ubilaz, have not. It appears that the risk is far greater for you than for me because my king promises me life forever, even if I die."

Ubilaz's evil countenance grew darker and his stare became more intense. As much as Clarion had him in her bow sight, he had all his power fixed on this pitifully weak, by comparison, archer. Clarion held her bow steady, her fingers turning white from the tension of the bowstring. She held the bowed arrow close to her face. Her eyes followed the length of the arrow to the sharp metal tip, which pointed to Ubilaz's black clad chest. She took a deep breath, slowly exhaled and quietly whispered, *"Altivolus!"* in anticipation for Ubilaz's next move.

Ubilaz looked down at Clarion and the corners of his lips began to curl up into a vile smirk of amusement at her challenging standoff. Suddenly the thunderous sound of galloping horses approaching in the distance, invaded the moment. The approaching warriors distracted Ubilaz from his delight, like a cat readied to pounce on prey, only to be shooed away by an ensuing broom. Tobijah's warriors were rapidly descending on the forest clearing.

Ubilaz quickly and strategically recalculated his options. He dared not engage the Warrior Knight's company for fear of losing the option of gaining his coveted Kalos Sapphire. Ubilaz's amusement at Clarion's challenge turned to evil hate. "We shall meet again, wench. It appears that your life and the lives of these boys have been spared in the nick of time by an approaching cavalry," he said. The Dark Lord gave a single thrust of his wings and vanished sending a torrent of wind through the glade, hurling dirt and debris through the air. Josiah watched the necrophim army disappear leaving their red visible mist for the others to see.

CHAPTER
FIFTY-EIGHT

A great white tiger bounded into the forest clearing with a ferocious roar. Themba was followed by a company of Knights in polished silver armor, on wild stallions that galloped over the ridge and halted at the edge of the forest clearing. The knight's breastplates, shields and banners were adorned with the crest that Caden wore on his shirt. It was a deep wine colored crest with a strong man's fist clutching a white flower. Each warrior had his sword drawn in preparation for battle.

The company of warriors stood silent as they encircled the clearing. The forest glade had become a solemn and sacred space. Wes sat on the forest floor with Maayin's bloodied broken body, propped against his chest. The young conciliator wept profoundly as the boy barely hung on to life. The wound in his chest was deep and flowed red with blood. Maayin began to turn ashen gray and his fingers and lips hued with death blue.

Caden knelt behind Wes. Still wailing in grief and clutching the boy, Wes leaned back into the strong support of his brother. Caden could feel the intensity of Wes' agony. Josiah quickly came to Wes' side. He put a gentle reassuring hand on his head. Wes glanced over to meet the loving empathetic eyes of his roommate. Josiah just lowered his forehead and pressed it assuredly against Wes' head without saying a word. Ian sat on the other side of Wes. He grabbed hold of Wes' forearm, still wrapped tightly around Maayin. Ian squeezed, as if to help carry the load of grief.

"Where we go one, we go all," Ian whispered, not fully knowing what to say in this situation. Each was moved by this tragedy but more so by the grief that their brother Wes was experiencing.

Caden turned to the line of warriors on horseback, "If only you had arrived a few minutes sooner," he cried. "And where is Lord Tobijah? Didn't he care enough to come with you? The right and decent thing would have been for him to come."

Themba slowly and solemnly walked over to Caden and pressed his head reassuringly against Caden's shoulder. Clarion didn't need to interpret the albino tiger's response. It became evident to Caden that everyone was sympathetic to the sadness of this occasion. Themba's action also communicated an attitude of redeeming hope. Deep down Caden somehow knew that Tobijah had full knowledge of the situation and hadn't compromised his good character.

Josiah suddenly came to new realization. "Ubilaz never had any intention of giving us a choice. All along, his strategy was to prey on Wes' heart. He predetermined that he was going to sacrifice Maayin to draw Wes out."

Clarion placed her hand on Josiah's shoulder and softly spoke, "Yes. But he underestimated the strong power of love, especially the committed, declared love that forms the type of bond you men share."

"That's great but it's not going to save Maayin's life," Wes cried. "I can feel the life leaving his body. Lord Serik told me that I would pay a price for being a loving man. He told me that I would be painfully broken and that love would lead me to feel the sorrows of the King. If this is what he meant, I'm not sure that I can bear it!"

CHAPTER FIFTY-EIGHT

"Where we go one, we go all," Ian spoke louder with more confidence. "You don't have to do this alone Wes, our love for you can carry you." There was something prophetically powerful and soothing in Ian's confidence and statement.

Wes found new freedom in the support of his brothers, allowing him to release his agony and he wailed louder. Wes rocked back and forth, hoisting the boy into a tighter grip. His tears flowed down his face and onto Maayin's chest. The entourage of warriors and friends stood in solemn empathy, watching, waiting and weeping.

Ian sat quietly as he watched Wes' tears wash cleansing trails on Maayin's dirty chest. As he followed Wes' tears, something else caught his eye. The wound in Maayin's chest began to close and heal. The skin was becoming new like an infant's soft skin, pink against the rest of the lad's ashen form. More of Wes' tears fell upon Maayin's chest accelerating the healing process.

"Look!" Ian shouted with excitement, breaking the quiet reverence of the forest sanctuary.

"He's . . . healing," Josiah said.

As the entire company watched, Maayin's wound closed fully and his color began to change from death gray to a more vibrant flesh tone. The lad began to breathe deeper as life reentered his body. Life also reentered Wes' heart, as he held the boy in his strong embrace. Wes could feel Elyon's mark burning on his chest.

"The love of a Conciliator Knight can bring healing," Clarion said, caught in the wonder of the moment, as if she were reciting the obvious truth she had known from some ancient creed.

Her words triggered Wes' memory of the conversation that he had with Doc about the girl in the cafeteria. "You may have brought healing to her by just joining her suffering. Your tears may have been the very thing that could have healed her brokenness." Wes looked down at the boy who opened his eyes to see Wes' face. Maayin smiled. This made Wes tear up again as his heart moved from suffering, to being overwhelmed by the King's joy.

CHAPTER
FIFTY-NINE

Maayin rested his face against the soft white fur of Themba's back. The Vitatha boy was weak and fatigued from the near fatal wound that he suffered. The band of brothers placed him on the back of the great cat to be carried to Tobijah's camp. He lay hunched over, clinging to the tiger's fur. Each step gently rocked the boy in a soothing manner.

Wes, Caden, Josiah, Ian and Clarion were each mounted on the backs of the wild stallions behind an able bodied warrior. Wes demanded that his mount stay close to Themba's side so that he could keep a watchful eye on the lad.

"You know he will have to go back to Lord Lemuel's fortress. He cannot stay in Lord Tobijah's camp. And he certainly cannot come along with us. The Dark Lord will assuredly prey on the boy to destroy you," Clarion whispered to Wes.

Wes diverted his attention from the boy and nodded affirmatively to Clarion.

"I sent one of our informants to summon Lady Daesis. She will come to Tobijah's camp to escort him back to Aanda," Clarion said.

The warriors followed a trail that ended at the base of a rocky cliff, which towered straight up out of the earth about sixty feet.

"This is a dead end," Caden said.

Clarion and the band of brothers dismounted to stretch. Wes immediately attended to Maayin who remained resting on Themba's back. "Lord Tobijah's camp is on the other side of this rock wall," Clarion replied.

Caden walked over to the stone wall and looked almost ninety degrees straight up as the cliff towered high above him. "You don't expect us to scale this?" Caden asked. By now, Ian was standing next to Caden, looking up the steep cliff side.

"Please, tell me we aren't climbing!" Ian pleaded.

"The wall is an entrance into the camp. It is covered with the cloaking blessing. We don't go over the wall. We'll pass through it. The cloaking blessing causes the camp to become a part of the terrain," Clarion replied.

"Cool, so this is a secret door into a mountain cave," Caden said as he pounded the palm of his hand against the hard solid surface. "Open it and let's meet the man, the myth, the legend . . . my mentor."

"It does not open. It will only allow those who are faithful to King Elyon to pass. You shall see, come over here." Caden and Ian walked to where Clarion was standing. As they arrived at her side, one of the mounted warriors charged the wall. Just as the stallion was a few feet from the barrier, it leapt and vanished through rock. The force of the stallion's entrance shook dirt and stony debris free form the rock wall's surface as if a mild earthquake occurred.

"Themba should go next," Clarion said. Maayin sat up straight on the tiger's back. Wes patted him reassuringly on the back. The tiger bounded toward the wall. Maayin lowered his head as Themba leaped. The white tiger and rider were absorbed into the mountain wall. One by one, the warriors quickly passed into the mountain. Clarion and the guys were each helped back onto their mounts by the warrior who commanded them. As soon as they were readied, the riders charged the wall. Each guy held his breath and closed his eyes as they passed through the rocky barrier.

The sight that welcomed them on the other side of the mountain wall was unexpected. They hadn't entered into a dark mountain cavern, like they assumed they would; rather they entered into a beautiful land with green glens and tall trees; waterfalls and bridge covered streams. The rock wall that they had passed through was a refreshing waterfall on this side. Tobijah's camp looked like an ethereal city in a dream. The dwellings were elaborate tent houses that appeared as if they were crafted of wood and lace. They were nestled into the terrain and hillside, some of which were connected by delicately constructed causeways. The great tent city was bathed in a bright pinkish-white light, created by an undetectable source.

The guys were immediately greeted by the sweet smell of patchouli mint that hovered in the air like the aroma of the continually burning incense in a great cathedral. Caden took a deep breath, "What is that amazing aroma?" he asked.

The warrior who shared the stallion with Caden spoke for the first time through his masked helmet, "It is the aroma created by the cloaking blessing. When the blessing is invoked, it covers its inhabitants with its own light source, the brilliant pink-white rays you see, and its own air supply, the wonderful aroma of exotic spice you smell."

"Wow I thought we were going to enter into a dank, dark musty cave that Tobijah used as a hideout but I forget that things aren't always as the seem to be in Salamgard," Caden said.

"We are very interested in talking with Lord Tobijah," Wes announced. "Can you take us to him directly?"

"As you wish," the warrior humbly offered.

Themba led the way. The company of warriors dispersed leaving five horsemen and their travel partners to follow Themba. They ambled through the tent city being greeted along the pathway by warriors, maidens and children as they passed by.

The travel party finally reached a dwelling in the center of the ethereal city. The canvassed door of this dwelling bore Tobijah's crest. Short of the crest, the tent dwelling looked like all the other homes in the city, elaborately refined and well crafted. The horsemen helped their companions off the stallions then each dismounted. Maayin also lit from Themba's back and was able to stand secure as long as he kept a grip on the cat's albino fur.

Without speaking, four of the horsemen graciously bowed and escorted their steeds away from gathering. "Please come with me," said the warrior who accompanied Caden. He walked through the tent doorway followed by Themba and Maayin.

"I have a feeling the inside of this tent is nothing like it would seem to be," Caden commented to his brothers. They followed Themba through the doorway only to discover that Caden was right. While the walls were made of canvass, the interior reflected a palace with many rooms and fine furnishings. Large candelabra chandeliers hung from the tented ceilings bathing the rooms in a soothing yellow glow.

The warrior led them into a room that was furnished with a round table surrounded by twelve chairs.

"Please sit and rest," he said. As he finished his invitation, a host of servants with trays arrayed with fruits and delectable foods entered the room.

Maayin took a seat along with Clarion and the guys. Themba sauntered over to flank the side of the warrior. The warrior placed his sword on the table and removed his helmet. "I am Lord Tobijah. Welcome to my camp and my home," he said.

Tobijah also removed his gloves and breastplate. He was a large muscular black man. His head was shaved and smooth like the taunt skin of his face. On the forearm of his right arm were tattooed seven small black stars, barely visible against his ebony skin. His ungloved hands glowed brilliant like burnished bronze that was being refined in a furnace.

The guys looked on him with wonder. Tobijah *had* come to their rescue. He was with them in the forest all along, although not distinct among any warrior.

Caden slyly smiled, "You deceived us! You *were* there in the forest clearing - why did you disguise yourself?"

"There was no deception or disguise. Deception is never a good thing," Tobijah replied. "Your perception is tainted and you fail to grasp the proper understanding that things are never as they seem to be in Salamgard. Your mind told you that I should be ranked higher and distinguished from among my warriors, but a good man sees others as more important than himself. He understands that rank only gives him power, which absolutely corrupts goodness."

"Then how do you lead?" Caden asked.

"As a servant to all; out of the goodness that the King instills in my soul. You have much to learn about being a warrior, Caden, my son. We had better attend to that without delay," Tobijah said as he stood from his position at the table and picked up his sword.

The great warrior turned and retrieved a spear that rested with many others in a rack against the taunt canvass tent wall. "While the cloaking blessing under which this camp resides, acts as a canopy to hide us, it does not protect us. Presidium Electus!" he said as he plunged the spear into the ground next to his chair. The spear's end began to spew the light of the protectus blessing against the tent ceiling. It crawled across the ceiling and into the other rooms of the tent palace.

"You must stay within the confines of my home," he said to the guys. "I'm sure that you will be well cared for and can get the peaceful rest and refreshment that you need here. Eat your full and be at home."

As Tobijah spoke, another warrior entered from a side room, "This is Iman. If you are in need of anything he will make sure that you are accommodated," Tobijah said as Iman bowed in humble servitude.

"Lord Caden, follow me," the great warrior said as he exited the dining hall followed by his young protégé.

CHAPTER
SIXTY

Ubilaz sat in contemplative thought on his large stone-carved throne at the top of the black slate stepped platform of his throne room. He and his necrophim captains had just returned from the ordeal in Ithcar and needed to strategize their next offensives. Daemonicus, Avah and Gath, stood silently before Lord Ubilaz, as they had done many times before, awaiting their next directives.

"My Lord you secured a great victory today with the death of the boy. You have weakened Elyon's stronghold on the Otherlanders," Gath said.

"You speak of things you know nothing about, Gath. I have great plans for the Vitatha boy," Ubilaz said.

"Don't you mean '*had* great plans', my Lord?" Avah questioned. "The boy is dead . . . what plans can you have for a dead Vitatha boy's body? Your strategy to kill the boy; drawing out the others, was a magnificent plan but . . ."

"The boy lives," Ubilaz interrupted as he slowly rose from his seated position. "It was never my intent for him to die."

"Sire, I don't understand," Gath replied. "You delivered a powerful death blow. We watched you slay him. Your dagger pierced his . . ."

"The Vitatha boy lives!" Ubilaz reiterated more deliberately. "Wes Litchfield discovered today, that he has power to heal."

"But my Lord, why would you want him to discover that? It would only reinforce the band of brother's resolve to unite with Elyon," Gath stated.

"They are already resolved, we shall not sway them. Our only recourse is to destroy them before they can reach King Elyon. I have perfectly set my plan in motion. Wes' healing powers definitely built a stronger bond between him and the boy. I want that bond to be very strong, because Maayin will be the pivotal player to bring down the most powerful and promising ambassador knights that Salamgard only hoped to see," the Dark Lord said. Gath and Avah were confused as to how this could be a victorious strategy.

"My Lord your cunning is to be reverenced," Daemonicus quietly proclaimed in a moment of enlightenment. "If you acquire the Vitatha boy it will make Wes Litchfield more vulnerable because the young conciliator will most definitely do anything to save the protégé that is now irrevocably knit to his heart."

Ubilaz's eyes glistened with an icy malevolence and he gave an impish smile, "How astute of you Daemonicus. You got it mostly right. Master Litchfield *will* give his life for the boy's, as he so willingly proclaimed. I will take him up on that offer before he reaches Elyon. Maayin will join our ranks and then betray and kill young Litchfield. He will not be our bargaining chip, he will be our assassin," Ubilaz stated.

"Maayin will kill Wes Litchfield? Did I hear you right, Lord Ubilaz?" Avah asked.

Before the captains could get clarity, Venem burst into the throne room from a side entrance. "My Liege, I have found it. I know that you will be pleased with me and I trust that you will be gracious in your reward. I beg your forgiveness for interrupting this council meeting but what I have found cannot wait. Last time I waited it didn't serve me . . . I mean *you* well, Most Exalted Wickedness."

"Have you found the Kalos Gem?"

"Something far greater, dear Majesty; not to imply that the Kalos Gem isn't a great thing. I have found Tobijah's Camp. I followed a company of Tobijah's warriors through the Valley of Ithcar. They were carrying Clarion, the four Otherlanders and the . . . Vitatha boy; I'm sorry to inform you, Sovereign, that the boy lives. I saw you strike him down with a powerful blow right into his chest – you are such a precise and skillful . . . dagger-user . . . daggersman . . . dagger-er . . ." Venem bumbled as he gestured stabbing blows into mid air. His nervous energy, verbose enthusiasm and incessant kissing-up was like a Pekinese puppy on the verge of wetting while waiting for its master to give him a dog treat.

"What I mean to say is that the precision of your blade handling – *primo magnifico*; but the young Conciliator's tears closed up the wound before death could take the lad. I heard Clarion say that Lady Daesis comes to retrieve the boy and take him back to Lemuel's fortress. Please don't hold that bad news against me because the good news far outweighs the bad, Your Royal Darkness."

"We know the boy lives. That was always the plan," Ubilaz said, rolling his eyes and giving a flick of his fingers for the necrophim to continue. "Tobijah's Camp?" the Dark lord inquired.

"It was always the plan? - Well then a great plan it was!" Venem said. "Yes, Tobijah's camp . . . it is cloaked under a hill in the Valley of Ithcar."

"The camp is under a cloaking blessing, my Lord", Avah smugly said in an attempt to thwart Venem's glory. "It will only allow those faithful to Elyon to pass."

"That's right we may not pass but, Highness, it is not a protectus blessing, which is impenetrable and disorienting. I have found a way to pass through the cloaking blessing," the necrophim gleamed. If Venem were a Pekinese, he would have been wagging his tail with unnatural velocity saying, *"throw me the treat, throw me the treat"*.

"I can't wait to hear this," Avah said anticipating that Venem was about to make the blunder of his existence.

"Well, my Lord, I noticed that warriors come and go on horseback. They pass through the cloaking blessing because they are faithful to Elyon. I thought that maybe I could grab the horse's tail just as it leapt into the camp. But that didn't work. I knew that I needed to be the horse or be *in* the horse not on the horse. Then it came to me! I simply transformed myself into a tick and burrow into the hide of the horse before it passed through. The host is faithful to King Elyon and thus can pass. Before the horse knew what bit him, I was off and on the other side of the cloaking blessing."

"Venem, it seems that I have underestimated you. I am impressed with your ingenuity. You have not failed me," Lord Ubilaz said.

"According to my humble estimation highness, not only have I found Tobijah's camp and found a way to get in, but I have also delivered the boys into your hands, because they take refuge there, *and* I discovered the location of the Kalos Gem. I trust that you will consider a small, tiny promotion, maybe to the rank of . . . *captain* - as sufficient reward for so monumental a discovery which, in my humble opinion, marks a turning point in our cause." Venem sneered at the other captains, then turned it into a smile and a low genuflect of worship as he faced Ubilaz.

"You have done well Venem. I will give it some thought. But now, we have to attend to more important things. We must move quickly. We should assume that Elyon's spies spotted you and have informed Tobijah. They will most likely make preparations to move the camp soon. Avah, you and Raith must go to the camp. Wait there and watch where they journey to establish camp next. Tobijah most likely wears the Kalos Gem. I am counting on your ability and Raith's cunning to get that precious stone. But before you move to acquire the stone, I want the Vitatha boy. Gath you and Venem will go to the camp as well, to acquire the Vitatha boy."

"The boy will be heavily guarded, and now with a stronger bond to the Otherlander, it may nearly be impossible to separate them. How can I get the boy without killing him? You cannot expect me to go up against Lady Daesis! I have never seen her power, but it is legendary. She is a virtuous woman, with the ability to defeat the strongest of foes. It is rumored that Elyon's power flows through her as strongly as it flows through Lemuel, Tobijah and Kesh combined," Gath said.

"Then you must get into Tobijah's camp before the Lady arrives. Escort the boy out by posing to be Lady Daesis," Ubilaz ordered.

"Even if I can get Maayin away, he will never join our ranks because, after all you did attempt to kill him my Lord. How do you propose to turn him to join our cause and then convince him to be your assassin?" Gath asked.

"The boy will certainly join us. Like Elyon, I have established powerful representatives of Eikondor in Otherland, who do my bidding and extend my kingdom. There is one very powerful representative, who I personally mentored. He is Maayin's father. I abducted the Vitatha tribal chief long ago because of his great ability to lead and influence. I saw him hide his son during the attack on the caravan. I have spared the boy's life as ransom for the chief's services and loyalty. Over time, the chief grew to forget his old life. He liked the power, authority and wealth that I gave him. He is a very persuasive man. He will convince the boy to join us because the boy loved him dearly. Gath, you just get the lad to the cave of Belial in Ataroth Woods. Daemonicus, you will journey to Otherland and summon the boy's father."

"Who am I looking for my Lord?" Daemonicus asked.

"Maayin's father is Charles Morelock. After he persuades Maayin to join us, I will have both of his sons in my ranks."

"As you wish, my Lord and King," Daemonicus bowed gratefully and then turned and disappeared in a red mist. Avah, Gath and Venem paid homage and quickly exited in the same manner as Daemonicus, leaving Lord Ubilaz to bask in the notion of the rise of Eikondor.

CHAPTER
SIXTY-ONE

Caden and his mentor, Tobijah stepped outside of the tented palace into the bright light of the blush hued cloaking canopy. Caden had awaited this moment since Clarion told them of their purpose in Salamgard. He had met his mentor and was now going to be shaped into a great warrior. Tobijah held his sword in hand and picked up a shield that rested outside the doorway of his tent. The shield bore Tobijah's crest.

"The crests of the other mentors had meaning. What is the significance of the strong arm and the flower?" Caden asked. "Is it symbolic of the prosperity that power brings . . . power used in a good way, of course?"

"Not quite. The arm represents justice grasping a flowering white lily of mercy. Both symbolize all that is good. You will come to understand this more fully as we talk. Come, we shall walk over there to that bridge," Tobijah said as he pointed the direction with his sword.

"It's a great day to learn the art of warfare," Caden blurted out with excitement.

They arrived on the bridge that overlooked the tented city. A powerful waterfall cascaded down the mountainside and under the bridge beneath them. *This bridge will be the lane that Tobijah teaches me the craft of swordsmanship*, Caden thought. He could picture the mighty warrior teaching him to lunge, thrust, parry, advance and riposte, high above the camp. Caden's excitement reached a frenzied pitch. He couldn't wait to have his weapon – which he expected to be the sword that Tobijah carried. Caden envisioned a familiar scene that he had dreamt of many times before. He pictured himself as an armor clad warrior charging into a battle with a powerful sword of truth. *My dream is about to become a reality*, he thought as he anticipated being schooled in the art of warfare. He was about to become a warrior commissioned to crusade justice, the most noble of all causes.

Tobijah walked half way to the center of the bridge, stopped and set down his shield and placed the sword on the flat beam of the bridge rail. "This is a great day to learn the art of being a *good man*," he stated.

Tobijah leaned against the guard rail of the bridge gazing onto the camp and the falling water below, like a father watching his children sleep. Caden stood next to him silently waiting.

"There is goodness deep within you, Caden. Goodness makes a man a warrior but very much unlike the notions that you believe a warrior should be. The goodness, deep within you, is covered by a desire to find a battle to fight or a cause for which to crusade. You believe that the battle validates you as a warrior."

Caden looked confused. This didn't sound like the beginning of a lesson on how to thrust and parry in fact it didn't sound like it was not going to be about warfare at all.

"You have come to believe that a man, who doesn't take a stand or fight a battle, is weak in every way. But I will tell you that the man who seeks to fight, no matter how noble the cause or how powerful the truth he believes he defends, is not a *good man*. A good man is one who seeks justice. That is what makes him a warrior. But he also loves mercy, and that is what makes him a *good* warrior. The man who seeks justice without loving mercy only sets himself up as a self righteous judge."

"I agree wholeheartedly," Caden expressed. "I believe that justice should be swift and powerful enough to eradicate evil. I also agree that mercy should be extended to those who have suffered, and a good man should go out of his way to do both." Caden's words echoed an air of confidence and pride. He wanted to impress upon Tobijah that he already had a head start on being a good warrior.

"My son, you are not yet speaking the words of a good warrior. Your words reflect your idea of what good is, not King Elyon's. Seeking justice and loving mercy are single directional, channeled to the same recipient. A warrior marked by goodness is an agent who administers reconciliation against evil; this is justice. He is also equally passionate to be an agent who champions mercy and grace to those who are victimized but more importantly to those who act unjustly."

"Wait, that's messed up, it doesn't make sense. You're telling me that I should fight against injustice then fight for mercy for the bad guys? How can truth ever prevail like that? Where's the justice? If someone does something wrong they should have to pay. How can any wrong be made right under the way that you described it?"

"You have come to think of a warrior as one who champions *truth*. A warrior defined by a character of goodness is not fueled by truth or a personal sense of piety. The tension of being just and merciful puts the good warrior in a position where he humbly waits on his king. I already told you that rank and status fuels power but so does a contrived righteousness that is generated by the notion that a man is operating as the guardian of truth and moral integrity. In Salamgard a grasp on truth and morality doesn't entitle any warrior to be a sword-wielding judge. Truth and power often become the stumbling blocks that rob a man of being good in character."

"Then how can you exact justice or bring correction? What's the sense in being a warrior? It sounds like the warrior you describe is a weakling who lacks conviction," Caden said.

"My boy, it has been engrained in you to think that your convictions are powerful. In your estimation, those convictions have been made sacred and have thus become your sword. You draw so much strength from your sword of conviction that you fail to draw strength from your king. You see a good warrior as a conviction-less, weakling because you are so swift to crusade for truth or the right thing, as you would define it; that you miss goodness. You are charged by King Elyon to *be* a good man who *does* good things. You will come to understand that the *right* thing may not always be the *good* thing. When all is said and done, King Elyon will not measure you for championing truth, but for being a good man."

"That makes no sense at all. If we do what is right, it is always good."

"You shall come to see this differently," Tobijah said with a confident tone that made Caden feel intimidated for the first time during this conversation. As the Warrior Knight spoke, he retrieved his sword and sliced through the air in a spectacular show of swordsmanship. Then he turned the sword and handed the grip to Caden.

"This is your weapon," the mighty warrior said.

Caden took the sword with dazzling excitement. He gauged its weight and balance in his hand then he attempted to mimic Tobijah's wielding exercise. Caden flailed the sword through the air, "I feel so powerful, like I've become a mighty man of valor. Is that the King's power?"

"It is not the king's power – you will know beyond a shadow of a doubt when Elyon's power comes upon you. The King's powerful goodness will flow through you into the blade, but you must know that you may only use this weapon to protect yourself from the attack of Ubilaz and his forces."

"Yes! I know. Serik and Lemuel told the other guys the same thing. Ian is the only one left to receive his weapon. After that we will all be equipped to fight."

"The charge to you is different, my son. You may *never* strike with your weapon at all – even in a battle, unless King Elyon is empowering you. You may only use this sword to block an attack. You are always forbidden to strike."

"Why?" Caden asked dumbfounded and annoyed. His dreams were being dashed. "I don't understand."

"A good warrior avoids a battle and doesn't take delight in crusading. A good warrior infiltrates dark places and lives out the ideals of Salamgard. He doesn't force those ideals on the unjust, or crusade against those who don't hold to those ideals; he just lives them. People will then see his goodness as a reflection of the King. That is what makes him powerful and separates him from all other warriors. The sword you hold is a powerful symbol of authority, which will bring about justice. Yet when wielded, it is always a tool of death and destruction. Unless the King explicitly orders its use, the outcome will never be *good*. Therefore you may never strike unless the King wills it."

"So how do I seek justice?" Caden asked again.

"You step into an unjust situation with full knowledge that you have been given authority, from the King, to bring correction. But you don't fight, instead you trust the King to pour his goodness through you. Goodness transforms terribly wicked situations into good situations. Then when you encounter those who are unjust, you continue to be a good warrior. This will create tension because even when people are recipients of all that is good, they want to do things that are not good to those who are unjust. You will want to do the same. The tension to be just and merciful will make you humble yourself before the king because you will conclude that you are at an impasse of conscience. Your conviction to be just will betray your conviction to be merciful and vice versa. A good warrior's only response is to kneel in homage and trustingly wait for his king."

"But don't people who act unjustly deserve to pay for their crimes? I mean shouldn't some even die for the atrocity of their crimes?"

"Probably, but who determines which crimes are atrocities and which are not. If people are required to die for their injustices, then all should die because all have acted unjustly at one point. As a citizen and Ambassador Knight of Salamgard, you are compelled by the knowledge that the King did die. He did pay for all crime, the crime inflicted upon us by Ubilaz. Only King Elyon has authority over death, even the death of the unjust, because he alone holds the mystery and secrets of death. Whenever you wield your sword, you become an agent of death, but if the king commands you to wield your sword then he has superintended it for good. A strong and good warrior is one who brings goodness into the darkness of injustice that constantly surrounds him. He will be like the sun as it crests over the mountain range in the morning, dispelling darkness and growing brighter, as he is fueled by his king."

"Then how will I know that the King has ordered me to use the sword?" Caden returned.

"You will know from the mark that the king bestows upon you."

"What mark? How will I be marked?"

Tobijah took the sword from Caden's hands and fiercely cut through the air again. Then he lowered the blade and pressed the point of the sword to Caden's abdomen. The tip of the sword pierced through the threads of Caden's vestment. He could feel the cold point of the blade against the surface of his skin. Caden held his breath in confusion. He looked down at the blade in full knowledge that this weapon, in one swift move, could end him. Then he looked up into the kind eyes of the Good Warrior. There was something reassuring about the goodness of the powerful warrior, which made Caden's heart and mind rest.

"Goodness is instilled in your soul, right here in your gut or the core of you being. It is deep within you," Tobijah said as he pressed the sword forward a bit. Caden could feel the tip of the sword slightly pierce his skin. He didn't move but kept his eyes glued to Tobijah's eyes.

"The sword of a just and merciful warrior is empowered by the goodness of the King when that warrior waits on, and humbly trusts in the king", Tobijah reiterated. "King Elyon infuses your soul with his goodness. People will see your good works and know you are Elyon's warrior. They will not know it by feeling the cold steel from the edge of your sword, or the power you demonstrate in fighting a battle, or the force that you bring to a crusade against evil morals. From this time forth your instinct will be to do good because you are characterized by goodness."

Caden could feel the tip of the blade becoming hot with a powerful energy. Then he began to feel that energy being transferred into the very core of his being. The goodness of the king was flowing through Tobijah's sword into Caden's soul. The young warrior straightened his posture, closed his eyes, took a deep breath and humbly bowed his head in awe as a fire began to burn deep within his belly. Caden never felt so alive and empowered.

Tobijah retracted and lowered his blade. Caden stood for a moment, with his eyes closed, still feeling the fire burning in his soul. "I feel like I'm on fire. Is this my mark? Will people see this fire?" Caden asked.

"Insert your hand into your shirt", Tobijah said. "Put your open palm against the place where that fire burns hottest."

Caden slipped his left hand into the flap of his wine colored vestment. He placed his palm against his abdomen and began to feel the fire subside.

"It's cooling off. The fire is going away," Caden said disappointedly. Tobijah reached in and pressed Caden's hand harder against his torso as if he were pushing it deeper into his soul. Caden could feel the warrior's hand burning hot as the fire began to rise again until Caden could feel his hand also being ignited.

"As a Knight of Elyon's Realm, I have been charged to act in the king's stay. King Elyon hereby has chosen you to be a warrior of Salamgard, marked by goodness. As a good warrior, you have been ordained to do good, evidence by the work of your hands. All men will see and know that you serve the King as a Good Warrior, administering justice and mercy." Tobijah released his grip on Caden's hand. "Now reveal your hand," he said.

Caden withdrew his hand revealing the same burnished bronzed glow that earlier marked his mentor's hands. "Your golden hands will be the mark of the goodness that has been instilled in your character."

Caden looked at his hands glowing brightly. "I see the mark but I don't understand how I will know when King Elyon has ordered me to use my sword."

Tobijah handed Caden's sword back to him. "Whenever you take up your sword, your hands will cease to blaze bronze," he said. Caden looked at his hands gripping the sword only to find them in their natural state. They had ceased to glow. He quickly placed the sword on the cross beam of the bridge. As soon as he released his grip, his hands glowed again.

Tobijah continued, "When King Elyon commands you to use your sword, your hands will blaze a burnished bronze as you grip the sword. Until then your hands will never glow golden as long as you hold the weapon. When your take up the sword with hands of gold it means that the King has deputized you to be his agent of judgment. Don't be deceived into thinking that you know the King's standard for justice and righteousness, leading you to wield the sword under your own power and authority. The warrior, marked by goodness waits on his Sovereign Lord and King, who alone is judge."

"Lord Tobijah, you have a reputation throughout Salamgard as being a powerful warrior. Is that because you have been deputized as King Elyon's agent of judgment?"

Tobijah took the sword from Caden again to show him that his hand ceased to glow when he also gripped the sword. "I have rarely used my sword. The times when I have used it was when I went into battle against Ubilaz's army. I fought alongside many of the King's knights, for the glory of the king. Even then, I had to wait for the King to emblazon my hands, while others fought around me. It was only during those times that I have been allowed to use my sword. These seven stars that tattoo my arm mark the seven times that the king has allowed me the use of my sword. They serve as a reminder that I am not a judge. It is important that you not confuse reconciling injustice with enacting judgment. Goodness brings about justice *and* mercy. Judgment never brings justice unless it is the final act of a good and righteous king. By the way, your observation of who I am answered your earlier question, people see a good man as a powerful warrior not a weak shell of a passive man." Tobijah set the sword down again and his hands glowed brilliantly.

"But what if you're staring into the face of injustice, I mean there are times that I see overt evil and hate it so much. You're telling me I should passively hold my sword and do nothing?"

"If you feel so strongly then swing away, Caden . . . and join the ranks of the unjust evil. But if you are going to be a good warrior then you will be aggressive to walk humbly with your king. You must cease to see, placing trust in the king, as a passive response, but an active discipline. In doing this, it will lead you to understand that the presence of evil affords you the opportunity to be a warrior who ushers in the goodness of the king which burns in you, rather than ushering in judgment which only stirs the evil passions of self-righteousness within you. That my son, is the difference between Elyon's power and your warrior power."

Caden picked up the sword again and watched as his hands ceased to glow. "I am starting to understand. The king's goodness in me will make me do good things."

Tobijah smiled, "I am confident that you will be the warrior, King Elyon has destined you to be. With that, I have been charged to give you your first task as a warrior." Tobijah reached beneath his armor breastplate at the neck line, and produced a magnificent gemmed amulet. The brilliant sapphire was larger than any precious stone that Caden had ever seen or imagined. Tobijah removed it from around his neck and placed it around Caden's neck.

"As the King's good warrior you have been charged to protect that which belongs to King Elyon. If you fail to keep this charge then you and your brothers will not be knighted and many will taste death," Tobijah proclaimed.

"Whoa, wait a minute. I'm not ready for this!"

"You are ready and King Elyon decrees that you be the guardian of the Kalos Gem."

"But isn't this the gem that increases the owner's power . . . the gem that Ubilaz is killing citizens of Salamgard for?"

"Yes, the very gem!"

"HA!" Caden blurted out a worrisome laugh. "You give me a sword that I can't use then you hang a target around my neck. Ubilaz will kill me. I don't see how this is good or how it can help me be a good warrior, unless it makes *me* seven times stronger while I carry it."

"Ubilaz cannot take the Kalos Gem by killing you. If he does, it renders the gem impotent. If he kills you to acquire the gem then he must kill Elyon before the gem's power can be transferred to him. The Kalos Gem must be given to him, in order for him to be its rightful owner. Ubilaz may torture you to the point of death, until you willingly give him the amulet. But you are a good warrior who avoids a battle and does what is good. The gem will not make you stronger seven-fold because it belongs to Elyon. Your strength must be the goodness Elyon instills deep within your soul."

"Ok, I guess I'll have to trust the king," Caden said as he concealed the gem under his shirt. "I'll never give the gem to Ubilaz and if I stay close to my brothers, I'll be safe from any damage he might want to do. I'm sure that if he tried to torture me into giving him the gem as he has been doing to other citizens of Salamgard, that Elyon will allow me to use my sword. After all that would be a great time to let me be an agent of judgment, right?"

Tobijah didn't say a word he just began to walk back toward his tented palace. Caden stood there dumbfounded for a moment trying to take in all that had just happened. Then he quickly caught up to his mentor. Neither said a word all the way back to their point of origin.

CHAPTER
SIXTY-
TWO

Lady Daesis sat at the banquet table in the great hall of Lemuel's fortress. She had the terrace doors opened wide, giving her a panoramic view of the garden. The morning was bright and cheerful. Daesis worked busily polishing the silver, a job that she personally took pleasure attending to. She enjoyed watching the transformation a tarnished unusable object went through, to become a stunning shimmering useful utensil. It reminded her of the many protégées that passed through Salamgard and Lemuel's fortress. She stopped her work occasionally to reflect on those young ambassadors, drink a sip of tea and take in the beauty of the hanging gardens in the cool gentle morning.

Her peaceful labor was suddenly interrupted by the approaching barks of Venn. Daesis rose and looked to see if she could identify where the barking was coming from. She quickly spotted Venn rounding the corner of the fortress into the garden. Venn's ears flopped with the cadence of his gait, as he barked up a storm.

Daesis smiled, "I'm so glad that you are home," she called. "I have missed you immensely. Was the boy found?" Venn didn't break stride until he reached the warm embrace of his lady who lavished love and affection on him.

"Tell me, was the boy found?" Daesis asked as she poured water from a pitcher into one of the silver bowls that she just polished and placed it on the floor for Venn to drink. Venn gave a few barks then began lapping up the water to quench his raging thirst.

Lady Daesis breathed a sigh of relief. "I'm so glad that you found him," she said. Venn barked again sending water slobbering all across the tiled floor.

"Oh, my word", Daesis gasped as she clutched her napkin to her breast. "Ubilaz attempted to kill the boy? You're sure that he is alright now?"

The hound told the entire story, slurping up water between barks. Daesis sat mesmerized, listening to every detail. As Venn continued, a turtle dove flew into the great hall and perched on a silver urn next to Lady Daesis. The dove cooed, causing Venn to stop his tale. Then the dove cooed again.

"Yes my dear," Daesis responded. "I shall leave immediately." Lady Daesis stood, perplexed to figure out what she needed to do first. She took inventory of the unpolished silver on the table in front of her. *There is no time to put this back in its proper place, it will have to stay where it is. I need to attend to a more precious vessel than these silver ones*, she thought.

"Venn it seems that Clarion thinks it wise that we go and retrieve the boy. I believe that she is correct. That boy is very valuable and can become a powerful asset to Salamgard or a destructive foe in the hands of Ubilaz. He has yet to understand the full significance of who he is. We must get him back to the safety of this refuge city and these fortress walls."

Daesis stepped outside through the threshold of the garden door and raised her calling charm to her lips. After giving it a few puffs of air, Trogen her devoted cheetah sauntered onto the terrace.

CHAPTER SIXTY-TWO

"Trogen, my darling, we have a very important task before us that requires your speed and devotion. You must quickly find Lord Cervus and summon him to the fortress. Please tell him that we must hasten to Tobijah's camp and return the Vitatha boy Maayin back to Aanda, before Lord Ubilaz gets to him. We believe that Ubilaz thinks the boy is dead but the dark Lord is very resourceful and will come to know soon enough that the child lives. We must hide the boy before Ubilaz knows any better. Long ago, the boy was hidden from Ubilaz by his father who has since become a powerful adversary in Otherland. We have no reason to suspect that Ubilaz knows the boy's identity and we need to keep that secret as secure as the boy. Tell Lord Cervus that time is of the essence. Go quickly with Elyon's power, sweet devoted Trogen."

Trogen turned and bolted across the garden lawns with blinding speed, and was soon out of sight. "I will quickly ready myself for the journey. I must get my riding stick. It has served me for many years as a powerful weapon against dark forces," Daesis said to Venn as she started to walk away. Before she left the grand hall she turned and said, "And Venn, I will need a faithful friend like you to accompany me on this journey. You know the exact location of Tobijah's camp. This time you can make the journey in Cervus' wagon." Venn gave a single bark of affirmation as Lady Daesis exited the grand hall to make her preparations.

CHAPTER
SIXTY-THREE

Caden and Tobijah entered the dining hall of Tobijah's palace. The band of brothers was together again, each seated around the large circular table along with Clarion and Maayin. Tobijah dislodged the spear from the floor and the protectus blessing ceased to spill its covering throughout the palace.

"Maayin you're looking good; healthier than you did when I left," Caden said as he entered the room. Maayin was alert, full of energy and eating a bowl of soup.

"I feel great, Lord Caden," Maayin replied.

"You're looking *good* too," Wes replied to Caden. Caden held up his glowing hands and turned sideways, jutting out his hip to show his brothers the hilted sword that graced his side.

"You are marked and armed," Josiah said.

"I'll tell you all about it later," Caden reported as he took his seat at the table.

As the band of brothers reconnected, Iman entered the dining room with a tray of luscious fruits. He set it in the middle of the table. He was immediately followed by a host of others who again lavished fine foods before their guests. The commotion of the servers and the delectability of the dining experience served as the perfect distraction for two deer ticks to enter the room and affix themselves to the canvass wall high above the dining party.

Venem and Gath had come into the camp just in time to see Tobijah and Caden enter the tented palace. The necrophim experienced the disorientation of the protectus blessing when they attempted to enter the palace but that was soon eliminated when Tobijah retracted the blessing. Now they could eavesdrop into the plans of their foe without being detected – or at least they hoped. Both necrophim knew that they were in a very vulnerable state as long as they remained insects whose lives could be obliterated with the swat of a shoe.

"We are one step closer to completing our mission," Clarion announced. "I think its best that we leave the camp before nightfall. We have one more mentor to meet and he can be very illusive. Kesh is Ian's mentor and he will be more difficult to locate than Tobijah was. He is a free spirit and roams throughout Salamgard. He could be anywhere but it was reported that he was last spotted at the north-western edge of the Ithcar Valley. If he is there, he will not be too far from our final destination. The forest of Ithcar Valley meets the Sargo Mountains on the west side of the forest, then opens up to beautiful fields just north of the Valley and mountain range. Those fields roll into the Dura plains that stretch out before Asilo. I suggest that we be prepared to leave within the hour. Lady Daesis should arrive before that time. We will leave when she returns to Aanda with Maayin," Clarion said.

"No! I am going with you. I'm not going back to Aanda," Maayin cried, shocked to hear this news.

"Maayin you cannot go with us. I have already explained this," Wes said. "Our journey grows more and more dangerous. Ubilaz already tried to kill you, and he found an opportunity to use you as bait in an attempt to destroy us as well."

"That would have never happened if you would have taken me with you in the first place," Maayin said holding back tears of pain and anger.

"Maayin, it wouldn't have happened if you would have stayed where you were told to, as well. We have been given powerful weapons to prepare us for a battle that may incur," Josiah said holding up his staff. "This isn't a game. You are not equipped for this."

"Not only that, but you're still a boy. You shouldn't have to think of engaging in a battle," Caden added.

"I can fight. Clarion taught me to shoot a bow. I am an archer and I am a man," Maayin replied. By this time, he couldn't hold back his tears. Wes began to feel the boy's heart ache.

"I risked being beaten when I came into Aanda to find you at the pub," Maayin said to Wes. "Then I traveled through the forest of Ithcar without a caravan and without you. I did it alone. I also saw the necrophim face to face. I can now be brave, I am not afraid. I'm not a boy, I'm a man," Maayin cried with passion.

"Maayin, it's okay to be afraid, lack of fear doesn't make you a man. I'm afraid but I know that I have a mentor who will prepare me," Ian added.

"Maayin, your heart is bound to ours, and even more to mine. I have grown to love you like a little brother. I know that you believe you will be abandoned again but you have a great family now. You will be cared for by Lady Daesis. I'm sure Lord Lemuel could be your mentor," Wes said.

"You should be my mentor but instead you treat me like I'm a weak little child. If our hearts are bound then you should take me with you and show me how to become the kind of man that you are," Maayin sobbed. The boy forced back his tears and replaced his grief with anger. "If you leave, then my heart is no longer bound to yours," he said.

As soon as he finished his sentence, he pushed his bowl of soup away and stormed from the dining hall. Maayin went running back to the bed chamber where he earlier convalesced.

Wes rose suddenly too. "Let him go, Wes," Caden said grab-bing his friend's arm to keep him from running after the boy. "You know this is the best thing and sometimes love must be tough."

"I *do* know that this is best. I won't change my mind on that. I'm not too sure about the tough love thing because I feel Maayin's pain and suffering. I just wish I could protect the kid's heart from any more pain. You guys can't begin to know the pain that I feel on his behalf," Wes replied.

"We really must prepare to leave," Clarion tenderly and ur-gently reminded. The band of brothers rose from the table and ex-ited the dining hall, still caught in the lingering web of their con-versation.

Josiah was pensive; the wheels of wisdom were turning inter-nally. "I feel like we may be making a big mistake," he announced without conviction because he was speaking his thoughts as he was formulating them.

"You don't sound too sure, 'Siah," Wes said.

"I'm not – but somehow my mind is leading me to think that we may be making a mistake by not taking the boy. I know the dangers and all, but hear me out. The first night we arrived in Salamgard, I lay in the bed at Clarion's cottage with my mind racing. I was processing through all that we had just experienced and had heard from Clarion. You know, the story of King Elyon and Ubilaz, life and death decisions, meeting mentors, along with all that Doc had said, and then something hit me. I came to the powerful conclusion that we . . . or. . . I, was no longer a boy – I was a man. Crossing over into Salamgard was somewhat of a rite of passage for me. I mean, I found myself in a place where I had to man-up, overcome fear, embrace the adventure and contribute to our survival, sustain-ability and success. Lord Lemuel confirmed that by reminding me that I was a man, *a man* who was wired up to seek wisdom. That was a powerful realization and I know that I can never go back to the way it was before. I think Maayin had that same kind of rite of passage experience in Ithcar. I think that by taking him we validate that he is a man. Somehow I got a feeling that if we don't, he may do something unwise to prove that he is a man, and it won't be good," Josiah said.

"What do you think he'll do?" Wes asked.

"I don't know – he might try to follow after us again."

"Siah, he can't go with us. We can't risk the harm that could come to him, besides I don't think I could survive if something else happened to him that could jeopardize his life. He's better off under the care of Lady Daesis in the safeguard of Lord Lemuel's fortress. We'll affirm that he is a man later," Wes said.

"But you do have a good point Josiah. Maayin may try to come after us again. It may be good to notify Tobijah to keep watch on the boy before we leave," Caden said.

"You guys might be right, Josiah added. "It all sounds logical but I still don't sense the wisdom in leaving him behind."

CHAPTER
SIXTY-FOUR

Daemonicus wasted no time in attending to his task. He was charged by Lord Ubilaz to enter into Otherland and bring back Eikondor's ambassador, Charles Morelock. The only way for any citizen of Ubilaz's kingdom to enter Otherland was through the dark magic of a powerful sorcerer named Belial. The cave of Belial was at the farthest outskirts of Ataroth Woods. Belial served as Lord Ubilaz's gate keeper into the realm of Otherland. Like Ubilaz, Belial was once given great powers and served in King Elyon's Court. When Ubilaz determined to overthrow Salamgard, Belial joined his ranks. The sorcerer discovered how to use his dark magic to open portals into Otherland, allowing Ubilaz the opportunity to counterfeit Elyon's program by sending his own ambassadors to expand the Kingdom of Eikondor. Without Belial's magic, the window to Otherland would be closed to Ubilaz and his loyal subjects. It was for this reason that the sorcerer lived in the seclusion of the cave far beneath the earth. Lord Ubilaz did not want to risk losing such a powerful ally.

Daemonicus stepped into the darkness of the cave, "I come in the name of the Dark Lord, King of Eikondor, Lord Ubilaz," he called. His words shattered the darkness and echoed through the caverns that extended deep into the belly of the mountainside. When the echo subsided, there was silence.

Daemonicus stood still, his hands clasped behind his back waiting patiently for a response like a delivery man who had just rung a doorbell. After a few seconds, he could see a pair of red eyes piercing through the darkness. He knew that someone was standing in the crevice of the cave.

"Sorcerer Belial, I would know your eyes anywhere. It is I, Daemonicus; I bring word from Lord Ubilaz. He is in need of your profound and powerful magic."

Belial stepped from the darkness of the cave's crevice into the shadows where he was more visible. He was clad in a dark tattered robe that was brocaded with a black velvet print. It looked like the robe that once adorned a king. His gray hair was dirty and matted but it was held in place by a diadem of black pewter. The diadem formed itself to fit the sorcerer's head just like Lemuel's had, giving him the appearance of a sage but absent of the essence that made him such. Belial's face was wrinkled, his form looked frail, and was hunched over. The lore of Eikondor speculated Belial to be four hundred years old, the oldest citizen in Ubilaz's realm. The years of living in the damp and dark of the cave had weathered the once virile looking magician. His skin was almost transparent, entirely absent of pigment, causing him to look as if his veins, muscles and bones were held in place by a milky white cellophane.

"Who are you?" Belial bellowed as he held his wand up in the direction of his visitor. His eyes failed and the light from outside the cave only silhouetted the form of the tall necrophim.

Daemonicus was wise enough to know that he should avoid being at the end of that powerful wand, "Daemonicus. It is I, Daemonicus, mighty wizard. Lower your wand. Lord Ubilaz sent me. I must pass over to Otherland. The Dark Lord has need of his servant Morelock."

"Ah, I see. It has been years since I let the Vitatha chief pass into Otherland". The sorcerer waved his wand. *"Exuro"*, he called, and a small orb of fire hovered above their heads dimly illuminating the cave.

"We must first locate the ambassador Morelock, so that we are sure to send you to the appropriate location," Belial said. Then he waved his wand again, *"Aquacretum"*, he proclaimed as a trickle of water began to ascend from the floor. The water's stream met the fireball overhead and produced a circular pane of steam before the sorcerer's face. He looked intently into the steam as if he were looking through a window. "He is in his throne room; I believe Otherlanders call it an executive office on Market Street. Tell me, why is the Dark One so interested in bringing this ambassador back?"

"Let's just say that Ambassador Morelock's unique abilities are needed to turn and persuade a person of interest, to join allegiance with Lord Ubilaz and our cause."

"The ambassador's son," Belial proclaimed.

"Yes, how did you know that?"

"Ah, I saw this event long ago. I knew the boy would serve as more than a leveraged hostage to keep an ambassador faithful to his cause. The boy can serve us well; not only by joining ranks with his father but also by the depth of the bond he has with the Otherlander's heart."

"If you have seen the future, will the Vitatha lad secure our victory and thwart Elyon's plans for the young Otherlanders to become the next great Knights of Salamgard?"

"I could not see that. The outcome is still to be decided. So you must go now while the ambassador is in my sights. But you cannot go in the state that you now appear."

"Metamorpho," Daemonicus said. The necrophim captain quickly transformed into a young corporate lawyer donned in a tailored black pinstriped silk suit with an alligator brief case. He

pulled at the collar and wrenched his neck, "I will never understand why those Otherlanders wear such inferior vestments," he said.

"I will keep watch," Belial quipped. "When you and the ambassador are ready to come back return to the place where you entered Otherland and I will snatch you back. Now, you must walk down that cavern." Belial pointed with his wand to a dark damp cavern off the right side of the cave.

Daemonicus stepped into the darkness and began walking deeper into the black earth. The old sorcerer raised his wand and began his incantation, *"Obscurum - permissum"*, summoning the darkness to allow the necrophim warrior to pass into Otherland.

A sudden gust of wind rushed through the cavern, hitting the old sorcerer with a force that blew his hair and garments back. Daemonicus was gone.

Belial scrambled to look into the steam window. He could see the dark lean figure of the necrophim emerge from an alcove in the underground rail of the Otherland city's metro system. Daemonicus stepped over one of the ground rails into the center of the underground tunnel and began walking toward the station. The tracks rattled and the air began to rush violently passed him, as a light from an approaching subway train loomed brighter and brighter behind him. Daemonicus remained unaffected and undeterred by the speeding blue line rocket. He kept a steady unhurried gait toward the brightly lit station platform ahead. The train sped closer and closer but Daemonicus didn't have any concern. His mind was fixed on his task.

Just as the train was about to overtake him, Daemonicus reached the station platform and leapt to safety with relative ease as the silver bullet shot passed him. The young corporate lawyer stood at the far end of the station platform, looking as if this was not his train to catch. He dusted off his jacket and straightened his tie. He got his bearings on the exit and followed the passengers who just disembarked the train, out of the subway station. He knew that Morelock's office was located in the skyscraper right above this Metro station.

"This shouldn't take long," he said. "I'll be back with the Ambassador shortly."

Belial was still peering into his window watching this scenario. He knew that the necrophim was speaking to him. "Oh I shall be here waiting, my friend. I know you say that this ambassador is vital to our cause but I believe that the Dark Lord should reevaluate his efforts and send you to collect a different ambassador – King Elyon's, Lord Darash. He is Elyon's gatekeeper in Otherland. He is the one who found the four whose hearts are bound."

The sorcerer's words were heard by no one. He continued to gaze into the window watching Daemonicus' every move, waiting for him to return to the metro rail platform with his prize.

CHAPTER
SIXTY-FIVE

Gath and Venem released their tick-like talons from the canvas wall in Tobijah's dining hall, jettisoning their insect bodies into a free fall. Before the two necrophim hit the ground, they changed into their invisible forms leaving a tinge of red vapor floating in the air. Nobody was in the room and it had been an hour since everyone had vacated the place, but the necrophim dared not take any chances. They were now standing on top of the large round dining hall table.

"So this is where Tobijah's warriors dine! Quite an impressive place wouldn't you say?" Venem asked.

"Keep your voice down fool," Gath scolded in a forced whisper. "While they cannot see us they still can hear your wretched cackling." The two stood there in silence for a moment to assess if anyone was in the palace. There wasn't a stir. "This kidnapping may be easier than I thought. Let's grab the boy like you and Avah did earlier and high tail it out of here," Gath said. "Maybe he will faint again. That would make it easier for us to carry him!"

"That could work but I think we could extract the boy in a more subtle way," Venem replied. "We don't even know where the boy is located. We need to worry about finding him and moving in a way that keeps us undetected. You recall we leave a red calling card everywhere we go. Once we have our bearings we can determine our plan of action."

The necrophim buzzed in slow short increments from the dining hall into the grand entrance hall of the tented palace, stopping occasionally to allow the red mist to dissipate quickly. Their entire scheme would be compromised if they moved too quickly leaving their marked trail throughout the dwelling.

They hovered in the grand entrance, watching and listening. After a few moments, Wes and Josiah came walking from a side corridor. The necrophim remained quiet and still. Both guys donned their weapons ready to leave on their journey.

If that young sage put on his spectacles we are doomed, Gath thought. He remembered how he was unmasked by Josiah back at the Victorium Morte celebration. Now his mind raced for an escape strategy, if by chance, Josiah put his discerning glasses on. But the guys seemed to be in a hurry as they walked briskly through the hall right under the invisible hovering nemesis.

"I'm glad that he fell asleep. I hope Lady Daesis arrives before he wakes up and realizes we are gone," Wes said.

"That would be best, but I'm still uneasy about leaving him here. I haven't had the chance to tell Iman to keep a watch on him. I'll do that before we take off," Josiah replied as the guys exited the tent palace.

Gath and Venem waited a moment until there was a silent stillness again and then they sprang into action. "The boy must be in a room down that corridor," Venem said. "I will transform into Lady Daesis and go to him. I'll take him out a back exit. You get outside the camp and morph into Cervus. We'll have the boy to Belial's cave in record time."

"Are you giving orders to a captain?" Gath growled. "I will be Lady Daesis and you . . ."

"There is no time to quibble, my captain. I would never think of giving *you* an order," Venem interrupted. "I was only thinking that I have more history with the boy since I have been tracking his every move, *AND* you did have a few . . . mishaps . . . that have not made the Dark Lord look favorably upon you. I was only thinking of you – should this attempt fail you could blame the whole thing on me."

Gath suddenly became more reserved in his plan, as a twinge of insecurity gripped him. Venem did have a point and the wrath of Lord Ubilaz would have fatal consequences. "Very well, I shall meet you outside the camp in the forest thick, south of the rock wall." Gath morphed into a horse fly and flew out the front entrance. Venem smiled with delight as he immediately took the form of Lady Daesis. He smoothed the wrinkles from the front of his dress and briskly walked down the corridor peering into the rooms until he came upon the sleeping boy.

The form of Lady Daesis quietly approached the boy who roused a bit at the presence of someone in the room. Venem sat on the edge of the bed and placed a warm gentle motherly hand on the boy's shoulder.

"Dear boy, wake up," the necrophim said in the sweetest, Daesis-voice he could produce. "Come child we must not waste time. You must wake up and come away with me."

Maayin rose from his nap. "I'm so sorry to be rude to you my Lady but I don't want to go with you, and I don't want to live in Lemuel's fortress."

"I know my child, and you shall not. If we leave here quickly I shall take you to your father."

"My fa . . .", Maayin's words were hushed by Daesis' hand place firmly over his mouth.

"Yes, your father," the deceiving necrophim whispered. "But you must be quiet and we must leave before anyone finds out. I have come to discover that the young conciliator Wes, has deceived you. Lemuel told him that we had located your father but in his jealousy, he wanted to keep you from reconnecting to him. Wes wants you to remain a little boy and he doesn't want your father to know you are a man."

This fueled more rage in Maayin, driving a wedge of distrust between himself and Wes. And yet the boy didn't want to focus his energies and attention on Wes because he was attempting to wrap his mind around the fact that his father, who he believed was dead, is now alive. It seemed unfathomable that he was being taken to his father. Any agenda or desire that the Vitatha lad had prior, was trumped by this news.

"My father is alive?"

"Yes, child and he longs to see you. Lord Ubilaz never killed your father as you were told."

At the sound of Ubilaz's name, the boy pushed away and shuddered. "Oh sweet boy, you need not fear. No harm will come to you. Hurry now, we must leave before Wes knows you are gone."

Maayin slipped on his shoes and the couple quietly slinked through the palace tent and out a back exit. They artfully dodged their way to the waterfall entrance of the cloaking blessing and disappeared behind it.

On the other side, Venem found Gath in the form of Cervus. As Lady Daesis, the necrophim climbed into the wagon and helped Maayin to his seat next to him.

Venem could only think that if he delivered the boy to Belial's cave, the Dark Lord would surely elevate him to the rank of captain. He gloated to be in a position of authority over another captain. This gave way to a lustful fantasy of the day when Gath and Avah would be subservient to him.

"Cervus take us quickly to the boy's father– and that's an order," the veiled necrophim commanded with a glint in his eye.

CHAPTER
SIXTY-
SIX

Iman walked through the grand hall of Tobijah's tented palace. He had orders to keep Maayin secure and make sure the boy didn't attempt to leave until Lady Daesis arrived to escort him back to Aanda. Moments earlier Wes and Josiah left the Vitatha boy sleeping in the comfort of one of Tobijah's guest beds.

Iman peered into Maayin's bed chamber. The lad was gone, leaving only an unmade bed as an indication that someone had found rest in the chamber.

"Maayin!" Iman called as he walked through the quiet palace seeking the lad. Iman walked through the dining hall and into the kitchen when he happened upon a chamber maid.

"Have you seen the young lad, Maayin," he asked.

"Yes, some time ago, my lord. I was in the garden attempting to have a conversation with a stubborn old billygoat about his rude behavior. He constantly thinks that he can just waltz in and help himself to the carrot bed. As we were having our conversation, I saw the boy and Lady Daesis leave from the back palace door. I waved, but they didn't see me as their backs were mostly to me and they were moving at a very hurried pace."

CHAPTER SIXTY-SIX

"Which direction did they go?"

"They were headed toward the waterfall entrance. I heard the Lady say that Lord Cervus was meeting them outside of the camp and she didn't want to keep him waiting. I do wish I could have spoken with her. She is very beautiful and always seems so delightful," the girl said.

"Thank you for being so observant dear girl," Iman said as he patted her cheek. Iman knew that there was something shady about the scenario. This matter needed Tobijah's attention immediately. He quickly mounted his stead and galloped off with his alarming news. He soon located Tobijah near the entry passageway of the camp. Themba, his albino tiger flanked his side. The Warrior was giving some last minute directives to the band of brothers who were about to leave the camp and resume their journey.

Iman stepped into the conversation. He had a commanding presence. His lean straight figure and perfect posture looked as if he was a soldier constantly at attention. Yet his gentle servant's spirit indicated that he was also a warrior with a soul characterized by goodness. He approached Lord Tobijah with a straightforward unruffled comportment.

"Lord Tobijah, the Vitatha boy is gone," Iman said.

Wes quickly became troubled. "We left him sleeping less than an hour ago and you went to him immediately. How can he be gone? This can't be happening. He must still be in the camp hiding, waiting to make an escape. We should find him."

"I'm sorry master Wes, but the boy is no longer in the camp", Iman corrected. Then he turned to address Lord Tobijah, "It seems that a servant girl saw the lad leaving with Lady Daesis. I thought it uncharacteristic for the lady to have entered the camp unannounced and leave without a word, in such a secretive manner. I fear that the camp has been compromised, my Lord."

"If it wasn't Lady Daesis with the boy, then who was it?" Caden asked.

"Only necrophim can take on the likeness of another being. I'm afraid Iman is right. Our camp has been compromised. The necrophim discovered us and found a way to penetrate the camp. They must have discovered our plans to have Lady Daesis escort Maayin back to Aanda," Tobijah replied.

"What about the protectus blessing? I thought they couldn't penetrate that?" Ian asked.

"They could have entered into the palace after I retracted the blessing. It was about that time when Maayin became aware that he would be returning to Aanda," The Warrior replied.

"So they may have been in the dining hall the whole time we were talking?" Ian shuddered. "Gosh, that gives me the creeps."

Themba let out a roar causing Clarion to gasp. "What is it," Ian asked feeling a little panicked now.

"I never thought of that," she said to the great cat. "Themba said that if the necrophim posed as Lady Daesis then she too may be in grave danger. Not only is Maayin's life at risk but hers maybe too."

Themba growled again and Clarion responded, "Yes Lord Themba, the King's power does flow strong through her but she cannot go up against a company of Ubilaz's forces alone. I do think it wise for you to go after her."

Tobijah nodded in agreement and Themba darted behind the waterfall and left the camp in haste to attend to the well being of the Lady.

Iman politely brought the situation back to task, "My Lord, your orders?" he asked.

"Alert our community. We will be moving immediately. Call all our warriors, both men and steed alike, to assemble. We will break camp and every warrior will search for the boy."

"Yes my Lord," Iman said as he produced a small glass crystal, which looked like a monocle, from his vestment pocket. He raised the crystal over his head and manipulated it so that it caught the light of the cloaking canopy. The crystal served as a reflector sending the beam of light to a tower just above the bridge where Caden and Tobijah earlier had their mentoring conversation. Within minutes, an ensemble of buglers emerged on the bridge and blasted a cadence that sent the entire community below into an organized frenzy. Women began gathering up their children and closing tight the windows of their tented homes. The animals found their place in the tented shelters and barns prepared specifically for them when such events like this occurred. Those animals who didn't need shelter prepared to run for cover into the forest tundra as soon as the cloaking veil was lifted.

Warriors on horseback began to assemble in companies of fifty on the pasture, right in front of Tobijah and the band of brothers. "We will also join the search," Wes said. "We can't let the boy fall victim again to Ubilaz."

Josiah put his hand on Wes' shoulder, "I think that the wisest thing for us right now is to find Lord Kesh and then get to Asilo. Ubilaz is counting on you to go after the boy. I'm sure he is baiting us again. He knows that we still haven't fully learned to trust King Elyon. He knows that you will rest in the power of your love, not your trust in the power of the King. Wes, I know that King Elyon can deliver Maayin from the hands of the Dark Lord, but even if he does not, we must stay faithful to trust the King and diligently hold the course of our mission. Lord Tobijah and his warriors are far more equipped and capable to find Maayin."

As Josiah spoke, the diadem glowed brilliantly on his brow. An inscription began to appear prompting Wes to read it out loud, "*Wisdom keeps one's feet from following a path of destruction.* I guess you are right, 'Siah – you have spoken wise words. We cannot fall into another trap."

"We must leave now," Clarion said. Wes nodded in resolved affirmation and threw his shield over his back.

Tobijah turned to address each of the guys. "We shall be vigilant in our search, Wes. The power of the King flows through you and your brothers. You must reach Asilo quickly. Josiah, you are wise and correct in your counsel to trust Elyon. Hold that course. Ian, your mentor awaits. He is highly acclaimed in Salamgard and among the most powerful of Knights in Elyon's realm. I wish you peace, in your search and encounters with Lord Kesh," Tobijah said. Then the warrior turned his attention to Caden,

"My son, remember to trust the King and go with your instinct, it will be goodness burning in the core of your being, your soul. Remember to protect that which belongs to King Elyon. You are a good man."

Caden put his hand against his chest to check and see if the amulet was there. He had almost forgotten that he was wearing the Kalos Sapphire. He could feel the amulet under his vestment. Caden bowed his head humbly in homage to his mentor. Tobijah removed his glove and placed his golden hand on the top of Caden's head in a strong gesture of anointing. "Until we meet again, good journey," the Good Warrior said.

Then Tobijah put on his helmet and mounted his steed. He turned the horse to take inventory of his warriors and the state of the camp. As he attended to his business, Clarion and the band of brothers slid behind the waterfall and exited the camp.

A moment later the band of brothers found themselves outside of the cloaked camp peering into the Ithcar Valley forest with the large rock wall at their backs. "If Kesh is at the western most part of Ithcar then we must head that direction," Clarion said pointing almost directly in front of her.

A short distance away out of hearing range, Avah and Raith sat undercover in the thick of some giant ferns. When they saw Clarion point in their direction, they both crouched lower behind the flora.

"Is she pointing at us? The white cat must have seen us and sent word to her. You think she knows we have been watching the camp since Gath and Venem left with the boy? She pointed rights at us!" Avah said.

Raith just calmly slinked lower and gave a quiet guttural growl. "You are right, Raith. If she suspected we were here, she would be pointing out our whereabouts to a company of warriors, not those pitiful Otherlanders. She doesn't see us and besides if they did, I could become invisible and you could slip away in the underbrush before they ever reached us," Avah whispered.

Raith caught the necrophim eyes and bared his teeth, communicating his message to the partner whom he despised, and who reciprocated the sentiment. "Again, you are correct, my hideous friend. They *ARE NOT* our concern; we must get that Kalos Gem for the Dark Lord. As soon as the Otherlanders leave I will position myself in a place where I can hijack my way into the camp under the hide of one of Tobijah's horses."

Suddenly there was a loud clap of thunder. The ground shook under the evil duo. The band of brothers also became unsteadied on their feet as the rock wall entrance of Tobijah's camp disappeared leaving only ten companies of mounted warriors and a forest full of trees and dense flora where the camp once stood.

Each company broke off into a thundering gallop, moving in every direction away from the former camp location, like a ripple when a rock is tossed into a calm lake. Tobijah's warriors were charged with canvassing the forest to locate Maayin and his captor's. The band of brothers huddled together as the horsemen darted off.

Avah's and Raith's eyes frantically darted from company to company and horseman to horseman trying to ascertain the identity of Lord Tobijah. All the warriors looked the same. No one emerged as the leader although each company stayed vigilant and on task.

"He's over there! No, he's over there," Avah kept saying.

As the warriors rode away Avah said, "I think it best that we just follow one of the companies. We should just play the odds that Tobijah is with the company we select. If he is not they will eventually lead us to him."

Raith didn't seem to be listening. In all the commotion, he kept his eyes on the brothers who were now walking straight toward them. He had another plan but he decided to play along with Avah's schemes. The sooner he got rid of the necrophim the better his chances of recovering the sapphire, or so he thought. The hyena made his quiet guttural growl.

"Good, I'm glad you see it my way. I will follow that company," Avah said indicating his choice. "You follow after me as quickly as you can."

Raith grunted again to warn Avah not to fly away in his invisible form. He didn't want the necrophim's red misty discharge to reveal his hiding place to the band of brothers. Then the hyena crawled deeper under the fern cover. Avah took Raith's advice transforming into a scarab beetle and buzzed after Tobijah's warriors. When he was a safe distance away, he changed to his invisible form in a pop of red mist.

Raith continued to stay still under the fern cover as the Otherlanders practically stepped over him while they passed by. The hyena thought, *that foolish necrophim can go on his cat and mouse chase but I will follow Warrior Tobijah's protégée. He most certainly would have knowledge of the gem's whereabouts. What mentor does not take his protégée into his confidence? At the appropriate time, I will get into the young warrior's psyche. He will come to believe that acquiring and giving up the gem is a GOOD thing. As for Avah, I am through with him.*

CHAPTER
SIXTY-SEVEN

Themba's mission was to find and protect Lady Daesis. He ran with magnificent speed through the Ithcar Valley forest toward Aanda. The powerful tiger's snow white fur against the deep greens of the forest flora made him look like white lightening bolting low against the wooded trail. Themba knew that he must stay this course. If Lady Daesis were unharmed and en route to Tobijah's camp, then he would intercept her. But if Ubilaz's soldiers had overtaken her, then Themba would find the aftermath of that altercation on this trail as well. Ubilaz would not be so unwise as to bring a fight into Aanda so he would have had to make a move while the Lady was traveling this path in the forest of Ithcar. Themba also knew of Lady Daesis's power. She would not be taken without a fight. The tiger quickened his pace. He only hoped that the first scenario was true and he would come upon Lady Daesis.

Themba could see a sharp left curve in the trail many paces ahead of him. That curve would mark the half way point between his journey's origin and Aanda. He had covered a lot of ground and still no sign of Daesis. Themba kept his pace, keeping a keen watch. Then he spotted her.

Rounding the curve, at a mighty gait, thundered Lord Cervus. Lady Daesis and Venn were seated in the coach seat of the wagon being pulled by the stag. Themba gave out a ferocious roar as he slowed his pace.

"Lord Cervus, it's Themba," Daesis said as the stag slowed his pace to engage his old friend. Themba roared and purred.

"Yes I am so glad to see you too, precious Themba," Lady Daesis replied. "And yes, I am well. No harm has come to me. But the news of Maayin progressively gets more grave, that dear sweet boy."

Themba roared again and Cervus gave a few snorts and whinnied.

"I should say so, it was the best and only strategy for Tobijah to move his camp in the light of such a perilous breech, Lord Themba. And Lord Cervus you are correct, it would not do us any good to continue on this journey. The camp is not there and Tobijah's warriors are engaging the search. But I fear for the young ambassador knights as well as the boy, Maayin."

There was a moment of quiet as Lady Daesis collected her thoughts. She closed her eyes and took a calming breath. Lady Daesis had the power of forward sight. She could see events before they happened although the outcomes were never always clear. The two captains and Venn watched and waited quietly for her. A few moments passed by. The forest was silent, save the rustle of the wind through the trees.

After a few moments, Lady Daesis spoke again, "We must not engage the search but rather take up another strategy. Ubilaz has orchestrated some events, which will level a destructive blow against Salamgard. Dark times lie ahead. The evil one will acquire Maayin and will intercept the young Otherland ambassadors before they reach Asilo. I'm afraid there will be a battle and one precious soul will be lost. We must move quickly."

CHAPTER
SIXTY-EIGHT

The lights of the Metro subway platform flickered as two darkly clad figures descended the stairs. Their footsteps echoed off the dirty white porcelain tile into the station below. The dampness from the underground, covered the stairs and walls with a thin film of sweat. A veil of cool heavy air caressed anyone who descended into the subway cavern. The cool air was infused with a dank and musty aroma, accented with the hint of urine and a bouquet of recycled ale.

The station was empty but within five minutes, the platform would begin filling with passengers who hoped to catch the 4:15pm blue line express. This offered the ominous duo a small but ample window of time to get back to Belial's portal. Daemonicus had little trouble convincing Charles Morelock to accept his assignment. The egotistical corporate lawyer was confident in his persuasive abilities and gladly welcomed the Dark Lord's request, although by now he cared little for the son that he left behind in Salamgard.

Charles Morelock was a broad shouldered, square jawed man. His temples were graying and the crown of his head salt and peppered. Morelock looked physically fit for a man who appeared to

be in his early sixties. He wore a charcoal suit with a black and red
striped silk power tie. Daemonicus and Morelock paused shortly at
the bottom of the station stairs. Daemonicus perused the platform,
first to the left and then to the right, to insure that they could make
their escape without detection. Charles Morelock waited, as a dig-
nitary would, on a body guard who was creating safe passage. The
powerful ambassador slipped his right hand into his trouser pocket
revealing his tailored shirt's finely starched, French-cuff and ruby
studded cufflink. The Metro was an unfamiliar place for Morelock
who had become accustomed to being shuttled everywhere by private jet and limo.

"I trust that you can turn your son to embrace our cause", Daemonicus said. "The boy has had some . . . let's just say, less than
pleasant experiences with the Dark Lord."

"My son will come to see that all of his experiences are part of
Lord Ubilaz's grand scheme to make him a powerful and wealthy
man like me," Morelock said. "Before I am done, my son will sit
by my side as my protégée. He will surely follow the bidding of
our master."

Daemonicus walked to the edge of the platform and stepped
off the side into the middle of the rails with ease, leaving Morelock
standing there with his hand in his pocket.

"Come, we have little time to waste," the necrophim said.

Morelock walked to the edge of the platform. Dirt and soot
from the trains blanketed the concrete underground tunnel. A small
stream of putrid sewer water ran down the center of the rail corridor making it a delightful water park for the city rats. Charles Morelock squatted down to steady himself on the edge of the platform
and then hopped down into the trench of the rail line.

"Belial could have picked a more suitable port of entry," he
said, as he brushed the dirt from his hands. His rebuke was cut
short by the conversations of a group of teenagers who were coming down the station stairs to the platform.

"Quickly, follow me. The portal is this direction," Daemonicus said with urgency as the pair ran down the center of the tracks into the darkness of the station tunnel and disappeared into the alcove.

Back in his cave, Belial watched the entire event unfold. He had been patiently waiting the return of the necrophim captain and Eikondor's noted ambassador.

"Good, good!" Belial chatted as he saw Morelock follow Daemonicus into the dark alcove. Belial stepped away from the steam window and walked to the cavern where he previously sent Daemonicus off. The old sorcerer raised his wand and began his incantation.

"Obscurum permissum," he said. There was a gust of wind and Daemonicus and Morelock emerged from the cavern. Daemonicus reappeared in his necrophim form and Morelock was no longer wearing his power suit. Instead he wore the colorful navy blue, burgundy and forest green cloak; the vestments of a Vitatha chieftain.

"Quickly, quickly, the boy arrives now even as we speak," Belial said pushing Morelock toward the cave entrance.

Charles Morelock stepped outside of the cave in time to see the wagon with Maayin, approaching. Gath and Venem remained in their form as Cervus and Lady Daesis so as not to alert the boy. It was important that they maintain the charade until the lad's father won him over. Daemonicus and Belial remained concealed in the shadows of the cave for the same reason.

The wagon came quickly alongside Morelock then stopped abruptly, kicking up leaves and dust. Maayin stood at his place in the coachman's seat and stared at the man. While the Vitatha chief looked older and more weathered, there was no mistaking that this was his father. Maayin didn't speak a word. He just studied the man's features recalling the loving father he once knew and adored.

"Maayin, my how you have grown," Morelock said, offering a hand to help the boy from the coach. Maayin refused any help. Instead, he boldly and defiantly jumped from his perch to the ground. After all, he had gotten along on his own for quite some time. He wanted this man to know that he was no longer a child, but rather a capable strong young man who certainly could dismount a wagon under his own ability. Maayin now stood face to face with his father, still not saying a word. He didn't know how to feel about this moment. He was angry that his father was standing before him looking robust and healthy.

Has he been well all along and never cared to come after me, the boy thought? But then his mind shifted, *but he is my father, the man I loved and adored. Why won't he just embrace me and tell me that he loves and misses me? Just give me something that tells me, that I am valuable to you.* Maayin was caught in the torrent of despising his father but yet wanting to have a deep relationship with him. To give into one side, meant that he would have to betray the other.

"You are no longer the boy I last saw. You have become quite a man, my son," Morelock said. This was enough to melt Maayin's heart, pushing him to give up his resentment and anger in exchange for a relationship with his dad. The young lad had longed for any kind of affirmation regarding manhood, from a significant male. His father's recognition that he was no longer a child made Maayin ready to pledge his allegiance once again to his father.

"Father!" Maayin said as he embraced the man.

Morelock pried the boy off him saying, "My son, you're a man now there is no time for this sweet affection that is common among children and women."

Maayin was caught off guard but he wanted the continued affirmation of his father so he quickly accommodated, straightening up at attention. "Father where have you been?" he asked.

"I have been in Otherland. Lord Ubilaz has made me a highly influential ambassador there with wealth and power beyond accountability."

"I don't understand, why didn't you come for me?"

"Maayin, sometimes a man must make sacrifices to give his

children something better. The Vitatha people are not looked favorably upon by Salamgard or Eikondor. I wanted more for you and now I can pass a mantel of wealth, respect and power to you. I had always planned to come back to you when the timing was right. I can now assure that people will fear and reverence you."

"But you left me alone and Lord Ubilaz terrorized me, even attempting to kill me."

"My son, the Dark Lord was testing you to see if you were a real man and you passed the test more bravely and powerfully than he or I, anticipated. You overcame pain and fear; and as the result of having to survive on your own, you learned to trust no one but yourself. You have become a man and now Lord Ubilaz is prepared to make you a mighty warrior, even greater than I. He has appointed me as your mentor, if you will have me."

Maayin began to feel a swell of emotion. His eyes began to well up because of his joy. He would have his father back who in turn would mentor him. Maayin didn't care if this was good or evil; he just knew that he was valuable and respected by his father for being a young man. He had his father back and his father wanted him.

"YES! Mentor me, my father and my Lord," the lad choked out as he began to tear up.

"I shall mentor you. The first thing you must know is that you never show your emotion. Women, children and weak men cry. Any emotion short of satisfaction or anger is unacceptable for a man. Any other time you remain . . . neutral, stoic and above all, controlled. You must hide your emotions because they are a sign of weakness and a real man never appears to be weak."

Maayin straightened up and wiped any tears from his eyes.

"Come stand next to me," Morelock said, putting his hand on the boy's shoulder. "We are going into battle and I will make sure you are prepared like I have done with your brother in Otherland."

Maayin looked up at his father with surprise. "My brother?"

"Yes, he is born of Otherland blood and while you are his elder, he will appear to be older because time in Otherland is not the same here. He is not as strong as you and he has not been selected by the Dark Lord for a special task as you have been".

"What is the task, father?"

"You must kill the Otherlander, Wes Litchfield."

Maayin gasped and pulled away from Morelock's side. "I cannot, he is my brother."

"He is not your brother," the Vitatha chief said angrily, startling the boy. Then he softened his tone, "The Otherlander has crippled you from becoming a real man. He would make you to think that love is virtuous and that power is not. This is the philosophy of a weakling, destined to be humiliated and taken advantage of, all his life. He would have you remain weak so that he can control you. Why did he not allow you to venture with him to see his king?"

"He told me it was too dangerous."

"What could be so dangerous about meeting a loving king? And why does he not recognize that you are a strong young man? Has he overcome the perils of fending for himself, or of tasting death and overcoming necrophim, as you have? You see my son, the Otherlander controls you."

Maayin stood silent. Morelock could feel the anger beginning to swell in the boy. He leaned down and whispered into the boy's ear, "But I know that you are a man and I know of your potential. Join me now and we will create an empire that we can rule together."

Maayin was burning with rage, "I will join you my father and I will pledge my allegiance to the Dark Lord. I will kill the deceitful Otherlander."

Morelock straightened up and caught a glimpse of Daemonicus who was standing in the darkness of the cave. The chief slyly smiled a gesture of confident accomplishment as the necrophim nodded in wondrous affirmation.

"We must go then to Lord Ubilaz," Morelock said. "I will take you to meet a real king."

CHAPTER
SIXTY-NINE

"Clarion, what does he look like?" Ian asked.

The guys had been walking in a north westerly direction for hours. Clarion led the way. She had removed the bow from her back and she was now using it as a walking stick. Wes and Caden followed closely behind her. Wes occasionally shifted the weight of the shield that was strapped to his back. Caden kept one hand on his sword, more because he wasn't used to wearing a weapon at his side, than out of a burning desire to use it. Josiah came next on the trail just a step in front of Ian who tended to lag behind. Josiah's staff, like Clarion's bow served as his walking stick. He gripped the powerful weapon that rose many inches over his five foot, eight inch frame.

Ian brought up the rear. He held a twig in his hand. He anticipated meeting his mentor and having a weapon more powerful than the stick, he held. Until then, he used his stick to swat at the grass and ferns along the way. When he wasn't swatting he was busy peeling the bark from the shaft of the stick.

Ian stopped for a moment to readjust his cape, rolling the sides up onto his shoulders, so that he would not become too over heated. The guys had continued to walk a few paces while Ian made his adjustments. Occasionally Ian's attention would be diverted by the rustling sounds of the forest behind him. With every sound, he expected to see Kesh but then his fear would peak of other things that may lurk in the shadows and underbrush and he would step up his pace to come along side Josiah. It was happening again, so Ian broke into a little jog and joined the safety of the caravan. None of the travelers realized that Raith was still following, concealed in the underbrush just a few meters behind them.

"What does, *who* look like?" Clarion called back.

"Lord Kesh! Is he a distinguished middle aged gentleman like Serik or an old sage like Lemuel; or is he like Tobijah, strong and muscular?"

Clarion smiled at Ian's descriptions, "Lord Kesh is a Wildman who is absent of any fear."

"That doesn't tell me anything about the way he looks. When I think of a wild man, the picture of a sweaty, hairy, masked, world federation wrestler, in a black body suit and tights comes to mind". The guys chuckled at Ian's description.

"Lord Kesh appears differently to different people. You will most definitely know him when you see him," Clarion replied.

The sun began to set as the entourage traveled on. There was still no sign of Lord Kesh. Clarion led with sure conviction that Lord Kesh, under the directive powers of King Elyon, would find them as much as they would find him. But now the forest was beginning to shadow over.

"Soon it will be dark. We are at the foothills of the Sargo Mountains in which, there are many caves where we can rest for the night," Clarion announced. "Come we will stay in that one ahead."

The guys agreed, so they made their way toward the cave. They had become tired from their journey and looked forward to a good night's sleep.

"I'm exhausted," Caden said. "I think I could fall asleep standing up and not wake up until noon tomorrow."

"I hear you," Josiah said, extending his fist, which was immediately pounded in a vote of affinity from Caden.

Clarion stepped into the cave to make sure that it was safe. She listened carefully for conversation or random thoughts that may come from any creature who claimed ownership on this cavern dwelling. After a few moments, she reemerged.

"Come in. This won't be as comfortable as the other bed chambers that you have slept in while in Salamgard but it will provide us with shelter and a good night's rest."

The guys stepped into the cave. Nearby in the brush, Raith kept watch.

I'll just wait right here and keep watch over you, he thought. *Tonight, when you are all asleep I will venture in and work my mind games on the one called Caden.*

The ground on the inside of the cave was soft and sandy. The band of brothers walked a few paces into the darkness. "We can't see a thing. I don't see how this can be safe for us, when we can't know what's in front of us," Ian said.

"Josiah can provide adequate light," Clarion replied. "Josiah, all you have to do is trust the power of Elyon and invoke an *illuminatus* blessing."

Josiah closed his eyes in an attempt to concentrate. After a few moments, he could feel the same surge of power that he felt when he was with Lemuel. The diadem on his brow began to emanate a faint glow.

"Illuminatus!" Josiah called and the crystal orb on his staff began to burn bright with a soft white light. Josiah chuckled at the sight of the torch that he now held in his hand. The crystal threw off enough light to engulf the circle of friends.

"This looks like a great spot to rest," Caden announced. "The ground is soft, it's deep enough from the front entrance and this little rock wall can serve as a nice protection from anything that might lurk from deep within the cave." He was of course referring to a formation of rock, about waist high that jutted out from the side of the cave blocking the path in front of them.

"I wonder what lies beyond this rock wall," Josiah said.

He took his staff and held it over the wall. The orb glowed brighter as if it had knowledge of its own accord. The crystal's glow illuminated an abrupt drop to a cavern below. It was difficult to see how expansive the cavern was because the floor of the cavern below receded into the darkness. The sandy path of the cave continued a few paces past the rock wall but then dropped off revealing a rocky crag that spilled down to the cavern.

The guys peered over the side of the rock wall. "Whoa, it's a good thing we stopped when we did. If we would have been walking on that side of the path, we could have fallen down there and been killed," Ian said.

"Or injured really bad!" Josiah corrected, giving Ian another reality check.

"This is perfect!" Caden announced. "We can rest here securely. Any enemy will have to scale that rocky crag to get to us from this direction." He removed the sword from his waist and plunged it into the sandy ground.

"I claim this spot for my bed," he said as he began to loosen the straps on his vestment. Caden pulled open his shirt and sat on the ground next to his sword. His bared chest revealed the Kalos Sapphire amulet that he still wore securely.

Josiah pushed his staff deep into the sandy floor of the cave so that it would stand alone. "There!" he said, "We have a Salamgard version of a campfire." Then each of the guys followed Caden's lead and found a spot to sleep, around Josiah's staff.

Clarion rested closest to the mouth of the cave. She tucked her bow under her arm and set the quiver of arrows in front of her face. She wanted to be ready should any dangerous foe venture in.

Outside the cave, one could see the ever-so- faint glow of Josiah's staff and hear the muted laughing and talking from the band of brothers as it occasionally broke the entrance of the cave. From a distance, Raith kept a fervent watch.

I can wait as long as it takes, he thought to himself. *Laugh and be merry now because soon your destruction will come.*

The noise from the cave began to die down as the night progressed. Soon there was no noise and the faint light that glowed from the cave began to diminish slowly until there was a quiet darkness in the forest broken only by the songs of the crickets and the harmonies of the night owls.

CHAPTER
SEVENTY

*I*t's *time,* Raith thought. The wicked hyena sat patiently waiting most of the evening in the darkness until it had lulled the inhabitants of the Ithcar Valley forest into a deep slumber. *The sun shall start to rise in a few short hours. Sleep has deeply swallowed the forest. It is time for me to seize the moment. When I am done with the young warrior, Caden, his mind will be so ravaged with confusion that he will gladly betray his mentor, Lord Tobijah to relieve his agony. He will come to believe that Elyon doesn't exist; the Kalos Sapphire is a piece of glass and that his brothers are fanatical crusaders who have no good in them.* Raith delighted in his cunning, which not only rid himself of his partnership with Avah, but also put him within reach of acquiring the gem.

Deep within the hollow of the cave, the travelers slumbered peacefully unaware that Raith was dangerously close. The ferocious hyena slipped out from his hiding place under the brush and lurked slowly and quietly into the mouth of the cave. Being a nocturnal hunter made his sense of smell more acute and his eyesight especially keen in the darkness. As he passed into the blackness of the cave, his eyes lit up like red spheres with molten yellow cores.

Raith crept quietly, hugging close to the cave's wall and low to the sandy floor as he ventured nearer to his sleeping target. He knew that the brothers where paces in front of him because he could hear their breathing as they slept. Slowly he peered around the corner of a rocky indentation in the wall. There they were, fast asleep in a circle around Josiah's staff. Raith carefully assessed the sleeping arrangements to locate Caden and plan his next moves. In order to get to Caden, the intruding hyena would have to step over Clarion who was ready for battle, gripping her bow, even as she slept. Raith plotted his trajectory and then took one slow deliberate step forward.

"What was that?" Caden yelled as he bolted upright out of his sleep, panting heavily. Raith quickly backed into the shadows. The brothers and Clarion were startled awake at Caden's sudden outburst.

"Caden - buddy what's the matter? I think you're having a bad dream," Wes said.

"No it wasn't a dream, I heard something. Someone is here in the cave."

"Illuminatus", Josiah called and the crystal in his staff glowed softly. Raith immediately pushed himself into the darkened recesses of the wall. Then he spotted it. Sparkling in the glow of Josiah's illuminatus blessing was the Kalos Sapphire amulet dangling from Caden's neck.

The sight of the gem made Raith, drool with delight. This was more than he could have hoped for. He quickly rethought his strategy. But then he saw that Clarion, who at the sound of Caden's distress, had her bow with an arrow securely strung ready to send it to its respected mark.

I must be prepared to make a quick escape in the cover of the shadows. Raith thought. *Surely, the young Warrior didn't hear me coming. I am more, light of step than his hearing is attuned too.* Raith didn't dare make any move so he stood silently and patiently watching.

"I don't hear anything", Ian said.

"Listen . . . there it is!" Caden said. The muffled sound of movement and the faint chatter of voices came from the cavern below. Raith now could also hear the same noises. The hyena listened intently and waited.

Caden and Wes peered over the rock wall to see if they could identify the sounds. From one of the tunnels that emptied into the larger cavern below, they could see the dim yellow light of torches growing brighter and brighter.

"Someone is coming," Caden whispered as he and Wes ducked back below the wall. Caden quickly tucked the amulet into his shirt and strapped the vestment secure. He grabbed his sword as Wes and Clarion both armed themselves too. Josiah pulled the staff from the ground, which went out as the intruders below stepped into the cavern. The light of their torches lit the expanse of the rocky room below sending light bouncing off the walls and ceiling, spilling into the space occupied by the brothers.

The guys peered over their rock wall hiding place, only to discover how immense the cavern beneath them was. The sides of the cavern had craggy slopes leading up to ledges and stone balconies similar to the one they were concealed behind. It was as if this was an underground amphitheater and they were in a VIP box seat high above.

"Hurry up." yelled one of the torchbearers. "Get in here and pile that wood in the center of the cavern." Six other torchbearers entered and stood around the sides of the cavern as soldiers carried in bundles of wood. It wasn't long before they had built a large altar of branches, twigs and logs.

"Now bring in the prisoners," barked the sergeant. Thirty shackled hostages where hurried in and herded onto the wooded alter. The prisoners ranged in age from adolescents to adults, both male and female. "We are ready to get this execution underway as soon as Lord Ubilaz arrives," the sergeant commented.

The guys looked at each other in horror. Josiah lifted his finger to his mouth as a gesture for everyone to remain silent and he slipped below the safety of the wall. The others followed his lead and huddled in close.

"We must remain perfectly still and quiet," Josiah whispered. "If they know we are here they will execute us too."

Raith also stayed quiet. If Lord Ubilaz were coming, this would be an opportune time to get the amulet. Raith knew that if he just sat patiently waiting, an opportunity would present itself.

There was a loud *whoosh* and a sudden gale of wind that filled the cavern below and rushed over the rock wall, chilling the backs of the brother's necks. Ubilaz had come and he was right beneath the young ambassador's hiding place.

"So these are the accused," the Dark Lord's voice echoed. "You are accused of the highest crime of treason against King Elyon who you once pledged your loyalty and devotion too. Up until this point I have been gracious enough to spare your pitiful lives."

As the Dark Lord talked, Caden whispered, "What is he talking about?"

Clarion replied, "He is correct. The high law states that if any citizen defects, giving their allegiance to another king, they become bound to that king and are subject to his will, even unto death. I assume that the prisoners were once loyal to King Elyon but because of their treasonous ways aligned themselves to Ubilaz."

"So that means that this execution is just? He can kill these people if he chooses?" Caden whispered back.

Clarion nodded her head in affirmation, "That is the high law of Salamgard."

They quietly listened as Ubilaz continued passing verdict, "My spies have told me that each of you has spoken contempt against me, or has waned in loyalty to the kingdom of Eikondor. As such, I no longer have need of you."

Ubilaz turned to his executioner, "Burn them!" he commanded.

Without thinking, Caden immediately sprang to his feet as if some reflexive reaction compelled him. "Stop!" he yelled pointing his sword with both hands around its grip, at the Dark Lord. The entire room directed their attention up to the roof of the cavern. Caden was brightly lit by the glow of the torches below.

"What the hell are you doing?" Ian whispered trying to pull Caden down by his pant leg. Josiah and Wes also grabbed at Caden from their seats on the floor but the young warrior brushed them off. Caden's sudden actions caught all the brothers off guard as well as the company below.

Raith saw this chaos as the opportunity he was waiting for. His cunning gave way to a perfect strategy and he quickly ran from the cave undetected by Clarion or the brothers.

"You cannot do this injustice," Caden yelled.

"Caden Boyd," Ubilaz droned, directing his attention to the opening high overhead. "Are you now a young warrior? I see you hold the sword of Tobijah. If you are going to battle *injustice*, dear boy, you ought to know how to interpret the law. You see, I *can* do this thing in the name of justice. Note that your hands do not glow as you grip your sword. You see, I am doing the right thing. Besides, I am king and I am sovereign over the law."

Caden looked at his hands in their natural state around the grip of the sword. *Could it be that the Dark Lord was speaking truth?*

"Maybe what you say is true," Caden yelled. "But you are a sub-ruler to the great King Elyon. Any sub-ruler must be just; ruling in the fear of Elyon."

"I will say it again: what I am about to do is just. This is a just execution and your demonstration of righteous indignation is impotent. All you have done is made it easier for me to attend to you when I have disposed of these traitors."

"Nothing that you do could ever be just or good," Caden called back.

"You impetuous fool," Ubilaz said as his anger began to burn. "You dare to stand against me without the protection of the circle of your brothers? You too shall die in my execution fires today."

"No he won't," Wes said as he stood up beside Caden, from his hiding place. Josiah and Ian both stood too, as did Clarion behind them.

"Ah, the circle is complete; such a joyous reunion. Each of you is armed and ready but I see that Ian has not yet come to meet his mentor. That means you can only use your weapons to defend yourselves and your circle only protects you from the attack of my necrophim, not these mortal soldiers here below. I am afraid that you gentlemen have made a very grave mistake, for you are greatly out-numbered. It seems I have you at a serious disadvantage. Seize . . ."

As Ubilaz was about to give the order for his soldiers to attack, Raith came sauntering through the tunnel into the great cavern. He gave a hideous laugh that echoed all throughout the cave, stopping Ubilaz's directive.

The hyena approached the Dark Lord who bent down to listen intently. "This changes things," Ubilaz said with a smile looking up at Caden. "Raith what do you suppose we should do?" The guys stood high above, dumbfounded as to what was happening.

Raith let out a deep guttural cackle. Ubilaz replied, "You are right, dear friend. It does become powerless if we kill them. What is your strategy my cunning advisor?"

Raith let out another laugh. Ubilaz smiled and stood upright. "I have decided to spare your lives," Ubilaz called.

The guys looked at each other in wonder. "And what about the lives of those hostages?" Caden called back.

"I will give them to you, good warrior . . . in exchange for the amulet that you wear around your neck."

Caden looked down at the faces of the hostages who now looked on him as the one who held their fate. He raised his chin and slowly pulled the amulet from its hiding place behind his vest-ment, letting it hang visible for all to see. The torchlight caught the sapphire sending blue sparks of light swirling through the cavern.

"No!" Clarion shouted at Caden. "As the King's ambassador, if you give it to him, you do so on behalf of the King. He will be-come seven times more powerful. Salamgard will be at his mercy."

"Caden this is a defining moment," Josiah reasoned. "You must do the good and right thing. Countless numbers will be terrorized if you exchange that amulet for the lives of thirty criminals."

"Don't give it to him," Wes affirmed. Caden then turned to see Ian.

"Don't do it, Caden," Ian said. "Consider the *greater good* of all those lives saved if King Elyon retains the powerful gem."

"What is your answer? I grow impatient." Ubilaz asked as he nodded in the direction of the executioner who prompted the torch-bearers to move to their positions close to the wood alter. As they did, there was a scuffle at the cave entrance behind the band of brothers. Ubilaz's troops moved in behind them.

"Don't be intimidated, Caden. You don't have to give him the gem. We will escape this dilemma," Clarion said seeing the soldiers. "It is during impossible times when King Elyon delivers his power. Remember, things aren't always as they seem to be in Salamgard."

"The amulet for your lives and the lives of these worthless criminals," Ubilaz growled.

Caden was perplexed as he removed the amulet from around his neck and held it firmly in his hand, "This is just a stone and a hunk of metal against the lives of thirty people. Are they not worth more?" he said to his brothers.

"Caden, think; think of what you are about to do!" Josiah said sternly as he grabbed Caden's arm.

"I need Elyon's wisdom", Caden said, "Help me, 'Siah."

Josiah held firmly onto Caden's arm, closed his eyes and began to concentrate. The diadem on his head began to glow. After a few moments Josiah said, "Follow the King's mandate; trust him with the core of your being and he will direct you."

Then Caden read aloud the inscription on Josiah's headband, "Protect that which belongs to the King".

There was silence in the cavern as every eye was fixed on Caden. The amulet swung from the chain held in his grip. Caden extended his arm and shouted, "The amulet is yours, Ubilaz." Ian grabbed Caden's shoulder but Caden pulled away. "Come and take it!"

The entire room watched as Ubilaz nodded for Raith to scale the slope and retrieve the gem. The hyena moved slowly and steadily upward. *Caden must have a plan. He has something up his sleeve,* the brothers thought. Caden stood firm with the amulet dangling from his extended left hand, and his sword raised in his right.

Ian stepped back a bit thinking that any minute Caden's hands would glow giving him the authority to take the life of the hyena.

Raith reached the top of the rocky crag. He sneered and let out a growling snicker. Then the hyena slowly and cautiously rose on his hind legs and guardedly closed his razor sharp teeth around the amulet chain. Both Caden and Raith remained frozen in the moment as the amulet's chain became taut from the firm grip that held both ends.

Caden released the chain and the hyena giggled with glee as he watchfully backed away from the band of brothers. After Raith felt he was a safe distance from his foe, he turned and rushed down the slope to present his Master with the trophy.

"Release the prisoners," Ubilaz ordered. He looked up at the band of brothers, "You are free to go for now. I shall give you an hour's head start before I send my warriors after you. Mark my words - You will not reach Asilo. You have made me stronger and next time we meet, you will not escape my wrath. One foolish decision has sealed your doom." The Dark Lord placed the amulet around his neck and soaked in the new surge of power. The soldiers in the cave opened a path allowing the band of brother's free passage, which they immediately seized.

CHAPTER SEVENTY-ONE

The brothers ran out the entrance of the cave. "Why did you give him the Kalos Sapphire, Caden?" Ian shouted in a panic. "You just made him stronger. I'm sure that's not going to rest favorably for us."

Wes looked at Caden with confusion trying desperately to make sense out of what just took place in the cave. Josiah put his hands on his head in disbelief. He immediately shook it off in an attempt to focus his mind on an escape strategy. Clarion just stared at Caden, like a mother waiting to hear an explanation from a teenage son as to how the front bumper of the car got smashed.

"I felt the king's power. 'Siah, you've felt it before and you too, Wes. Clarion, you know the power that guides your arrow and flows through Lord Cervus. It is unfathomable. I experienced that same power when I let go of the amulet. I guess I just thought that if King Elyon is as powerful as everyone claims he is - as we have experienced he is - then he doesn't need a magic sapphire to increase his power. I believe that he is more powerful than Ubilaz – even if

Ubilaz's strength is increased sevenfold. The lives of those people hung in the balance. Even though they did something unjust, they deserved mercy."

"In your defense Caden, we *were* instructed to trust the power of the King and not our own power," Wes replied. "I guess you did that boldly."

"But are you sure it was the King's power you felt?" Josiah asked. "I just find it hard to believe that the King would empower you to disobey his command; '*protect that which belonged to the king'*. The task given to you wasn't to discern if King Elyon's power needed to be enhanced by the gem; it was to protect the gem from falling into the hands of anyone who would use it for evil, like the Dark Lord. You may have jeopardized your knighthood and maybe ours as well. Remember - Where we go one, we go all?"

Caden's countenance fell and he got a sick, sinking feeling in his stomach at the sound of Josiah's wise words. Doubt began to well up in him like bile in his throat.

"I think I'm going to be sick," he said. "I'll plead my case before the King and beg his mercy on your behalf. You shouldn't have to be penalized because I acted disobediently. I believed that I was doing the good thing. I felt the King's power burning in my soul."

By now, Clarion was paying little attention to the conversation. She was on high alert, communicating with the forest creatures in an attempt to plot the next move. Her back was to the huddle of guys as she watched the forest landscape in front of her.

"Gentlemen, we have little time to quibble over events that have past," she said. "We need to leave here now, lest we become locked in a battle with a deadly enemy. The eyes and ears of the Ithcar Forest have no knowledge of the whereabouts of Lord Kesh. I'm afraid that he hasn't been seen for days in these parts. At this point, I think that we should head directly to Asilo for your protection. I cannot say for sure, but the tables have been greatly turned against us. Ubilaz will surely mount an offensive maneuver within the hour as he so villainously promised."

"But what about my mentor, Lord Kesh?", Ian said. "I have to meet with him before we arrive at Asilo".

"I'm sorry Ian, but we cannot afford to wait for Lord Kesh to show up. The unfortunate turn of events mandates that we go directly to Asilo. From all appearances, it seems like your mission has been severely compromised. The only option before us is to get safe passage for you to Asilo and then back to Otherland."

"But things aren't always as they seem to be in Salamgard," Caden quickly interjected, in hopes that the situation could, in some way be redeemed.

"You are right, Caden," Clarion said with a soft reassuring smile. "If King Elyon intervenes he will do it as we travel to Asilo. That is still our best option. Asilo is about a half day's journey in that direction. We must move quickly and staying alert," Clarion returned.

Before anyone could say another word, Clarion raised her calling charm to her lips and blew a soundless melody. "Quickly follow me, we must leave this place. I have summoned for assistance."

Clarion pointed the direction of Asilo to the left of where the guys were standing but then she broke into a run the opposite direction, down a trail deeper into the woods. The guys followed her, trying to remain sure footed as they jumped over fallen tree limbs, dodged rocks that littered the forest path, and traversed up and down steep areas of the terrain.

After running for about ten minutes, Clarion stopped at the bottom of a ravine to listen again to her hidden friends who watched over their travels. Wes found that to be an opportune time to clarify something.

"Clarion," he said as he tried to catch his breath, "I thought you said that Asilo was the other way. We have been running hard but not in the right direction. What's the plan?"

"We are running to the Natsal River. That river runs through the Ithcar Valley and meanders around the Sargo mountain range all the way to the City of Wreingor where it becomes the Natsal Falls. The river will take us to the edge of the Ithcar Forest and will put us in closer proximity to Asilo. It is the quickest route to get us to safety. Help awaits us at the river." Then Clarion got quiet as she listened. A bird began to chatter high above the guys. Clarion looked up and then returned her attention to the brothers.

"You need to run faster than you have ever run before. Ubilaz knows that his necrophim are powerless as long as you keep your circle of brotherhood in tack but he also knows that your circle is relatively powerless against his mortal army. And because Ian is weaponless, he knows you can only defend yourselves. He has already begun to mobilize his mortal warriors. It seems that he is not going to wait an hour as he promised. Ubilaz plans to outnumber us and kill us. The good news is that they must catch us," she said with a sly smile and a redeeming twinkle in her eye.

Clarion began to run down the center of the ravine. The guys followed in aggressive pursuit. After what seemed to be a good mile's run, Clarion followed the path up the right side of the ravine. The trajectory uphill slowed the guys down to a pace that resembled a less than brisk jog.

"I . . . have to . . . stop," Ian said winded and in pain over how out of shape he suddenly realized he was.

"The Natsal River is just beyond the top of the ravine. Don't stop now, Ian!" Clarion called.

Caden reached back and offered Ian a hand. Ian grabbed hold and Caden pulled, grunting as his brother joined his side. "C'mon buddy, I feel the same way but we can do this," Caden reassured.

Clarion reached the top of the ravine and stopped. Wes quickly joined her side, followed by Josiah and then Caden and Ian. Before them flowed a great river.

The Natsal River cut through the forest parting the trees on either side. The river glistened, a deep blue-green, which again taunted the guys to take a refreshing dip, as the mountain stream did earlier in their journey. But the lure of taking a cool swim was overshadowed by the gravity of their predicament.

Clarion stepped to the edge of the river bank so closely that the water lapped up at her boots. She again raised the calling charm to her lips and blew. The guys watched and waited. Nothing! Clarion looked up one side of the river and down the other as one would if she were crossing a busy street. She raised the charm again and repeated her call. A moment past and then a large white river dolphin shot up out of the water in the center of the river with a loud click, whistle and giggle. At the apex of her ascent, she did a full flip and jovially plunged back into the water.

Clarion smiled and called, "Lady Soteria, you are a wonderful and welcomed sight. I'm so glad that you answered my call." The dolphin rose out of the water on her tail and cackled a joyful salutation in return. As she rose up, the guys could see King Elyon's mark emblazoned on the breast of the graceful mammal. Soteria giggled and clicked again.

"Yes these young men are the ambassador-knights that you have heard about," Clarion replied. The dolphin cackled again.

"The scouts were right in telling you that our journey has taken a dreadfully urgent turn. We must get to the northern most part of Ithcar Valley where the river bends. The Dark Lord is in rapid pursuit of the young men and time is of the essence. He will surely destroy them if we cannot reach the safe haven of Asilo. We need your help to get us quickly up river. That would put us within an hour's journey closer to the plain of Dura, which spreads before Asilo. Once we get there, we can journey across the plains by staying hidden in the meadow grass. I have called for Lord Themba to meet us with an entourage as well. Soteria, are you prepared to give us passage?"

Soteria cackled her answer back. Clarion turned to interpret for the guys. "Lady Soteria commands King Elyon's forces in the waters. She has arranged to give us faster passage. We will travel on the river. It's a bit more risky because we will be in the open, but it will be much faster."

Soteria cackled again prompting Clarion to give instruction to Ian and Wes. "Remove your belts," Clarion said. Wes untied the sash from his waist and Ian did the same with long leather strap he wore. As they did, Clarion searched the banks of the river to find two solid girthed sticks that fit her specifications.

"Here," she said handing them the branches. "Tie the ends of your belts to the either end of the stick. You are making reigns to harness yourselves."

As she finished giving instructions, three giant stingrays swam up to the river edge at the place where the guys stood. Clarion stepped onto the back of one of the stingrays.

"Josiah and Caden your rides are here. I trust that you guys can surf."

Caden stepped onto one of the stingrays, "I've never surfed, but we both snowboard. This should be fun."

Josiah also took his place on the back of the third stingray. As he did, Soteria came close to the shore. Clarion instructed Wes to give her the branch, which the dolphin took in her mouth. Then Wes was instructed to step onto her back. He held the middle of the sash like the reigns he once held that bridled Cervus. Another Dolphin came near and Ian mounted the mammal in similar fashion.

Moments later the party was skimming across the top of the water as if they were on jet skis. Soteria lead her company. Wes stood tall on her back. He could look ahead and see the river stretched out far in front of him to meet the horizon. Clarion rode just slightly behind him to his right and Josiah was to his left. Ian and Caden followed to the right and left putting the travel party in a perfect inverted "V" formation. This allowed the sea animals the ability to break through the water quicker while avoiding the wake created by the others.

Wes looked down at Soteria. Her head bobbed up and down, just barely skimming beneath the surface of the water. She was aware of keeping the rider on her back as dry as possible. The dolphin and her escorts cut through the water with powerful speed sending their unified wake crashing against the shore.

Wes shifted his weight to his back leg, which kept him more balanced and the reigns tight. That seemed to give Soteria a bit more leverage to increase her speed. He looked over his right shoulder to see that Ian had discovered the same stance on the dolphin he rode. Ian's cape was unfurled in the wind behind him, making him look like he was some kind of comic book super hero. Caden, Josiah and Clarion discovered quickly to put their weight forward to balance themselves on the backs of the stingrays.

The forest on both banks whizzed by as the band of brothers were whisked down river. They could see the river begin to turn far ahead.

"We will stop just beyond that bend in the river," Clarion yelled in Wes' direction, over the sound of rushing water. She motioned to the others who observed the river bend ahead and prepared to dismount. Each nodded or gave thumbs up in understanding of exactly what Clarion was communicating. *Apparently her gift of communication was not limited to animals,* Wes thought.

Soteria set her sights on a drop off spot. Clarion's stingray moved closer to Wes. "When you get near the bank of the river, jump," Clarion yelled to Wes. Soteria then moved quickly ahead of the pack. The others followed in single file, each now positioned in the center calm of the wake from the escort ahead.

The white dolphin slowed a bit then gave a click and whistle releasing the stick from her jaws. Wes jumped and his forward momentum made him hit the sandy shoreline running. He slowed his pace and stopped as Soteria kept right on swimming to clear out of the way for the others. Clarion came next followed by Josiah, Ian and Caden. Everyone ended up relatively dry and secure on the banks of the Nastal. Wes and Ian transformed their reigns back into the belts they once wore.

"That was a rush!" Caden said as he landed safely on the river bank. Clarion thought that his comments would be a repeat of their escape on the Gilbreath Plains but she was surprised at Caden's response.

"Thank you, Lady Soteria and thanks to your entourage. Because of your faithful service to the King, you brought salvation to us. The King's power is evident in you," he said.

Soteria rose up on her tail and gave her dolphin giggle. "And may you live in the peace and prosperity of King Elyon as well, dear Lady," Clarion returned.

The dolphin did a quick aerial dive back into the river and she and her guards disappeared into the deep.

CHAPTER
SEVENTY-TWO

"We must get into the cover of the woods again," Clarion urged. "Soteria provided us with a good head start but that will be easily diminished if we don't continue to move. Lord Ubilaz's loyal horses are likely to carry his warlords. They will make short work of our lead. He will also dispatch his great cats, wolves, hyenas and any other ferocious beast that can quickly navigate the woods. His spies will surely inform them of our whereabouts and they will soon pick up on our scent."

"Can't we stop Ubilaz or at least slow him down?" Caden asked as the guys darted into the cover of the trees.

"I alerted King Elyon's spies before we got on the river. They carried an urgent message to Lord Cervus and Lord Themba. I have asked them to send reinforcements to interfere with Ubilaz's troops. It is my hope that Lord Themba will meet us where the woods open to the Dura plains, if they can get the message in time. He may be our only hope of reaching Asilo safely. Now quickly, we must head north into the woods to pick up the trail that leads to Asilo."

They found the trail straight away and set a steady brisk pace toward their destination. The trail seemed well traveled as it cut through the forest. It soon passed through an opening in the forest tundra and quickly meandered down a small slope that again, required the guys to mind their steps. At the bottom of the slope, they could see the trail cut through the tree line and open many paces ahead onto a road that stretched across the plain of Dura. In the distance, the spires of Asilo could be faintly detected. A new surge of exhilaration came over the guys.

"We're almost there," Wes said.

"Yes, but we dare not take the road lest we be too exposed," Clarion warned. "Follow me. We will travel off this path and remain in the cover of the woods until we can emerge into the high grass on the plain, over there". She pointed in the direction of her plotted trajectory. "That is where Lord Themba will rendezvous with us".

The guys looked ahead. They could see in the distance where the trees ended and the golden browns and greens of the grassy meadows began. Again, Clarion led the way, deviating from the forest trail. The woods weren't as dense as they had once been. The trees began to thin out and the terrain began to roll softly as if to create a perfect blending transition between the Ithcar Forest Valley and the Dura plain. Clarion's brisk walk suddenly came to an abrupt stop, bringing the guys to an unexpected halt. She stood very still as she once did when they met the Dark Lord before.

"It may be too late," she whispered. "I fear we are not alone!" She quickly brandished her bow and pulled the arrowed string tight. Caden drew his sword from the hilt as Wes brought his shield in front of him and bared the blade of his dagger. Josiah also readied himself for and encounter by gripping his staff firmly with both hands as he would if he were gripping a battle mace.

The group stood silently still watching. An eerie déjà vu fell over the guys. They had a similar encounter like this before that nearly ended tragically. Without saying a word, each guy determined that he would follow Clarion's lead and instincts. The deafening quiet of the forest was suddenly broken by the snap of a twig to the right of the guys.

"There!" Ian yelled. "I saw someone there." They all turned their direction to hear a shuffle and then silence again. The quiet was unnerving and seemed to linger long in the forest air. It was finally broken by the sound of movement, which came again on the reverse side of the band of brothers. In reflexive consensus, they turned to face their foe.

Nobody was there. There was quiet again. Each guy's heart was beating so fiercely, that one wondered if it audibly echoed throughout the forest. The adrenaline that coursed through their veins had increased their respiration to the point that it became painful to hush their breathing.

All of a sudden, they heard a giggle, which then turned to laughter. In one accord, the guys turned again to face their stalker. Their fear was dissipated by the sight of the source of the commotion.

"It's a glowing - naked guy," Ian stated. There before Ian, about one hundred paces into the cover of the flora stood a young man who looked to be within a decade older than the brothers were. His wild, dreadlocked hair was dirty brown and he stood smiling with his hands on his hips. His tanned skin glowed as if it was its own light source. Unusually, he wasn't wearing a stitch of clothing and he didn't seem to be concerned about that, or that Clarion was present.

"A naked guy? You must be seeing things, Ian!" replied Caden. "It's a child dressed colorfully like the Vitatha children we saw in the market. But you did get one thing right; she is glowing. How did a five year old child get out here?"

Josiah quickly said, "Something strange is happening here. I don't see the naked guy or a colorfully dressed Vitatha child but I do see a glowing . . . caveman. Standing right there is a large bearded, hairy, beastly glowing man, wearing animal skins. Am I right Wes – isn't that what you see too?"

"I see the glow too, but it's the glow of a white robed, winged man with a golden sash around his waist," Wes said. "He almost looks like a very pure version or opposite of Ubilaz."

"Lord Kesh!" Clarion said with resolve, as she pushed past the brothers to stand face to face with the final mentor and last great Knight in King Elyon's realm. "I believed that we would not encounter you before we reached Asilo."

Kesh didn't say a word he just smiled. Then he reached down to the ground and picked up a stone from the floor of the forest. The guys each watched as their transfigured representation of Kesh flung the stone high into the air and yelled, "Presidium Electus"!

The stone soared upward and exploded into a protectus blessing, like a big round firework Chrysanthemum covering the expanse of the forest.

"Wow!" Caden exclaimed. "That's an outrageously wide protectus blessing. It's almost looks like we are free to roam the entire forest without fear."

Lord Kesh let out a laugh and then gestured for Ian to follow him as he began to jog away from the group. Ian stood frozen watching his mentor playfully summoning him to a cat and mouse chase. When Ian didn't begin the chase, Lord Kesh became more animated, dancing a little jig and waving his arms for Ian to join him.

"This is just my luck, of all the mentors possible I get a naked lunatic who is probably as old as some of my peers . . . I may be wrong but he doesn't look like he's equipped to give me a weapon. As a matter of fact it's probably safe to say that he doesn't look like he's carrying any weapon at all."

"Ian, don't be deceived. Lord Kesh is far from lunacy. He is a mighty Knight of King Elyon's realm, a Wildman; and this wildman is never a lunatic," Clarion corrected. "Remember things aren't always as they seem in Salamgard."

Ian took a step toward Kesh who then turned and broke into a full run, away from the band of brothers. Instinctively, Ian started to chase after the mentor generating enough speed to send his cape flailing behind him.

"Go, Ian!" Caden yelled as he watched his brother engage the chase. As Ian and Kesh ran farther, Caden looked up at the protectus canopy that stretched across the sky. It felt very reassuring and safe.

"I'm going to take a walk," Caden announced thinking that he needed time to reflect on what he was going to say when he encountered King Elyon.

"I'll go with you, bro," Wes said.

"Um . . . I think I'd like some alone time. I'll be safe. The blessing is wide," he said pointing to the sky. "I hope you don't mind. I just need time alone to think."

"Oh, sure," Wes said, respecting Caden's wishes. He knew that Caden was going to contemplate the consequences of his action and try to determine if there would be any redeemable way that he could make the situation good. As Caden began to walk away, Wes called, "Hey, I love you bro. Always have. Always will."

CHAPTER SEVENTY-THREE

Caden often thought more clearly, when he walked or went on a good run. Since they spent most of the day running, he felt that a leisurely stroll would adequately do the job. The expanse of Lord Kesh's protectus blessing afforded him the luxury of taking his walk alone. Caden replayed the events that occurred over the past day, in his mind. He wondered how or if his actions had compromised their mission in Salamgard.

Caden walked until he disappeared from Wes and Josiah's view. Ian had also run out of view as he chased Lord Kesh. No matter how fast Ian ran, the gap between him and Lord Kesh remained calculatedly the same.

Ian quickly winded and stopped to catch his breath. Lord Kesh stopped and faced Ian who was buckled over with his hands on his knees attempting to suck in more air and alleviate the burning in his thighs and the stabbing pain in his side.

"What the hell, man; this is ridiculous," Ian said. "All the other mentors acquired the guys, but I have to catch my mentor. It's messed up; I've been running away from Ubilaz all day. I've used all my strength to surf on the back of a dolphin, and now I'm chasing a buck-naked dude who is ten times more athletic than I am. Something is wrong with this picture! Why are you naked and why am I *chasing* you?"

Lord Kesh still stood on the path, well ahead of Ian. He was smiling jovially, his hands on his hips, not having broken a sweat or even the slight bit winded.

"Lose the cape," Kesh yelled. "Throw it off – you don't need it. Get rid of your cape."

"What? But I like this cape it's the only thing that distinguishes my Salamgard clothing."

"It impedes you and easily entangles you. Lose the cape!" Lord Kesh said deliberately with a sly smile. Then without waiting for Ian to respond, he began to run again.

Ian stood for a moment, contemplating if he wanted to engage this foolery anymore. He glanced in the direction that he had come. He was so far out of sight from the brothers and had not paid attention to the way he had traveled, that he dare not turn back. Then he glanced toward Lord Kesh who was not waiting for him, running farther away. Ian felt an anger beginning to grow in him because he knew that he had no choice but to follow his mentor, as crazy as it seemed.

Ian unclipped the cape from around his neck, wadded it up and threw it into a bed of ferns nearby. As soon as the garment left his hands, a burning rush surged through Ian's body from the bottom of his feet to the top of his head, then back again. Ian held his breath with surprise as fatigue evaporated from his heart and lungs, and new supernatural energy infused his muscles, regenerating his legs and thighs. He chuckled, and with a new found confidence, believed that he could catch Lord Kesh.

Ian sprinted toward the mentor, gaining closer and closer with every stride. He was beginning to close the gap, coming within reach of Kesh, when the mentor broke away again with almost no effort. Ian stopped abruptly. He began to feel fatigue seeping back into his body.

"Get rid of your boots, you have no need of them," Kesh yelled back as he again stopped to wait for his protégée.

"Are you kidding? If I go barefoot, I'll never be able to run. There are sharp twigs, thorns and stones all along the path. This terrain will cut up my feet. You're used to running without shoes – or, from the look of it, anything else on, for that matter; but I don't go around barefoot enough for my feet to toughen up like yours."

"Have it your way," Lord Kesh said. He smiled and turned to run again.

"Wait, wait!" Ian yelled. "I know what you're doing. I start throwing things off and then I'll be totally naked like you. I'm not going to play your naked game. It's just way too weird. It's not even – moral. Aren't there decency laws in Salamgard?"

"In Salamgard, things aren't always as they seem to be," Kesh called back. "You have learned to place your trust in things you know, not in a powerful unseen King. You are imprisoned by worry, to the extent that you make it logical. Then you trust your logic."

"You're telling me that my logic is faulty when I say that running on the rough, sharp path will tear my feet to shreds? That doesn't make sense. How can my logic be faulty when that is fact?"

"No, I'm telling you that you trust your boots will protect you in a greater way, than an all powerful King! That doesn't make sense! Throw off your boots. You have no need for them." Lord Kesh laughed again and started to run.

At the sound of Lord Kesh's laughter, Ian uncharacteristically felt amused. Lord Kesh's free spirit was beginning to resonate with Ian's spirit in some strange way. Ian plopped down on the trail, with a determined smile. He hurriedly began to pull at his right boot as he watched his mentor running farther away. He could begin to feel the same surge of energy welling up in him as before, but this time it was accompanied by a new sense of wildness. Ian began to think that his spirit was breaking free. He pulled off his right boot and tossed it into the woods. Then he quickly tugged at the left boot all the while watching Lord Kesh increase the distance between them. Ian pulled and smiled. "No holds barred, Wildman. You shall not escape me," he said through the strain of his labored tugging.

Ian's boot finally came off and he pulled the socks from both his feet. He tied them together and from his seated position, he flung them as hard as he could. When the socks left his hands, Ian felt like he was on fire. The same burning that his brothers had described, he now experienced. He felt like his spirit was finally unleashed.

Ian sprang to his feet and began to run effortlessly. He soon started to gain on Lord Kesh until they were running side by side. Kesh quickened the pace as he did before, but this time Ian remained by his side, running without any weariness. They both laughed at Ian's new freedom. Lord Kesh slowed his pace and came to a stop right where his protectus blessing met the floor of the forest. They had run to the edge of the blessing's dome.

"I'm not even tired," Ian said.

"And how are you feet?"

Ian looked down to see that his feet were unharmed and in better shape than they were before, having been conformed to his tight boots. "My feet are fine," he chuckled.

"You are a free man, Ian because King Elyon has made you free. That freedom is in you regardless of whether you live into it or not."

"This whole freedom thing doesn't make sense to me – don't get me wrong, I've never felt more alive and on fire as I do now. But I'm confused about how freedom is a character trait. Doc said . . . oh, he's our professor and mentor in Otherland . . ."

"Yes I know Dr. Ashe very well."

"Oh, yeah I guess you would. Anyway, Doc tried to explain it to me but it's just not computing."

"Ian, King Elyon conquered the very thing that is most feared, death. With that, he also conquered fear. To those who trust him, he instills a free and wild spirit, which he empowers; not a spirit of worry and fear. He made you free. You *are* free! But often you don't feel free because you continue to put yourself back in bondage."

"That's crazy! I don't put myself in bondage! Who in their right mind would put themselves in bondage?"

"Only someone in their *right* mind," Lord Kesh said with a wink and a smile. "You see Ian, faith or trust is not logic, reason or rationale, and logic is not faith."

"So you're telling me that faith is irrational and I should just throw caution to the wind, do whatever I want and trust that King Elyon will make it all good."

"There is a difference between being a wildman and being a lunatic; between living free and living irresponsibly. The line that divides it lies in an understanding that faith is *non-rational*, not *irrational*. You will still be called on to think critically, but not to trust your own understanding. Your spirit is unleashed to be it's free self when you exercise a reckless abandon of everything to place your faith solely in the King. If you trust anything else, you begin to enslave your spirit again. It's kind of like covering yourself or hiding who you are. You need to throw off anything that would bind you: worry, concern, doubt, fear and many other things – even death."

"Kind of like throwing off the cape and boots . . . and everything," Ian said as he began to understand. Ian suddenly came back to the realization that his mentor was not clothed.

"You have to admit that running around naked isn't decent, although it really is freeing and fun." Ian paused for a moment to drink in the profound juxtaposition of the words he just uttered. His mind wandered to the time when he and his brothers went to Wild Gorge Canyon about two miles from Mason University one evening. They sat on the edge of the canyon wall watching the sunset and looking into the deep clear blue water about forty feet below.

It just began to get dark when Caden said, "How cool would it be to just jump off these cliffs into that water?" They knew that the park district had approved the area as a safe place to dive but they had never gotten the nerve to jump. Without hesitating, Ian stripped down buck-naked, said, "Real cool", and leapt off the rocks yelling "Yee-Ha" all the way down into the water.

The exhilaration of flying through the air unencumbered was a brief taste of freedom. The brothers all followed Ian into the water.

"I remember thinking, I wish I could feel this free all the time," Ian said.

"You can because you are that free," Lord Kesh said. "Ian, many well meaning people will look at your freedom and have an opinion or pass judgment about it. Some may caution you, seeing freedom as indecent, lacking wisdom, questionable, heretical and even bordering on immoral. Those precious people are in bondage, they are weak in their trust of King Elyon."

"This sounds reckless to me! For example, Josiah has been given wisdom, are you telling me that if he warns me of something then I should just pass it off or throw it off, disregarding what he says in the name of freedom? Doesn't the King also give wisdom?"

"Yes the King gives wisdom and no I'm not telling you to just pass it off. A Wildman is not reckless, he calculates, plans and orders his ways. He seeks out input from others and lives obediently to the King. But he only remains free when his trust lies solely in the king and not his own power, understanding, reason, plans or abilities. The only thing reckless about a free wildman is his abandonment to hold strong on anything that would give him security over the King's power. You must let go and rest in King Elyon. Let me show you something."

Lord Kesh placed his hand over Ian's eyes. "Faith or lack of it will determine how you see things," the wild mentor said. He removed his hands giving Ian sight.

Ian opened his eyes and saw Lord Kesh standing before him clothed. Kesh was still the young man with wild dreadlocks and tanned glowing skin, but he was wearing a maize colored vest, no shirt, brown suede pants that ended at his shins, and he had a long leather strap that tied around his waist. Kesh stood there barefoot, just like Ian. But that's not all Ian saw. The color of the forest was gone. Everything was crisp and clear but it was all black and white. Ian reached down and plucked a piece of a once, green fern. The gray fern was starkly drab against the flesh color of his hand.

"There are many who see clearly, Ian, but they don't see in color. Their lives lack the vibrancy that comes with living into the wildness of the King. They are not truly free. Now close your eyes again," Lord Kesh said. Once more, he placed his hand over Ian's eyes. When he removed his hand, Ian saw things as he had before only this time the color was richer and more intensely vivid. Lord Kesh was naked once again but the glow that emanated from him was also much more intense.

"Ian, faith or lack of it determines how we see things. It colors our views or better put, it restricts or unleashes our freedoms. The more you trust the king the more you will live into the freedom that so aptly is instilled in you. But I know that you worry about the opinions of others."

"Yeah, I guess I'm a people-pleaser."

"There is only one person's opinion you need to be concerned about. That is the opinion of King Elyon. Don't you know that his opinion of you is high? He chose you to be a knight in his realm. He highly values you, regardless of what you do, because he is making you the man that you are to become – a great man. When you come to understand this, your confidence will be in King Elyon and not in yourself or your abilities. You should also know that the opinions of others are just small things. Others who trust the King will value what he values . . . and if he values you, they will too. A Wildman is not a loose cannon who does whatever he pleases. Nor is he a man who has shifting morals or values that drives him to live in bold defiance of other's opinions. He is a man who knows the one who owns his spirit and he understands that because he belongs to the King and trusts the King, he will never be in want. With King Elyon he has everything, without the King, he has nothing."

"What do you mean?"

"You worry about losing your scholarship so you trust *your* abilities to keep it. Look around you, Ian. All of this is the King's and he freely gives it to you and me. He makes sure that the smallest of creatures in his realm are fully sustained, and yet you are more valuable than they. Will he not provide for you? Study hard because you are equipped to do so, but then trust that the King will provide for you."

"That's incredibly freeing," Ian said. He felt a tremendous weight lifted off him again. "I feel like I could run forever and never get tired. Lord Kesh, you said that I could experience this freedom all the time; how?"

"Come with me," Lord Kesh said. He then stepped outside of the protectus blessing. Ian followed him. On the other side was a field. Ian stood in awe at the vibrant green pasture. It was spotted with brightly colored wild flowers. Ian took a deep breath and inhaled the sweet smell that came from the lavender hyssop, lemon mint, alyssum and monardella.

"Rest," Lord Kesh commanded. "Let go of everything and rest."

Ian smiled. He unbuttoned his vest and lay on his back in the lush field looking up at the brilliantly blue sky. The warmth of the sun washed over him as a gentle breeze kept him refreshingly cool and served him with a generous helping of the wildflower's aroma.

Lord Kesh lay down next to Ian. "Rest is the exercise of faith," he said.

"You mean I need to sleep more or get alone in nature and that will help me be free all the time?"

"Not necessarily, although those things will give you a different perspective. Rest means that you need to quit worrying, stop struggling, cease striving so hard, surrender, be still . . . and then deep within your soul you will come to know and trust the King."

"Trust in the King . . . rest in the King . . . they are one in the same," Ian said. Lord Kesh smiled in affirmation. Ian took a deep breath again and could feel the fire deep within. Everything around him was more vibrant and smelled so sweet. Fear and worry was replaced by strength and confidence. Ian's spirit was free. This new found wildness overwhelmed Ian. Quiet tears of joy and relief rolled off his face into his ears as he lay still on the soft grass.

CHAPTER
SEVENTY-
FOUR

Ian didn't want to leave the field but Lord Kesh was already on his feet. "Come. There is one other thing that you must experience," Kesh said. Ian rose to his feet with the help of his mentor who offered his hand.

Both mentor and protégé stepped back through the protectus blessing into the forest again. "Give me the leather strap from around your waist," Lord Kesh commanded.

Ian untied the strap and handed it to his mentor. Lord Kesh took the belt and stepped behind Ian. "Close your eyes," he said. Ian did and Lord Kesh tied the strap behind Ian's head, covering his eyes with the makeshift leather strapped blindfold. The broadest portion of the strap that set on Ian's back now fit snugly across the bridge of his nose, covering his eyes completely.

"Now Ian, I would like for you to run with me again," Lord Kesh said.

Ian laughed, "You're kidding! I can't see anything."

"You don't need to see, you just need to trust."

Ian tried to recall what the terrain looked like. He remembered a fallen log that stretched across the path a few yards in front of him, but he would never be able to judge exactly where it was. In his mind, he could picture the direction he needed to run and envisioned other obstacles that would be in his way. Ian held out his hands, groping to feel for Lord Kesh or anything else that might be in his path. He shuffled his foot forward knowing full well that he would find it difficult to walk without sight, let alone run. Then his mind went back to his bare feet and the hazards that lurked on the forest floor.

"Can't we just take this a bit slower so that I can get used to it," Ian spoke into the open space of the forest. He didn't know any longer, where Lord Kesh was standing. "Let me just take your arm and walk for a minute before we start to run. I'd feel more comfortable if I could ease into it." Ian reached out his hand again to grab Lord Kesh but couldn't find him.

"You just need to trust," Lord Kesh said. His response was some distance away and it sounded like he was running as he shouted back to Ian.

Ian took a deep breath. The fire in his spirit began to burn. *King Elyon will keep me from falling. He is my protector. He will guide my steps,* Ian thought. Then with a new sense of confidence, Ian broke into a sprint. As he ran there came moments where he was compelled to shift direction slightly with a little dance move, or leap because of the freedom he felt. He didn't realize that he was bounding around and over obstacles.

After a few moments, Ian could hear the running steps of Lord Kesh. He had caught up to the mentor and was now running alongside him.

"You will know that you are truly free when you trust the King without seeing what lies ahead or without vision of the outcome," Lord Kesh said.

"This is great!" Ian exclaimed.

They kept running and Lord Kesh said, "Ian Bound by the authority given to me as a Wildman Knight of King Elyon's realm, because of your reckless abandon of all things to hold on to and place your faith in the King; and because King Elyon has made you free indeed; I proclaim that you are Lord Ian Bound a wildman Ambassador-Knight in King Elyon's realm."

"That's so amazing," Ian said, but there was no further response from Lord Kesh. Ian began to slow down. "Lord Kesh?" he called, waiting for a response. Ian called again and reduced his pace to a walk. "Lord Kesh, are you there?" he asked, now reaching up to untie his blindfold.

When the blindfold came off, Ian found himself standing alone on the trail in the woods. He turned all the way around but could not see his mentor anywhere in the forest.

"Lord Kesh!" he yelled, but there was no answer. Then Ian heard a faint call.

"Ian, hey buddy is that you?"

"Over here!" Ian called back as he walked in the direction of the voice. Ian recognized that it was the voice of his friend and roommate Caden.

"What are you doing out here, alone?" Ian asked.

"I just needed time to clear my head and I thought I'd take advantage of the protectus blessing's vast coverage. But the real question is what are *you* doing out here alone? Where is Lord Kesh and where is your cape and your boots, bro?"

"I'm not sure where Lord Kesh is. He was here a minute ago," Ian returned. Both guys looked around and there was no sign of Kesh.

Caden began to look Ian over. "Bro, how did Kesh mark you and what weapon did he give you?" he said as he walked around Ian lifting up the back of his vest and examining him for some tattoo or adornment that would distinguish him.

Ian stood stupefied. He had been so caught up in his new freedom that he didn't even remember that he would be marked, nor did he give any thought to having a weapon. "I – I didn't get either," he said.

There was a sudden crash of thunder, which made both guys nearly jump out of their skins. Ian and Caden looked skyward to watch the protectus blessing disappear. The realization of the implications of this event suddenly gripped Caden with fear.

"Dude, you don't have a weapon and we are not even close to Wes and Josiah. The circle is broken. We're all open targets. This is definitely not good."

"We need to run. Let's get out of here," Ian said.

The two brothers began to run as fast as they could in the direction that they remembered Josiah and Wes to be. The trail wound around and began to look more familiar to Caden. "This way," he said shifting direction down a side trail, which curved through a pass that cut between two rocky ridges.

"This doesn't look familiar at all," Ian yelled. "Are you sure we're going the right way?"

"I'm positive! I stopped and sat over on those rocks for a while. There is a mountainous cliff up ahead, on the left. We need to take that trail to the right of the cliffs which leads back to the opening where I left the Wes and 'Siah," Caden called as he continued to run.

Caden and Ian ran through the pass and took a sharp right on the trail just as Caden had recalled. As they darted around a curve in the trail, they were halted abruptly in their tracks. Ian ran into the back of Caden who was now face to face with terror. Both guys slowly began to take a step back as Raith let out an evil laugh. The horrific hyena was blocking the trail along with a fierce wolf and a vicious mountain lion.

Raith snarled and bared his teeth with delight. He began to drool at so easy an opportunity to inflict destruction on the guys. Earlier, Raith saw Caden leave the company of his brothers. The hyena had been lying in wait for his return. He hadn't expected that he would have the opportunity of killing two of the Otherlanders.

Raith let out a blood curdling laugh. He was joined by the howl and roar of the wolf and mountain lion, who harmonized with their battle calls. Ian took the opportunity to whisper in Caden's ear, "We will trust the King for strength, grab the back of my vest and don't let go."

Caden reached behind his brother and grabbed a fist full of Ian's maize colored vest. As soon as he had taken hold Ian yelled, "RUN!"

Ian and Caden turned and broke into a sprint. Caden held tight to the bottom of Ian's vest as it whipped up from the the wind behind Ian. There was a surge of power, that flowed through Ian into Caden and both ran with speed that kept them calculatedly ahead of the treacherous trio's chase. The faster the ferocious animals ran, the faster Ian and Caden were carried. It was as if there was an invisible wedge put between them and their pursuing foe.

Ian diverted off the trail and took a path that led up the mountain cliff. As they ran uphill, the ferocious beasts began to slow and tire but they remained pursuant. Ian's vest stayed clutched tightly in Caden's hand and they began to distance themselves from the beasts. The brothers rounded a curve on their way up the slope losing visibility of Raith and his posse. After a moment, the trio came back into view, relentless in their hunt. Ian ran higher and higher up the trail but the sure footed carnivores continued undeterred in their pursuit.

The two brothers took a quick left through some bushes and found a new trail. This trail became a ledge walkway that jutted from the wall of the cliff. Navigating the walkway took great care because one false slip would send a traveler plummeting to his death far below. Ian ran the tight walkway, hugging the mountain wall closely. Caden stayed close behind, still being empowered by his connection to Ian. Neither could see the end of the walkway because it proceeded around the side of the mountain out of their view.

"They won't be able to traverse this path," Ian called. He and Caden rounded the trail only to find themselves at a dead end on a ledge high above the forest. They could look out and see the end of the forest, the great Nastal River, the plain of Dura and Asilo standing stalwartly between the two mountains at the end of the plain.

"We're trapped," Caden said. Then he heard Raith's grotesque laugh. "Ian, they are coming around the trail".

Ian suddenly felt the power drain from him as fear flooded in. He looked over the side of the ledge at the steep abrupt drop to the rocks and forest below. There was no way down. He looked up the side of the cliff but that provided no way of escape either. "I thought Elyon was leading me," Ian said bewildered.

"Well now you know how I felt," Caden returned. They could hear the animals inching closer as they carefully walked the trail. Caden drew his sword and immediately his hands ceased to glow.

"King Elyon will surely let me fight," he said waiting for his hands to glow again. There was nothing. Caden's hands remained in their natural state as they heard Raith's laugh coming dreadfully near.

"I'm going to fight, regardless of the state of my hands," Caden stated in panic.

"No, you can't. You must remain faithful to the King," Ian said, only because it was right, but he hoped that Caden would wail on each predator as it rounded the corner.

Raith leapt from the trail onto the opening of the ledge, catching the guys off guard. The guys backed up perilously close to the edge of the precipice. Caden held up his sword as the hyena growled. Raith was quickly joined by the mountain lion. They both seemed to be savoring the moment of their victorious hunt. Soon the wolf would find his way onto the ledge too.

Caden gripped his sword with both hands. "C'mon glow!" he said with frustration as he kept his eyes on his hands and on the enemy that inched closer. Ian stood behind Caden keeping watch on their footing. There was no more room for another step.

CHAPTER SEVENTY-FOUR

"Don't back up or we go over the edge," Ian cried.

Raith laughed and took another slow deliberate step forward. He was taking great delight in terrorizing the duo before he took their lives.

"I'm fighting!" Caden called. "I've disobeyed the King once already. I may not be knighted but at least I'll be alive."

Ian closed his eyes and remembered Lord Kesh's instructions to rest. He took a deep breath and said, "Hold your sword, Caden." His words were spoken with such peace and confidence that Caden instinctually obeyed. Then Ian quickly took off his vest and threw it at Raith who caught it and shredded it with his razor sharp teeth in seconds.

As the hyena ripped the vest apart, Ian reached around from behind Caden and clasped his arms across Caden's chest, holding him in a bear hug.

"What are you doing, Ian?"

"I'm not sure, but you need to trust me. Elyon can save us if he desires, but even if he doesn't, we don't need to fear death." As Ian finished his sentence, he fell backwards off the edge of the cliff with Caden caught in his grip.

Ian let out a "Yee-Ha" as they plummeted to the rocks below. Just before they were about to encounter a terrible fate against the rocks, snow white wings, double Ian's arms length, burst from his back and caught the wind making him and Caden soar upward. They flew past Raith and his henchmen, who stood defeated on the ledge.

Caden began to laugh with amazement as he watched Ian's wings powerfully cut through the air and lift them higher. "I guess we all know how you are marked, Ian, and I'd say that's quite an outstanding mark for a free wildman."

Ian soared in the warmth of the sunlight high over Salamgard.

CHAPTER
SEVENTY-FIVE

Ian spotted Wes, Josiah and Clarion standing in the forest clearing, each armed and alert. They too had heard the thunderous boom as Lord Kesh released the protectus blessing and feared for their vulnerability without Caden and Ian. They were so busy keeping watch over the forest that they didn't notice Ian and Caden circle overhead.

"Hey guys, up here!" Caden yelled.

Josiah looked up and quickly pointed. Clarion and Wes didn't see them at first because the foliage of the trees blocked their view. Ian swooped into the clearing.

Before he and Caden landed on solid ground, they heard Ian say, "We are about to make our descent on the forest glade. The captain has turned on the fasten seatbelt sign. Please remain seated until the aircraft has come to a full and complete stop".

They touched the ground running from the momentum of their descent. Ian released his grasp around Caden who said, "I hope this airline didn't lose my luggage." He raised his arm showing his sword still in his hand. "Nope! Luggage arrived with me. I may fly this airline again."

CHAPTER SEVENTY-FIVE

Caden hugged Ian, "Thanks bro, your freeing faith saved us."

"Ian, you're amazing," Josiah said as he reached out and ran his hand along the smooth soft pattern of the white feathered wing. "Can you feel that?"

"Yeah!" Ian chuckled.

"You are magnificently marked," Wes said.

The four brothers stood in a circle facing each other. Wes' open shirt revealed the glorious palm print with King Elyon's name, visibly burned as a banner of love over his heart.

Josiah reached up and ran his finger over the smooth surface of the glistening platinum diadem that crowned his brow with wisdom.

Caden returned his sword to its hilt and immediately his hands glowed a burnished bronze, marking his goodness.

Ian stood barefoot and shirtless, as his white feathered wings folded neatly behind him, arching well over his head and cascading to the ground behind him. He could run without getting tired, soar like an eagle and be free from anything that entangled him.

"We can go to Asilo now," Clarion said. "If we encounter the Dark Lord and his forces we can now fight."

"Wait!" Ian interrupted. "We can't fight. Lord Kesh never gave me a weapon."

"That is because you have always had your weapon with you," Clarion responded.

"What weapon?"

"The strap around you waist - It is a sling," she said.

Ian reached down and untied it once again. The strap had been used as his belt; as reigns to keep him standing on the back of a dolphin, and as a blindfold to teach him trust, but Ian never realized that it was a weapon. He noticed that the large center leather, which aptly fit against the small of his back, was really the sling that would caress any projectile he wished to fire. Ian quickly stooped down and retrieved a stone from the ground. He wrapped it in the sling and twirled the slingshot around, above his head.

"I think that I understand how it works but I'm probably a terrible shot."

"You don't have to be a good shot, Ian. You need to trust the King to carry your stone to its mark. Just invoke the *altivolus* blessing and King Elyon will guide your stone like he does my arrows."

"Now I'd say we are all *marked* and *armed*," Caden said.

"Then that will certainly make for an interesting battle! Now all you need is the enemy," said a low deliberate voice from behind the band of brothers. The air suddenly chilled and the guys turned to see Lord Ubilaz standing at the top of the ridge. His Dark figure was now accessorized with the Kalos Sapphire.

"It's a shame that you will not live long enough to see Asilo," he said.

With agile reflex, each guy readied his arms. Wes stood in the front center with his shield positioned in front of his chest; dagger drawn. Clarion had her arrow trained in Ubilaz's direction and the bow string was tautly pulled. Caden's sword was in his hands that ceased to glow. Josiah held firm to his crystal topped staff and Ian scooped up a handful of rocks and already had one in the sling.

Daemonicus, Avah, Gath and Venem flew to Lord Ubilaz's left side. They were visible in their red ugliness. Two figures came from behind the ridge to flank the Dark Lord's right side. It was Maayin and Charles Morelock.

Morelock wore the hood of his Vitatha Chief's robe over his head to conceal his face. He didn't want the guys to recognize him, revealing his identity as an Eikondor Ambassador and Knight of Lord Ubilaz. He wanted to remain incognito, lest he ever would encounter the guys, back in Otherland. As Morelock stepped to Ubilaz's side, he pulled the hood of his robe down lower to conceal even more of his face. His white French cuff and ruby studded cuff link peeked past his robe sleeve for a second, as an uncharacteristic representation of both realities: Otherland and Salamgard.

Maayin stood at his father's side. The boy was dressed in black. His hair was slicked back and his face was painted with red and black war paint. His shirt was opened like Wes' shirt and the guys could see that the wound Lord Ubilaz inflected on Maayin's chest was now tattooed over with the Dark Lord's name, a vile counterfeit to Elyon's banner of love.

The sight of Maayin caught the guys off guard, especially Wes. They had thought the boy was safe with Lord Tobijah's troops or under the care of Lady Daesis.

"Maayin, what are you doing?" Wes asked.

"I have joined my father and mentor, a great knight in Lord Ubilaz's realm. Together we serve the Dark Lord. I am now a knight in his realm. I have come here to kill you".

"Maayin, you will only be badly hurt if you stay here. And you'll come to know pain and destruction if you give your allegiance to Lord Ubilaz. Come down here and join this circle of brothers where you belong and where you are loved," Wes pleaded.

"LIAR! You declare your love to me but you abandon me. You just want to manipulate me. You don't love me and you never will."

Wes could feel the King's love burning in him. It was so powerful that he winced with pain as it burned in his chest. "Maayin, you're my younger brother and I love you. If need be, I will fight here and die here to save you."

Maayin's face remained filled with rage as tears streamed over his war paint and down his cheeks. He was confused because Wes' love was so compelling but the lad willfully gave into his anger and hate. Someone had to pay for all the terrible things that he experienced and Wes became the object of the boy's rage.

"NO! You shall die, and I will kill you," Maayin shouted.

Maayin reached around his back, as if to remove a bow from its resting place there, but nothing was visible. Then he reached over his shoulder as if to retrieve an arrow from its quiver.

"What's he doing?" Caden asked.

"I don't know," Ian replied. "I don't see a weapon. Is he pretending to have a bow and arrow?"

Maayin drew the invisible strings of his bow tight. Wes stood still, looking unflinchingly into Maayin's eyes. Wes could see that the bow in Maayin's hand was real.

"Will someone tell us what is happening here," Caden asked.

"I believe Maayin is pretending to kill Wes with an invisible bow and arrow," Clarion returned. "Pay no attention to the boy. Keep your eyes on the others. I'm sure this is a diversion so that they can stage an offensive."

Maayin's hand trembled as he wept, looking down at the ground rather than Wes. Morelock placed his hand on the boy's shoulder causing him to swallow his tears and straighten up with rage again.

"Your King cannot save you. Die, Wes Litchfield!" Maayin proclaimed with hateful fury as he released the invisible bow string.

As the boy was talking, Josiah reached into his pocket and produced his discerning glasses. He put them on just as Maayin said, "Die, Wes Litchfield!" In that same moment, Wes lowered the shield that was in front of his chest, willingly giving the boy a clear target.

"The arrow is real," Josiah yelled as he lunged toward Wes. Caden quickly and blindly put his sword in front of Wes' heart in an attempt to block the attack but it was too late. Neither could intervene against so swift a shot. Wes' body convulsed from the impact of the invisible arrow. He fell backwards into Josiah's arms. His chest and white silk shirt rapidly turned red from the blood that profusely poured from his wound.

Caden began to breathe heavily and began to get weak kneed as if he were about to go into shock. Ian quickly moved behind him, to steady him. He put his arm around Caden's chest, like he had when they were flying, infusing him with power. Caden immediately regained the boldness needed to face Ubilaz and his bullies. Clarion moved to the other side of Caden and the three formed ranks between Wes' fallen body and Ubilaz's entourage.

"It looks like your venture is over; where you go one, you go all," Lord Ubilaz stated. "Maayin is an excellent shot. Clarion, you taught him the basics very well. I just perfected his form and aim. The young conciliator will be dead in a few moments. You cannot save him."

Josiah attended to Wes while the Dark Lord talked. He could see the invisible arrow protruding from Wes' chest. He quickly broke off the shaft of the arrow near the chest and then removed Wes' sash to create bandages.

"You lowered your shield!" Josiah said frantically attempting to keep his brother alive. "How could you be so foolish? I know you saw that the arrow was real. Why did you lower your shield?" He stuffed the sash into the wound to stop the bleeding but he couldn't. Wes had slipped into unconsciousness as his life began slowly slipping away.

CHAPTER
SEVENTY-SIX

Just before Maayin got his shot off, Wes' mind was whisked back to his earlier encounter with Serik at the Rose and Raven pub.

"Wes there is one more very important instruction that I must give you regarding love's highest power. I will tell you about it as we return to your friends, it is the most crucial of any instruction that I will give you," Serik said.

Serik raised his hand, *"Restituo Vicis"* , he proclaimed bringing the pub out of their time lock and into the present again. The noise level returned to its blaring decibel in the pub. The glass of ale that was suspended in air, shattered on the floor and the patrons of the Rose and Raven never missed a second of time.

Serik put his arm around the young conciliator's shoulder as they walked through the corridor from the back room to the common area of the pub. Serik leaned over to whisper in Wes' ear. "There is one very powerful act of love but it is extremely costly," Serik said.

CHAPTER SEVENTY-SIX

Wes stopped in the corridor and faced his mentor. "What is it?"

"It is rarely experienced because many conciliators choose to compromise who they really are and fail to allow King Elyon's love to pour through them during this experience."

"I can't imagine that, especially when I've experienced the exhilaration of having the King's love flowing through me. Why would I or anyone want to compromise that?"

"Love ceases to be exhilarating in the shadow of betrayal."

Serik's sobering statement dramatically extinguished the mood like a person who extinguishes the wick of a candle with a pinch, leaving an ember to smolder and smoke until it succumbs. Wes had never thought that anyone would reject love. His mind raced to his brothers and others that he loved. Would he love them if they turned against him and betrayed him?

"I don't know if I could bear the pain of rejection if someone who I invested in and loved deeply, betrayed me. I would probably want to even the score by getting some level of retribution."

"Then you will cease to love. You will compromise who you are. If you are to remain a loving man then you must love through the betrayal, painful as it is. You must willingly count the cost and pay the price."

"But I think that that would kill me," Wes said and he started to become emotional at the thought of how much he loved his brothers and the agony he would endure to love them through betrayal.

"To love like this means to experience the fullness of King Elyon's love, and become more like him. It was his love that willingly let Ubilaz cut him down on Mt. Aphesis. The King suffered the rejection of those he loved. His love compelled him through that betrayal, to give his life. That act of love defeated death and evil. When one of King Elyon's conciliator's lovingly sacrifices his heart in the face of betrayal, that Ambassador Knight diminished the stronghold that evil has on the life of the betrayer. But be forewarned, love in the face of betrayal will cost you your life."

Wes' mind was jolted back to the present moment in the forest clearing. He could clearly see that Maayin had a bow and arrow and that the arrow was trained on him. He looked directly into Maayin's eyes and concentrated on communicating just as he had seen Clarion do.

"No matter what you do I will always love you, little brother," Wes thought as he concentrated on Maayin's face.

Maayin's hand trembled as he wept, looking down at the ground rather than Wes. He had heard Wes' profession, as clearly as if Wes had been standing next to him whispering it into his ear. Then the darkly shadowed man placed his hand on the boy's shoulder causing him to swallow his tears and straighten up with rage again.

Wes watched as the boy drew the bow strings. Then he heard the words that shattered his heart; words of deep betrayal.

"Die, Wes Litchfield."

Wes closed his eyes, lowered his shield and everything went black.

CHAPTER
SEVENTY-SEVEN

Wes lay moments from death on the floor of the Ithcar Forest Valley just within a short journey of reaching Asilo. His breathing was now shallow and labored. The band of brothers had come this far only to be defeated by Lord Ubilaz.

"You are finished," Lord Ubilaz said as he caressed the Kalos Sapphire amulet that hung around his neck. "I have destroyed the one from your little group, who carries the most powerful trait. You are no longer bound together, making you open prey for my necrophim."

"Shall we do quick work and destroy the rest of them, my Lord?" Daemonicus asked.

"No, I think we shall let them suffer a slow death. Before they taste death, they must know that my power is far greater than King Elyon's, thanks to the young warrior." The Dark Lord looked directly at Caden as he raised the amulet to his lips and kissed it.

"Let's see how they fair against my mortal army."

Morelock looked behind the ridge and gave a nod summoning Ubilaz's forces. Hundreds of men and ferocious beasts lined the ridge encircling the band of brothers.

Josiah promptly covered Wes' body with his shield and stood ready for battle as the four formed a circle around their fallen brother.

"If we fight back to back we are by far, stronger," Josiah shouted.

"Yes," Clarion returned. "And don't lose heart; the power of our King flows through us and our weapons. Remember things aren't always as they seem in Salamgard."

"Let's make this more interesting," Ubilaz said. "I have little time in wasting the efforts of my entire army on so pitiful a group when one hundred of my best warriors can make sport of you." He nodded and one hundred warriors stepped from the ranks of the masses that encircled the group. Among those warriors were skilled swordsmen, archers and gladiators who could rip them apart with their bare hands. Lions, bears, wolves, snakes, hyenas, rhinos, alligators and a host of other beasts joined the ranks of the fiercest warriors. The hundred surrounded the four lone warriors.

"Kill them!" Ubilaz commanded, with sweet delight.

The warriors rushed the inner circle. Immediately Clarion's arrows flew as fast as she could grab them. "Altivolus", she yelled before releasing each arrow. One by one the arrows hit their mark but she needed to work fast to keep the enemy from overtaking her.

Josiah pointed his staff at the charging foe. He was determined to hold the line where he stood, protecting the backs of his brothers. *"Excessum neco"* he called as his staff spewed forth a bolt of lightning, destroying any warrior that Josiah aimed at. Repeatedly he called, *"excessum neco"* and repeatedly it was followed by a flash of lightening and the death of his foe.

Caden held his sword securely. He waited for his hands to glow but there was nothing. He began to wonder if his hands didn't glow because his former action of giving over the Kalos gem disqualified him. Then he remembered Lord Tobijah saying that he almost never struck with his sword. As Caden pondered these things, a large wolf lunged at him. As the wolf was flying through the air, Caden lifted his sword and held the blade with both hands as if he was bunting a baseball. The wolf soared, opened mouth, right into the steel. Caden held firm and watched as the blade broke many of the animal's teeth and knocked it cold at his feet. A strong gladiator charged Caden on the heels of the wolf. Caden turned and dropped to one knee, pointing his blade toward the warrior and he too could not stop his momentum, impaling himself on the blade.

Ian followed Clarion's lead and slung stones as fast as he could all the while invoking the *altivolus* blessing. He wasn't a good shot, often sending rocks flying in many directions. Sometimes the stone left the sling prematurely and flew in the direction, opposite his charging enemy. But as Ian trusted the power of the King and yelled, *"Altivolus"*, each stone righted its trajectory and squarely hit its mark.

After a very intense few minutes, one hundred of Ubilaz's best warriors lay dead or incapacitated. Ubilaz looked less than amused.

"It seems Elyon's power is great with you," he leered. "You may have enough power to handle a small band of warriors but you shall not last against the full ranks of my mortal army."

Morelock leaned over and whispered to the Dark Lord, "Your loyal warriors from the region of Wriengor have just arrived to join ranks with you, my Lord. We have thousands more than we need." Morelock delighted in giving the Dark Lord an up-to-the-minute battle report.

"Make short work of these four and make sure the one on the ground is dead as well," Ubilaz whispered back.

"Yes my Lord," Morelock replied. Then he shouted the order, "Destroy them!"

There was a deafening roar of attack as the Dark Lord's army crested the ridges surrounding Caden, Ian, Josiah and Clarion. Lightning flashed, arrows flew, rocks and stones soared with accuracy to their marks. Clarion and the brothers fought with all their might in the power of Elyon but there were too many soldiers to maintain the battle.

"We will not be able to hold them long," Josiah yelled.

"Things aren't always as they appear to be", Clarion yelled back as she kept releasing arrows. "When things look impossible that is when King Elyon's power is made evident."

"Well, I'd call this vey impossible!" Caden yelled as he still waited for his hands to glow.

All at once, there was a great quake, which shook the earth beneath them. Ubilaz's troops fell to the ground, as did Clarion, Josiah, Ian and Caden. Everyone fell at the quake. The only one who remained standing unaffected was Lord Ubilaz. The quake neutralized the battle temporarily. Everyone looked around trying to see what or who caused this commotion.

Ubilaz looked amusedly at the ridge across from where he stood. "This is about to get more interesting," he said.

Clarion lay on the ground and began to push herself up when she too spotted someone. "Lady Daesis!" she said with relief.

There on the ridge stood Daesis with Lord Cervus on one side and Lord Themba on the other.

"Don't you think this battle has skewed odds, Lord Ubilaz?" Daesis called.

"I assume that was your quake, dear Lady", the Dark Lord chuckled. "Nice touch."

Daesis nodded graciously and remained silent.

"Have you come to even the odds?" the Dark Lord shouted.

"Yes . . . me and my friends."

"What friends, a stag and a tiger? I believe that you have miscalculated the battle and underestimate me. Unfortunately *your* friends will die with the Otherlanders."

Lord Ubilaz lifted the Kalos amulet to his lips and whispered, *"Nikao"* unleashing a shock wave of power that gave new strength to his warriors.

"Bring on your friends," he yelled across to Lady Daesis. Then he yelled, "Destroy them all. Kill everyone loyal to Elyon!"

Josiah, Caden, Ian and Clarion all sprang to their feet as Ubilaz's army advanced to resume the fight. Cervus and Themba bolted down the hill into the battle. Lady Daesis raised her calling charm to her lips and blew. Seconds later hundreds of King Elyon's warriors crested the ridge to join the battle, led by Eleus and Virtus.

"Ha, yes! Bring it!" Caden yelled at sight of the reinforcements. "I guess she did come with friends to even the odds."

"Dude look at your hands," Ian called back abruptly.

Caden looked down and his hands glowed bright gold as he held his sword. "The power of King Elyon now flows through my sword," he yelled.

Caden swung fiercely at his enemy. His sword became King Elyon's weapon of judgment, as did Josiah's staff, Ian's sling and Clarion's bow. The four remained in tight formation around Wes' body, assuring his safety. They didn't know whether he was still alive or if his wound had taken its fatal toll. The enemy kept pressing in too aggressively for any one of them to check on his condition.

The battle started to turn against Ubilaz and his troops. The Dark Lord raised his amulet again to his lips to summon more power. As he did, Lady Daesis flicked her riding stick toward the ground and chanted, *"Elyon interfere maleficus."* As soon as she said those words, a wall of ice shot up out of the ground encasing Lord Ubilaz, rendering the use of the amulet impotent.

The Dark Lord raised his arms, held his palms outward toward the icy hedge, and yelled, *"Destructus!"* The ice wall exploded in every direction.

Across the way, Lady Daesis was anticipating Ubilaz's counter attack so she flicked her wand again and another ice hedge surrounded him. Lady Daesis was prepared to do this as long as she needed, keeping Ubilaz from engaging in the battle with the amulet.

The Dark Lord knew that Daesis power was great, but he was determined to engage the battle in any way he could.

"Unleash my necrophim," Lord Ubilaz commanded Daemonicus from behind the icy confinement. Then he again obliterated the icy prison only to find another quickly rise up. Gath, Avah, Daemonicus and Venem disappeared and positioned themselves at the four corners of the battle. They each produced trumpets and blew a cadence summoning hundreds of necrophim. The sky began to turn blood red from the mist that they exuded.

"We cannot see the necrophim," Clarion yelled. "They remain invisible and their mist is too thick. They move too quickly for us to single out any attacker."

Josiah had on his discerning spectacles and could see the necrophim attacking and destroying countless numbers of Elyon's warriors. He saw one coming directly at Clarion.

"Straight in front of you, Clarion. Shoot!" he yelled.

Clarion called, "Altivolus" as she blindly shot in that direction. There was an explosion of light as the arrow destroyed the necrophim.

"Caden, One-O'clock," Josiah yelled. Caden slashed through the air as he yelled, *"Excessum neco"* sending particles of light scattering from the destroyed necrophim.

"Don't worry about me," Ian yelled as he slung his stones and called *"Altivolus"* hitting the necrophim with accuracy.

"Can you see them, Ian?" Josiah asked.

"No, faith is trusting King Elyon for the battle even when you can't see the enemy. I just wildly release my projectiles and the King carries them so that they always hit their targets. It's great fun and totally free," he called back.

Josiah kept calling instructions to his friends as more and more necrophim descended into the battle. "We cannot hold them and I can't keep calling directions to you," Josiah cried to his brothers. *If only the faithful army of King Elyon could see,* he thought. Then he remembered.

At the Victorium Morte celebration, Lord Lemuel had many of his warriors ready to do battle against the necrophim. He was able to make them see by pounding his staff down against the ground and chanting a blessing that sent out a force empowering his warriors with sight.

What were the words that he spoke? Josiah ravaged through his mind to recall the blessing. *King Elyon, I need your wisdom,* Josiah thought as he attempted to concentrate in the midst of battle.

Josiah suddenly began to feel the powerful wisdom surge through him again. Above the battle's din, still engaging in the fight, he yelled, "Caden, is my headband glowing?"

"What?" Caden yelled as he sliced at an attacking bobcat.

"My headband, is it glowing?"

"Yeah!"

"What's it say?"

"I don't know! I can't see it. Turn your head this direction."

Josiah pointed his staff, yelled *"excessum neco"* destroying an incoming necrophim, then turned his head quickly for Caden to see the inscription in the diadem.

"Visum Fidelis," Caden yelled. "It says *Visum Fidelis!*"

Josiah raised his staff and brought it down with full force against the ground. As it struck the earth the young sage called, *"Visum Fidelis!* Give sight to the warriors faithful to King Elyon." A white light flashed and rippled from Josiah's staff. Immediately the invisible necrophim became visible to King Elyon's warriors.

The grotesque forms of the necrophim filled the air and blanketed the battlefield. Elyon's warriors fought with greater accuracy. For a while, it looked as if the battle began to turn in the brother's favor. But the necrophim continued to come in droves.

"We are still outnumbered. The necrophim are coming too fast," Clarion yelled as the battle raged. Lord Ubilaz continued to destroy Lady Daesis's hedge and it seemed like the lady was beginning to weaken under his power. Lord Ubilaz shattered another barrier of ice and before Lady Daesis could get another in place, the Dark Lord invoked a curse from the amulet.

"Nikao", he said quickly and distinctly. His troops began to increase with power. His necrophim were able to avoid the onslaughts of Elyon's warriors. The battle swiftly began to turn against Elyon's army.

The band of brothers also grew weary. They didn't expect to hold on much longer. Elyon's warriors were beginning to lose hope.

"Maybe the amulet does have the ability to make Ubilaz as powerful as Elyon," Caden muttered. Nobody heard him. Nor did they hear him say, "I'm sorry that I ever gave up the amulet."

Caden swung his sword as Ubilaz's warriors pressed in from every direction. He cut through a necrophim that attacked him at his right. As he swung back to meet another attacker, a sharp pain ripped through his left shoulder sending him crashing to the ground. Caden rolled over quickly to see the powerful gladiator who punched him, now standing over him ready to plunge a sword into his chest.

Josiah turned just in time to see the gladiator. *"Excessum neco,"* he yelled as he swung his staff toward the attacker. Lightning blasted, striking the dark warrior with such force that it hurled him ten feet away to an instant death. Josiah had little time to turn back before a charging bull attacked.

The young sage dodged the charging animal but fell to the ground dropping his staff. Themba roared and intercepted the bull with a powerful leap to its back. The white tiger swiftly brought the bull down.

While Themba took care of the attacking nemesis, Josiah's vulnerable position, on the ground without his staff, was the opportunity that a leopard immediately seized. The great cat leapt and landed on Josiah.

"'SIAH!" Caden yelled groping for his sword.

The leopard flailed on top of Josiah then rolled over and didn't move. Josiah lay on his back breathing heavily. He held Wes' dagger, now stained with the blood of his attacker. Josiah had fallen close enough to Wes that he could see the dagger from under the shield. As the leopard attacked, Josiah quickly grabbed the dagger and impaled the animal as it landed on him.

The fatigue was almost too great for Josiah and Caden to rise up and reengage the battle. Ubilaz's troops grew more powerful as Elyon's army weakened.

Just as the battle reached its darkest point, thunder crackled from the north corner of the battle field. A large eagle swooped down from the sky carrying Lord Lemuel. When the bird came close to the ground, Lemuel jumped from its back. He was immediately joined by reinforcements that came over the ridge. Venem was directing the necrophim from that corner. At the sight of the Lord Lemuel's powerful staff, the necrophim's cowardice gripped him. Venem decided that this was a good time to retreat and quickly abandoned the battle. Many of the hosts that he led followed his example and also retreated.

At the same time on the south ridge of the battle, the wind began to kick up and a white winged Wildman appeared with a slingshot and a myriad of the King's hosts. Lord Kesh caught Avah's eye.

"I think I would leave here if I were you," he said as he twirled his sling around over his head. Avah didn't want to taste the projectile in the Knight's sling, so he disappeared in a mist of crimson taking all of the woodland necrophim with him.

At the eastern corner of the battle there began to rumble the sound of hundreds of charging horses. Gath was orchestrating the city necrophim from this corner. He knew that that sound couldn't be good. Seeing that Venem and Avah had retreated with a host of necrophim, he abandoned his post before he could find out the source of the noise. Lord Tobijah promptly, appeared on the ridge with countless mounted warriors in shining armor.

From the west, a bright light began to glow. It grew brighter and brighter blinding anyone who looked in that direction. The silhouette of Lord Serik was seen standing in the light. He had his shield and dagger ready to do battle along with another battalion of the King's troops.

At the sight of all four powerful knights, the remaining necrophim fled along with a third of Ubilaz's mortal forces. Daemonicus defiantly stood his ground until he heard Lord Ubilaz say, "This is not the battle that we want to engage in, Daemonicus. Get the boy and his father out of here quickly. We were victorious in destroying the young conciliator. We have crushed the hopes of Salamgard and the promise of her future. Where they go one, they go all. The problem with hearts bound is that if one dies so does the promise of the others. King Elyon shall not have his successors."

Ubilaz laughed and disappeared in a flash of sulfuric smoke sounding a retreat, which sent the remaining necrophim and mortal warriors scattering. The four powerful Knights descended into the forest valley clearing to secure the victory for their King.

CHAPTER
SEVENTY-EIGHT

The beautiful forest clearing, which once served as the threshold for the plains of Dura, now laid waste from the ravages of battle. Dead and wounded warriors, both men and beast, littered the forest floor.

Caden swiftly left the trauma of the fight to rush to the side of his brother Wes. No one knew Wes' condition. Before the battle commenced Maayin's arrow had ripped through Wes' chest, punctuating the tattoo of King Elyon's beautifully encrypted name. Throughout the battle, Wes' body lay lifelessly under his shield as his brothers fought valiantly around him.

Caden threw the shield off Wes to reveal his bloodied ashen body. Josiah and Ian immediately joined Caden. Because of Josiah's *Visum Fidelis* blessing, everyone had the ability to see the broken arrow still protruding from Wes' chest. The sash that Josiah had used to arrest the bleeding was drenched in deep scarlet. The wound in his chest no longer pulsed with blood but remained still and lifeless.

There was no sign of life. No breathing. No wince of pain. No response to touch and no heart beat. Wes' head was turned to the side and his mouth was partially opened. His skin was a bluish gray and his eye lids were half closed, fixing a ghostly postmortem stare into nothingness.

"He's gone. Wes is dead," Caden wailed as he began to sob. Josiah covered his mouth with both hands, choking back an agonizing howl. His body convulsed as tears washed the dirt of battle from his face.

Ian turned his back and hung his head. The agony of the moment hit him like a punch to the stomach. He doubled over, dropped to his knees and wept. He couldn't believe that the journey had come to this.

"Even if we were victorious in battle, we lost here," he said. "This was far too great a price to pay," he said through his agony.

Clarion came near Caden and placed her hand on his head. He threw his arm around her and clung to her tightly as he wept. He had never felt this demoralized and unstable in his life.

The forest creatures watched in reverence, sharing the sting of grief that the brothers bore. Serik, Tobijah, Lemuel and Kesh also came near. The guys looked at their strong mentors and realized that these larger than life Knights were helpless to do anything.

Themba and Cervus quietly joined the circle. Themba pushed his head against Wes' head and gently licked his forehead in an attempt to stir him. There was no movement. Any hope of reviving the fallen knight was gone.

The mentors parted allowing Lady Daesis to enter their circle. Lemuel helped Josiah to his feet and Daesis replaced him at Wes' side. She slowly extracted the arrow from the young conciliator's chest. It was true; Wes had succumbed to the wound of Maayin's deadly arrow. Daesis held Wes' hand and quietly wept. Wes was dead.

"We all have lost a lot here today. Salamgard lost many sons and daughters, and a long awaited dream," she said, and then she pressed her lips against Wes hand.

Serik came and knelt next to her. He looked into the faces of Ian, Caden and Josiah who now stood together at Wes' head. They were broken and pained by the agony of loss. He was moved with compassion over the unbearable grief that the guys were experiencing.

Serik placed his hand over Wes' eyes to shut them in peaceful slumber. Then he closed Wes' shirt over the wound and gently placed his hand upon the spot that once, so beautifully bore his palm print. Wes lay as still and lifeless as he had before. The reverential moment was broken by Josiah.

"He lowered his shield!" Josiah cried in painful frustration. "Lord Serik, I saw Wes deliberately drop his shield. Why did he do that?"

"Wes offered his heart as an act of selfless compassion. He let King Elyon's love flow through him in the face of betrayal."

"So the King let him die! How could that be loving or good?" Caden cried directing his comment to his mentor, Lord Tobijah.

Tobijah placed his hand on Caden's shoulder to console him. "Wes' selfless loving act broke Lord Ubilaz's stronghold on Maayin and as such, also saved each of you from destruction," Tobijah said.

"How did he break Ubilaz's power when the Dark Lord was still able to use the power of the amulet? I don't understand," Ian said.

"He had limited use of the amulet. It was powerless over you," Lady Daesis said. "The amulet acts as a magnifier of power from the one who possesses it. When Ubilaz's power was broken over Maayin, it weakened the Dark Lord and thus diminished his power. That allowed me to maintain the icy hedge around him. Lord Ubilaz could only use the amulet to strengthen his warriors, not to destroy any of Elyon's forces. Wes' love greatly affected all of us."

"I still think it was far too great a price to pay," Ian cried. "I wish we had never come here."

"Wes held us together," Caden sobbed. "He was the great man among us. I would rather have died than him. If I hadn't given Ubilaz that damn amulet maybe things would be different and Wes would be standing here with us."

"I greatly doubt that possessing the amulet or not, would have stopped the evil one from his attack on you. He has far too much to lose from so great a binding of hearts and virtues as yours," Lord Lemuel said.

Caden was grabbing at anything to make sense of so painful an outcome. He felt suffocating guilt, thinking that his act of disobedience was the cause and effect, which lead to this tragedy. His doubts, questions, beliefs and a cadre of emotions pounded him in a torrential internal battle that was worse than the physical battle he had just engaged in. Everything that he began to believe seemed to be dying as well.

"I thought that King Elyon conquered death. If he did, then why is our brother dead?" Caden asked.

"His spirit is alive and he dwells in the halls of Asilo," Lady Daesis responded. "This is one of the great mysteries of Salamgard. He is free from the needs and limitations of his body. In truth, Wes is more alive right now than you or I. At the appropriate time, in the distant future, King Elyon will reunite those hallowed spirits with new bodies. You will surely see Wes again someday."

"Somehow that doesn't console me," Caden returned.

"The hollow ring of words thus spoken shall only give way to the deeper knowledge of *defeated death*. Thus shall come with profound resolve, comfort and courage to continue your journey," Lord Lemuel said

"What journey? It's senseless for us to go on to Asilo. Everything is lost," Ian said. "Besides I don't think I want be an Ambassador-Knight without Wes."

"I feel the same way," Josiah said. "We knew that this was a mission of all-or-nothing. We knew that we were in this together. We failed our mission and lost. We weren't cut out to be great men. I just want to get home. How do we get home? What will become of Wes?"

"King Elyon must send you home. There are ambassador knights in Otherland who will attend to the details of Wes death. His body will be retrieved by them and returned to Otherland. Otherlanders will come to view Wes' death as a tragic accident that led to the untimely death of a young life," Lord Kesh said. "We will make sure his body is cared for. You must go on to Asilo."

"No! I'm not leaving without him," Caden ordered. "We will take him to Asilo. King Elyon will have to send him back with us. I'm sure one of the Ambassador-Knights can meet us when we get back."

"As you wish, but you must quickly go to Asilo, lest Lord Ubilaz returns and there are more casualties," Tobijah said feeling an uneasiness beginning to stir in the forest.

"You will all accompany us, wont you?" Ian asked the mentors.

"This alone, you must do," Lemuel replied. "For in doing so you will see, as if a veil were lifted to give you unobstructed sight; that each of you possesses something that your brother has and the whole is greater than the parts."

"We will stay here to hold the line lest Lord Ubilaz return to finish a battle. No necrophim or warrior will pass us onto the plain of Dura," Lord Serik stated.

"You will never be able to carry his body all the way to Asilo," Lord Tobijah said. "Lift your brother and place him on the back of Lord Themba, my loyal captain. He will carry Wes and escort you into the throne room of King Elyon."

The guys lifted Wes onto Themba. His limp body was difficult to balance on the tiger's back. The brothers had to keep a firm grip on Wes' body, to help steady it as Themba walked.

Clarion stepped up next to the guys. "This is where I must leave you too," Clarion stated. She gently placed her hand on Wes' head as a gesture of valediction. Then she kissed each brother on the cheek. "Go in the power of Elyon. I am confident that we will meet again very soon."

The guys flanked the sides of the white tiger, each having a firm grip on Wes' lifeless body, like pall bearers in a funeral procession. While they wished they could have had more time for proper happier farewells, the permanent farewell of their friend seemed to drain the joy and hope out of any happier days. As the guys left the Ithcar Forest, their mentors slipped from view to hold the line in the forest.

CHAPTER
SEVENTY-NINE

When the band of brothers first arrived in Salamgard, they learned that their mission was to journey through Salamgard to Asilo where they would meet King Elyon. Once they arrived there, the King would knight them as Ambassador Knights, sealing each of them with a character trait distinguishable among great men of integrity. But the events of the past day had dramatically changed the trajectory. Lord Ubilaz had the Kalos Sapphire and Wes was dead. The guys couldn't think or care much about knighthood or characters of integrity.

Caden, Ian and Josiah walked for a long time in silence. They each held tight to Wes' lifeless body, steadying it on the back of Lord Themba. They were empty and lost in the convoluted caverns of their mind. Nothing seemed to make sense as random disconnected thoughts bounced around in their heads.

"It was so easy to trust King Elyon when things were going well," Caden blurted out. I really felt his power in the core of my soul, just as Tobijah said I would. I guess I'll never be a good warrior."

"Yes you will," Ian said. "I've been thinking a lot about this. This is the time that we should really trust the King. Only he can make us men of great character, just as Dr. Ashe and our mentors said he would. If we really believe that we are the men that we claimed to be and were destined to be, then we should stay true to that."

"Ian you're right," Josiah said. "I've been thinking about Wes and how he deliberately dropped his shield. He knew what the outcome would be and yet he willingly gave his life. He counted the cost and did the loving thing. That was the strength of his character. He didn't back down or compromise who he was. I'm going to miss him for the rest of my life but I'm not going to do it as a mediocre man."

The determination and passion in Josiah's voice began to be infectious. He continued, "Sometimes bad things happen to good people. I don't understand why that is, but being a wise man, or a good man or a free man of incredible faith can counteract the evil in the world. Wes showed us true character in the face of adversity. We should do the same."

Caden stopped walking and stared affectless at Ian and Josiah. Then his face began to change as if an epiphany was beginning to overtake him.

"We need to become Ambassador-Knights so that we can advance the kingdom of Salamgard and put an end to Lord Ubilaz's reign. We would make Wes proud if we did that. It would also avenge Wes' death. When we get to Asilo, I will appeal to the King's goodness and request that he mercifully reconcile us as Ambassador-Knights."

For the first time since Wes' death, the brothers began to feel some sense of joyful resolve and renewed purpose. Themba sensed their anticipation to get to Asilo and began to walk more briskly. The guys picked up the pace alongside Lord Themba's rhythmic gait.

Asilo loomed large on the horizon. Built between two great mountains, Asilo resembled a fortified palace, with high rising towers, ornately sculptured buttresses, lofty spires and intricately crafted domes. But Asilo was not just a palace. It was also the royal city. Many of Salamgard's citizens came and went during all hours of the day. Business was conducted outside the drawbridge and in Asilo's inner courts. Musicians filled the courtyards, halls and gardens of Asilo with the cheer of their music. In the midst of the bustle, there was an overwhelming peace, which was indicative of the palace when the King was there.

The details and artistry of Asilo became clearer as the guys got closer. The massive drawbridge was as large as the gates of Aanda. Over the lintel arch of the draw bridge hung a tapestry adorned with the King's crest, for all to see. The crest was the same that adorned the sword in Doc's office. Each of the four quadrants of the King's royal crest was the individual crest of their mentors.

Lord Themba came upon the entrance of Asilo and slowed his pace. The citizens who congregated near the outside of the draw-bridge and in the entrance of the palace walls parted ways to allow the brothers to pass. There was a hushed reverence that came over the crowd. The musicians stopped playing and conversations ceased. Slowly a somber affect rolled through the palace like a black fog, as the small funeral procession passed. The citizens bowed in respect to the fallen conciliator. Ian, Caden and Josiah observed the deep disquietedness of the crowd, unaware that the citizen's expectations of the four brothers succeeding the mightiest Knights, whose crests so richly comprised the King's crest, was visibly shattered.

In the center of the palace courtyard was a white marble statue erected to commemorate King Elyon's defeat over death. The stonework depicted two tigers with the once slain body of King Elyon draped across their backs. The statue served as a reminder that the king was once dead. It marked the place where his body was laid just before the Dark Lord's archers launched their fiery arrows over the palace walls.

Onlookers in the midst of the courtyard and in the balconies above, watched as the slain body of the young conciliator solemnly passed beneath the shadow of the commemorative statue. The citizens bowed in respect and many joined the procession behind the young Ambassador-Knights and Lord Themba.

Themba walked through the courtyard to a long arcade on the other side. The left side of the long arched corridor opened to a beautifully manicured garden. At the end of the arcade were two artistically carved doors each bearing the crest of the King. Two attendants in brightly colored uniforms served as sentries posted before the doors.

As the entourage moved closer, the attendants swung open the doors as if they had been expecting the party's arrival, and then bowed in respect. The doors gave entrance to an elaborate throne room. Themba continued forward and the guys stayed close to his side. The citizens who followed stopped outside the throne room and watched from there.

Just inside the vestibule, there were many statues of some of the great Lords and Ladies in King Elyon's court. The guys stopped shortly to drink in the awe of these faithful citizens. They immediately recognized the statue of Lord Cervus and one of Lord Themba. They noted the statue of Lady Clarion and Lady Daesis and Lady Soteria. There were statues to others they had not met; Lord Ruah the wild goose, Lady Eirene the pasture ewe; Lord Gaudium the hyena. There were many others; men, women and creatures who were faithful to serve King Elyon.

"Look here", Josiah said. In the midst of the stone works, immortalizing the great Salamgard nobles was a statue of Dr. Darren Ashe.

"Lord Darash, seeker and gatekeeper of Otherland," Ian read aloud from the face plate at the base of the statue.

"Dr. Darrin Ashe is Lord Darash," Caden whispered.

Lord Themba began to move again past the vestibule into the throne room. The room looked like a great cathedral with high elaborately painted ceilings. Statues of other noble Lords and Ladies bordered the ledges that ran down the length of the nave. The sculptured nobles resembled saints who were looking down on the proceedings that took place in the room. Arched columns separated the nave from the aisles. The pillars that supported the arches were white marble, veined with ruby, sapphire, emerald and amber. The King's crest was inlayed in the center of the throne room floor. The crest was made with the same precious stones that bled through the support pillars.

Themba and the guys walked slowly down the center of the nave. The citizens of Salamgard began to crowd the aisles on either side of the nave. They wanted to watch the procession and grieve the loss of the fallen would-be knight. The silence and the sacred space impressed the somber final realization that the brothers were now in Asilo's grand throne room for a funeral.

At the end of the great hall, high above the throne room was a dome set upon pendentives. The oculus in the dome allowed a shaft of light to illuminate the magnificent royal chair beneath it.

White marble stairs led up to the throne, which set it high above the nave floor. The stairs and platform ran the width of the nave creating an alter-like hallowed podium for the king. A single white tiger, Lady Thanda, lay at the right side of the throne. The throne was empty. No monarch was present in the throne room.

Lady Thanda roared and an attendant stepped to the center of the nave at the bottom of the stairs. "Lift the young conciliator from Lord Themba's back," he announced.

Ian, Josiah and Caden raised Wes's body and Themba stepped out from under its weight. Themba then proceeded to climb the stairs to the throne and lay prone on the left side of the symbolic seat of authority. The brothers were instructed to lay Wes to rest on the floor. His body set perfectly in the center of the inlayed crest; the length of his body and his extended arms accentuating the lines that divided the quadrants of the crest.

Lady Thanda and Lord Themba stood from their restful positions. Their beautiful white fur with its black stripes enhanced the gold throne. Lady Thanda let out another roar and the crowd of citizens and nobles bowed low facing the throne. Upon seeing this,

Caden, Ian and Josiah followed the response of the crowd. When they looked up again, King Elyon stood in front of the throne.

"Lord Tobijah!" Caden gasped.

"No he's Lord Lemuel," Josiah whispered.

"He also looks like Lord Kesh and Lord Serik," Ian said.

King Elyon was tall and fine featured like Lord Serik. He had the same eyes of fire as Serik. His skin was brightly luminescent like that of Lord Kesh and his hands were glowing a burnished bronze like Lord Tobijah.

"Rise, sons and daughters of Salamgard!" he said with a voice that sounded like rushing waterfall in Lord Lemuel's voice. The guys suddenly realized that the King had always been with them. Separately, their mentors each represented a part of the king. Together, the mentors created the whole representation of the king.

"This is what Lord Lemuel meant" Josiah whispered. "He said, *'each of you possesses something that your brother has and the whole is greater than the parts'*. He was telling us that like our mentors we each possess a quality of the king and together we create a more complete picture of him".

"You are correct in part, my son," the king said to Josiah. His comment caught Josiah off guard because he didn't think that anyone, besides his brothers, was listening.

"Together you create a more complete picture of me but you each possess all of the qualities of greatness; love, goodness, wisdom and freedom. One may be more dominant but all are present in the noble Ambassador-Knights of Salamgard."

The guys looked at each other and then down at their slain brother. The loving conciliator was missing. There wasn't a complete picture any longer and the sadness began to rush in.

"You are sad over something that is joyful," King Elyon said.

"Forgive me for speaking, my king" Caden began. "There is no joy without our brother, Wes. I know that one day we may come to find closure over his death and joy may return, but not today. All I ask is that you be merciful and forgive my error. I beg you not to hold my disobedience to my brother's account. Allow us . . . but if not I, at least them . . . to be the great men you have deemed us be. Then please allow us to carry the body of our dear brother back to Otherland."

"Dear Caden, don't you know that you are so precious to my heart?" the king said. "Even now, your selfless request for your brothers reflects the goodness I have already instilled in you. You see, you were created to this end."

King Elyon began to descend the grand marble staircase to the floor where the young knights stood. "Lift your brother," he commanded.

Caden reached down and grabbed Wes' left arm. Josiah quickly reached under Wes' right arm to lift. Ian took hold of Wes at his knees and the three lifted their dead brother.

"Your brother Wes lives in these hallowed halls. You only hold a carcass that housed the real person. Do you believe that?"

"Yes, my Lord", the boys responded in unison.

"Then don't sorrow without hope," the king said as he put his left hand on Caden's shoulder. "I defeated death," he said clutching Josiah's shoulder. Then he looked into Ian's eyes and said, "You need to trust that you shall be reunited with your brother."

King Elyon leaned down and kissed Wes' forehead. A bright light began filling the room, blinding all the congregants. Just as the light reached its brilliance there was a clap of thunder, which startled the guys from their posture and left them empty handed.

The light immediately diminished and Caden, Ian and Josiah stood side by side clothed in new garments. Their vestments were the same with exception to the color. Each wore the color of their mentor's crest. The guys donned brightly polished boots and long capes. The king's crest was embroidered full, in the center of each vestment. No longer were Ian's wings, Josiah's diadem and Caden's bronze hands visible.

On the platform of the throne stood their mentors each side by side, dressed similarly to their protégés. Lord Kesh and Lord Serik stood to the left side of the throne next to Lady Thanda. Lord Lemuel and Lord Tobijah stood to the right with Lord Temba.

Caden looked into the eyes of the king. "We gratefully and faithfully wear the crest of our King along with the red wine, royal blue and golden maize of our mentors. But our hearts are still heavy in the absence of the hunter green that marks our mentors standing up there, but not our band of brothers here."

The king placed his hand around the back of Caden's neck and smiled. He didn't say a word, instead he nodded in a direction, prompting the guys to turn around. Standing right behind the trio, wearing hunter green vestments, was Wes.

He smiled the grin that so typically distinguished him and said, "Hearts bound boys! Where we go one, we go all."

The brothers fell on Wes, embracing him. Caden hugged him so hard that he thought he might break him. They laughed and wept tears of the greatest joy they had ever experienced. The court erupted in cheers, sharing their joy and in awe of the magnificent power of the King.

"My sons!" the King spoke. The room silenced and the guys stood together side by side. "Well done. I have longed for this moment."

As he spoke, four attendants stepped forward each carrying a platinum tray. On the tray was a velvet cloth, in the color of each mentor's crest and a beautiful double-edge silver sword. The sword was the same one that they had seen in Doc's office. Its grip was wrapped with a deep midnight blue-dyed leather. It had a blue sapphire medallion with an inlayed ruby stone fleury cross, set in the center of a silver pommel. The blade of the sword was inscribed with the familiar words:

HEARTS BOUND: MEN OF LOVE,
GOODNESS, WISDOM AND FREEDOM

On the ricasso of each sword set King Elyon's royal crest.

King Elyon took the sword from the blue cloth clad tray. "Step forward and take a knee, Josiah Nestor."

Josiah stepped to face the king and bowed in adoration. "My Lord and my King," he said as he knelt.

"Josiah Nestor because of your faithfulness to me and to the ideals of Salamgard I crown your brow with wisdom. You have shown yourself to be wise beyond measure in your selection of Lady Sabedoria, your continued discernment of the counterfeits manifested by dark forces and your passion to relentlessly pursue wisdom. I also bestow upon you a measure of love, goodness and freedom. From this day forth you shall be known as a Wise Ambassador-Knight of the realm".

The king placed the sword on Josiah's shoulders and said, "Rise, Lord Josiah Nestor, Knight of the King's realm". Josiah stood and the king presented him with the sword. Then Josiah returned to his place next to his brothers.

"Step forward and take a knee, Ian Bound". King Elyon took the sword from the attendant with the maize colored tray

Ian moved to his rightful place. As he knelt he said, "My allegiance to you my King".

"Ian Bound because of your faithfulness to me and to the ideals of Salamgard I release your spirit to soar in freedom. You have shown yourself to be free by your unrelenting faith, blind trust and complete rest in your King. Your desire and practice of living into the wildness of Salamgard makes you a great man. I also bestow upon you a measure of love, goodness and wisdom. From this day forth you shall be known as a free and faith-filled Ambassador-Knight of the realm."

The king placed the sword on Ian's shoulders and said, "Rise, Lord Ian Bound, Knight of the King's realm."

Ian accepted the King's sword and returned to stand next to Josiah.

King Elyon took the third sword from the green colored tray. "Step forward and take a knee, Wes Litchfield".

Wes stepped forward and as he knelt he said, "My heart, my love and my life for my King."

"Wes Litchfield because of your faithfulness to me and to the ideals of Salamgard I write my name as a banner of love over your heart. You have shown yourself to be compassionate, even to the point of death. You now wear the scar of betrayal because of your love, and have thus shared in the suffering of your king. I also bestow upon you a measure of goodness, wisdom and freedom. From this day forth, all will know that you are an Ambassador-Knight of the King's realm by the demonstration of the powerful force of the King's love through you. Rise, Lord Wes Litchfield, Knight of the King's realm."

King Elyon then took the final sword from the wine colored tray and lowered it to his side. "Step forward, Caden."

Caden stepped forward and fell on his face before King Elyon. "My Lord I know I am not worthy to be called an Ambassador-Knight in your realm. There is no good in me and I have grossly disobeyed you."

The gracious monarch stooped down and raised Caden to his knees. Then he tenderly lifted the young man's head to look full in his face.

"My son, you show deep humility. Tell me, what was my order to you?"

"Your mandate was: 'Protect that which belongs to the King', my Lord. But I gave that which belongs to the king, to the vile and wicked Dark Lord."

"Yes you did and in doing so you protected that which belongs to the king." The king gestured to the side aisle of the great hall and thirty noble citizens, clad in regal robes, stepped forward. Caden recognized them as the hostages who he ransomed.

"These are my devoted seers who have penetrated Lord

Ubilaz's ranks. They have and always will belong to me. Out of goodness, you protected them and thus allowed them to remain in anonymity as my seers. You did the good thing as opposed to the presumed, right thing. You will never be disobedient or compromising when you seek to be a good man."

King Elyon raised his sword and placed it on Caden's shoulder. The young warrior raised his tear filled eyes to look into his Sovereign's face.

King Elyon smiled and said, "Caden Boyd, because of your faithfulness to me and to the ideals of Salamgard I ignite the fires of goodness deep within your soul. You have shown yourself to be a good warrior by trusting in the king and placing goodness as a virtue higher than the conviction of power or the quest to champion truth. From this day forth, all will see your good works as a reflection of your King. You shall be known as a Good warrior and an Ambassador-Knight of the realm. Rise, Lord Caden Boyd, Knight of the King's realm."

Caden held firm to his new sword and joined his brothers as King Elyon turned to address his citizens. "These men secure the hope of Salamgard. We have long awaited the day when Lord Darash would find four whose hearts were truly bound and who demonstrated the virtuous character traits that exemplifies Salamgard. As your King I proclaim that these young men; a Conciliator, a Sage, a Warrior and a Wildman, to be the successors to my greatest Knights, Lord Serik, Lord Lemuel, Lord Tobijah and Lord Kesh."

The mentors bowed to their king and then descended the stairs to encircle the brothers. They bowed in respect to the guys who felt overwhelmed by so humbling an act. The brothers were delighted but not surprised by the king's announcement. While they didn't know or expect to be their mentor's successors, they did know that they would someday be required to pay it forward and be mentors.

King Elyon ascended the stairs and stood before his throne.

"Now, you must take our spots beside the King's throne," Serik said to the guys. The four brothers, with swords in hand, ascended the stairs and each stood where their mentor once stood. The throne room exploded in applause for the mentors and their protégés.

King Elyon quieted the crowd of joyful onlookers. "At the appropriate time these men will be summoned to permanently stand here at my side, in the place of their mentors. Until that time, they will return to Otherland as Ambassador-Knights to live as the virtuous men they were destined to be. They will greatly influence Otherland for the glory of Salamgard and their King," Elyon said. Then he addressed the young ambassador knights directly, "You will continue to have access to Salamgard as I deem fit. Your mentors will also continue to pour into you. But you must remain vigilant because Lord Ubilaz will not cease to seek your demise."

The king again turned to address his loyal citizens. "While we celebrate the joy of this long awaited moment, I must warn you. The days that lie ahead will be dark. Lord Ubilaz will grow more powerful and destructive. He will increase his stronghold in Otherland and here, in Salamgard. Eikondor will grow more prominent and threaten to suffocate the ideals of our kingdom. Many will succumb to his demands and join his ranks. Hope will die. Nonetheless, I charge you to stand firm and don't be afraid. To these great Knights at my side and their mentors before me, I charge you to remain faithful. Salamgard has a bright future in our loyal sons and daughters, like these young men. Tomorrow may bring peril but today we celebrate great victory! Let there be a joyful resound throughout all Salamgard as we leave this room to celebrate in the courtyard, streets, cities, woodlands and the remotest parts of our kingdom."

The throne room burst into applause again. The four brothers humbly bowed. When they rose from their obeisance, an ensemble of trumpeters sounded their antiphonal introit at the throne room doors.

The four mentors, Lords Serik, Lemuel, Tobijah and Kesh turned and began a processional out of the throne room. The crowd of onlookers watched and waited as Lord Themba and Lady Thanda slowly descended the marble stairs to follow in place behind the great mentor Knights. They were joined by Lord Cervus who suddenly emerged from a corridor off the side of the throne room.

As they processed out, Lady Daesis stepped from the same corridor and fell into line. She was followed by Lady Clarion who held two red glass orbs burning brightly with a sweet smelling incense. The smoke from the incense began to fill the throne room.

"My Lords, you are to follow next," she said to the four brothers with an endearing smile. The brothers stepped down the stairs in perfect unison. Once they got to the base of the stairs, they turned to face their King and bowed in humble gratitude. King Elyon smiled and nodded his delighted approval.

Clarion waited and swung the incense orbs releasing a torrent of smoke as the guys walked slowly behind her.

"I can't see a thing through all the smoke," Ian whispered.

"I can't either," Caden said quietly. "It looks like the smoke is getting more dense."

"Just keep your eyes on the red lights," Josiah whispered.

"Walk toward the red lights," Wes softly said. Then he chuckled, "Where we go one we go all."

Clarion swung the orbs again releasing another thick opaque cloud of incense smoke. The only thing visible was the red orbs. The brothers continued their slow gait toward the lights.

"Are you guys still there? I can't see anything!" Caden said.

"Yeah I'm here bro," Wes said.

"Me too," Josiah called.

"I'm right here too," Ian said. "Clarion is still right in front of us because I can see the red lights."

At the sound of their voices, the brothers moved closer to one another. They were now tightly grouped side by side. They could see the red orbed lights of Clarion's incense burners closer and clearer. Then a gust of wind came, cleaning the air of any smoke that would cover their view. Caden, Wes, Josiah and Ian suddenly found themselves standing behind Ian's car in the parking lot of the Mystery Brews Coffee Shop. Ian had left the lights on in haste to get to their meeting. The red glow of the tail lights illuminated the dark corner of the lot. The outside lights of the coffee shop were dark and the baristas where turning off the last remaining lights inside. Across the street, Mason University peacefully slumbered. The campus lights, no longer enshrouded by fog, burned bright in the darkness of the late evening.

The guys looked around in wonder. There was no throne room or crowd, no king or mentors, no lords or ladies. There was no forest, just the quiet of an early autumn evening and the asphalt of the parking lot.

The brothers were wearing the same old T-shirts and jeans that they wore before the venture began. Wes looked at his watch, "Twelve-O-five," he said with a chuckle.

"Was that real?" Ian asked. "Did you guys experience what I just did?"

Wes raised his hand to reveal a sword clutched in his grip. Each guy held his sword. They quietly stood awestruck by the wonder of their experience. Each felt the kindling of profound joy churning in the middle of their chests. This joy was the kind of joy that makes you want to laugh out loud, but they dared not break the reverence and awe that accompanied their experience. All they could do was looked at each other without saying a word and smile.

Wes took a deep audible breath and softly said, "Hearts bound boys! Where we go one, we go all!"

THE CREST